DEAD AND GONE

DEAD AND GONE

A Detective Annalisa Vega Novel

JOANNA SCHAFFHAUSEN

MINOTAUR BOOKS
NEW YORK

First published in the United States by Minotaur Books, an imprint of St. Martin's Publishing Group

DEAD AND GONE. Copyright © 2023 by Joanna Schaffhausen. All rights reserved. Printed in the United States of America. For information, address St. Martin's Publishing Group, 120 Broadway, New York, NY 10271.

www.minotaurbooks.com

Designed by Gabriel Guma

Library of Congress Cataloging-in-Publication Data

Names: Schaffhausen, Joanna, author.
Title: Dead and gone / Joanna Schaffhausen.
Description: First edition. | New York : Minotaur Books, 2023. |
    Series: Detective Annalisa Vega ; 3
Identifiers: LCCN 2022059544 | ISBN 9781250853370 (hardcover) |
    ISBN 9781250853387 (ebook)
Subjects: LCSH: Women detectives—Fiction. | LCGFT: Detective and mystery
    fiction. | Novels.
Classification: LCC PS3619.C3253 D43 2023 | DDC 813/.6—dc23/eng/
    20221213
LC record available at https://lccn.loc.gov/2022059544

Our books may be purchased in bulk for promotional, educational, or business use. Please contact your local bookseller or the Macmillan Corporate and Premium Sales Department at 1-800-221-7945, extension 5442, or by email at MacmillanSpecialMarkets@macmillan.com.

First Edition: 2023

1 3 5 7 9 10 8 6 4 2

For Larry and Cherry, my A+ bonus parents

DEAD AND GONE

PROLOGUE

....

FLIES ARE ATTRACTED TO DEAD THINGS, LIKE HE IS. One buzzes through the open window and lands on the sweaty orange cubes of cheese some girl from Delta Gamma Nu put out in an effort to make the party seem classy. The fly performs a leggy dance, inspecting this unexpected bounty, and he smiles in appreciation within the humid confines of his gorilla mask. Calliphoridae, the blowfly, arrives within minutes of death, drawn by the gases and fluids of decaying flesh, and its patterns are so established that scientists use the fly's timing to solve murders. He admires the constancy of it. You can set your alibi for Friday night, but it's no good if Calliphoridae says your wife was dead Thursday morning. He's read that warmer temperatures have forced southern blowflies northward, confusing several species and making it harder to tell which fly got to the body when. *Climate change is coming for everyone*, he thinks.

It's a mild night for late October. Maybe they have climate change to thank for that, too, or maybe it's the presence of more than a hundred grinding bodies in a room that might comfortably hold forty. He's hanging around near the punch bowl by the open windows because the inside of his costume is about a thousand degrees. He doesn't dare take it off. He's wearing only boxers underneath, but the reality is, he'd never come to this party as himself. The campus studs are maskless and bare-chested—one was walking around in a thong and a pair of swimming goggles, calling himself an Olympic diver. He's also seen a werewolf, a Ghostface, and some guy in a hockey mask waving a rubber butcher knife. The girls are dressed like some sort of hooker: witch hooker; cheerleader hooker; Dorothy from Oz, if she was a hooker.

A trio of them bursts free from the crowd, leaning on one another and laughing, staggering in his direction. They stop at the drink table and he recognizes them as three first-year girls: Quinn, Natalie, and Sarah Beth. Quinn is the only one who's ever spoken to him. The other two act like he is part of the physical campus, like a recycling bin or a flower bed. Something you pass by on your way to somewhere else. So he isn't surprised when they don't even glance his way as they grab another round of drinks. He sidles closer so he can hear them. It isn't hard since they have to shout over the pounding music.

"What even are you?" Sarah Beth yells as she wrinkles her nose at Natalie. "You look like a British schoolgirl."

"I'm Clarice Starling!" Natalie brushes back her red hair. "Like, from the movie? Didn't you see Logan dressed as Hannibal?" She looks in vain at the crowd, trying to find her boyfriend.

"No, I didn't see Logan," Sarah Beth replies, like she's designed it that way. "But that's not a couple's costume. Clarice and Lecter aren't, like, boyfriend and girlfriend."

"Oh, yes they are."

Sarah Beth rolls her eyes and takes a big swallow from her red Solo cup. She nudges Quinn, who is glued to her phone, texting. "Q, tell this idiot that Clarice wasn't trying to get in Hannibal Lecter's pants."

"I wish I could," Quinn replies without looking up. She has on a silver sparkly jacket and a fifties-style poofy skirt, and her hair is in a bouncy blond ponytail.

Sarah Beth puts a hand on the scrap of white cloth covering her hips. She is dressed like Cleopatra, if the Egyptian queen had been turning tricks on the Nile. "I saw that movie in eighth grade and it scared the crap out of me. I remember every second of it, and Clarice and Hannibal most definitely didn't screw each other."

"There's a sequel," Quinn says, still eyeing her phone, and Natalie shoots Sarah Beth a triumphant smile.

"That's so gross." Sarah Beth shudders. "Who'd want to fuck a serial killer?"

The little hairs on the back of his neck stand up.

"Ha, well, you'd be surprised," Quinn informs her without looking up. "My aunt Annalisa gets weird shit in the mail all the time about the Lovelorn Killer."

"Kinky," Natalie says, jostling Sarah Beth with a nervous giggle.

"I'll tell you who *isn't* getting any," Quinn declares, irritated. "Jason. He hasn't replied to any of my texts all night."

"What? I thought you said he was coming." Sarah Beth sounds disappointed.

"He said he would when he and Gavin finished their stupid video game."

"Gavin Beckwith?" asks Natalie, with raised eyebrows. "He's here somewhere. I saw him in the kitchen. He's wearing a Cubs hat and calling it a costume."

"What?" Quinn whirls in the direction of the kitchen, ponytail flying. "And Jason isn't with him?"

"Forget Jason. Who needs him?" Sarah Beth pushes a cup of bloodred punch into Quinn's hand. "There's a hundred other guys here to choose from, way hotter than Jason Wilcox. Find someone who prefers your box to his Xbox."

She gestures southward on Quinn's body and Quinn scrunches up her face. "You're so disgusting."

Natalie grabs her arm. "Who needs the boys, anyway? Let's dance!"

"Yeah, screw him," Quinn proclaims at the top of her voice. The other girls let out a whoop of agreement and they all throw back their cups. Quinn clasps Natalie's hand, tugging her into the crowd with Sarah Beth right behind.

Part of him wants to follow. His eyes track Quinn's shiny jacket into the crowd. *Not her*, he corrects himself. *Anyone but her*. She mentioned her aunt, and it wasn't the first time he's heard her name on campus. *Annalisa Vega*. With Quinn here, everyone hopes to get a glimpse of Annalisa. *Maybe she'll visit her niece. Maybe she'll even guest lecture in a criminology class*. He's hoping if Annalisa shows up there will be some warning so he can be far away. He doesn't want her to look at him. She would know immediately what he is and who he is becoming.

Just the thought of locking eyes with her makes sweat break out across his body, which causes the gorilla suit to cling to his skin. His heart pounds out of rhythm with the booming bass and he plasters himself against the nearest wall. The floor feels like it's shaking. His ragged exhales blow back across his flushed face and he will suffocate if he doesn't get out of here right now. He staggers toward the stairs, pushing past bodies until he crashes into a tall girl dressed in goth attire. He steadies himself, and in the process, he grazes her breasts with one hand. "What the hell are you doing, pervert?" Her speech is slurred, her cheeks red. She shoves him off her. "Don't touch me."

He has a flash of himself wrapping his hands around her throat and squeezing until she goes quiet. Instead he gulps in air, mumbles an apology, and trips over his gorilla feet as he heads for the stairs. It's not too late. He can still go through with the plan. He has to find a girl. Isolate her. He's rehearsed the scenario a million times in his head, but he visualizes it once more, imagining her gasp of surprise when the needle pierces her flesh. He's been careful his whole life, and he's being careful now. There's not enough drug in the syringe to kill her. Just enough to make a convincing facsimile and let him play a little. It's better if she wakes up and realizes what happened to her. She won't know who did it. She'll have to watch every guy's face and wonder if he's the one. She'll have to pay attention to the ones she didn't notice before.

He waits until he's sure, until his blood quiets, and he walks sure-footedly up the stairs. The sweet, acrid stench of pot intensifies as he reaches the second floor. There's a cloud of it coming out of the first bedroom, illuminated by a blue light spilling out from inside. He hears male voices but does not look to see who it is. He goes up to the third floor, which he knows is all bedrooms. He tries the second door and finds it locked. The third is partway open, but when he peeks in, he sees a male behind pounding away and female legs wrapped around it. Drifting onward, he passes a bathroom where a guy in a pink rocker wig lies curled up, groaning on the floor. At the end of the hall, he encounters another closed door. It yields when he turns the knob and he freezes when he sees he's in luck: lying on top of a rumpled bed is an orange-haired girl all alone. The only illumination is from the moonlight slanting in through the curtainless window and a lone fat candle flickering on the bedside table. Her eyes are closed and she's not moving.

He slips inside and shuts the door behind him. She doesn't stir when he prods her with one furry paw. He moves his hand higher, under her skirt. She still doesn't wake. This is it. His heart starts beating so fast it feels like it's turned to liquid in his chest. He removes one paw and unzips the costume enough to grab the syringe and take it out. He holds it between his teeth to uncap it. His hand shakes as he moves the needle closer to her naked thigh, and he pauses to steady himself. He has to find a vein. The tip hovers over her flesh and he tenses, preparing to thrust it in, when the door opens behind him so fast it reverberates and bangs the wall. The girl's eyes fly open as the lights come on.

He hears something like a hiss, and when he turns his head, he sees a woman dressed as a black cat. Where the hell did she come from? "Get the fuck off of her!" the cat woman hollers as she picks up a chair and throws it at him. He ducks, but the chair hits his shoulder and he drops the syringe. His mask goes askew, partially blinding him. *Gotta get out of here.* He gropes blindly at the floor for the syringe.

"What the fuck are you doing?" She's on him now, clawing to remove his mask.

"I'm sorry. I'm sorry." He trips on a pair of gym shoes and his face catches the edge of a bookshelf as he falls. He whacks his jaw and tastes blood in his mouth.

The cat woman kicks him in the ribs, but the bulky costume absorbs most of the blow. "You're a sick freak."

"I didn't do anything." He pants through the mask and crawls toward the door. The cat woman follows, chasing him down the hall. He half runs, half falls down the stairs and races out into the woods. He finds the nearest clump of pine trees and ducks behind them, gulping in air. His heart is beating so fast he thinks he might be sick. He yanks off the mask and spits blood. Then he collapses, lying in the cold and waiting to be found out. But no one comes. The party gradually goes quiet.

He lies there a long time, feeling sorry for himself. The cat woman did this to him. She ruined everything. He'd spent an hour at that party watching people and he hadn't glimpsed her once. She appeared out of nowhere like some sort of avenging angel. Like she'd been watching him the whole time. He crawls to the edge of the pine trees and peers around the branches to look for her.

Footsteps. Someone *is* coming. The branches rustle as he makes a swift retreat, holding his breath at the intruder's approach. A girl walks by, her legs passing right in front of his face, but she does not look down. It is hard to see her well in the dim moonlight but she has light-colored hair and a shiny silver jacket. It's Quinn Vega.

Not her, the voice in his head reminds him. At the same time, he imagines how she would look, silent and still as he stands over her.

She stumbles in the dark, muttering to herself. He creeps forward to keep watching her and his fingers touch something cold and hard. A rock. He has big palms, large enough to hold the whole thing in one hand. He picks it up and begins to follow. She hears him and turns and now he has no choice. He raises the rock high in the air and brings it down on her head. She crumples immediately on the dirt path and he stands there, breathing ragged, stunned at what he's done. His hand goes limp as he drops the rock.

He sees her face and realizes he was wrong. But the voice was wrong too. She is perfect. It is better than anything he ever dreamed.

ONE

....

I'M LATE," ANNALISA SAID INTO THE PHONE AS SHE STOOD IN THE SHOWER, BARE-
FOOT BUT WEARING HER PAJAMAS, WITH THE CURTAIN CLOSED FOR EXTRA PRIVACY
DESPITE THE FACT THAT SHE'D LOCKED THE DOOR AND NICK WAS STILL SNORING IN
HIS BED.

"It's not even seven," her friend Sassy replied with a groan. "Your shift
doesn't start till eight."

"Not that kind of late," Annalisa said darkly, and after a beat, Sassy
caught on.

"Oh! How late?"

Annalisa blew out an anxious breath. "Two days?"

Sassy turned disappointed. "That's all? Two days is nothing." Annalisa
heard her flop back down on her bed. "My cycle is twenty-eight days,
plus or minus a week."

"Not mine." Annalisa pressed herself against the tile wall like she was
trying to pass through it. "I'm never late."

"So go to the drugstore and take a test."

"I don't want to take a test."

"Why not?"

"Because what if I am?"

"Anna. I know you got an A in biology because I sat next to you sophomore year, so I'm positive you're aware that whether you're pregnant does not depend on if you pee on a stick. It's an entirely different kind of stick that's involved here."

"Oh my God. Could you not right now?" Annalisa's stomach had dropped at the word *pregnant* and now she started sweating as Sassy giggled on the other end of the phone.

"I'm sorry. Really," Sassy said as she tried to pull herself together. "But what do you want me to say? I'm not an oracle. I can't tell you if you're pregnant or not."

"You had two babies. You know about this stuff." Annalisa's littlest nieces, Carla and Gigi, were the loves of her life.

"Yeah, and you know how I knew I was pregnant with them?"

"How?"

"I peed on a stick."

"Okay, okay. I get it."

Sassy rustled the bedcovers. "Would it be so bad?" she asked tentatively. "If you were?"

"Well, it wouldn't be good." Annalisa heard Nick whistling from the other room as he began his morning routine. Any moment, he'd be banging on the bathroom door.

"I thought you wanted kids."

"I did. I do. But—not like this. We're not married. We don't even live together." She'd been sleeping with Nick for eight months now, but she kept all her stuff at her place, save for a toothbrush and a bathrobe. Nick had cleaned out a dresser drawer for her and made room in the closet without asking or explaining why he did it. The empty space just sat there, waiting for her, like a question she had yet to answer.

"You were married to him," Sassy pointed out. "Once."

"Yeah, and look how that turned out."

Nick rapped on the door. "Hey, Vega, you redecorating in there or what? I need the john."

"Gotta go," Annalisa whispered to Sassy. "Talk later."

She stepped out of the shower and opened the door, finding herself face-to-face with her bare-chested ex-husband. He was unshaven with his hair standing partly on end, and when he smiled, he looked as sexy as the day she'd met him at age nineteen. "Good morning," he said to her with a hint of a growl. He took her face in both hands and kissed her soundly on the mouth. "You were primping a long time for a woman who's already this beautiful."

"I was in the shower." He did a brief double take at her dry hair and pajamas, but she shoved him over the threshold before he could respond. "I'll make eggs," she called through the door as she heard the shower turn on.

She unzipped the hanging bag she'd brought and put on her usual inexpensive gray suit. Her holster and weapon lay on the dresser next to Nick's. She left them there while she went to start the toast and eggs. The slide of the whites across the pan and their vaguely sulfuric scent triggered a wave of nausea. A symptom? Or maybe she'd slept poorly. They had been working long hours on the Chicken Bandit case—a lone male in a chicken mask was holding up corner stores and late-night delis— and all she had to show for it were the rings under her eyes and a pile of empty coffee cups in her car. Her body chemistry was off. Sleep involved hormones, right?

The toast jammed and burned, sending black smoke up to the ceiling and triggering the alarm. She cursed and unplugged the toaster but the alarm continued to shriek. Nick came running bare-assed into the kitchen just as she climbed on the counter to fan the smoke alarm with a dish towel. "The broom," he hollered over the noise. "You need the broom." He grabbed the broom from the closet and used the handle to poke the "reset" button on the alarm, ceasing the alarm, but a sharp trill carried on from the next room.

"My phone," she said, still looming over him on the counter. Smoke started to rise again, and she looked down to see the eggs turning to charcoal. "Oh, no, the eggs!"

"Answer your phone. I'll handle this." He helped her down with one hand as he removed the pan from the stove with the other.

The caller ID read *Zimmer, L.*, which meant the commander was on her personal phone, not at the precinct. Zimmer rarely did fieldwork, especially not at this hour, so Annalisa braced herself for bad news before she answered. "Morning, boss."

"Vega." The commander's voice sounded thick as wet cement. "Sorry about the early hour."

"No problem. What's up?"

"I need you to meet me at Rosehill Cemetery. Probable homicide, special circs."

"Special circumstances" could mean multiple victims or a hate crime. Or the deceased was a kid or someone famous. Annalisa started kicking out of her pajama pants even as she held the phone to one ear, hopping on one leg. "Okay, but I'm already on the Chicken Bandit thing."

"I'm leaving Carelli on the Chicken Bandit for now. You're with me and I'll show you why." Zimmer sent her a picture. It showed a dark-haired man hanging from a tree. His face wasn't visible but there was a word written in white paint across his gray shirt: PIG.

Annalisa eased backward until she found the edge of the bed and sank down on it. "It's a cop?"

"Ex-CPD. Been a PI for more than a decade."

But the slur said *pig*. Annalisa rubbed her head with her free hand. "With all due respect, boss, I don't know if I can take another dirty cop case right now."

"He wasn't dirty."

"But—"

"He was a friend."

Annalisa shut her mouth. After a beat, she said, "I'm leaving now." She hung up with Zimmer and pulled on her suit. Nick, now wearing pants, caught up with her as she was trying to comb her hair and brush her teeth at the same time.

"I take it there really is a fire," he remarked, noting her hurry.

"Zimmer called. She wants me at a scene in Rosehill Cemetery."

"Just you?"

She met his eyes in the mirror. "For now, yeah." Their gaze held as she told him the rest of it. "Probable homicide, and the victim is an ex-cop. A friend of Zimmer's, apparently. She swears he's clean."

"But she asked for you," he said.

She spat in the sink and rinsed her mouth with a handful of water. When she raised up, she met his reflection again. "I'm guessing she has doubts." Annalisa had turned in the most notable ex-cop of all: George Vega, her own father. Since then, Zimmer deployed her like a specialized weapon in tough cases involving other officers, and with predictable results. Annalisa had become the kid alone at the lunch table. Even Nick joked that she slept with him just so she'd have one friend on the force.

She gathered her unruly brown hair into a thick knot with Nick still crowding her from behind. He wrapped his arms around her as she moved to go. "Watch your back."

"I will." She couldn't, of course. She'd be out there alone. As much as her fellow officers no longer trusted her, she no longer trusted them. Even the one holding her so sweetly. Nick had told her so many lies when they were married. He kissed her neck now, almost in apology, and she tilted her head to let him do it. They made a pretty picture in the mirror—even half-dressed and unshaven, Nick was always pretty. But she had a wedding album full of beautiful photos and knew what they were worth. When his hand stole over her middle, low across her belly, she sucked in a breath.

He drew back. "You okay?"

"Fine." She disentangled herself and gave him a perfunctory kiss. "See you later."

....

As SHE DROVE WEST THROUGH RUSH-HOUR TRAFFIC, SHE WOLFED DOWN A PRO-TEIN BAR SHE'D FOUND IN THE GLOVE BOX. She made only lurching progress on the road, but her mind raced ahead to the crime scene. Based on the picture Zimmer had sent, the victim appeared to be an above-average-sized male, well built. It would have taken someone, or multiple someones, of considerable strength to wrestle him into a noose and suspend him from the tree. Also, the *P* in PIG on his shirt was backward. Perhaps it had been painted backward on purpose to underscore the slur: cops aren't just pigs; they're stupid too. Or maybe the killer was dyslexic. Or maybe it was a mistake, done in a hurry by someone perched in the dark on a tree branch. Rosehill Cemetery's name was a mistake itself. Some clerk had written it down wrong ages ago, when it was supposed to be named Roe's Hill, after nearby farmer Hiram Roe. Roe had sold his land to the city on the promise that the cemetery would memorialize him, but a slip of the pen had rendered him as anonymous as the worn-down old gravestones dotting his land.

Annalisa reached her destination and slowed to a crawl. At a hundred acres and a hundred thousand graves, Rosehill was the largest of Chicago's cemeteries, and it contained hundreds of mature trees. The victim could be suspended from any one of them. She circled the perimeter until she found the telltale black-and-white units parked outside. She slid her Honda in behind them and entered through the nearest path. In early November, the usually lush trees looked like half-eaten turkey legs, brown and missing chunks of foliage. Annalisa located Zimmer, a half dozen uniformed cops, and Joe Biggs from forensics. He wore a full-body protective suit, as though the crime scene might be on Mars, and he crouched to take photos of the corpse. Zimmer spotted Annalisa and wandered over to greet her. Her boss held a paper cup half-full of coffee and Annalisa's mouth watered at the sight of it. "The coroner's been here and gone," Zimmer reported, squinting past Annalisa to the trees beyond her.

"Time of death?"

"The body's in rigor. Best guess right now is twelve to twenty-four hours."

"Witnesses?"

"Just the groundskeeper who found him early this morning, but I don't think he'll be much help to us. There was no one at work here yesterday, so we can't be sure when Sam was brought here."

Sam. Annalisa glanced at the man suspended from the tree. He had a name. A day ago, he'd been a person, and now he'd become an inanimate thing, a puzzle to solve. Annalisa scanned the area, checking the sight lines to the body. A pair of oak trees shielded it from view on the west side, and a mausoleum blocked it from the east. You would need to approach from the southern path to see it, and even then, the body would blend with the wide trunk of the tree from which it was suspended. Whoever put him there had chosen this relatively isolated spot on purpose. Annalisa glanced sideways at her boss, who looked every bit of her fifty-two years, the lines deep around her down-turned mouth. "I'm sorry about your friend. Sam."

Zimmer studied her coffee cup. "We rode together back in the day. He used to say he picked me as a partner because he could tell I was going places and he wanted me to drive." She smiled a little, and Annalisa's gaze went to the silver oak leaf on Zimmer's uniform denoting her high rank. Sam had been right about her. "But I knew the truth. None of the white boys wanted to work with the only Asian guy. They sure as hell didn't want to ride with a Black woman. So Sam Tran and me, we formed a team. Turns out, catching bad guys usually means talking to the right people, and on the streets, those people didn't always want to talk to the white boys."

Annalisa nodded. The public liked to think that policing meant shoving bad men into the wall until they confessed, but really, it was about getting the right person to talk to you. Zimmer was a good talker. Sam Tran, Annalisa didn't know about yet. "He left the job," she said. "Went into business for himself?"

"About twelve years ago, yeah."

Annalisa regarded her with mild surprise. "He must've been shy of his twenty." They had to do twenty years on the force to qualify for a full pension.

Zimmer shifted her feet as though trying to keep warm. "Left with five years to go," she said grimly. When Annalisa gave her a questioning look, Zimmer continued. "Sam found out one of the lieutenants in his division was having his unit pad their overtime stats—work two hours, get paid for four. City foots the bill. Sam wanted to tell the deputy chief about the scam, but I said he should keep his head down till his pension kicked in. He reported it. One guy got fired and a couple more got transferred. The lieutenant who okayed the whole thing kept his post."

"And Sam got the boot."

"Someone planted a baggie of coke in his locker. It was total bullshit. It didn't have his prints on it and he came up clean on a drug test, but Internal Affairs hassled him for weeks about it anyway. They finally cleared him and then someone stuck kiddie porn in his car."

"What?"

"Disgusting, right? Sam quit then and I almost followed him out the door."

"Why didn't you?"

Zimmer's nostrils flared with emotion. "That lieutenant who kept his job? He went up for commander of the north-side detective squad. I decided I would make sure he didn't get it. If we all quit, then they win, right?"

"Right." Annalisa gave her boss the ready agreement she seemed to need. Ten years on, Zimmer clearly felt torn by this decision. After what the thin blue line had done to her friend, Annalisa couldn't blame her. "What about Sam's personal life? Married? Single?"

"He's divorced, with one son. Benjamin. He's about thirteen or fourteen now. God, this is going to kill him. It's going to kill all of them, especially his mom. Sweet lady. Sam and I had a thing going about whose mother made the best fried chicken. One day, Sam decided we would have a contest at the end of shift. His mom would make her chicken and mine would make her recipe. We'd bring it to the precinct and put it to an anonymous vote whose was better. Stan Figgins brought potato salad and Bert Reyes contributed a case of beer. We all ate like kings." She gave a ghostly smile at the memory.

"So who won?"

"His mom did—by one vote." She looked over her shoulder to Sam's body. "Don't you ever tell anyone, but it was my vote." When she turned around again, there were tears in her eyes and she blinked them back rapidly. "Biggs is wrapping up his initial pass," she said, nodding in the direction of the scene. "You should take a look."

Annalisa reached down to pull gloves from an open box and walked up the grassy slope to the tree where Sam Tran still hung suspended about eighteen inches from the ground. The rope around his neck appeared to be white nylon. "Watch it over there," Biggs said, pointing at a yellow marker he'd placed on the ground near the base of the tree. "We have a possible shoe print." Annalisa nodded and walked to the other side of the body. Lividity in Sam Tran's hands made it difficult to be certain, but she thought she saw abrasions on his right knuckles, which could be a sign he'd fought with his attacker. The PIG scrawled across his chest was more jarring in person. The letters were even, despite the backward P, meaning Sam had been motionless when they were applied. Either the killer rendered him unconscious somehow before dragging him out here or he'd waited until Sam went unconscious before whipping out the spray can in public. Annalisa looked around again. Pretty ballsy to linger like that.

The sound of a ringing cell phone made Annalisa reach for hers reflexively. "It's his," Biggs said helpfully, pointing at Sam. "Second time so far."

Annalisa held her breath and maneuvered the ringing phone out of Sam's back pocket. "Hello," she said, holding it gingerly in her gloved hand. "This is Sam Tran's phone. Who's calling?"

There was a funny pause on the other end. Then a familiar voice said, "Anna?"

She yanked the phone away from her head to stare at it for a second. Sure enough, the caller ID read *Vega, V.* "Vinny?"

Zimmer folded her arms. "You want to tell me who's on the line?"

Annalisa stretched the phone away from her body in a helpless gesture. "It's my brother."

TWO

············

"WHY ARE YOU ANSWERING SAM TRAN'S PHONE?" Vinny demanded when she spoke to him again.

"Why are you calling it?" Annalisa countered.

"Because he and I have business to discuss. Is he there? Let me talk to him."

Annalisa eyed the corpse and stepped away from it, like Vinny might sense the truth through the phone. "Not right now. Tell me about this business you have with Sam Tran."

"It's personal."

Annalisa ducked her head and lowered her voice. "Personal? I'm your sister."

"No, you're a cop. Don't bullshit me because there's no other reason why you're answering a private investigator's phone. Are you hassling him? Did you raid his office or something?"

"Sam was a cop too," Annalisa said.

"Yeah, and he knew when to walk away."

Annalisa looked over her shoulder again at the body. Apparently, he hadn't. She bit her lip and tried to sound conciliatory when she spoke again. "Look, if you hired him for something, you may as well tell me. The quicker we can rule you out of this—"

"Rule me out of what?"

She hesitated. "Sam Tran is dead."

Vinny responded with stunned silence. "Dead?" he echoed finally. "How?"

"I can't tell you that right now."

"If you're there, it's got to be bad. Traffic accident?" Annalisa said nothing. His voice got rougher and she heard him swallow. "Murder?"

"I can't discuss it."

"Fine. Then I can't either." He clicked off the phone and Annalisa let out a frustrated groan.

Zimmer sauntered over to join her. "Trouble on the home front?"

"I think my brother Vinny may have been one of Sam's clients."

"Small world," Zimmer offered. "What's the job?"

"He won't say," Annalisa said, and Zimmer's mouth thinned. Whatever it was, Vinny hadn't breathed a word to Annalisa. As far as she knew, things seemed fine between Vinny and his wife, Carrie. They joked that they were newlyweds again with their daughter, Quinn, off at college. It seemed impossible Carrie might be cheating. Maybe it was job-related, Annalisa reasoned. Vinny ran a landscaping business that had grown to more than fifty employees. If one of them was claiming on-the-job injury, Vinny could have hired a PI to investigate. But then why not say so?

"Maybe I should switch you out with Carelli. You work the Chicken Bandit and he can handle this."

"Commander, no. Whatever this thing is with Vinny, I'm sure it's not mixed up in Sam's death. Sam probably had dozens of recent clients." Zimmer did not look convinced. "Well, he didn't do that," Annalisa said, gesturing to where the ME's team was preparing the body for removal.

Zimmer made a calming motion with her hands. "I believe you. But Vega, you've already got one brother doing twenty to life on a homicide charge."

Two years later, the truth still hit Annalisa like an icy wave to her face. "Yes," she managed at length. She kept her gaze level. "And you know better than anyone if Vinny was somehow involved here—which he isn't—I'd be the first to bring him in."

"If he's implicated in the slightest, you're off the case. So he'd better have a stone-cold alibi—I mean like he was on the Jumbotron at United Center doing the cha-cha in front of twenty thousand witnesses—or I'm pulling you off."

"Got it."

Zimmer's shoulders rose and fell with her heavy sigh. "I have to notify Lara and Benji Tran before the press does."

"You want me to come with?"

"No, it's better if I do it alone. I know the family."

"Okay, then I'll start with the business angle. Did Sam work alone or did he have associates?" She hoped for a partner or second investigator who could help her figure out Sam's current caseload.

Zimmer handed a simple white business card to Annalisa. It read SAM TRAN, CRIMINAL INVESTIGATOR, with a phone number and an address in Oak Park. No mention of anyone else involved with the business.

Annalisa tucked the card into her jacket pocket. "I'll check it out."

She paused to watch the men load Sam's body into a bag to preserve any evidence and then place him onto a stretcher. His physical form disappeared from view, and with it, the PIG on his chest. Annalisa had been called worse. But she got up every morning to the possibility of change, that her best or worst deeds need not define her. Someone had stopped Sam Tran's story prematurely and tried to script the final words across his body. Annalisa couldn't undo the damage, but she was determined that this sad little show in the cemetery would not be Sam's ending.

············

SAM TRAN'S OFFICE WAS A TWO-ROOM OUTFIT IN A REDBRICK BUILDING, NEXT TO AN AUTO BODY SHOP AND ABOVE A NAIL SALON. Annalisa arrived to find the door partially open and the sound of cabinets being rifled through on the other side. She put one hand on her weapon and nudged the door with her foot until it widened enough for her to pass through without noise into the waiting room. The person searching Sam's office cried out in agony and kicked a metal cabinet, creating a hellacious bang and causing him to yell even louder.

"Easy there," Annalisa called as she entered the office and found a teenage boy attacking the file cabinet. "It's unarmed."

The kid jerked his head up in surprise at her arrival. He had gangly limbs and giant sneakers on his feet, like a puppy who hadn't yet grown into his paws. "Who're you?" he demanded, chest puffed up, ready to defend his territory.

She showed off her ID and introduced herself. "I'm guessing you're Benji. Shouldn't you be in school now?"

He scowled at her. "I'm trying to find my dad. He hasn't answered my texts or calls for three days. Mom said he's probably busy working a case, but he always tells me ahead of time when he's going to be out of touch. Always." His bravado slipped when she didn't reply, and he swallowed visibly. "Do you know my dad? Is that why you're here? Do you know where he is?"

Annalisa's heart lurched in her chest. She'd done dozens of death notifications over her career, but she'd never had to tell a fourteen-year-old kid that his father wasn't coming home. This wasn't news that should come from a stranger. She took a few steps closer to him. "When's the last time you talked to your dad?"

"Saturday. He came to my basketball game and then we had burgers after. Well, I had a burger. Dad ate some tofu thing like he always does. He didn't say anything about leaving town."

"Did he seem like he might have been worried about anything?"

"Like what?"

Annalisa shrugged one shoulder. "Like anything might be weighing on his mind."

A crease appeared in Benji's forehead as he considered. "He seemed normal to me. I mean, he told me I played a great game when I only scored four points, but he's always like that—hugging me, telling me he's proud of me."

"That's great." Annalisa forced a smile.

"I mean, sort of. The guys give me crap about it, but they don't get where he's coming from. Dad had cancer when I was a little kid, like only four years old? I don't even remember it, but Mom says he almost died. Dad tells me God must've known how much I needed a dad so he let him live. How am I supposed to tell him not to hug me and stuff?"

To fight through cancer and end up hanging from a tree, Annalisa thought. She hoped the horror didn't show on her face. "So he wasn't having any trouble with anyone?"

"You mean like the guy next door?" he said, and she perked up.

"Which guy is that?"

"His name's Willie Doyle. He owns the garage next door, and he's always parking cars in Dad's reserved place. He says since Dad has two spots in back, he can spare one of them, and Dad told him it's for clients. Mr. Doyle said if there was no one using it, what's the harm? I guess he parked one of the cars he was working on in the spot and Dad had it towed. Doyle cussed him out and called him a bunch of names. Then Dad's car got a slashed tire one night when he was working here, and he's pretty sure Doyle did it. Did Doyle call the cops on my father or something? Is that why you're here?"

"What kind of names did Willie Doyle call your dad?"

Twin spots of pink appeared high on his cheeks. "I don't know if I should say."

"You can tell me."

"He called him an effing asshole, a—a goddamned Chink. A pig."

"I see," Annalisa said, carefully neutral. "Thanks for telling me." She stepped forward to look down at Tran's tidy desk. "I'm trying to find out information on the cases your dad has been working on lately. Any ideas?"

Benji gestured at the desk, where three manila folders were lined up. "That's them, as far as I know. The dates are current. It's all local stuff, so I don't know why he'd take off on me like this."

Annalisa picked up the closest folder to her. The tab read OSTEEN, NINA. She opened it to find a picture of a woman with thick, curly brown hair holding a small child, both of them smiling. The style of dress, with high-waisted jeans and white sneakers, and the woman's poofy hair said the picture wasn't current, perhaps dating to the 1980s or early 1990s. Underneath was a copy of a missing person report on Charlotte Osteen, indeed dated January 4, 1990. From what Annalisa could see, Nina was Charlotte's daughter and she had hired Sam Tran to try to find her mother. She set this folder aside and picked up the next one.

The tab read MORRISON, BRAD. When she opened the folder, a queen of hearts playing card slipped out. "What's that for?" Benji asked, straining to see.

"Not sure," Annalisa replied as she retrieved the card. It had a hand-written note on the back that said *Springwood Inn*. She put the card down and caught her breath when she flipped open the folder again. It showed copies of graphic crime scene photos depicting a naked couple lying face-down, male and female, who had been killed in bed. The amount of cast-off blood along the walls and ceiling suggested bludgeoning, although she saw no weapon in the photos. She closed it before Benji could see.

The third folder read VEGA, VINCENT, and Annalisa braced herself for what she might find inside. Screw Vinny for making her find out this way. She flipped the cover open with her eyes shut and then forced herself to peek. *Harassment*, she read. Potential stalking? The complaint said there was a possible Peeping Tom or stalker on the Illinois University campus, and that her niece Quinn had been a victim of anonymous threats. Vinny hadn't breathed a word to her about any of this. She was family. A cop. Instead, he went behind her back and hired some PI to protect Quinn. She flipped through the notes to find the stalker's identity. Nothing. Tran hadn't cracked the case.

"Is that the one about the college girl being stalked?" Benji asked.

Annalisa slapped the folder closed. "You know about it?"

"Just that some guy called and reamed out Dad for not doing more on the case. He said the girl's roommate was being followed now, too, or something. I could hear him yelling on the other end of the phone. He said for what he was paying, Dad should park his ass on campus and watch the dorm around the clock. Dad said he'd look into it." He turned anxious eyes to her. "Do you think that's where he is now? Like on a stakeout?"

Annalisa tamped down her anger and her concern—both for Quinn and for Vinny, who'd apparently had a shouting match with a murder victim—and regarded the boy with a heavy sigh. She would drop him off and go find Vinny. Like Zimmer, she hoped he had an unshakable alibi. "I think it's time I took you home," she said to Benji as she scooped up Sam's files. "You know my boss, Lynn Zimmer? She's visiting with your mom."

He brightened. "The Hammer? Yeah, she and my dad are tight. She plays ball with us in the driveway sometimes. My dad goes easy on me, but not the Hammer. She brings it."

"Hard," Annalisa agreed. "She's tough and she doesn't quit, no matter what. You should remember that, okay?"

He gave an uncertain nod as he collected his backpack from the floor. "My mom is going to kill me for ditching school."

"I think she'll understand." Annalisa put an arm around his narrow shoulders as she shepherded him out of the office, and he did not shrug her off. The poor kid was in a waking nightmare and didn't know it yet. She resisted the urge to pull him tighter, to shield him, but she knew it wasn't possible. In a few minutes, Benji's world would change and she'd be marked in his memory forever on the line between before and after.

THREE

....

QUINN VEGA AWOKE WITH A GASP, LIKE SOMEONE EMERGING FROM UNDERWATER. She sat straight up in bed, heart trembling until her eyes adjusted to the familiar dorm-room surroundings. Her tufted blue ottoman. The giant mosaic sunflower print that hung next to her on the wall. Across the way, her roommate Natalie's bed was unmade and empty. The room felt still and silent, like Natalie had been gone for a while, and Quinn couldn't figure out what had awoken her. She reached for her phone and saw she had seven missed texts from Jason, her boyfriend, but she expected that, since she'd been ignoring him ever since he failed to show at the Halloween party. What surprised her were the four missed texts from her father. The last one said, ANNALISA AND I ARE COMING TO TALK TO YOU.

Quinn let loose a string of cuss words as she leaped from the bed and started picking up dirty clothes from her floor. Each shirt, each pair of pants, she swore anew. The door opened and Natalie appeared, flushed from a run, sneakers on her feet and a damp T-shirt clinging to her body. She removed her earbuds and watched Quinn whirl around the room cursing for a few seconds with amusement in her eyes. "Did you develop Tourette's or something while I was gone?"

"Worse." She shoved the armful of clothes in the hamper. "My father's coming. He's bringing my aunt with him and they want to talk about the stalker thing."

"I thought your dad hired a PI for that."

"Yeah, and I told him not to do that either. It's not a real stalker. It's some idiot trying to get attention. But now my aunt's involved, and she's a cop, so it's going to be a whole big thing."

"Well, maybe she can actually get the creep. He's back, you know."

Quinn halted her frantic cleaning. "What?"

"Look for yourself." Natalie grabbed her shower caddy and gestured with her free arm at the door.

Quinn hesitated for a second and then yanked the door open with her eyes shut. She forced herself to peek. On their whiteboard, someone had written SLUTS R US with a crude rendering of male genitalia added. "You didn't remove it?" Quinn demanded as she grabbed a tissue.

Natalie shrugged and threw a towel over her shoulder. "I just saw it. It wasn't there when I left."

Quinn froze as she realized this meant the person had been here while she slept, maybe minutes before. The door wasn't strong. Maybe an inch thick, with a flimsy lock. A guy emerged from the room across the hall, scratching his bare chest with one hand as he held a towel around his waist with the other. She didn't know him. Probably one of Emma's latest conquests. He stopped when he saw Quinn and he read the note on her door. His eyes turned appraising and he gave her a suggestive half smile. "Morning," he said.

Quinn removed the writing with a furious swipe. "You'll have to wait or use a different bathroom," she told Natalie when she was back inside the room. "Emma's one-night stand is in our shower."

Natalie sat on her bed with a sigh. "I'm just saying—maybe it's not the worst idea to have your aunt look into it. Who knows what might have happened to me the other night if Officer Ken hadn't shown up?"

"No one was following you," Quinn said, rolling her eyes. "You have to stop listening to all those podcasts." Natalie loved anything with a serial killer in it.

"Hey, Officer Ken believed me."

Officer Ken's name was really Officer Kent, but he had blond hair, blue eyes, and a chiseled jaw like a Ken doll, so everyone called him Offi-cer Ken. "Oh, let's be real—you wanted an excuse to talk to him." Quinn made her voice high and girly. "Oh, Officer Ken, will you walk me home? I'm so scared."

Natalie threw a pillow at Quinn. She blew her bangs off her forehead before cracking a grin. "You gotta admit he's sexy in a huncle sort of way."

Quinn had a slew of uncles and she didn't find any of them hunky. "It's the uniform that gets you going," she replied as she tugged on a pair of jeans. "And trust me, the blues don't do anything for me."

Natalie sobered. "You really hate her, don't you? Your aunt."

Quinn wilted under the question. She had been sixteen when Annalisa blew apart the family. Alex and Pops on trial for murder. Her father sobbing in the bathroom at night when he thought no one would hear him. Her parents had fought over the legal bills, over how much they could give to Alex and Pops. For a while, Quinn wasn't sure she'd be able to afford college, but she'd managed to scrape together enough scholarship money to pay for a state school. "Annalisa? I don't hate her. But I sure don't trust her." Fully dressed now, she eyed her friend. "Shower's probably free."

"Shouldn't you be at your meeting with Professor Hottie?"

"Hawthorne," Quinn corrected absently as she checked the time on her phone. Natalie was right that she had to hurry if she was going to make it all the way to the life sciences building by nine thirty to meet with her biology professor.

"I stand by what I said. He totally looks like that guy from *Bridgerton*. The Duke? Yummy."

"Nat, ew. He's like, forty."

"I'm not saying you've got to peg him. But if you have to sit there watching some guy drone on about chlorophyll or whatever, it helps if the view is good." She left to find the bathroom and Quinn finished getting ready, fixing her hair into a messy topknot. *Focus*, she told herself. *You can't worry about Dad or Annalisa right now.* She'd bombed the first bio exam and she needed to make sure she got at least a B on the midterm to keep her grades up. Her scholarship depended on it. She jogged down the stairs and out of the dorm into the sunshine. Winter would win November eventually, but so far, the sky still shone blue—no need for a heavy coat yet. Quinn felt optimistic about her meeting with Professor Hawthorne. He wasn't a fossil like so many of the professors; maybe he would remember what it was like to be crushed under a full load of classes.

Her phone buzzed with a text and she dug it out to look, praying it wasn't her father. She halted when she saw the words. **I see you.** She checked the sender's number and didn't recognize it, but it was simple to spoof a number these days to disguise the sender. All that talk with Natalie about the "stalker" made her jumpy. She glanced around. Students walked past her in both directions, some lost in whatever was playing on their headphones, others chatting in pairs or small groups. She saw one guy in a Cubs hat sitting on a bench swiping at his phone. He glanced up and looked right at her, but he was no one she knew. She sucked in a breath and walked faster. After a few minutes, her phone pinged again. She made herself look and gave a soft cry when she saw the words. **The pink top is sexy. Tighter would be better.**

She texted back, **Fuck off.**

She started walking again, phone in hand, looking for anyone tracking her. She had to cut through the center of campus with its many trees. Around her, students sat on the grass chatting or studying. Her heart sped up and her face turned hot as she increased her pace. She heard a stick crack to the left, somewhere among the trees, and it made her jump. She whirled to see who it was and someone grabbed her shoulders from behind. "Found you!" She screamed and jerked away.

Her boyfriend, Jason, stood there grinning at his cleverness. "Why aren't you answering my texts? I went by the dorm and Natalie said I just missed you."

"Your texts? Is this you?" She held up her phone to show him. "You scared the crap out of me."

"That's not my number."

"I know that. But you were following me just now."

"Following you? I was trying to catch up to see if you wanted to have lunch later."

"I can't." She pushed past him in the direction she was originally headed. The cold sweat that had come over her when Jason jumped her had not evaporated.

"Why not?" He fell into step beside her. "Come on, Q, you can't be mad at me forever about some stupid Halloween party."

"My dad and my aunt Annalisa are coming, and they want to talk to me about the stalker." She shot him a glare. "I should tell them it's you."

"The stalker? You mean the guy drawing dick pics on your board?"

"Look, I can't get into this now," Quinn said. "I'm late for my meeting with Professor Hawthorne."

He took her arm to stop her. "Hey, if someone is threatening my girl, that's more important than a stupid bio test. Who's texting you? Let me see if I know him."

"The number is anonymous." She tried to pull free from his grasp but he held her tight.

"Let me see it. Why won't you show me?"

"Jason! Let me go."

"Just show me the phone." He tried to get it from her with his free hand but she held it back.

"Is there a problem here?" Officer Ken appeared as if from the ether.

Jason dropped his hold on her. "No problem." He raised his palms and stepped back. She could still feel the finger marks on her skin. "Me and my girlfriend were just having a conversation."

Officer Ken turned his blue eyes to her. "Are you all right, Ms. Vega?"

Quinn's heart missed a beat in momentary confusion. She hadn't realized he knew her name. "I—I'm fine," she stammered, hoisting her backpack higher on her shoulder. "I'm late for a meeting."

"I'll text you," Jason called after her as she put her head down and hurried on her way.

She practically sprinted to the biology building, where she took the stairs two at a time. Breathless, she found the door to Hawthorne's office partially open, so she knocked and peeked around the edge. "Professor?"

He had the window open and a breeze hit her in the face. His chair was empty. Quinn heard yelling out on the quad and she drifted to the window to see. A group of guys was playing football. Her phone chirped and she jolted at the noise. With trepidation, she looked at the screen. **WE'RE ALMOST HERE**, her father wrote. **WHERE ARE YOU?** He texted in all caps like a grandpa half the time because it let him read the screen without putting his glasses on. She was about to answer him when she noticed Professor Hawthorne's computer screen. His browser was open and it wasn't showing anything related to plants or DNA.

He had been looking at a picture of Annalisa.

FOUR

···········

VINNY SAT STONE-FACED IN ANNALISA'S PASSENGER SEAT AS THEY DROVE SOUTH TO QUINN'S CAMPUS. Annalisa had three older brothers, but Vinny was the oldest, almost eight years her senior. By the time she had memories, he'd been in high school, off making his way in the world. Alex, only two years older than she was, had been her coconspirator. Tony was in the middle, the peacemaker and protector. Vinny had played on the football team, and the whole Vega clan came out to cheer for him, huddled together on the cold benches. She hadn't understood the rules, but she understood the thrill of the win, the way the crowd roared as one and Vinny's sweaty face shone with pure joy. Sometimes after a victory he'd put her on his shoulders while still in uniform and parade her around the field. *He's my brother,* she'd shout down at anyone who passed them, and Vinny would squeeze her legs, holding her tight so she wouldn't fall.

"I need to know where you've been for the past forty-eight hours," she said as they drove. She braced her hands on the wheel, ready for blowback.

He snorted. "Aren't you supposed to tell me I can have an attorney present?"

"Do you need one?"

"You tell me. You say Sam Tran is dead and then nothing else. I don't know what I can tell you. I just talked to the guy a few days ago. He seemed fine."

"What did you talk about?"

"I hired him to find out who was harassing Quinn at school and he hadn't done it. I know he had other investigations going, but he took my money and I wanted an answer."

"He didn't have any leads?" She hadn't been through the full file yet, but the case looked open from what she saw in the folder on Sam's desk.

"The girls on Quinn's floor all told him it was probably some idiot boy in the dorm trying to be funny."

"The dorm is coed?"

"Yes. Sam said he talked to the guys in the dorm and they all denied writing the messages."

"And that's that?" Not much of an investigation.

"He said we could put up a camera to try to catch the guy in the act. I said go for it but Quinn freaked out. She didn't want Sam watching her and her roommate in their underwear. I told her the camera would be pointed outside the room, but she swore she'd remove it if Sam put one in, and he wouldn't do it without her cooperation."

Quinn probably didn't want her comings and goings reported back to Vinny. Annalisa couldn't blame the girl. She cleared her throat. "So what was Sam's plan?"

"He said we had to wait to see if the stalker made another move. Then last week Quinn's roommate, Natalie, got followed home at night by some creeper hiding in the trees. I wanted Tran to park his ass here on campus until he figured out who the stalker was. He said he'd keep on it, but when I talked to Quinn she said she hadn't seen him. So yeah, we had some words."

She gripped the wheel tighter. *Please tell me you have an alibi*, she thought. "And this weekend? You didn't see him or talk to him at all?"

"No. Saturday I was at work, and I stayed late to do some work in my shop. I've been refinishing a set of dining room chairs." Vinny had a workbench at his landscaping business where he liked to work on furniture as a hobby and a side gig. "Sunday I was at dinner at Ma and Pops's place, as usual, which you would know if you were there."

"I was working."

"Sure, you were." It wasn't a lie. The Chicken Bandit case had been running them ragged. But the real truth was she found these family meals almost unbearable now, with Pops in his wheelchair and the ankle monitor strapped to his leg. His crimes had put it there, but they both knew he'd still be free if it weren't for Annalisa. "Is that why you didn't tell me what's going on with Quinn? Because I missed Sunday dinner?"

"It's not your problem. I was handling it."

"Sure, you were." She tossed the words back at him and he turned his head away from her. "What about after dinner? What did you do then?"

"What is this?" he demanded finally. "Why are you grilling me like some suspect?"

She said nothing but her silence filled in the blanks for him. Horror broke out over his features.

"You said Tran's dead. Someone killed him. Is that it?"

"We're investigating it as a homicide, yes."

"Jesus." He ran his hands over his bald head. "And you think I did it? Is that how you operate now? Someone gets murdered and you figure it has to be one of us. Thanks a lot, sis."

"Hey, your name is in his files. You're one of the last people to talk to him, and it wasn't friendly."

"He was working for me! How's that supposed to go if he's dead? What sense does that make?"

"Murder doesn't make sense. God, Vinny, you should know that by now."

He glowered, arms folded, shaking his head at her. "It's because of Alex. You think if he could do it then maybe so could I."

"I don't think that. I'm just doing my job."

"Super cop, Annalisa Vega. Everyone's hero."

She jerked the car to the side of the road and stopped. "Hero? You've got to be kidding me. Half my squad room thinks I'm a traitor. You should have seen how my boss looked at me when your name came up in a dead guy's phone. Everyone around us was like, *Oh, here we go again*. Don't you dare claim I want this, because I never wanted any of it."

"At least you had a choice. The rest of us didn't. Not me, not Ma, or Tony or Carrie or Quinn. I lost a third of my business. Clients were dropping like flies and I had to lay off six people—guys with their own families to worry about. But did you know or care about any of that? Of course not. It's always about you and your feelings."

After Alex, it was hard to trust her instincts anymore, and Vinny looked more the part of a killer than Alex ever had. Alex had been a doughy middle school math teacher who cracked jokes all the time. Vinny had real muscles and a gruff demeanor. He had the physical strength to string Sam Tran from a tree and maybe enough hatred of her profession to write PIG on his chest. But like Vinny said, his motive seemed thin. "I don't think you killed Sam," she said quietly, surprised to find she meant it.

Vinny unclenched slightly. "Then why the hell are we here?"

"Because someone did kill him. Maybe someone who didn't like him coming around asking questions."

"Someone like the stalker," Vinny said as he followed her thought. "Shit."

Annalisa turned the car back on. "Let's talk to Quinn. Find out how worried we need to be."

"I'm worried all the time," he said, more to the window than to her. "Seems like the world isn't safe for anyone anymore."

They met up with Quinn as she was coming out of the life sciences building. She wasn't alone. An older man in a green sweater-vest was with her, his expression expectant. "Hi, Dad," Quinn said as Vinny enveloped her in a hug. "This is my biology professor, Wendell Hawthorne. He wanted to meet you."

"Call me Wen," he said, extending his hand to Annalisa and not to Vinny. "I'm a big fan."

"Uh, thanks." She shook his hand.

"How's my girl doing in your class?" Vinny said as he squeezed Quinn around the shoulders. Quinn looked embarrassed.

"She's a hard worker," Hawthorne replied, his eager eyes still on Annalisa. "A very motivated student. Kind of like her aunt, yes?"

"Oh, I never loved biology," Annalisa said to Quinn. "I didn't like the lab where we had to dissect the frog." She added a shudder, hoping to coax a smile from her niece, but Quinn remained impassive, avoiding her gaze.

"And yet you had no trouble dispatching the Lovelorn Killer," Hawthorne said with admiration. "Sending him six stories to his death and saving who knows how many lives in the process." He put a hand to his chest. "Forgive me, I'm a bit of a true-crime enthusiast. I even have a podcast as a little hobby on the side. I'd love to have you on sometime." He produced a card and handed it to her.

"Thanks, but I don't give interviews. Nice to meet you." She gestured away from him to a bench along the quad. Quinn and Vinny started walking in that direction, and Annalisa followed after a beat, feeling Hawthorne's eyes on her as she went. She was used to people around Chicago recognizing her and asking about the Lovelorn case, but Hawthorne's words niggled at her. She had sent the Lovelorn Killer tumbling through a skylight, but that part of the case had never been made public. Everyone assumed she'd shot him and not the glass from under his feet. Her unease lingered as she caught up to Vinny and Quinn, who sat on the bench. Quinn was showing her father something on her cell phone.

The top of Vinny's head turned purple and he thrust the phone in Annalisa's direction. "Tran thought I was being paranoid, but look at this. This guy is sick."

Annalisa read the texts and looked at Quinn. "And you have no idea who sent them?"

"No?" Quinn didn't seem sure.

"Who has your number?" Annalisa asked.

Quinn squirmed and glanced at her father. "Well, kinda everyone. I mean, not everyone, but we did a number exchange in our dorm during orientation. We have a group chat going . . . see?" She took the phone and called it up for Annalisa to review. "It's silly stuff mostly."

"Send me the anonymous texts and I'll see what I can find out."

"And then pack a bag because you're coming home with us," Vinny said.

"What? Dad, no." Quinn leaped off the bench and away from him. "That's insane."

"No, it's insane to stay here. I'm not leaving you with some lunatic following and threatening you."

Quinn turned to Annalisa with an imploring gesture. "No one is threatening me. I'm sure it's just a stupid joke."

"She's right," Annalisa told Vinny with regret. "There's no actual threat here."

"See?" Quinn said, turning on her father. "No threat."

"That's bullshit." Vinny rose to his feet. He was taller than Annalisa. "It says right there he's watching her. Following her. That makes him a creepy little fuck, and maybe the next time, he delivers his message in person."

"It says 'I see you' and then there's the remark about her sweater. I agree it's concerning that we don't know who is sending the texts, but the content on its face is not threatening." She turned to Quinn. "What about your door? Have you received any more lewd messages?"

She looked at the ground. "Uh, a few, I guess. But other girls get them too."

"Uh-huh. What about this story your father was telling me about someone being followed the other night?"

"That was Natalie, my roommate," Quinn replied with a roll of her eyes. "I think she freaked herself out over nothing. Nat comes from a farm in a small town, so she's not used to noises at night, except like cows and stuff. She told Officer Ken someone was following her, but he checked it out and didn't find anything."

Annalisa wondered if there had been any similar reports from other girls on campus. "I'd like to talk to Officer Ken. Where can I find him?"

"Oh, his real name is Officer Kent," Quinn began, and broke off with a touch of surprise as she looked across the way to a man loitering by a recycling bin. "You know, I think that's him right over there."

FIVE

....

OFFICER "KEN" TURNED OUT TO BE CALLED OWEN KENT, BUT ANNALISA COULD
SEE WHERE HE'D GOTTEN THE PLASTIC NICKNAME. It wasn't only that he
sported short blond hair, light blue eyes, and a square jawline; he held
himself with a slightly rigid posture and his forehead didn't seem to move
with the rest of his face. He insisted on bringing Annalisa to his office for
their chat, dragging over extra chairs from the unoccupied desk in the
room to accommodate Quinn and Vinny. Officer Kent kept a tidy work-
space, almost spartan, with a desktop computer and monitor, a phone,
and a university-branded coffee mug that held six matching blue pens.
The only nod to personalization was a wall calendar he'd tacked up on the
concrete wall next to his desk that showed a pair of orange kittens inside
a pilgrim's hat. The calendar had nothing written on it.

"Yes, I talked to the man," Kent replied when Annalisa asked him
about Sam Tran. "He wanted to know the same thing as you do, about
whether we'd had reports of females being harassed on campus. I told
him we hadn't seen anything out of the usual."

"What's 'the usual'?" Annalisa asked.

"We mostly get property crimes—theft, vandalism. Beyond that, we
answer nuisance complaints, usually noise-related, and we handle med-

ical emergencies. Those mostly involve alcohol, and every year when we get a new crop of students who don't know their limits, we end up sending a bunch of kids to the hospital." He fixed Quinn with a stern look and she turned her gaze to her lap. "We did get one report of sexual assault last month, a date-rape situation. The perpetrator and the victim knew each other, which is typically how these crimes occur around here. Nothing like what you're saying with a stalker hiding in the trees."

"Date rape," Vinny said, his voice tight. "You say that like it's no big deal."

"On the contrary, we take the allegations very seriously. The incident has been turned over to the local DA's office for further investigation."

"So you have nothing similar to what Natalie Kroger reported about being followed," Annalisa said.

He considered for a beat. "The only thing that even comes close is a report last Saturday we had of a female who says she was attacked in the woods behind the Greek houses on Fraternity Row. But we investigated and could not confirm the report."

Annalisa sat forward. "What do you mean you could not confirm it?"

"The girl said she was on her way home from a fraternity party when someone hit her with a rock from behind. But there were no witnesses and the alleged victim was obviously intoxicated at the time of the incident. There isn't a paved road in those woods. The kids use it as a shortcut and they've worn kind of a dirt path, but it's hard to navigate in the dark. You've got tree roots and loose rocks everywhere. Easy to trip and fall, especially if you're not walking too straight to begin with."

"But she was hit with a rock. She must have been injured."

"Yes, ma'am, she had a bump on her head and a cut lip from where she fell. But she still had her phone in her pocket, and there was no sign of sexual assault. The health clinic on campus patched her up and sent her home. No treatment necessary other than an ice pack and maybe a real strong cup of coffee." He grinned at his own humor.

"I want to see where it happened," Annalisa said briskly, and his smile evaporated.

"It's been several days and we had rain Sunday morning. I don't think there's much to see there."

"Then you don't need to come," she said as she stood up. "Just point me in the right direction."

He rose as well and put a hand on his hip, drawing her attention to his gun. "Begging your pardon, Detective, but your jurisdiction stops at the city limits. Even if there was a crime here, it wouldn't be yours to investigate. We're not some rent-a-cops. We're sworn officers who went through the same training as you did. Your meddling could be classified as interference with our investigation."

Annalisa held his gaze. "What I'm hearing is that you did investigate and found no crime."

"That's correct," he said, seeming glad she was agreeing with him.

"So then your investigation is concluded and I couldn't possibly be interfering." She turned to Quinn. "Do you know this place, the woods behind the Greek houses?"

Quinn gave a cautious nod. Vinny pivoted to look at her, askance. "You've been to these parties? With the drinking and some girl getting attacked?"

"Dad! No." Quinn squirmed in her seat. "But everyone knows where the Greek houses are."

"Great," Annalisa said flatly. "Let's go."

Officer Kent, frowning all the way, joined them as they trooped across campus to the wooded area behind the fraternity and sorority houses. The trees were densely packed but not that numerous. In the light of day, Annalisa could clearly see the worn path the students used as their cut-through. She estimated it was perhaps an eight-minute walk from one end of the woods to the other, which probably made it feel safe. There wasn't a lot of room for trouble to start.

"This is where she said it happened." Officer Kent indicated a patch of dirt under his feet.

Annalisa surveyed the scene. It was roughly at the midpoint of the woods. The fraternity houses had disappeared behind them and the paved path to the main campus was not visible on the other side. If you were dropped blindfolded from a plane, you might think you were alone in the world. Someone planning an attack could hardly have picked a more opportune spot. She paced about five feet in one direction and then the other. "I don't see it," she announced.

Officer Kent tilted his head at her. "See what?"

"The rock she supposedly hit her head on when she fell." She pointed at the tree roots. "You could stumble there, I agree. But where's the rock?"

"Maybe there was no rock," Officer Kent countered. "Maybe she hit the tree. She was highly intoxicated."

Annalisa didn't doubt the young woman had been drunk. She'd already spotted two empty beer cans among the trash in the woods, and she'd attended a frat party or two in her day. She examined the bark of the tree he had indicated, finding nothing obvious at the roots and then gradually working her way up. She spotted something four feet off the ground. "It's got something stuck here," she said, leaning closer to observe. "Silver threads, maybe."

"Yep, see, that jibes with what I was telling you," Officer Kent said. "She had on a shiny silver jacket, like part of her costume. It got ripped when she fell."

"She was wearing a silver jacket?" Quinn blurted, and Annalisa turned to look at her.

"Yeah, fifties style, silver with white trim," Officer Kent said, looking back and forth between them. "Kinda reminded me of that movie *Grease*."

"You know this girl?" Vinny demanded of his daughter. "You know what happened to her?"

"No," she replied quickly.

Annalisa made a noncommittal noise in reply and continued her search. "See, look at this," she said, pointing out the sagging end of a nearby pine-tree branch. "Someone broke this off recently. How could she fall on both sides of the path at the same time?" The tree was healthy, the branch sturdy; it would have required some force to snap it.

"If she were stumbling around, she could," argued Officer Kent. "Besides, a hundred kids come through this way every day. We can't determine when that branch was damaged."

Quinn shivered inside her pink sweater and looked around like she wanted to be anywhere else. It was cooler in the woods, hidden from the sunshine. Without saying anything, Vinny put an arm around her and rubbed her vigorously to warm her up. Quinn tolerated his touch for a few seconds before she broke away. "Can I go now? I have to get to class." She asked the question of no one in particular. She was eighteen, a legal adult, but she didn't carry herself like one yet. Annalisa could see the vestiges of the child Quinn had recently been in her grumpy slouch, in her bitten nails, and in the posturing for an authority she didn't quite have.

"You don't know anything more about what happened here?" Anna-lisa asked her.

"How could I?"

She held Annalisa's gaze, her brown eyes steady. Annalisa remem-bered the Christmas four-year-old Quinn sneaked into a box of candy and then tried to deny it while her cheeks were still stuffed, chipmunk-like, full of chocolate. She was a better liar now, but not a practiced one. Honest people didn't like to lie outright. They didn't want to say yes when they meant no. So they would stall, change the subject, or, like Quinn, answer a question with a question.

"Out of curiosity," Annalisa said, "where were you?"

"What's that got to do with anything?" Vinny interjected. "Quinn didn't attack this girl."

"Answer the question," Annalisa said to Quinn, her voice still calm.

"I was in my dorm hanging out with Natalie and Sarah Beth. Now can I go, or do you want to take me in for questioning?"

Annalisa let the dig slide. "If you get any more anonymous texts, send them to me immediately."

"And me," Vinny added pointedly. "Come on, I'll walk you to wher-ever you're going."

"Dad . . ." She let out a groan and stalked off, leaving him to pick through the trees behind her.

Annalisa watched them disappear and she had a sudden vision of another watcher, someone standing here when a different young woman passed this way. "I want to talk to the girl who made the complaint."

"I can't give you her name," Officer Kent replied, rocking on the balls of his feet.

"We both know that's bullshit."

"It's the truth," he said, not sounding sorry. "University policy. We protect the student's privacy."

"If she made a complaint, she wants it to be investigated and the po-lice involved."

"Well, when she calls up the Chicago PD and makes her case to you, then you may follow up on it. Until then, you'd have to get a warrant."

The gleam in his eyes told her he knew she couldn't. The odds that this attack was connected to Sam Tran's death seemed slim at best. But she couldn't shake the image of Quinn walking these woods, that it could have been her to call the campus cops and get the brush-off. "It doesn't bother you that a young woman could have been assaulted on your watch?"

"I do everything I can to keep these girls safe. But I can't make up evidence. Maybe that's how you do things in the big city . . ."

"It's not."

He gave an expansive shrug. "No witnesses, no motive, no signs of sexual assault. What do you want me to do, Detective? Haul every male on campus into my office for interrogation? Check his socks for pine needles?"

"I wouldn't presume to tell you how to do your job," she replied evenly.

"Then I guess we're done here."

"You go on," she said. "I'm going to take another look around."

"Suit yourself." He gave her his best plastic smile. "If you run across any used condoms, feel free to toss 'em. The groundskeepers would be mighty appreciative."

He walked away whistling and she gritted her teeth so she wouldn't say anything she would regret. When he was out of sight, she went for a closer look at the tree he suggested might have caused the girl's fall. It didn't show any signs of scraping or trapped hair. She sifted through the surrounding decayed leaves and found nothing, as he'd indicated. She discovered a sizable rock about ten feet down the path. She could lift it but only with effort. It, too, bore no signs of blood, hair, or tissue. Maybe she really was chasing a mixed-up memory.

She examined the damaged pine tree. There, she did find a single strand of orange hair, which she removed and bagged. Venturing behind the tree to the other side, she discovered it formed a sort of sheltered nook with its neighbors. The students took advantage of the privacy. She discovered two empty beer cans, one with cigarette butts in it. Something else caught her eye, dark, furry, and unmoving. A dead animal? It was hard to see in the dim light. She used her phone as a flashlight and crouched down for a better look. The fur was fake, she saw up close. Gingerly, she lifted it up and saw it was a kind of glove covered in black faux fur, like from a costume. *Halloween*, she thought, and she put it back down where it had laid.

SIX

··········

BACK AT THE PRECINCT, ANNALISA UNWRAPPED A COCHINITA TACO COURTESY OF THE FLASH TACO TRUCK, BUT SHE HADN'T EVEN TAKEN A BITE BEFORE NICK WANDERED OVER AND COLLAPSED IN THE CHAIR ACROSS FROM HER. "Chicken Bandit still on the loose?" she asked with a note of sympathy.

"You're not going to believe this. Patrol arrested a guy early this morning, some nineteen-year-old punk skateboarding down California Ave. wearing a rubber chicken mask. Not just any chicken mask—a dead-on ringer for the one the bandit wears when he's holding up corner stores. Naturally, we're all thinking this has to be the guy. Same build, same mask. He's even wearing the same shoes with the three gray stripes on the sides. But when they search the backpack, it's got a T-shirt and basketball shorts, a water bottle, a banana, and no gun or wad of cash."

"So it's not him?"

"Nope. I didn't tell you what else was in the backpack. A bunch of crumpled receipts. One of them was from an all-night deli for a large sub and soda, and the time stamp matches the second robbery almost exactly. He was across town on Archer when the store was hit on Milwaukee. He decided to jerk our chains with a look-alike mask."

"Sorry." She paused. "I guess you laid an egg on this one."

He wadded up a piece of paper and threw it at her. "What have you got? The ex-cop looking as clean as Zimmer says?"

"He practically squeaks." She looked at the array of Sam Tran's folders she had spread across her desk. "No debts, no vices. He rented a two-bedroom apartment on Francisco Ave. and drove a four-year-old Nissan Sentra. Divorced years ago, one kid."

"Aw, hell. There's a kid?"

"Tran had a boy, aged fourteen. His name is Benji and he seems sweet. He actually gave me the best lead I've got so far. Tran had an ongoing beef with a guy named Doyle at the repair shop next door. They fought over his parking spaces and Doyle may have vandalized Tran's tires. I've got him coming in here for an interview in fifteen minutes. Maybe I'll get lucky and he'll confess."

Nick snorted as she took a bite of her taco. "Then you can rejoin me chasing around the Chicken Bandit."

She didn't tell him about Vinny, Quinn, and the possible campus stalker. Her family had starred in all the precinct gossip for the past two years and she didn't want to give them any more fuel by talking about it out in the open. Plus, deep down, she suspected Nick wouldn't approve of her wandering off the path of the Tran investigation, especially since it had to do with her family. As far as Nick was concerned, Pops had screwed up trying to protect the Vega family and Annalisa was left to deal with the fallout. Better to draw a sharp boundary between her and them. The problem with sharp boundaries, Annalisa found, was that they hurt when you bumped into them.

"Detective Carelli?" The soft female voice made Annalisa look up, taco still in her hands. Nick glanced back from his computer at the same time. A girl with honey-brown hair stood there in a jean jacket with a bunch of pins all over it. The half smile and air of diffidence about her made Annalisa's skin prickle. She'd been here too many times in the past, back when they were married, with one of Nick's conquests showing up all wide-eyed and hopeful that maybe she was just Nick's sister. But this girl looked not even eighteen. "Detective Nick Carelli?" she clarified when neither of them answered. Annalisa shot Nick a "what the hell did you do" look, but he appeared perplexed, not guilty.

"Yeah, that's me."

"Oh, good. My name is Cassidy Weaver."

Nick straightened his tie and smiled at her. "And how can I help you, Cassidy Weaver?"

The way the girl flushed with happiness the instant he said her name was like watching a magic trick come alive onstage. *Presto, change-o. You are now under the spell of Nick the Magnificent.* Annalisa chewed her taco and pretended to look through the nearest file folder. "I got your name from my mom. Summer Weaver?" She said the name with an expectant lilt and paused for his reaction.

"Okay," Nick said patiently. "Is your mom in some sort of trouble?"

"No. Well, yes." She waved her hand dismissively. "That's not why I'm here."

"Why are you here?"

She took a deep breath. "You knew my mom back when she worked at the Screwdriver."

"Yeah? That place closed, didn't it?" He looked to Annalisa. "More than ten years now."

"You would've known Mom about sixteen years ago. She has brown hair like mine and a rose tattoo on her shoulder. I have a picture of her here." She took out her phone and swiped to show him.

Nick barely gave it a glance. "I'm sorry, I don't remember."

"Yeah, that's what she said you'd say," the girl replied, sounding fretful. She shifted from side to side. "She told me not to bother, but I had to come see for myself. I had to know."

"Know what?" Nick asked.

"Know my father." She looked right at him and held his gaze, waiting for his reaction. His mouth fell open and then he abruptly closed it again. Annalisa dropped the remnants of her taco.

"Uh, what?" Nick looked at Cassidy like a Labrador retriever trying to understand its human. "Did you say *father*?"

She nodded quickly. "You're my dad. Biologically, I mean. But don't worry, I don't want anything from you. I'm not here for money. I just—I had to see you."

Nick put both hands on his head and rolled his chair backward, away from her. "Wow. I don't . . . I mean I didn't . . . How?" He looked bewildered and blindsided.

Cassidy was prattling on. "I'm sorry to show up here at your work. I didn't know where you live."

Summer Weaver. Annalisa didn't remember the name either, but the story about the bar sounded familiar and she could do the math. Nick had been wearing the wedding band she'd put on his finger when this girl was conceived. Now Annalisa might be pregnant and he already had a kid. Annalisa stood up and felt the ground shift under her feet. Her heart started to pound so hard she thought she might be sick. "Excuse me," she muttered, fleeing with no direction in mind except *away from here*.

"Anna," Nick called, his voice pleading. "Wait . . ."

She didn't slow down. The nearest restroom had a yellow sign outside that read CLOSED FOR CLEANING, so she detoured to the hallway by the vending machines. She braced her back on the wall and took several deep breaths. Her arms felt shaky and she tried to still them against her body. *You knew he cheated*, she reasoned with herself. *This isn't news.* She'd processed his infidelity, accepted his apology, and she trusted him now. Didn't she? She put a hand on her belly and considered the irony of her situation. She'd been worrying how to tell Nick he might become a father and some teenage kid wandered off the street to do it for her.

"There you are." Officer Marta Hernandez appeared in the hall and Annalisa jerked to attention.

"What?"

"Some guy named Willie Doyle is looking for you at the main desk. He says you have an appointment."

"Uh, yeah." She wiped her clammy palms on her thighs. "I'll be right there."

Willie Doyle turned out to be a large man who resembled Mr. Clean, if Mr. Clean wore baggy jeans and a Bears jersey with half the lettering worn off from age. His grumpy expression didn't change when she introduced herself and thanked him for coming for the interview. He grunted and refused her handshake, shoving his hands into his pockets. "Let's get it over with, okay?"

"As you like." She took him to an interview room.

He slouched in the chair, which somehow looked smaller with him in it. "Look, whatever Sam Tran said I did, I didn't do it. The guy's had it in for me just because I put a car in one of his spaces sometimes. It's not like he was using it. But he goes and has it towed without even warning me first."

"I understand you had a disagreement with Mr. Tran over the parking spaces. I also heard someone slashed his tires recently."

"Wasn't me." He sat back, satisfied. "He came over to my garage a couple of weeks ago, hollering about it, and I told him the same thing. Only my phraseology might've been a little more colorful."

"What did you say?"

He sniffed. "I told him to shove his tires up his ass. He said he'd sue me for damages. I told him I'd sue him back for harassment. Friggin' cops think they make the laws, not just enforce them."

"Vandalism is against the law."

"So is accusing someone of something they didn't do!"

"Actually, that's not a crime."

He waved her off with both hands. "Shoulda known you'd take his side. Do I get a lawyer or what?"

"You're not being charged with anything. Do you want a lawyer?"

"I don't want to pay for one. This whole thing is a friggin' scam and you can't tell me otherwise. Cops round people up, charge 'em with whatever they feel like so their records look good. Lawyers come after to cash in, and everybody wins. Except the poor innocent fucks stuck in the prisons."

"What do you know about prison?"

"My dad did a stint in Joliet and I got a cousin locked up. So, what's the charge here, Officer? What did that pig say I did this time? Throw a rock through his window? TP his house?"

"Have you been to his house?"

His face twisted. "Hell no. You think we're buddies or something?"

"Where were you last weekend?"

"Working," he said without hesitation. "That was Saturday. Sunday I took my girlfriend to visit her mother in Indiana. We watched the game and had a barbecue. Didn't get back till late because Debbie and her ma spent like four hours arguing about the Thanksgiving menu."

"I see." She slid a piece of paper and a pen toward him. "Could you do me a favor? Could you print the word *pig* in capital letters?" She wanted to see if he made the same backward *P* error present in the slur on Sam Tran's chest.

He looked suspicious. "You're trying to trick me."

"How would I do that?" She made her eyes wide and guileless. "It's just a single word."

He weighed this and then picked up the pen. With apparent concentration, he printed out the three letters so large they filled the whole page. He held it up to her with a humorless smile. "How do you like my work, Officer? Do I get a gold star?"

All the letters were correctly rendered. "It's very nice, thank you."

He flicked the paper in her direction. "Are you going to tell me what this is all about?"

"Sam Tran is dead," she said, watching closely to see how he absorbed the news. He froze for a second, genuine surprise on his features.

"No shit?"

"No shit."

He shifted in his seat, still processing. "And he was killed? That's why you brought me here and asked me all these stupid questions?"

"His death is being investigated as a potential homicide, yes."

He folded beefy arms across his broad chest, demonstrating again that he had the required strength to outwrestle Sam Tran if he wanted. "Well, if I'm the best you got, you cops are fucked. I didn't kill him."

"Yeah? You got a better lead? Because so far, you're the only one I've found who had screaming matches with him on the regular."

The words triggered a memory for Doyle because he sat forward. "No, I'm not," he told her smugly. "There was a guy last week. Tran threw him out on the stoop, and the guy was yelling at the door after Tran went back in. Called him a fraud. He said something about murder, too, now that I think about it." He put his chin on his hand and made a show of batting his eyes at Annalisa. "Do you think that sounds like a clue, Officer?"

She ignored his attitude. "Do you remember what this guy looked like?"

"He was ordinary, except for the yelling. Maybe six feet, dark hair, dark jacket. On the younger side. He drove a blue Mazda3 like he was trying out for those Fast and Furious movies."

"You think you'd recognize him again if you saw him?"

"Uh, maybe." He leaned in close enough that she could smell the traces of oil and exhaust on him. "Listen, if Tran's kicked it, does that mean the spaces are free? Like, no one's going to take over his office immediately . . ."

"Goodbye, Mr. Doyle." She stood up. "We'll contact you if we need you." She would check his alibi, but he didn't feel like the killer. He had no record of violence. He'd come in voluntarily to speak to her. The display Sam Tran's killer put on in the cemetery felt personal. She'd seen men come to violence over less than a parking space, but this was heat-of-the-moment stuff, where one guy bloodied another's nose over losing a twenty-dollar bar bet. If they'd found Sam Tran with a bullet in him, lying next to his car, then maybe Doyle would be a viable suspect. As is, she'd keep him in the mix but start looking elsewhere.

She glanced to Nick's desk as she left the interview room and saw he was gone. So was the girl. Marta Hernandez was leaving a message memo at Annalisa's desk, so Annalisa moved to intercept her. "What's up?"

"You've got a full dance card today, Detective. There's a man out front who wants to see you. He says his name is Andrew Powell."

"Powell," Annalisa repeated. She'd heard the name recently. Her gaze slid to the folders on her desk and she realized it had been in one of Tran's files. "Tell him I'll be right out, thanks." She opened first one folder, then the other. Here it was in the Queen of Hearts case, as she already thought of it. The male victim's name in the double homicide had been Stephen Powell. She looked at the crime scene photos again, the ones that depicted the couple nude, facedown on a blood-soaked mattress. Spatter coated the walls. The photos were dated more than twenty years ago, so they seemed logically unconnected to Sam Tran's death, but the fury she saw in them and the flair for the dramatic with the added playing card—these matched the scene she witnessed at the cemetery.

She went out front and a man in the waiting area stood up at the sight of her. "Detective Vega." One side effect of her infamy was being recognized by people she'd never met.

"Mr. Powell?" She accepted his handshake. "What can I help you with?"

"It's me who's come to help you." He had an urgent tone and anxious posture. "I heard Sam Tran got killed, and I know who did it."

"Oh, really?" She was about to invite him back for an interview when she heard a shout from across the room.

"Hey, that's him!" She turned and saw Willie Doyle, ostensibly on his way out. He pointed in her direction and then shifted his finger slightly to Powell. "That's the guy I saw screaming about murder on Tran's doorstep."

SEVEN

....

ANNALISA DIDN'T CARE WHETHER ANDREW POWELL WANTED A POP; SHE RE-
QUIRED ONE FOR HERSELF. She was not going to get through this conversation otherwise. She slid a Coke across the table to him and opened
her own can of ginger ale. "Who was that guy?" Powell asked of Willie
Doyle. "What was he saying about me and Sam Tran?"

"He says he witnessed an argument between you and Mr. Tran."

"Oh," said Powell, sitting back in his seat, like he'd just realized he wasn't
invisible and could be seen by other humans. "Yes, well, I guess that did
happen. But you can't blame me for being upset. Tran harassed my father
at church—at his church!—trying to insinuate that he killed my brother."

"Wait a minute. Tran said your father killed your brother? His own
son?" She peered into the top of her soda can and wished she could add
something harder.

"He asked him for his alibi. Again! We've been going round and round
with that pit-viper family of hers for twenty-two years now, and it never
stops."

"I'm sorry . . . whose family?"

"Kathy Morrison's. Her family's been after Dad for years about the
murders, saying he did it because Stephen brought shame to the family,

shame to the church. Dad condemned the affair, yes, but he never would have murdered anyone for it, and especially not Stephen. Murder's a sin, too, you know."

"I know," Annalisa said drily. She took a deep breath and exchanged her drink for a pen. "Suppose we start there, okay? With the murders. Your brother Stephen and Kathy Morrison were the victims. They were having an affair?"

He hesitated and then gave a tight nod. "Yes. They were both married to other people at the time. Stephen was the choir director in the church and Kathy sang in the choir. I think this was Dad's shame. He urged Kathy to join up. She was new to the area and lonely. Dad knew she was unhappy in her marriage, with her life. . . . He thought it would give her a distraction, help her make friends. He sure didn't think she'd end up seducing his son."

"Kathy pursued Stephen, then?"

"Of course she did," he scoffed. "Stephen and Elizabeth were married eight years, had two kids, and there wasn't a whisper of trouble between them. They were high school sweethearts. Best friends. Lizzie was bro-kenhearted when she found out."

"How did she find out?"

His mouth tightened briefly. "The murders. Can you imagine? A cop shows up at your door one night and says your husband has been found dead in bed with another woman? Lizzie couldn't even believe it at first. She made them show her the body."

Annalisa remembered the first shock when she found out Nick was cheating. She came home early and caught the other woman literally leaving their apartment. He'd been inside, shirtless, and fixing himself a ham sandwich. He'd made up some story about dropping his wallet during lunch at the café down the street, and how the server saw that the address on the driver's license was only two blocks away and so she returned it to him directly. Annalisa knew he'd been lying, but she didn't call him on it or ask any pressing questions. The minute she admitted the truth, she'd have to leave. It would be over. So she'd eaten half the sandwich and let him kiss her mouth before he stepped into the shower.

"I'm sure it must have been awful for all of you," she said to Powell.

"It got worse when her husband started accusing my dad of doing it."

"Brad Morrison? Why did he think that?" Powell looked away and said nothing. She waited, toying with her pen. "Whatever it is, it's going to be in the files."

"Dad killed a guy once," he admitted finally. "Once, a long time ago, and it was an accident. He was in the service, stationed in Mississippi. There was a guy in his unit named Plunkett, and to hear Dad tell it, he was a piece of work. Foulmouthed, lazy. Nobody liked him. So when they got leave, the rest of the unit went out to the bar—Plunkett wasn't invited. I guess there were some cute girls in the bar who liked the uniforms and started getting friendly. Dad had his arm around this one gal when Plunkett showed up and found them all there drinking without him. He'd gotten plastered all on his own somewhere, and he started shooting off his mouth about how the girls were whores. Dad told him to get lost and Plunkett took a swing at him. Now, Dad's a big man. Not too many would take him on. He laid Plunkett out flat, right there in the bar. The bar owner says then that they have to leave, all of them, and so Dad and his buddies start to go. Only Plunkett comes up behind Dad with a switchblade. He cuts Dad's arm, and Dad retaliates by throwing him into the bar. Plunkett cracked his skull on the cement edge. He died three days later in the hospital."

"What happened to your father?"

"Dishonorable discharge." He said the words like they had a sour taste, even after all these years.

"That's all?"

"What do you mean, 'that's all'? Plunkett came after him. Was he supposed to stand there and let the guy murder him?"

"So Kathy Morrison's family thought this meant your father has a temper."

"They've tried for years to ruin him. They picketed outside the church. They went to the media. They even tried to sue him. It's disgusting."

"I'll look into it." She made a few notes. "You say you know who killed Sam Tran. Who is that?"

"Brad Morrison, obviously."

"What?" She looked down at what she'd written so far. "Didn't you say it was Brad who hired Sam Tran to look into the case? Why on earth would he kill him?"

He jabbed at the table with one finger. "Because Tran must've found out the truth. Brad's been guilty all along."

"You sound very sure of that," she replied, skeptical. The police must have investigated the husband at the time.

"He had motive, didn't he? He has no alibi. I know there was a playing card found at the scene. Brad's in finance now, doing risk analysis, but back then he was finishing a PhD in computers. Guess how he made his money? Playing poker—he'd go to Vegas for tournaments and everything. Plus, a witness saw a blue Taurus that night at the motel, the same kind of car Brad Morrison drove."

Annalisa laid down her pen and observed him. He'd worked up a flush in his tirade, sweat beading across his considerable forehead. "You are impressively informed on the details of this case, Mr. Powell. Did you hire your own investigator?"

He colored further and cleared his throat. "We sued him," he said at length.

"Sued Brad Morrison?"

"In civil court. Wrongful death. Part of the motivation was to get legal discovery, so we'd have access to the police reports. When you look at them, you'll see. The cops should have arrested Brad at the time. We still want him in prison for what he did. It's not about the money for us, but we had to sue for money to get the files."

"And how did the case turn out?"

He shook his head, his disgust obvious. "Judge threw it out. That damn family just keeps on getting away with it. I'm sure Brad thought he could dispose of Mr. Tran, too, and why not? It's been decades of no consequences."

Annalisa had been raised in the Catholic Church, and an old line came back to her. "Vengeance is mine, so sayeth the Lord," she suggested to Powell.

Powell leaned over close to her and his voice took on a hard edge. "In His realm, no question. Here on Earth, sometimes the Lord needs help."

Annalisa took his contact information and sent him on his way, promising to look into Brad Morrison. When she exited the interrogation room this time, Nick had returned to his desk. She would have ducked him again, but he turned around just as she looked over and their eyes met. Her mother liked to say that if you loved someone at age eighteen, you would love them forever. Anna had met Nick when she was nineteen— off by one year—and some part of her felt their entire relationship could be captured in that slight gap. They were almost perfect. The *perfect* kept her coming back to him. The *almost* kept her from staying.

Reluctantly, she made her way back to her desk, the mirror to his. He watched her approach. "Heard you might have gotten a confession," he said.

"No such luck." She looked around without taking a seat. "Where's the kid?"

"She had to get home to her mother." He paused and looked at his lap. "Her mom is sick. ALS."

Annalisa couldn't hide her wince. There had been a sergeant in the 7th district diagnosed with ALS at age forty-seven. He hadn't made it two years after that. "Ouch, that's rough. Is that why . . . ?"

"Why she came to see me now? I think so, yeah."

Annalisa gripped the back of her chair so tightly her nails made marks in the faux leather. *I don't want money*, the girl had said. Her mother was dying, and so she was after something much more valuable—a father. "I have to go," she said abruptly, picking up Tran's Queen of Hearts file from her desk. She wanted to drive out to the Springwood Inn and inspect the site of the double murder herself. Tran's notes said he'd been there, and she wanted to see what he'd seen.

"I'll come with," Nick announced as he picked up his own coat.

She halted in surprise. "Nick, this isn't your case."

"So? My case is stalled. I could use a change of perspective for a few hours." He plucked the folder from her hands and found the playing card Tran had clipped to the notes. "What's this about?" he asked as he showed it off to her.

"A card like that one was found at the scene of the murders. Tran put it right there on top, so I'm guessing it meant something to him. I'm hoping this little trip will provide the answer."

"Queen of hearts." He pulled the card free and studied it. "You know, that's what my dad used to call my mom, the Queen of Hearts. He said it was because of all the guys she turned down before she married him."

"Oh yeah?" She took the card from him to examine it. "I guess it could be a romantic sort of nickname."

"No," Nick said, his expression sober. "He was angry when he used it." He picked out a picture of the slain couple in the motel bed and showed it to her. "Same as whoever did this."

EIGHT

....

Sarah Beth lay on her stomach across Quinn's bed, doing her nails with Quinn's Berry Naughty deep red polish. "If you think it's Jason who sent you those texts, you should break up with him."

"I might anyway," Quinn said, peering out the window by her desk. She'd managed to convince her father to let her stay, but she didn't trust him not to spy on her. Or send some other PI to do it for him.

"You got someone else waiting in the wings?"

Quinn dropped the curtain. Jason was like a huge, goofy teddy bear, if the bear had a six-pack. He was two years ahead of her, so she'd felt like Cinderella at the ball when he'd plucked her out of all the freshmen and asked her to a party. At a huge school where she knew no one, she suddenly had someone to hold on to—a popular hockey player, no less. But now she had other friends, and Jason had endless practices and video games with the guys. "No, there's no one else. I just—we met during orientation, that first night. We're supposed to be exploring our options here, right? I don't want to be married to the guy or anything."

Sarah Beth rolled her eyes. "Figures. You nail one of the hottest guys on campus and you're still not satisfied."

"I have to focus on my grades. If I don't get them up by the end of the semester, I'll be put on academic probation and could lose my scholarship. That's all my dad would need to yank me out of here."

"You're eighteen. You can do what you want."

"Not without the scholarship money, I can't." Sarah Beth's parents paid for her to live in an off-campus condo, so she didn't understand. There was supposed to be a first-year residency requirement, but *money makes its own rules*, as her father liked to say. Quinn sat next to her friend on the bed. "Hey, did you hear anything about a girl getting attacked in the woods behind Delta Gamma Nu the other night?"

Sarah Beth held out her right hand to admire her work. "No. Why?"

"There's a girl who reported that someone hit her with a rock on her way home from the party, but Officer Ken says she was just drunk and fell down. My aunt found out about it when she was here earlier."

"Do you know how many drunk girls fall down in those woods? I bet tons." Sarah Beth looked sideways at her and arched a perfect eyebrow. "You were walking pretty funny on the way home that night yourself."

"The thing is, the girl had a silver jacket."

"So?"

"Mine is missing. The one I wore to the party. I took it off when I got hot and then forgot about it. I didn't even think about it until Officer Ken said the girl was wearing one just like it."

Sarah Beth sat up carefully to avoid damaging her wet nails. "And you want to find this girl and get it back?"

I want to find out what happened, Quinn thought. If it was true that this girl had just fallen down, then it didn't matter. If she'd been attacked wearing Quinn's jacket . . . Quinn repressed a shudder. "What if Officer Ken is wrong and she really was attacked? The stuff about the stalker could be true."

A hard knock at the door made Quinn jump, but Sarah Beth laughed. "Maybe that's him now—the stalker. Ooooh!"

Quinn cracked the door and saw Jason's best friend and roommate, Zach, on the other side, wearing his usual grungy sweatshirt. He held a single red rose wrapped in clear cellophane—the kind they sold in a bucket near the checkout counter at the student union. "Zach?" She widened the door but didn't let him inside. "What's up?"

"Uh, nothing. I'm here for Jason. He said you're not answering his texts."

"Yeah, well, I've been busy."

"He wanted me to give you this," he said, handing her the rose. His ears had turned a matching color. "He says sorry for scaring you earlier. He was just joking around."

"Yeah, well, tell him thanks, I guess." She fingered the edge of the plastic wrap.

Zach shoved his now-empty hands into the pockets of his jeans. "I told him he was being an asshole. You've already got someone graffitiing your board here." He gestured at her door. "That's creepy enough. You don't need him making more trouble."

"I appreciate it, thanks."

He stood there awkwardly another moment. "Okay, then I'll get going. See you around."

"Zach, wait," she said, and he turned with an expectant look.

"Yeah?"

"You were at the Halloween party this weekend, right? The one at Delta Gamma Nu?"

He shuffled back in her direction. "Uh, for a bit, yeah."

"Did you hear anything about a girl getting attacked in the woods after?"

He looked shocked. "What? Who said that?"

"It's just something I heard. No one said anything to you about it?"

"No. Nothing like that." He scratched his shaggy hair with one hand. "Well, there was one weird thing. You know Sienna Soto?"

"No. Who is she?"

"She's in my Spanish class. I think she's a sophomore. She's got dyed orange hair and a nose ring and she wears, like, combat boots half the time?"

She made an impatient gesture. "Okay, yeah, I think maybe I've seen her once or twice. What about her?"

"She showed up in class today and her face was all bruised down one side." He indicated the left side of his own face. "Someone asked her what happened, and she said she went skydiving and her parachute didn't open. But when you say some girl got attacked . . ." He broke off with a shrug.

"Do you know where she lives?"

He looked wary again. "No idea. Why?"

"Maybe I want to go skydiving."

He shook his head at her, dismayed. "You shouldn't. A person could get killed like that."

NINE

....

O N THE DRIVE TO SPRINGWOOD INN, ANNALISA KEPT GLANCING AT NICK, WAITING FOR HIM TO RAISE THE SUBJECT OF CASSIDY NOW THAT THEY WERE TRAPPED IN A CAR TOGETHER, BUT HE SAID NOTHING. Finally, she could take the silence no more. "She could be wrong, you know."

"Hmm?" He was studying a gruesome close-up of the Powell-Morrison murders. The photos showed the original queen of hearts card found at the scene, which had a pair of Renaissance cherubs on the back, baby angels with fat faces.

"The girl. Cassidy. Maybe her mother got it wrong." She steeled her hands on the wheel. Annalisa hadn't studied the teenager for more than a minute, but it was long enough to see she didn't have any particular resemblance to Nick. She had dark eyes like him, but his hair was almost black, while hers was light brown. Nick had a dimpled chin, and Cassidy didn't.

"Maybe." He sounded unruffled by this possibility and continued studying the file. "Says here the victims' wallets were found emptied at the scene. Cash removed."

"You don't bludgeon two people to death for petty cash." This crime was about the killing. The theft was an afterthought, or maybe a deliberate attempt to obscure the motive. "So are you going to have a paternity test, then?" She pressed him.

He shut the file with a sigh. "You know, I was thinking maybe I could get coffee with her first—save the buccal swabs for our second visit."

"Nick—"

"Anna. I don't know what you want me to say here. I don't know this girl. I only know what she's telling me, but we both know her story is . . . plausible."

"But you don't remember her mother. Summer?" Annalisa made it sound like she was searching for the name, but she doubted she'd ever forget it.

"No," he said, his voice rich with regret. "But that's plausible too."

She swallowed and nodded, her gaze fixed ahead. He'd told her back then that the other women hadn't meant anything to him. Seems he had been truthful about that part, at least. He reached for her, but she moved her arm to gesture at the motel sign in front of them. "We're here."

The Springwood Inn was a budget motel option nestled among its midlevel counterparts around Midway airport. Long and boxy like a LEGO block, one row of units stacked directly atop the other. Rooms exited to a shared parking lot, where Annalisa slotted her Civic. Through a single-glass door at the front, she and Nick found a small lobby with two chairs, a fake fern, and a narrow faux-wood table that held a carafe of hot water, tea bags, and packets of instant coffee.

"Can I help you, Officer?" The guy at the desk looked up from his phone, his eyes on the shield clipped to Annalisa's belt rather than her face. He was a baby-faced Black man who would have been in grammar school at the time of the Powell-Morrison double homicide.

"Detective Vega, and this is Detective Carelli. You are . . . ?"

"Rondell Hayes."

"Mr. Hayes, we're wondering if you recognize this man." She pulled up a photo of Sam Tran on her phone and showed it to him.

He studied it for a long moment and then shook his head. "He doesn't look familiar to me. Did he stay here recently?"

"I doubt it." She took the file from Nick and pulled out the queen of hearts playing card. "What about this? Does this mean anything to you?"

He flipped it over and then back again. "Nope."

She sighed. This lead was so thin it could walk a Paris runway. But Tran had put the card on top for a reason. "Do you have anyone here who was working back around 2000?" She aimed for the timing of the Powell-Morrison murders.

He let out a low chuckle. "Two thousand? Like more than twenty years ago? Around here, an old-timer is someone on the job more than six months."

Nick gave her a look that suggested they were wasting their time. She wasn't ready to give up yet. "Okay, thanks. Could I speak to the manager or the owner?"

"Oh, the owner," he said, realization dawning. "I thought you meant someone who, you know, works here. Mr. Tolliver goes back at least twenty."

"How can we get in touch with him?"

He looked around her at the door. "Well, if you hurry, you can find him right out there. That's him getting in the Acura."

Nick reached the door before she did, barreling through it and letting her jog to catch up with him. "Mr. Tolliver!" he called, and the short man in a disheveled raincoat turned from the driver's-side door to look at them. "Thanks for waiting." Nick smiled at the man as Annalisa arrived, slightly breathless, behind him. Nick showed his ID. "My colleague and I had a couple of quick questions for you, if you don't mind. I know you're probably at the end of a long day." Nick's goal was to charm everyone out of information, even the men.

Tolliver grunted, apparently not charmed, but he didn't seem disagreeable. Just tired. He had a salt-and-pepper fringe around his weathered dome and swollen knuckles from what looked like arthritis. Annalisa pegged him as about sixty-five years old. "State your business."

"We're investigating the death of this man," Annalisa said as she again showed Tran's picture on her phone. "Do you recognize him?"

He took the phone and gave the picture a dispassionate glance. "He's dead? Not an old fella. What happened?"

"That's what we're trying to find out," Nick said. "Do you know him?"

"Know him? No." He handed the phone back to Annalisa. "But I did talk to him once, about three or four weeks ago. He came around here asking about the murders."

Annalisa and Nick exchanged a quick look. "Do you mean Stephen Powell and Kathy Morrison?" she asked.

"Yeah, them two. They got killed in their room about twenty years ago, and it wasn't ever solved as far as I know. This fella was trying to get to the bottom of things."

"What did you tell him?" Annalisa asked.

"Same as I'm telling you." He scowled at her. "It was horrible what happened to those kids, but whoever did it was a first-rate psycho."

"What makes you say that?" Nick wanted to know.

"He went way overboard if alls he wanted was to rob them. No need to do what he did. There was blood from one end of the wall to the other, up around the headboard, and those two poor kids, facedown, side by side."

"You saw the crime scene?" An actual witness, twenty years later. She couldn't believe her luck. He looked suspicious at her excitement and she reined it back in. "I mean, that must have been terrible for you to see that."

"What's terrible is you lot never caught the guy. The cops at the time, they tried to pin it on Marvin."

"Marvin," Annalisa repeated. She paused to consult her notes. "The maintenance guy? He found the bodies." She had checked and there were never any arrests in the case, so whatever suspicions the investigators may have had about Marvin, they couldn't gather enough evidence.

"He was in that room because I sent him up there." Tolliver drew himself up to his full height, about level with Annalisa's chin. "Marvin was deaf, see. It didn't matter none for the work he did around here. I'd write down what needed doing, and he'd do it. We had a broken AC in room 229, but I wrote it down wrong, as 226. Marvin went to the wrong room." He shook his head. "Got the worst surprise of his life."

"We'd like to talk to Marvin if we could," Annalisa said. "I don't suppose he still works here."

Tolliver snorted with disbelief. "He died about six years ago. He was never the same after your lot got done working him over, accusing him of God knows what. He spent all his time clipping crime stories out of the newspaper, looking for the killer you all couldn't catch. When he found out about those other murders over in Homewood, he figured that was it—proof he didn't do it."

"What other murders?" Nick asked, looking quizzically to Annalisa to see if she was tracking this story. She shook her head almost imperceptibly.

"A young married couple got beat to death in their motel room a few years after what happened here. Marvin saw the story in the paper and brought it to me all excited. He figured this was vindication for both of us, see. The killer didn't have anything to do with our motel or anyone who worked here. He was some psycho preying on whoever he could find. Marvin made me call up the detectives and tell them about these second murders."

"And what happened?" Annalisa asked.

"A big fat nothing. The detective who was here about Stephen Powell and Kathy Morrison had retired. The case belonged to some other guy now. Someone took a message and said he'd get back to us. He never did."

"I see," Annalisa said. She closed her notebook. "Did you tell this story to Sam Tran?"

"Every damn word. Made him a copy too."

"A copy?"

"Of the original newspaper story about those second murders."

"You still have it?" Nick asked with some surprise.

"Oh, I saved everything." He hoisted his thick briefcase from the ground as if to illustrate. "Come on, I'll make you a copy."

TEN

···········

THE SUN TURNED THE SKY ABLAZE WITH ORANGE AS IT SANK TO THE HORIZON, DISAPPEARING IN ANNALISA'S REARVIEW MIRROR AS SHE DROVE THROUGH THE SLUGGISH LATE-AFTERNOON TRAFFIC. "Well?" she asked Nick impatiently as he worked his phone for information on the Adkins case. "Anything?" The faded newspaper clipping had not provided details beyond what Tolliver had already told them. It did name the murdered couple, Bonnie and Todd Adkins, who were visiting from Wisconsin when they were killed at the Crown Gate Motel.

"The Crown Gate was bought up ten years ago. It's a Days Inn now and under completely new management."

"Great," she replied flatly. "What about the investigation? Did you find out who had the Adkins case?" Their best hope of learning more would be to talk to the original detective, although he was unlikely to be on the job after twenty additional years.

"Yeah, but you're not going to like it." He grimaced at his phone.

"Dead?"

"No, he's alive. It's your dad."

"What?" She jerked her head to gape at him and he looked back at her, alarmed.

"Anna, stop!" He pointed out the windshield.

She hit the brakes hard, just in time to avoid hitting the bumper of the car stopped in front of her. Nick snapped hard against his seat belt and back again. "Sorry," she muttered as traffic started moving again. "You're telling me Pops caught the Adkins case?"

"Him and Rod Brewster, yes."

Brewster was also dead. Cops in Chicago, it seemed, didn't have a very long shelf life. Pops was her only lead. There was a time when this news would have been the best she could hope for—Pops had a keen memory for his cases, especially the ones that had gone unsolved. But now he was off the force, disgraced and homebound from Parkinson's disease and with an ankle monitor that said he wasn't allowed to leave the house except for medical treatments. Accessory to murder. He'd pled guilty but still held Annalisa responsible for his fate. *I can't even go to church*, he'd groused at her recently. *How am I supposed to pray for my soul?*

Try praying for Katie Duffy's soul, she had replied tartly, naming the dead woman who'd put him there.

Squinting, he'd raised one shaky finger and pointed at her. *I'll pray for you*, he'd said, and somehow, it sounded like a threat.

"You want me to talk to him?" Nick asked her.

"No, I can handle it."

"I only meant he might be more cooperative with me."

"It's my case." She eyed him. "You're on the Chicken Bandit."

"Yeah, but this thing just got big. Maybe a serial killer, one no one even knew about. The press gets ahold of this and it's got the potential to go national."

"I know how it works," she snapped at him. They'd been down this road before.

"The point is, you're going to need help. I'm supposed to be your partner."

"Yes," she agreed darkly. "You're supposed to be."

He sat back in his seat and stared straight ahead for a long moment. "Is this about earlier? The thing with Cassidy?"

"You mean the girl who could be your daughter? Who, if she is your daughter, was conceived when we were married."

He didn't answer for a few moments. "I can't go back and fix it. The only question is whether you believe me when I say I'm sorry."

All the anger deflated out of her. "I believe you." She swallowed the lump in her throat and looked determinedly out the windshield.

"But you can't forgive me."

"I do forgive you. I just—I can't forget."

....

Back at the precinct, Annalisa had a stack of messages on her desk. The one she was most interested in was the one from Joella Fuentes in the tech department. Annalisa had charged her with learning anything she could about the anonymous number texting Quinn. Annalisa picked up her desk phone to return the call. "Joella, thanks for jumping on this so quickly. What've you got?"

Across the desk, Nick had his head bent over his own work, but she could tell from the set of his shoulders that he was still uneasy with her. *Back at you*, she told him silently, turning away to listen to Joella's assessment. "It's a prepaid burner phone," Joella said. "But purchased recently from a Walmart." The store location was near Quinn's campus. "If you're lucky, they charged it rather than paying cash. If you're even luckier, the whole thing's on camera and you can see the face."

"Got it, thank you." She tried to sound thankful rather than resigned. Joella's information was helpful, but Annalisa would need a warrant to probe further, and currently, she did not have cause to get one. She made a note of the store's location and hung up the phone. She looked up to find Nick watching her.

"What was that?" he asked.

"Running down a phone number." When he retained his expectant look, she sighed. "Vinny hired Sam Tran to look into someone harassing Quinn on campus."

"Harassing?" Nick's full mouth turned downward with concern. "What did he find out?"

"Not much. Someone left dirty messages on the dry-erase board on her door. Now she's got someone sending her anonymous texts. You know, of the 'I'm watching you' sort. It could be some idiot boy jerking her chain, thinking he's cute, but someone needs to tell him to knock it off. More concerning, a girl reported someone attacked her on the way home from a frat house Halloween party. The campus cops say she got drunk and fell down."

"What do you think?"

Annalisa picked up a pen and toyed with it. "I think on a campus that big, you've got probably a hundred drunk girls falling down every weekend, and none of them reports an assault. Something made this one go to the cops. But they wouldn't give me the girl's name to check it out."

"You're thinking the university might want to keep it quiet, if it was an assault."

"Doesn't look good on the brochures," Annalisa agreed. She picked up the phone and dialed again, this time calling her niece. Quinn picked up on the third ring. "Hey, kiddo, good to see you today," Annalisa said, meaning it. "How are you holding up? Any more strange messages?"

"Uh, no. Nothing. Did you find out who sent them?"

"Not exactly, no. They're from a prepaid phone purchased at the Walmart close to campus. Do you know anyone with a connection to the store?"

"Sure, lots of kids buy stuff there. But . . ." Her voice trailed off.

"What is it?" Annalisa pressed her.

"My boyfriend, Jason, he works there part-time."

"I see." Annalisa tried to keep her tone neutral. "Do you think he could be the one texting you that stuff?"

"He'd better not be," she said, the threat evident in her voice. "Thanks for letting me know." She seemed ready to end the call, and Annalisa stopped her.

"Quinn . . ."

"Yeah?"

"You know you can talk to me, right? About anything."

"Sure," Quinn said, too quickly. She'd been old enough to understand everything that went down in the Vega family, from her uncle's murder conviction to her grandfather's cover-up and the aunt who turned them all in. "I gotta go," she said, and hung up.

Annalisa sifted through her other messages and found one from Nina Osteen. It took her a moment to place the name, and when she did, she pulled out the third folder she'd taken from Sam Tran's office. Nina Osteen was Sam's last open case, the only one Annalisa hadn't looked into yet. Nina had hired Tran to find her mother, who had disappeared on New Year's Eve in 1989—a lifetime in cop years. Wherever Charlotte Osteen had gone, the trail she left would have turned to dust and blown off in the Chicago winds long ago. Annalisa glanced over Sam's notes: an alcoholic woman who went to a New Year's party at a bar near Lake Michigan and never came home. Husband and young daughter Nina left behind. The theories were that she found another guy and ran off with him or that, in an alcohol-induced stupor, she had fallen into the lake and drowned. *She got drunk and fell down*, Annalisa thought with bitter irony, reflecting on Officer Kent's assessment of the girl in the woods. *Seems like there's a lot of that going around.*

She closed the folder and put it aside. She would return Nina Osteen's call eventually, but a case this old and thin was not a priority. She did not see any reason it would be connected to Sam Tran's death. Easing back in her seat, she closed her eyes and rolled her stiff neck, stifling a groan as she did so.

"Hey, it's late," Nick said. "Why don't we grab dinner?"

She folded her hands over her stomach and regarded him, contemplating a truce if it would get her some food. Her stomach answered with a loud rumble, and Nick grinned.

"That's an affirmative," he said as he snatched his coat from the back of his chair. "You feel like Thai? I could go for drunken noodles."

"Yeah, I'd love a yellow curry." She got up more slowly and Nick waited for her. The slight delay gave time for Zimmer to emerge from her office, calling Annalisa's name. She was walking across the room with another woman at her side.

Annalisa hung back and so did Nick. Zimmer indicated the other woman with a delicate sweep of her hand. "Detective Vega, please let me introduce Lara Tran, Sam's ex-wife. I told her I would let her meet the detective working Sam's case so she could know we are giving Sam our best effort."

"Mrs. Tran," Annalisa said, extending her hand. "I'm sorry for your loss."

There was no way she could duck out for dinner now. She shot Nick a helpless glance and he held up his hands in a "no worries" gesture as he backed away toward the door. "I recognize you from the news," Lara Tran said, her eyes crinkling in what wasn't quite a smile. "Lynn told me you're the best. The newscasters would seem to agree."

"The commander's opinion is all that matters around here," Annalisa replied. "Let's go somewhere we can talk for a bit. Can I get you a coffee?"

Please say yes, she thought. Then Annalisa could get one for herself.

"Thank you, but I can't drink any more coffee today. I'm jittery enough as it is." She held out her arms to illustrate.

Annalisa gave the coffee machine a sad glance as they passed it on the way to the interview room. Zimmer had retreated to her office, leaving Annalisa and Lara Tran on their own. Annalisa made a point to sit with her on the same side of the table. She knew that Mrs. Tran was probably older than she was by about ten years, although she did not look it. Her face was fatigued but unlined, her dark shoulder-length hair pulled back in a ponytail at the base of her neck. She wore a mauve pullover sweater and her hands showed no jewelry. "Do you have any leads?" she asked Annalisa.

"We're exploring a number of angles right now, but you can help us. Anything you can tell us about Sam would be useful right now."

Her dark eyes grew wet. "I can't imagine who would kill him. Sam was a good man—the best I ever knew."

Annalisa nudged a tissue box in her direction and Lara withdrew one, drawing it into her lap. "But you were divorced?" Annalisa asked gently.

"Yes," Lara conceded, bowing her head. "He was—he was sick."

"I heard he had cancer."

Lara shook her head. "Not that kind of sick." She drew a shaky breath. "Sam always had very strong ideas about right and wrong. I think it's a big reason he went into law enforcement. Also as a way to belong. I was born here, but Sam's parents emigrated from Vietnam when Sam was a baby, before the fall of Saigon. They are citizens now, but I think he wanted to prove himself fully American by becoming a police officer. His parents were less than pleased. They don't trust the police."

She gave Annalisa a tight, apologetic smile. Annalisa smiled back. "Sometimes I don't trust us either. Please tell me more about Sam's illness."

Lara bit her lip. "I first glimpsed it when Benji was born. Sam's a great dad. He adores that boy. You should have seen him driving home from the hospital so carefully, his eyes checking on me and Benji in the back every few seconds. He washed everything, all the linens, three times before they touched Benji's skin. I thought it was sweet. But then he also had to check the fire alarms each night before bed three times. And the locks on the doors. I would wake to feed the baby and find him already up, standing over Benji's crib, watching him sleep. He worried so much that something might happen to him."

"I hear that's usual for new parents."

"That's what I thought, too, at first. But the rituals didn't seem to make him calmer. They seemed to drive his anxiety and lead to more and more 'rule of three' games we had to play to keep us all safe. Sam wasn't sleeping well. His anxiety was making me anxious. I suggested he might need to see a doctor and he refused. But then he got injured on the job."

"As a police officer?"

"Yes, he was chasing a suspect and he tripped on the curb and messed up his left knee. It wasn't too serious but the doctor prescribed pain medication and rest. It was like . . . I don't know . . . the spell broke. When his knee healed, his mind was calmer too. He still had rituals but they weren't as bad. For a couple of years, we were very happy." She smiled with genuine joy at the memory, and Annalisa could see the love she still had for Sam. "Sam was forced out of the department—I know Lynn told you about that."

"How did Sam feel about that?"

"To tell you the truth, I think he was relieved. Your job, the people who do it—sometimes there is more gray than Sam was comfortable with." She shifted as though she weren't comfortable either. "He was excited to start a private investigative practice. He promised me better hours and more time for our family. But then, the cancer. Lymphoma."

"He beat it, right?"

"He did," she said wistfully. "But the rituals came back with a vengeance. He couldn't just park in front of our house. He had to circle the block three times. He had to wash Benji's hair three times, even with Benji crying. It was too much. Sam used to cook us such wonderful meals. Now they took forever, everything needing to be checked and rechecked. Washed and rewashed." She took a deep breath. "I asked him again to get help. My own doctor said it sounded like obsessive compulsive disorder. She said there were good treatments that would help Sam, but he wouldn't go. I begged, I pleaded. He said he was doing what he needed to stay safe, and if I loved him I would support him. I was supporting him—his condition left no way to start his practice."

Annalisa put down her pen. "But he did start a business."

"Yes." The one little word held so much regret. "I—I left him. I took Benji and got my own place. I felt like if I stayed there, I would go crazy with Sam, and then where would Benji be? At first, Sam got worse. The stress of the separation and the divorce. I was granted full custody, and I think that was a real blow. You have to understand—he loved us, he really did. Especially Benji. There was nothing he wouldn't do for his boy."

Annalisa reached over and squeezed the woman's hand. "I understand. I do."

"It was his love for Benji and his desire to be part of his life that forced Sam to get help. Like my doctor had said, there are good treatments. He got a lot better in only a few months' time. But by then we'd been apart more than two years. I was seeing someone." Her hand fluttered to her neck. "Paul is another good man. He's asked me to marry him several times and says he understands when I say I can't." She broke off with a small sob, crumpling the tissue in her hand.

"Was Sam seeing anyone new?"

Lara blew her nose. "No. His work and Benji, they're his life. And he . . . he would bring me little gifts, for my birthday, for Valentine's. He never pushed. But I could tell he was hoping . . ." She broke off, closed her eyes, and shook her head. Tears leaked out from behind her eyelids and she opened her eyes to plead with Annalisa. "You have to find who did this. I have to know who took Sam away from us."

Never make promises to the victims or their families, Pops had told her. *God will hear you, and you do not answer prayers.* Annalisa didn't attend church these days. She had worshipped her father and followed his advice like it was the Ten Commandments.

Annalisa reached over to cover Lara's hand with her own. "I promise," she said.

ELEVEN

··········

SHE HAD BECOME THE STALKER. The irony wasn't lost on Quinn as she waited in the shadows outside Gibson Hall, one of the dorms on campus reserved for returning students, not first-years like her. She'd asked around and found that Sienna Soto was a sophomore, an art major, and she lived in Gibson. She didn't know which room, however, so Quinn waited outside, watching the people coming and going, hoping to catch a glimpse of Sienna and her orange hair. It was dark, freezing, and her fingers and toes were starting to go numb. *This is stupid. You should be studying for your calc exam*, she told herself as another young woman who wasn't Sienna exited through the front door. Quinn hadn't breathed a word to Sarah Beth or Natalie about her plan, partly because she didn't know what the plan was.

Her phone pinged and she dug it out. Natalie. **Q where r u? Masked Singer is on.**

Library, Quinn texted back, adding a frowny face.

As she slid the phone back into her pocket, it pinged again and she looked at the screen. **It's late to be out all alone.** She gave a sharp yelp and dropped the phone into the grass. Her chest tightened like someone had a fist around it and she backed up against the tree. But then she remembered what Annalisa told her about where the phone originated. *Jason is being an asshole again.* She had to dump him. *Only wait*, she remembered. *Jason is at hockey practice.* On the ground, her phone flashed with a new text. She couldn't read it from this distance. Instead, she looked around wildly to see who was watching her. The dorm windows glowed with light but she saw no faces peering out. The paths were empty. She couldn't see in the dark to the trees beyond. With a gulp of cold air, she bent down and snatched up her phone. Want some company . . . ?

The sound of male voices made her jump. Two guys, heading into Gibson Hall. She didn't know them but she didn't care. She just wanted to get inside. She darted for the door and followed in behind them when they used a student ID to buzz through. Once inside, she sagged against the worn-out couch in the lobby. The guys walked up the stairs without paying any attention to her, and soon she was alone again under the fluorescent lights. The doors and windows looked completely black from the inside, but anyone out there could be looking in at her. She felt a whimper of fear rising in her throat and she clamped her jaw to hold it back. *Think like Annalisa*, she told herself. *What would she do?*

She'd have a gun, Quinn answered herself, eyeing the blackness outside. She was in no hurry to go back out there, so she decided to look for Sienna. She didn't want to go knocking door-to-door, but maybe she would get lucky and Sienna would have hers labeled somehow. Plenty of people did. Quinn took the stairs to the first floor and walked the hall slowly. The floor was coed. Lots of kids had their doors open, some with music playing. She saw a couple of guys gaming together. A girl with dark hair lay on her bed reading a textbook, her head bent with headphones on. Quinn studied the names on the doors as she went: Charlie, David, Ella, Mikayla, Brayden, James . . . most had labels, and none read SIENNA. The few doors that did not have names were not open.

Quinn repeated the process with the second floor, then the third. She was not feeling hopeful when she got to the fourth floor, and sure enough, she didn't see any door with Sienna's name on it. She was about to give up when she remembered something else: Sienna was an art major. Quinn went back over the unlabeled doors with a fresh eye and stopped in front of one that had been covered top to bottom in paint swatches. They were crisscrossed and grouped so they formed a vivid rainbow. Quinn raised her hand, hesitated a moment, and then knocked. She held her breath and waited so long she decided no one was home. As she turned to go, the door cracked open. She saw one green eye peering out at her and a wild swatch of orange hair. Sienna. "Who are you?" the girl asked.

"My name is Quinn Vega."

Sienna chewed her lip. "I've heard of you. You're related to that cop."

"That's right. She's my aunt."

When Quinn didn't say anything further, the sliver of face Quinn could see turned suspicious. "What do you want?"

Quinn took a step closer and lowered her voice. "I lost my silver jacket at the Halloween party the other night. I heard you might have it."

Sienna took a sharp breath. She looked away. "Come in," she said finally, widening the door.

"Oh my God, it's true." Quinn's jaw fell open when she saw the girl's full face. She didn't mean to stare, but Zach's description hadn't done Sienna's injuries justice. Her left eye was ringed with purple and there was an ugly brown-green bruise down the side of her face. A cut around her temple had scabbed over. She had a scrape across her right hand.

"Here." Sienna grabbed the silver jacket from the floor of her closet and threw it at Quinn. "I didn't know it was yours. Sorry it got kind of wrecked."

Quinn looked down at the brown stains on the back of the jacket. The stains on the collar were reddish in color, maybe blood. She felt sick looking at it. "It's okay," she stammered. "I got it secondhand anyway."

Sienna gestured at the door. "Is that all?"

"I—" Quinn licked her dry lips and started over, the words coming in a rush. "I heard you were attacked."

Sienna gave a slow blink. "Where'd you hear that?"

"Just . . . around."

"I don't know who said I was attacked." Sienna shrugged one shoulder. "I got drunk and fell on my ass. Ask the campus cops."

"Did you?" Quinn stepped closer to her, still clutching the jacket. "Is that really what happened?"

Sienna folded her arms and fixed Quinn with a hard look. "You don't even know me. Why do you care?"

"Because you were wearing my jacket."

Surprise flickered over Sienna's face and she dropped her defensive posture. "Wait . . . you think someone jumped me, thinking it was you?"

"I don't know. Someone's watching me. My roommate got followed the other night. I wasn't sure it meant anything serious, but then I heard what happened to you, and now I don't know what to think."

Sienna let out a humorless laugh and she sat on the edge of her bed. "Well, I don't think you have to worry. I know who got me. I mean, I don't know his name or anything—if I did, I'd have had him arrested or strung up by his balls on the main quad."

Quinn perched on the end of the bed next to her. "What do you mean?"

"The asshole tried to get me earlier. At least I think he did. I wasn't feeling so good at the party and one of the guys I know there, Adam, let me use his room to lie down. I woke up to someone groping me. I think he was wearing a gorilla suit."

"You think?"

She flopped back with a sigh. "That's what I see in my memory. Anyway, before I had time to react, this cat woman came in and scared him off. I was still pretty out of it. I tried to sit up, but I was so dizzy. I lay back down, and when I could move again, the party was pretty much over. I must have grabbed your jacket on the way out. I took the short way back home through the woods, and that's when I felt something hit me from behind." She indicated her head. "I have a huge lump back there that still hurts when I lie down. It was fucking bleeding and that cop said I did it to myself."

"Okay, so we find this guy," Quinn said, feeling energized with the injustice of it. "This gorilla man. We figure out who he is and turn him in."

Sienna sat up and rolled her eyes. "How? He had a costume on."

"Yeah, but someone must know him. He can't hide inside a suit forever. He's already screwed up, right? Because the cat woman is a witness. Maybe she knows who he is or how to find him."

"Ha, that's no help. I don't know who she is either."

"Then we find her too." Quinn was determined now.

"And what makes you so sure we can do that?" Sienna asked, skeptical.

"Well . . ." Quinn smiled and spread her arms. "I found you, didn't I?"

Sienna looked sideways at her and shook her head, but her expression suggested admiration. "Jeez, you're a real firecracker, huh? Think you're a detective like your auntie? Okay, let's say I'm in. How do we find the gorilla guy?"

Quinn considered. "Pictures," she said after a moment. "Did you take pictures that night?"

"A few, but I already looked at them. No gorilla man. No cat woman."

Quinn got out her own phone, bracing herself for more menacing texts. She relaxed when she saw none. She went to her pictures and started flicking through them. Her and Natalie getting ready, mugging for the camera. Sarah Beth making a peace sign. Carved jack-o'-lanterns glowing in front of the Delta Gamma Nu house. She got a few of the crowd, but mostly she'd been dancing, not taking pictures. She flicked to the last picture and her heart seized in her chest. "Oh my God."

Sienna leaned over, intrigued. "What is it?"

Wordlessly, Quinn showed her the selfie she'd taken with Natalie by the punch bowl. They both made kissy faces for the camera, their cheeks pink from dancing and booze. Over Natalie's shoulder in the back was the gorilla, and he'd been staring right at them.

TWELVE

···········

By the time Annalisa had finished with Lara Tran and debriefed Zimmer, the late shift had rotated on duty. Nick was gone, his jacket missing from his chair. He'd left her a paper sack on her desk and she opened it to peer in at the contents: yellow chicken curry with rice, now congealing and tepid. She took Tran's file on the Powell-Morrison homicide and her forlorn dinner out to her car, but she didn't drive to her condo. She drove to Norwood Park, to the two-story brick house she'd grown up in, the place she always considered home even when she wasn't welcome there. As expected, she saw the light on in the den. Pops slept down there now that he couldn't manage the stairs. Most nights, she knew, he couldn't manage to sleep either.

She retrieved the spare key from the fake rock by the back bushes and let herself in through the kitchen. Pops must've heard her coming because he didn't look surprised when she appeared in the doorway to the den. Blue light from the TV played on his face, but the sound was on mute. "You're lucky I don't carry anymore," he said to her. "Come creeping in at this hour, a person might get shot."

"Hello to you too," she said as she took a seat on the couch next to his armchair.

He squinted at her, looking her over. "You hungry? Ma made meat loaf for dinner. Leftovers are in the fridge."

His speech was clearer than it had been recently. A new medicine, maybe. "You know, that sounds good. I'm going to make a sandwich. You want anything?"

"Ice cream."

He wasn't supposed to have it. Pops had diabetes to go with his Parkinson's. She used to sneak some in and not tell him it was sugar-free. "Ma doesn't keep that stuff in the house. You know that."

"Beer then." He shouldn't have that either but she figured she owed him this much.

She got a sandwich and a soda for herself, as well as a cold beer for Pops. She opened it before handing it over. His arm trembled, but he got it to his mouth without trouble. She ate and they sat in silence as the TV flickered through the top news stories. Finally Pops nodded at the file folder she'd brought with her. "What's that?"

"Cold case. A couple beaten to death in a motel room. Ring any bells?"

"Sure," he said immediately, interest in his eyes. "Todd and Bonnie Adkins. I worked that one."

She shook her head. "Different couple. This one is Katherine Morrison and Stephen Powell. They were killed about three years before the Adkinses."

"No shit?"

"You didn't know?"

"Wait a sec, yeah. I do remember. I talked to the detective on that case—Doug Acker."

"Acker's dead," she interrupted, and he looked at her, surprised. "Heart attack."

"We're dropping like f-flies," he said, his head bobbing with a tremor.

"You talked to him, though? About the case?"

"It—it wasn't related."

Two couples found beaten to death in their motel room, a few years apart. "You sure about that?" she asked, opening the folder on her lap.

"Acker was. He told me they were having an affair, his victims. He said they knew who the doer was but they couldn't prove it."

"They did?" There was nothing in Tran's file about a clear suspect.

"Acker said the husband did it. The husband of the female vic."

"Brad Morrison?" Brad Morrison was the one who had hired Tran in the first place.

"Yeah, yeah, him. He had no alibi. He knew his wife was running around on him, and he was real steamed up about it. Acker was real POed he couldn't nail the guy, but it was a domestic thing. It had nothing to do with my case."

Annalisa took out the photocopy Tran had of the original queen of hearts playing card found at the scene. She showed Pops the back, with the cherubs on it. "What about this? Have you seen this before?"

He looked at it with mild surprise. "Sure, they were all over the floor of the motel room. Cards everywhere. The place was a t-total mess."

"Wait." She scooted closer. "You found playing cards at the scene of the Adkins murders?"

"Yeah, the whole deck scattered all over the floor. With little angels on them like you got in that picture." He pointed a shaky finger at the paper in his lap. "Except that one."

"What do you mean except that one?"

"There was one card missing from the deck. Queen of hearts. Where'd you find it?"

"At the scene of the Powell-Morrison murders."

He jerked like his armchair turned electric. "No shit?"

"No shit. Pretty big coincidence, don't you think? Two double homicides, both at a motel, both with this same deck of cards?"

He glared at her. "You saying I messed up?"

She snatched the paper away from him. "You were hardly the only cop on this case, Pops. Or the Powell-Morrison investigation. Everyone missed it, not just you."

"Figures this is w-what gets you back in the house," he groused at her. "Don't come to Sunday dinner. Just show up in the middle of the night to rub my nose in my mis-mistakes. You got a perfect record? Solve every case?"

"Of course not." The playing cards probably wouldn't have seemed significant at the time amid the chaos of the crime scenes, but Acker zeroing in on Brad Morrison as a suspect hadn't helped. Neither had Pops's easy acceptance of the original theory. She didn't blame him for the miss exactly, but frustration was winding its way through her gut like a constrictor. Now the case was her problem, twenty years too late.

Pops stewed, not looking at her. Her gaze went to the family photos that hung all over the walls. They showed her and her brothers in various stages of growing up, on holidays and family camping trips. Graduations. Vinny at age eighteen with his new car. Pops in uniform with some of his buddies around Ma's kitchen table. In pictures, at least, the Vega family remained perfect. No wonder Pops lived in this room.

"I don't get it," he said finally. "Why are you digging into the case now?"

She couldn't resist a barb. "Because it's never been solved."

He harrumphed but gave a weak wave of his hand in surrender. "You—you clean up all my messes."

Her flesh quivered somewhere south of her stomach. She let her eyes linger once more on the pictures, the ones of the girl she'd been and the family Pops had lied to save. "Did you always want kids?" she asked him.

"Of course," he answered without hesitation. He followed her gaze to the photos.

Even now? she wanted to ask. *Knowing how it all turned out?* "Nick may have a daughter," she said, the words slipping out of her before she could stop them. At his questioning look, she told him the story. He let out a long sigh.

"What'll you do about it?" he asked, his voice gruff.

"Me? She's not my kid."

"If Nick's your guy, then she's your kid," he said, as though this should be obvious.

"You make it sound easy."

He chuffed an amused breath. "Kids are a lot of things. Easy ain't one of them."

"I've got to go."

"Yes. You always do."

Their eyes met and she saw the grief in his watery gaze. She leaned down to kiss his grizzled cheek. He squeezed her arm with surprising strength. "Night, Pops," she whispered. She left him alone with his TV and his memories.

Tired as she was, she was determined to make one more stop. The corner store's lights shone bright in comparison to the shuttered darkness of its neighbors, a trinket store for tourists and a cigar shop. She went inside and nodded at the clerk, a Sikh man reading a paperback thriller. She did a slow walk of the place, which wasn't all that big to begin with, frowning at the chips and leaning in to study the fine print on the laundry detergent. Eventually, she hit her target: pregnancy tests. Sweat broke across her neck just looking at them. *You're thirty-eight*, she told herself. *Not sixteen*. She cleared her throat and grabbed a test, but on her way to the counter, she added in a bag of chips, a half gallon of milk, a packet of dish sponges, and some gum.

"Will that be all?" he asked her. He glanced up as he said it and his face became frozen in fear.

Annalisa barely had time to register the shift before she felt a gun barrel at her back. "Get on the floor," said a muffled voice. "Do it now."

Annalisa looked down at the grimy tile. "Okay, just stay calm."

"Don't fucking talk!" He jabbed her again, pushing her downward.

She got down at shoe level, her face in the grit. The man with the gun was ordering the clerk to empty the register. She saw the stripes on his sneakers and a smear of mud along the cuffs. Her gaze traveled up over his jeans, past his hoodie, to the rubber mask over his face. She'd found the Chicken Bandit.

THIRTEEN

....

HE WAS YOUNG AND SKINNY, BUT THEY KNEW THAT FROM THE TAPES. He smelled like weed. Between the gloves and the tiny eyeholes on the mask, she couldn't even see his skin color. "That's right," he said to the clerk. "All of it." Annalisa's gun was hidden beneath her black wool overcoat. With his mask on, he wouldn't have great peripheral vision. She tried moving her arm slowly. She got about four inches before he whirled on her. "Who the fuck told you to move?"

She froze again, her chin hard against the ground. By her right hand, she saw the tub of mint gum she'd been about to buy. It had come open when she dropped it and two pieces were in reach of her fingertips. Steeling herself against the germs, she quickly popped the closest one in her mouth.

"You don't hear very good," the kid said, looming over her.

"You got your money," she replied. "You can go now."

"Who the fuck are you, telling me what to do?"

She didn't like his calm or the way he remained in the store. He should want to flee at this point. She kept her mouth shut and did not make eye contact. He kicked her anyway. Her breath left her in a sharp *whoosh*. As she recoiled from the pain, he kicked her again and his toe hit the weapon at her hip.

"What the hell's that?" he demanded. "Turn over."

He drew back his leg to kick her again so she turned over, breathing hard through the pain. He saw the badge and the gun. "You're a cop."

"My partner's going to be wondering why I'm not back with the coffee. He'll be coming through those doors any second."

His gaze flicked the counter, where the rest of her would-be purchases sat. "I don't see no coffee. Just a bunch of junk and a pee-stick test." He moved closer, leaning down to look in her face. The big cartoon chicken eyes seemed garish up close. "You pregnant, cop?"

She held his gaze and said nothing.

"Take out your gun. Two fingers. Real slow."

She swallowed and hesitated. The other robberies had been in-and-out jobs. Why wasn't he leaving? She complied with reluctance as he pointed the gun at the clerk and then back at her.

"Push it to me. That's right." He picked it up alongside the sack with the money in it. "Nice piece," he told her.

"You can't use it for anything," she said, trying to reason with him. "It's completely traceable."

"I could use it right now." He swapped his pistol for her automatic and aimed at her head.

The barrel seemed to grow in size; it looked three feet long. Her heart beat so fast she felt dizzy. Her mouth went utterly dry. "Don't," she pleaded with him. "It's stupid. They—they would find you."

"They ain't found me yet."

She heard it then, a siren. The Chicken Bandit cursed and ran for the door. She had one move and less than a second to make it. Grabbing the gum from her cheek, she threw it at his feet. He didn't even notice it catch his heel as he ran out the door. She fell back on the floor, spent and shaky. He had her gun now and who knew what he'd do with it. "I punched 911 on my cell phone," the clerk said, his face pale as he peered over the counter at her. Blue flashing lights appeared outside.

"Thank you." She struggled to her feet. "That was . . . that was smart."

She met the responding officers and sent them off in search of the Chicken Bandit. Two units became four as patrol spread out around the surrounding blocks. Annalisa stayed inside the door with the clerk, whose name was Raveneer Singh, and both of them gave initial statements to the sergeant on the scene. He called an ambulance for her but she waved off the medics. "I'm fine." Her ribs were sore on one side but she would live. They were still hovering, however, when Nick crashed through the door.

"Jesus, Annalisa," he said as he grabbed her shoulders. "Are you all right?"

"I guess I'm back on the case," she said drily. "Of all the gin joints in all the world . . ."

"Glad you can make jokes. Are you sure you're okay? Was anybody hurt?" He looked around and spotted Singh, unharmed.

"No, but he's going to hurt someone," she said. "This isn't some nervous kid trying to make a quick buck. He's dangerous. And now he has my gun."

Nick swore and turned away. "I want this asshole nailed to my wall."

"Yeah, well, I can't give you much more than we already knew. Except the stripes on his shoes aren't gray—they're red." The footage they'd harvested from the convenience stores was all black-and-white. The stripes appeared gray on camera. "And when you find this guy," she said, stooping to retrieve the rest of her gum, "he'll have gum stuck to his shoe. I made sure to tag his left sneaker on the way out." Even if he scraped it off, forensics would raise traces, possibly even with her DNA on it.

Nick grinned at her with admiration. "You're a quick thinker, Vega. You could be a detective, you know that?"

"Yeah, I'm really going places. Zimmer'll have my head when she hears I lost my weapon."

Nick sobered. "I think she'll be glad your head doesn't have a bullet in it."

Behind them, Singh cleared his throat. "Ma'am, would you like to finish your purchase, or . . . ?"

"Oh," she said, patting her pockets absently. "Sorry, I totally forgot."

Nick pulled out his wallet. "I've got it. It's the least I could do after you may have helped crack my case."

"Nick, wait." The pregnancy test. She tried to throw herself between Nick and the counter so he wouldn't see her items. Too late. He leaned around her, his eyes widening.

"A pregnancy test?"

She sagged, defeated. Her bad night was about to get one hundred percent worse.

FOURTEEN

....

ANNALISA WENT HOME BUT SHE DIDN'T GET MUCH SLEEP. She flopped around in the bed like a fish out of water, breathless each time she awoke in the darkness. *Not here*, she'd muttered to Nick under the bright lights of the convenience store when he'd noticed the pregnancy test among her purchases. *Not like this*. The tendons in his neck had gone rigid and his eyes had bulged out of his head. He hadn't seemed to hear her. He did hear, belatedly, the crackle of his radio that signaled a possible sighting of the Chicken Bandit four blocks away. *I've got to go*, he'd said vaguely, more to himself than to her. He hadn't given her a backward glance as he'd loped out the door.

At 4 a.m. she heard the scrape of his key at her door. She sat up in bed when his silhouette appeared in the room. "Did you get him?"

"It wasn't the guy." He peeled off his layers of clothes and his holster until he was down to only his T-shirt and underwear, at which point he slipped into the empty space she'd left, hoping he'd come. He stared at the ceiling and said nothing.

Tentatively, she put a palm to his chest. "You'll get him soon. I know it."

He covered her hand with one of his own, warm and sure, and relief flooded through her. She scooted closer and he shifted to wrap an arm around her. She closed her eyes and listened to the steady thrumming of his heart. "Why didn't you tell me?" he asked eventually.

She tensed but kept her eyes shut. "Life has been so crazy. And I didn't know there was anything to tell." That was the point of the test, after all.

He waited a beat, and when she didn't say anything more, he prompted, "And now?"

She sighed, opening her eyes with reluctance and shifting away. "I still don't know."

"But the test . . ."

"I left it there. I left everything." She'd fled the scene almost as soon as he had. She hoped the uniformed guy and the lingering EMT standing there hadn't heard her exchange with Nick. The last thing she needed now was more gossip.

"So we get another one," he said, trying to get up. She grabbed his arm and pulled him back down.

"It's four in the morning. Let's just . . . let's try to get some sleep, okay? A few more hours one way or the other won't make a difference."

He looked down at her but she couldn't read his expression in the inky shadows. "It would be a good thing, right?" He sounded unsure. His hand searched out her face, cupping her cheek, and she leaned into him briefly. "You always wanted kids."

She had wanted her own childhood. A big family gathered every night around the table. Everyone talking and laughing, teasing one another over plates heaped high with chicken piri-piri or stuffed peppers and rice. Always something going on and someone at home when you came through the door. The big games and piano recitals. Swim meets and dances and camping in the summer up in Michigan, catching fireflies in a jar. They'd lain out in sleeping bags and marveled at the stars. Pops pointed out constellations, while Alex and Annalisa had preferred to invent their own. Now when she looked up at the sky she knew the starlight was years old by the time it reached her eyes. That maybe the stars you saw weren't there at all.

In the morning, she eased out from under Nick's arm and dressed silently in the gray light. She made strong coffee and contemplated her day. She would need to replace her license, cancel her credit cards, and get a new weapon. More paperwork. She also wanted to track down Brad Morrison, the supposed number one suspect in the Queen of Hearts homicides.

Brad had hired Sam Tran to investigate, which meant he'd been one of the last people to talk to her victim. It also meant he was unlikely to be Kathy and Stephen's killer. He'd have to be a psychopath to set a PI on his own trail.

She poured a cup of coffee for Nick and took it to the bedroom. He lay slack-jawed and dead to the world. She set the steaming mug on his bedside and sat near his hip. He stirred at the weight of her and regarded her through slitted eyes. "Leaving already?"

"It's past seven. Got to go." She leaned down to kiss his prickly cheek, and when she moved to leave, he caught her hand. "Maybe you should pack a bag, stay with me for a few days."

"Why?"

He gave her a look. "You know why. That asshole took your wallet, so now he has your address. Not to mention your gun."

"I can get another gun."

"Yes, but I can't get another you." He laced his fingers through hers and squeezed. "Think about it, okay?"

She squeezed back and gently disengaged. "Catch him today and then I won't have to."

··········

ANNALISA DID NOT REACH BRAD MORRISON'S OFFICE UNTIL AFTER TWO, AND HE KEPT HER WAITING NEARLY HALF AN HOUR AFTER THAT. She had plenty of time to enjoy the view from the eighteenth floor. The financial services firm boasted a sweet suite near the edge of Millennium Park. She could see the cold blue expanse of the lake out of the east window and a straight shot down Michigan Avenue out of the west. From this height the metal Bean sculpture looked like a large silver egg, a downed UFO inspiring awe among the ever-present spectators. "He's ready for you," said the woman at the front desk, finally, setting down the phone. "It's the first door on the right." She had box-blond hair swept up so tight Annalisa wondered if the woman could even move her eyebrows. *Nature's Botox*, Sassy used to joke when they'd fixed their ponytails so tight it hurt.

Annalisa found the office with no trouble and Brad Morrison jumped up behind his desk at the sight of her. "Detective Vega," he said with an easy smile, coming around to shake her hand. He looked like a Brad. Trim, close-cropped salt-and-pepper hair, with ice-blue eyes and a nervous energy about him. He indicated the sitting area with its leather sofa and glass coffee table. "Sorry to keep you waiting. Please, come have a seat. Can I get you anything—coffee, tea, scotch and soda?" He chuckled at his own humor.

She looked beyond him to the expansive lake view. "I'm impressed," she said, because she could tell he wanted her to be. "My office view is a bunch of filing cabinets and an old coffeepot."

He smoothed his narrow tie over his white shirt. Crossed and uncrossed his legs. "Hey, if you have to work eighteen-hour days, may as well have something to look at while you're doing it. Am I right?" Another smile, crinkling his eyes. "So tell me, what can I help you with?"

"I'm investigating the death of Sam Tran."

"Wait." He sat back in shock. "You're telling me Sam's dead?"

"You hadn't heard?"

"No. What happened to him?"

"We're still figuring that out. When was the last time you talked to him?"

"A week ago," he said immediately. He sat forward, his posture open. "We were due for another check-in conversation this evening. I can't believe he's dead."

"You hired him to look into the death of your wife," she said, making a show of consulting her notebook.

"That's right. She was murdered twenty-three years ago, and the cops didn't solve it." He looked right at her, no apology for the barb. "Amos Powell has been walking free for more than two decades now. So yeah, I decided it was time to do something about it."

"Amos Powell." She consulted her notes for real this time. "You're speaking of Stephen Powell's father."

"That sonofabitch murdered Kathy and his own son and got clean away with it. I was a grad student at the time. Didn't have a lot of money back then so there wasn't much I could do about the problem. Now I have enough to buy and sell that run-down old bunch of stones Powell calls a church. I'll spend every penny of it to prove he's a liar and a killer."

"That's interesting. His son Andrew says you did it."

He jumped up and went for his water bottle. His suit had a subtle sheen to it, like an oil slick. "I know what he says," he said as he uncapped the bottle. He paused to take a big swig. "I told Tran to look into him too. He was a teenager when Kathy was killed, but it's possible he was in on it. He's under his daddy's thumb even today."

"Why would Amos Powell kill his own son?"

"Stephen was a sinner. Drinking to excess. Cheating on his marriage, helping another woman cheat on hers. I've seen the notes from the original investigation. The cops had a witness, someone cleaning the church who heard Amos screaming at Stephen that he was beyond redemption, that he was going to hell. What does his son do? Does he repent and come clean? No, he goes off with my wife to a cheap motel for sex."

"That must have made you angry too," she said mildly. "Your wife cheating on you like that."

He paused and seemed to choose his words carefully. "I didn't like it. Who would? But Kathy didn't deserve to die. She started going to that church because she was lonely, and that was partly my fault. I was either at school or going to tournaments to earn extra money. She was alone a lot. I was glad when she said she was singing in the choir. I thought she'd find friends."

"Was she upset about that? Your being gone a lot, I mean."

He eyed her a minute. "It was a source of tension. Like I said, I was happy when she found an outlet, something to keep her busy."

He'd enjoyed the sudden lack of nagging, that much was clear. "How did you find out she'd started seeing Stephen?" Annalisa asked. Brad had hired one PI to look into the murder. Maybe he'd hired one back then too.

One end of his mouth curved in a smile and he came back to join her in the sitting area. "Reading people is a strength of mine," he said.

"You mean from playing poker."

"Oh, I was good at it before I started playing cards. Still am to this day." He gave her a speculative look. "I'd bet, with your line of work, you're pretty good at it too."

She let that remark go by. "You're in computers now. AI?"

"It's the same thing, Detective. People like to imagine they're more complicated than machines, less predictable, but really the opposite is true. We're all just a sum of inputs and outputs."

"If that's true, you should have seen Kathy's murder coming." She watched him closely for his reaction. He seemed intrigued by her supposition, not offended. She found his whole demeanor somewhat puzzling. Maybe it was the intervening two decades or the infidelity that had preceded his wife's murder, but he did not seem pained by her death. His predominant emotion appeared to be anger and his motivation a desire to best Amos Powell, as though Kathy's and Stephen's murders were part of an intellectual chess match he was determined to win.

"I didn't know about Amos Powell," Brad said finally, pointing at her like she had to admit this key fact. "I didn't have all the data. But Kathy knew. She knew she was going to church and screwing the minister's son. If anyone should have seen it coming, it was her."

"When you figured out Kathy was cheating, did you confront her about it?"

He worked his jaw back and forth. "Didn't get the chance."

She looked at his hands and did not see a wedding ring. No obvious family pictures on his desk or hanging on the wall. Brad Morrison kept a sleek office, with only the million-dollar view for company. "You must know that Detective Acker shared Amos Powell's suspicions of you. There was a witness who saw a car matching yours at the motel the night of the murders."

He let out a derisive laugh. "Acker. That guy was three months from retirement and about three years from the grave, if I recall correctly. He decided I was the husband so I had to be guilty."

"I think there was more to it than that."

"The witness . . . some handyman, I recall? He saw a blue Taurus, not my blue Taurus. There were thousands on the road back then. But that was enough for Acker to zero in on me. Well, that and the cards."

"The cards?" Annalisa played dumb.

"There was a card found at the scene . . . the queen of hearts? Acker found some old pictures from a tournament I did in Indiana—at Four Winds? They used a deck with like, Renaissance paintings on the back or something. I guess it was similar to the card found at the motel where Kathy and Stephen got killed. But Acker searched our apartment four times, and he never found the deck he was looking for."

Saying the cards weren't found wasn't the same as denying he'd ever had them. "You were home alone that night."

"I'm home alone lots of nights." He flashed her a white smile. "Hazards of the job. But I didn't kill Kathy. Amos Powell did. I hired Sam Tran to find the proof of it. Why would I do that if I was the guilty one? It makes no sense."

She had to admit it did not. And now, of course, there was the second double homicide. If he had a solid alibi for the night of the Adkins murders, that would go a long way to ruling him out. "I wonder if you could tell me your whereabouts on November 15, 2003? It was a Saturday, if that helps."

"You've got to be kidding. That's twenty years ago. Where were you?" He gave her a challenging look.

"If you'd like to consult your calendar . . ."

"That was the year I was writing my dissertation. I was probably at the computer lab or in my apartment working. Why do you want to know?" When she did not reply, he rose again, becoming fidgety. "Was it Powell? Did he say I did something else? He fell down once and tried to blame me for it, you know."

"Blame you how?"

"There was black ice on his stairs that caused him to slip one morning. He said I went to his church and put water on the steps so it would freeze. That's crazy, right? I told you he's nuts."

"I'll look into it. Do you know if Amos is still preaching?"

"He's retired but still rattles around in that old church like the Holy Ghost. Here, I'll give you the address." He went to his desk and pulled out a notepad with company letterhead on it. He jotted down the information from memory. "In my wine fridge at home, I have a bottle of champagne worth more than a thousand dollars. I've been keeping it ever since the judge threw out the ridiculous civil suit they brought against me. If you can prove Amos is guilty, we'll drink a toast together."

She wondered idly if thousand-dollar wine tasted any better than the twenty-buck version she usually had. "Thanks. I'll be in touch."

Leaving the office, she had the elevator car to herself, allowing her a moment alone to catch her breath. The elevator panels were solid wood, the buttons shiny and modern, but she could feel the building's age in the car's slow pace and slight wobble. She tapped an impatient toe and nudged open the folded paper Brad Morrison had given her. *Calvary Chapel*, he'd written, with the man's number. The car touched down and the doors opened, but Annalisa remained inside staring at the paper in her hand. The *p* in *chapel* was backward. Just like the *P* in PIG that had been painted on Sam Tran's chest.

FIFTEEN

....

THE FIRST THING ANNALISA WOULD DO WAS VISIT THE SCENE OF THE CRIME, QUINN DECIDED. She only had to convince Sienna to go with her. Sarah Beth and Natalie argued over the wisdom of her plan to go back to the frat house. "If there is a stalker, you'll just antagonize him," Natalie reasoned, sitting cross-legged on her bed while Quinn got ready. "Let Officer Ken take care of it."

"He's not even looking for the guy." Sarah Beth swiveled back and forth in Quinn's desk chair. "At least Quinn is doing something. I think it's cool."

"I think it's dangerous," Natalie replied with a shiver.

Quinn fixed her ponytail and nodded at herself in the mirror. "If the gorilla guy attacked Sienna thinking she was me, I need to know. Like you say, Officer Ken isn't going to save me."

"What about the texts?" Natalie asked. "Did you get any more?"

Quinn put on her jacket. "My aunt thinks it's Jason. She traced the number on the phone back to the Walmart where he works. The phone was bought there recently."

"They can trace that stuff?" Sarah Beth asked with interest. "The phone, I mean."

"Sure, you can trace anything now."

"Oh my God," Natalie said with faux dramatics. "Jason's your stalker?"

"No, he's just an ass," Quinn replied with a roll of her eyes. "I gotta go. I'm meeting Sienna at the student center and then we're heading over to Delta Gamma Nu."

"Be careful," Natalie called, her tone turning worried.

Sarah Beth tossed a stuffed dog at Natalie. "You sound like my mom. She practically yelled 'Don't get pregnant' whenever I went out the door."

Natalie caught the dog and giggled. "Don't get pregnant!" she yelled after Quinn. Quinn shut the door on their laughter.

············

IN LINE FOR COFFEE AT THE CAMPUS CENTER, QUINN TRIED TO BUCK UP SIENNA, WHO STILL HAD DOUBTS ABOUT RETURNING TO THE SCENE OF HER ASSAULT. "I'll be with you. It's daylight hours. What could happen?"

"Some guy in a gorilla suit could bash us over the head and rape us."

Quinn's throat closed off at this horrible new detail. "Did he—?"

"No, no," Sienna assured her in a rush. "But he was groping me when I was in the bed. Who knows what would've happened if he had more time? We don't know who this guy in the gorilla suit is. What if it's his house . . . like, he lives there?"

Quinn hadn't considered this possibility and it sent a chill through her. She straightened her spine. "All the more reason for us to check it out. If we find a gorilla suit in his closet, he's toast."

Sienna looked doubtful. "The DGN brothers aren't going to let us in and show us their closets."

"Oh, yes they will." Quinn ordered a double espresso for fortitude, and they drank their coffee on the way to Fraternity Row. It was colder today, and windy, a swirl of dead leaves beneath their feet. Students hurried to their classes rather than lingering to chat outside.

Beside her, Sienna huddled inside her oversized army jacket, her orange hair a flash of color against the gray sky. She walked slowly and Quinn forced herself not to charge ahead. Sienna had been attacked here. Of course she would be nervous about going back. Quinn did her best to radiate quiet support. When they reached the brick house of Delta Gamma Nu, Quinn linked her arm through Sienna's. "Whoever he is, he doesn't have a mask on today," Quinn told her. "He's the one who should be afraid."

Sienna considered this and took a deep breath. "Okay, let's do it."

Quinn tried the front door and found it open, so the girls stepped inside, out of the wind. They didn't get beyond the entryway before a tall skinny guy with a tight Afro fade and wire-rimmed glasses appeared. She recognized him as Randy Nichols, the fraternity's president. Jason played on the hockey team with Randy, and Quinn had seen him at the games. He had a backpack slung over one shoulder and a denim jacket on, like he was on his way out the door. "Who are you?" he demanded, obviously not recognizing Quinn from her time in the stands.

She remembered Randy from the party. He'd worn a white T-shirt with primary color circles painted on it—the Twister game. He definitely wasn't their gorilla man. Quinn cleared her throat and indicated Sienna. "My friend and I were at the Halloween party here the other night. She lost a diamond earring."

He narrowed his eyes at Sienna, who touched the four multicolored rings in her left ear and nodded to back up Quinn's assertion. "I haven't seen any earrings," he said. "But there's a lost and found box over there." He gestured at a cardboard box sitting by the stairs. "Knock yourself out."

He left through the front door, a burst of cold air behind him, and Quinn exchanged a look with Sienna. *Stairs*, she mouthed, and Sienna nodded. They crept up one flight and paused. Quinn heard the muffled sound of male voices behind one of the nearby doors. Someone said something that triggered loud laughter, making Sienna quiver. She pointed upward to indicate she'd been on the third floor. They climbed onward, and at the top, they found silence. Sienna looked right and then left. "I think it was this way," she whispered as she started to drift down the hall. The hardwood floors creaked as they walked.

"What the hell are you doing?" A guy popped out of an open room, his white face angry. He was slim with longish brown hair and Quinn didn't know his name. "You can't be up here."

"My friend lost an earring at the party," Quinn said.

"Yeah, it was my grandma's," Sienna added.

The guy didn't look appeased. "The party was downstairs."

"I came up here to lay down," Sienna said. She pointed at a closed door. "I think it was that room."

"That's Adam's room," he told them. "He's not here."

"Can't hurt to take a quick look, right?" Quinn said with a smile, spreading her arms. "I'm sure he wouldn't mind."

The guy stood up a little straighter, stuck out his bony chest. "I say he would mind. I think you need to leave."

"Listen . . ." Quinn looked at him, at his luminous gray eyes and lanky hair. He did not seem like the usual muscled-up bonehead frat boy. "What's your name?"

He didn't reply for a moment. "Byron," he muttered at last.

"Byron," Quinn repeated, her tone cooperative and collegial, "I know you don't want any trouble, right? We don't either. That's why we came on our own like this. We didn't go to the campus security. We didn't call my aunt. She's a cop, you know."

He eyed her. "I know. I know who you are."

This made her blink and draw back. She knew Annalisa was semi-famous after the whole Lovelorn case, but Quinn was relatively new on campus and she didn't realize word had spread quite so fast. She recovered from her surprise enough to give him a tight smile. "Then you know what she can do. One call from me, and she's here with a warrant."

"A warrant for what?" he scoffed.

"Stolen property. Her missing earring is a diamond. If you're holding it here and not letting us take it back, that's grand larceny." She was totally bullshitting him now. "And we don't know where the earring is exactly, so she'd need to search the whole place . . ."

"Okay, okay." He raised his hands in defeat. "You can look. But don't touch anything."

Byron chaperoned them to Adam's door and stood there unsmiling as they entered and began to search. It smelled like musk and gym shoes. Adam had a poster of a half-naked blonde on the wall and a framed photo of a Labrador retriever on his desk. The place was tidy, though. Adam's momma had trained him well. He'd made the bed, pulling up a red plaid comforter, and there were no clothes strewn about the floor. "What was Adam at the party?" Quinn asked. "Like, what did he go as?"

"A pirate, I think," Byron answered. "Why?"

"Just making conversation." Sienna searched through the items on the nightstand while Quinn examined the desk. A laptop charger, notebooks and folders, a book on trigonometry. She eyed the closet door. It was closed and she wanted to get a look inside. "What about you?" she asked Byron casually. "Did you dress up?"

"Are you done here or what?" he said, ignoring her.

"We're still looking," Quinn said airily. She moved to the closet, feeling him watching her. She decided the hell with it and jerked open the door.

"Hey!" Byron objected. "You don't need to be in there."

"You don't know where the earring might have rolled." Quinn ran her hand over the hanging shirts, kicked lightly at the pile of shoes on the floor. She stuck her head fully into the dark space but did not see any sign of a gorilla suit.

"I think—I think we should go now." There was a note of alarm in Sienna's voice that made Quinn poke her head out of the closet. "I don't think it's here." Sienna had been looking under the bed and now her face was deathly white.

"Maybe we could check your room," Quinn said to Byron.

He righted himself from where he'd been slouching against the door-jamb. "She wasn't in my room, so the earring wouldn't be there either. I guarantee it."

Quinn walked over to him and he blocked the door to prevent her from moving to his room. "If you were at the party, how can you be sure who was up here in your room?"

"I just know."

Sienna appeared and grabbed Quinn's arm, hard enough to leave marks. "Let's get out of here," she said under her breath.

"Do you mind?" Quinn turned back to Byron. "We'd like to go now."

"It's all I've ever wanted," he said as he stepped aside with a sweeping gesture.

He followed them down both flights of stairs, all the way to the door. As they stepped out onto the porch, he called Quinn back. "Hey, Nancy Drew." She turned and regarded him. He held her stare. "Whatever you're looking for, it's not here."

"I told you. We're looking for an earring."

"Sure." He rapped the edge of the door and nodded goodbye to them. "You ladies get home safe, okay? It's getting dark out there."

Quinn saw he was right. The pale gray sky had darkened to slate and the wind rattled the trees. She grabbed Sienna and they left without an-other word. Once they were safely away from the house, Quinn stopped to check in. "Are you all right? You were looking pretty pale back there."

"Look what I found under the bed." Sienna pulled her hand out of her sweatshirt pocket to reveal a tuft of black fur. "I didn't make it up. The gorilla guy is real. He was in that room."

"I didn't think you made it up."

"Really? I did. Or at least I hoped I did." Sienna gave a watery laugh. "I didn't want it to be true." She sniffed hard and Quinn patted her. "But what now? We still don't know who he is."

"We'll figure something out." If they couldn't find the gorilla man, maybe they could find the black cat. She might know something that could nail him. Quinn's phone buzzed in her pocket and she dug it out to look at the glowing screen.

You shouldn't walk alone in the woods.

She whirled around to look back at the house. She saw a dark figure standing in a lighted window, watching them.

....

BYRON WATCHED FROM THE WINDOWS TO CONVINCE HIMSELF THEY WERE RE-ALLY LEAVING, BUT THE TIGHTNESS IN HIS CHEST DID NOT GO AWAY ONCE THEIR FIGURES HAD MELDED INTO THE SHADOWS. He went to the dresser to get the pills the shrink had given him. His parents' idea. He knew better than to say anything real to the guy, an earnest bearded dude with a fondness for knit sweaters. *Tell me what you're feeling*, he urged Byron, and Byron knew he could never confess the truth. For one thing, the shrink had to be a narc. He'd go running back to Byron's parents with whatever Byron told him. So he made up vague concerns like *I worry that some of the frat brothers don't like me* or risible lies like *I'm afraid I might fail trigonometry this fall*.

He didn't lie about the panic, the constant fear that his carefully built house of cards would come crashing down at any second. He'd be fine one moment and the next his palms would sweat and his heart would start to pound right out of his chest. So the doctor gave him drugs. He was useful for that, at least.

Byron popped a pill and checked the hall. It was empty. Adam wasn't back yet, nor Seth or Griffin, the other two guys on his hall. He'd seen the way they looked sideways at him. Byron had pledged Delta Gamma Nu because his father had insisted he do so. *You'll love it. These guys, they'll be your brothers. Your friends for life.* Byron had no real brothers, not anymore. Eileen and William Lambert had pinned all their hopes and dreams on their only son, Byron Allen. There was no one else to take on his father's love of sailing or his mother's passion for fashion. Byron hated the briny, fishy smell of the sea—hated being wet and cold—but he could never tell his father that. As for his mother, he could never breathe a word to her what he really thought when he looked through the fashion magazines . . .

Satisfied he was alone, Byron closed the door with a firm click. The drug was fast-acting. He could feel it cooking his veins, mellowing him from the inside out. *Quinn Vega is gone*, he told himself. *She's not coming back*. God help him if she really brought her aunt down on the place. He went to his dresser and opened the top drawer, pulling out his neatly balled socks and stacking them on top. There it was, untouched at the back, and he yanked it out to hold in his palm. He felt himself exhale at the sight of it.

The syringe was safe.

SIXTEEN

....

THE COOK COUNTY MEDICAL EXAMINER'S OFFICE EMBODIED BRUTALISM WITH ITS BLOCK STYLE AND ENDLESS POURED CONCRETE. A short iron fence surrounded the place, protecting a measly strip of half-dead grass. As the hour was late, Annalisa had no trouble getting a spot in the barren parking lot. She donned a gown and mask to join the autopsy suite, where she found Lynn Zimmer already on the scene and the autopsy of Sam Tran's body underway.

Her boss gave her a curt nod. They stood clear of the ME, whom Annalisa recognized as Raj Namboothiri. He was one of the newer docs in the rotation, but he already had a strong reputation for extreme care and detail in his work. Last year he had unearthed a murder that the cops had been ready to rule a suicide, in part because the guy who called it in was a cop himself. Travis Hale said his wife Karen had shot herself right in front of him. Karen had previously attempted suicide, with pills, ten years prior. A single gunshot wound to the head and her prints on the gun, and CPD was ready to rubber-stamp it. But Namboothiri had listened to Travis Hale's recorded statement and discovered that his account of the angle of the gun in Karen's hand did not match the trajectory of the bullet. Annalisa sneaked a sideways look at Zimmer and wondered if she had requested Namboothiri personally.

"No surprises on cause of death," the ME told them as he gently tilted Tran's head back to reveal the dark ligature marks around his neck. "The jugular veins on either side of the neck are superficial and easily compressed. Obstruction of blood flow from the brain induces hypoxia—a lack of oxygen—and loss of consciousness in as little as fifteen seconds. Ultimately death results from cerebral hypoxia and global ischemia."

"Ischemia," Annalisa said. "Like a stroke."

"Yes, same idea. Blood flow is restricted and the brain dies from oxygen deprivation."

"No broken neck? Spinal injury?"

"You see that mostly in judicial hangings," Namboothiri replied, "when the victim is hanged from a height greater or equal to his own." He raised his hand over his head to illustrate.

"What about defensive wounds?" Zimmer wanted to know.

"He has abrasions on his right hand, here." He lifted it to show them. "From the position of his watch on his left, I am presuming he was right-handed."

"He was," Zimmer affirmed.

Namboothiri nodded. "They were sustained antemortem but fairly recently. Beyond that, I'm not seeing much."

"No head injuries?" Annalisa asked.

"No visible damage and the X-rays were clear."

"Drugs?" Maybe Sam had not been subdued by force, but by chemicals.

"Full tox screen to come," he replied. "But there was this." He held up a jar full of amber liquid. "Stomach contents reveal 430 milliliters of alcohol and nothing else. I'm betting bourbon."

"That's not possible," Zimmer said. "Sam didn't drink." She looked to Annalisa. "After he got over his cancer, he went for a totally clean lifestyle. No processed foods of any kind. No soda, and definitely no booze. He was kind of obsessive about it."

"Yeah, his ex-wife mentioned that to me."

Namboothiri pried open Sam's mouth and used a light to look inside. "No obvious wounds to the lips, tongue, or inside cheek. No chipped teeth. If someone force-fed him, it was smooth."

Zimmer shook her head faintly as she regarded the man spread out on the metal slab. "Who did this to you, Sam?"

Annalisa regarded Namboothiri. "Doc? Manner of death?"

The ME's brown eyes showed sympathy behind his goggles. "So far? Suspicious but undetermined. Find me someone strong enough to string him up, maybe someone with a can of white paint in their garage. I'll sign off on homicide."

....

IT WAS DARK AND ANNALISA WAS HUNGRY WHEN SHE REACHED SAM TRAN'S WALK-UP APARTMENT IN HUMBOLDT PARK. Nick had texted about dinner plans, but she had not yet replied. If she had dinner with him, he would want to know if she had bought another pregnancy test. She hadn't. So she kept working the case, telling herself the first forty-eight hours were too important to waste on anything else. She parked in an open slot across from Tran's place. He lived on North Francisco Avenue, a tree-lined street featuring rows of brick town houses with pretty iron gates. Annalisa eyed the place as she shut her car door. As she did so, she heard an echo, like someone down the road had shut their door at the same time. She glanced down the shadowed street, first in one direction and then the other, but she did not see anyone else nearby.

Fishing out Sam Tran's keys from her pocket, she opened the main door and then the one leading to the first floor where Tran had lived. She braced herself for the smell. Murder victims' homes tended to be ripe with garbage after a few days of moldering. Sam Tran's place, however, smelled faintly of dust and dead air. Intrigued, she checked the kitchen and found the garbage empty, no liner in the bin. The refrigerator held what she would expect from Lara's description of Sam's habits: plain yogurts; organic, cage-free eggs; some lemons; a wilted head of lettuce; and a water pitcher with a built-in filter. She didn't see any alcohol. She checked all the cabinets and drawers and came up empty there as well. Wherever Sam had gotten his drink, it wasn't his own kitchen.

The place had two bedrooms. Sam's was plain and tidy. The other one had to be Benji's. She saw sports posters on the walls and a ratty old stuffed rabbit sitting on the bed. The highlight of the apartment was the office. It had a wood inlay ceiling with an intricate crisscross design in differing shades. Carved wood paneling came down over three walls and there was a bay window with a view of the street below. Annalisa checked the file cabinet and desk for any sign of a bottle and found nothing. Sam wasn't hiding his booze anywhere she could find.

She took a seat at his desk. He had a file folder sitting there with a sticky note. It read WADE ARMSTRONG and gave a local phone number. Inside the folder there were photocopies of what looked like handwritten work schedules, with names and hours, dates and times. At the top, printed text read SPRINGWOOD INN. "Wade Armstrong," Annalisa murmured. She dug out her notebook and paged through it until she located the reference. Wade Armstrong had worked as a handyman at the Springwood Inn at the time Kathy Morrison and Stephen Powell were murdered. He was the witness who had spotted the blue Taurus. Annalisa spread out the copies of the time sheets and examined them. They were for the week of the murders. Wade Armstrong's name showed up multiple times, highlighted in yellow, presumably Sam Tran's doing. He'd worked Tuesday through Friday and again on Sunday. Nothing for Saturday, July 22. "Armstrong wasn't working that night," Annalisa said to the empty room. "He couldn't have seen the car." Maybe he'd misremembered and seen the Ford another night. Maybe he made up a story to seem important somehow. People occasionally did that with big murder cases like the double homicide in question.

Her phone pinged with a text. It was Nick. **Picked up a sausage pizza and salad. Dinner at my place?** Her stomach rumbled at the idea, but her brain didn't want to argue with him about the pregnancy test. **Working late**, she texted back, adding a frowny face to show her regret. **I'll crash at my place so I won't disturb you.**

She saw the floating dots to indicate he was typing something. Then they disappeared. He said nothing else. With a sigh, Annalisa returned to Tran's kitchen, where she checked the expiration date and then helped herself to a plain yogurt. She wandered his place, listening to the creak of her own footsteps, imagining Sam there walking the same floor. He had numerous framed photos of Benji displayed on the hallway wall. A gap-toothed smile here. A first bike ride there. In the bedroom, she opened the nightstand drawer to find a Glock pistol, unloaded, a half-empty pack of batteries, an old phone charger, a few loose condoms, and some more photos. These were candid snapshots of Lara from years ago. Annalisa took in the worn edges and the fingerprint smudges on the surface. A closer examination of the condoms revealed they had expired six months ago. Sam Tran had room for only one woman in his drawer.

At the thought of Lara, Annalisa dug out her phone and texted her.

Hello, Mrs. Tran. We have a question that's come up in our investigation. Did Sam ever drink alcohol?

Dots danced right away as Lara formed her reply. When we met, yes, occasionally. Not in many years. Not since the cancer.

Annalisa wrote back. When he drank, what did he favor?

Beer, mostly. He would have a glass of wine with me sometimes. Why?

What about bourbon? Annalisa asked.

Only with his father on special occasions, Lara replied.

Annalisa let the phone sag in her hand as she considered this. If Sam had seen his father recently, it would explain the alcohol in his stomach and would also be a key to his activity right before his death. Can I speak with his father?

He passed away two years ago. Heart disease.

Ok, thank you. Annalisa put the items back in the drawer and did another slow turn of the apartment. There were only three real motives for murder: sex, money, and revenge. So far, she couldn't make Sam Tran's death fit into any of these categories. This suggested her hunch was correct: someone killed Sam to keep him quiet about a secret he'd uncovered. But which secret . . . and whose?

She walked back to the desk where the folder lay, with its details of Wade Armstrong's work history. She would follow up to see if Sam had spoken to Armstrong about the discrepancy in his account. Picking up the folder, she reached with her free hand to turn off the desk lamp. As she did so, she noticed the light reflecting off the white memo pad on the desk. She could see indentations from where Sam had written something on a previous page. She hunted around until she found a pencil, which she rubbed over the indentations to reveal the words. *Sally Johnson*, it read, and underneath a date: *1999*. None of this held any meaning to Annalisa, but she pocketed the note anyway.

She turned out the desk light, leaving only the overhead fixture in the office for illumination. She'd turned out all the other lights in the place, preparing to go, but she couldn't bring herself to shut off the lamp that showed off the gorgeous wood ceiling. Chicago had plenty of shiny modern condos, but she loved the history of the old homes where generations had come of age. This one had housed a lonely PI for too short a time, but she liked to imagine the walls would remember Sam. As she glanced over them, she noticed for the first time a slight shadow by the window. She went to examine it and found it was a shallow indentation in the Sheetrock about the size of a fist.

She ran her fingertips over the dent, measuring it as the wind howled, a big gust battering the window and making it shudder in its wooden sash. Suddenly, a crack exploded from outside and the glass pane shattered in front of her. Annalisa gasped in shock as shards hit her face. She reacted on instinct, hitting the floor and shielding her body with the front wall of the house. A second explosion further destroyed the window and sent a rain of glass down over her head. This was no lightning strike or branch caught in the wind, she realized. Someone was trying to kill her.

SEVENTEEN

···········

SHE CALLED FOR BACKUP, AND BY THE TIME SHE GOT OFF THE PHONE, THE SHOOT-ING HAD STOPPED. She cautiously raised up to peek out the window. Porch lights were coming on up and down the street. She took out her new department-furnished weapon and went out the front door. A lone figure dressed in black was running in the distance, and she took off after it. "Chicago PD," she hollered as she passed the curious neighbors. "Get back inside."

House by house, she waved them off, not stopping to see if they complied with her orders. The running figure turned a corner and vanished. She slowed as she reached the same point, ducking low and bracing herself against the rough brick as she rounded the corner in case there was some-one waiting on the other side. She saw nothing. Chicago Avenue had brisker traffic, headlights whooshing by at speed. There was a big parking lot and a squat taco place, and beyond that, the Metra yard and maintenance station. The running figure had disappeared into the night.

She stood motionless, trying to catch her breath and figure out her next move. Sudden footsteps behind her made her whirl with her gun drawn. Nick came to a skidding halt and raised his hands. "Whoa, there."

She lowered her weapon. "What the hell are you doing here?"

"Nice to see you too."

"Sorry. I'm just—there was a person running away from the scene. I lost them."

He squinted in the direction she'd indicated. "Man or woman?"

"Too far away to be sure. But whoever it was took several shots at me while I was inside Sam Tran's apartment."

He searched her face, his hand coming up to touch her cheek. "You're bleeding."

"There was a lot of glass," she replied as she pulled away from him and started walking back to Sam's apartment. Nick fell into step beside her. "You beat the cavalry," she observed as she saw the arriving black-and-whites rolling up.

"When you said you were working, I asked Zimmer where you were. Figured you might need backup." He cast her a meaningful glance. "Seems like I was right."

She bristled at the idea that he could have seen trouble coming where she had not. "It was dark out here and light inside the house. No way to see the shooter." Whoever it was must have followed her to Sam Tran's, or they were watching his apartment to see who showed up.

Nick nodded toward the town house. "Did you find anything?"

The most interesting thing was what she didn't find—the booze. "Nothing that explains why he got killed."

They went back inside Sam's place. "It's clear," one of the patrolmen told her as they walked through the doors. She was about to retort that she knew this, that she'd been inside and the shooter was outside, when it occurred to her it might have been a ploy to get her outside so someone could break in. She quickly assessed the office, now in disarray with glass shards all over the floor. The papers she'd been holding from Sam's desk had blown about the room, but they were all accounted for, as far as she could see.

"Check this out," Nick's voice called from deeper inside the apartment. He stood in the living area with his flashlight out, and he pointed it at the floor as she neared him. "It looks like a bullet ricocheted off the beam across the ceiling, hit that TV cabinet, and landed here."

She crouched down to look. "Nine millimeters."

"Maybe we'll get lucky and it will be in the system."

She stood up and looked him in the eyes. "Maybe it's mine." The Chicken Bandit had her weapon.

Nick didn't have a chance to reply because the medics caught up with her. "Detective Vega," said the shorter one, a Black woman whose name tag read SHELTON. "We understand you've been injured. We'd like to take you in for a full checkup."

Annalisa tried to wave them off. "I'm fine. Nothing's broken or severed."

Shelton gave her a dubious look. "At least let us treat the cut on your face."

"Maybe you should go with them," Nick told her. "I can hang here."

"I said I'm fine."

Nick pulled her to the side, away from the others, his hold on her elbow gentle but firm. "You should go," he said, keeping his voice low in deference to their audience. "In your condition . . ."

"I don't have a condition," she broke in swiftly, yanking her arm from him. At least no condition she was sure about. She didn't want to find out otherwise while wearing a paper gown, surrounded by strangers.

"I mean trauma," he replied with a frown. "You were attacked yesterday too."

"I don't need a doctor. I need to bag this evidence and go home to take a long, hot shower."

Nick held up his hands in defeat. "Suit yourself."

She let Shelton clean her cheek and put a bandage on the cut, but she sent the ambulance on its way. Zimmer arrived and was not pleased at what she found. "This is two crime scenes in two days where you've had a starring role," she told Annalisa.

"Yeah, well, they might be related. Ballistics should be able to tell us more."

"You think it's the Chicken Bandit? Not related to Sam?"

"I don't know what to think yet," Annalisa answered. She told Zimmer what she'd found in the apartment, the notes on Wade Armstrong and the lack of alcohol anywhere. "I'd like to have a couple of uniforms take Sam's picture around to the bars in the area. Maybe he wasn't drinking alone." If Sam's killer had been buying the booze somewhere in public, there might be security cameras that caught them together.

"Good idea," Zimmer said. Nick cleared his throat pointedly. The women turned to him. "You got something to add here, Carelli?" Zimmer asked him.

"Look, someone has to say it. Sam Tran was in the process of maybe linking one double homicide at a motel to a second double homicide that appears to be very similar in nature. Two plus two equals four. We may be looking at a serial offender here, one that slipped under the radar. I think you've got to pull all other motel-related homicides for the past twenty-five years at least, along with all double homicides where the victims were a couple, and give them a fresh look. If it is a serial killer who's been walking free all these years . . . well, we all know what happened in the Lovelorn case." He looked at Annalisa, and she looked away.

Zimmer motioned for Nick to keep it down. "No one's saying serial. Not yet."

"But—" Nick objected.

"We'll look into it," Zimmer told him tightly.

He hadn't softened his stance. "We?"

"Yes, I'm pulling you from the Chicken Bandit for the moment. You'll be doubling Annalisa on the Tran case until we know what we're dealing with here."

It was Annalisa's turn to object. "Commander, I don't think that's necessary."

Zimmer frowned. "Someone's taking shots at your back, Vega. The least you can do is let me assign someone to watch it."

Annalisa didn't have the energy to argue further. She didn't argue with Nick, either, when it was finally time to clock out and go home. He insisted on his place, where he got his pizza and she got a hot shower. When she emerged, toweling her hair dry, she found him standing in the kitchen with a slice in one hand as he went through his mail with the other. She draped the towel over a stool and grabbed a piece of pizza before it got cold. "What's this?" Nick asked. He slid a plain white envelope in her direction.

She turned it around and saw her name hand-printed on the front, no other identifying marks. "I don't know." She did not get mail at his place, but then again, this hadn't been mailed. Someone had dropped it off at Nick's box. She put the pizza down and opened the envelope. Inside was a flyer with a sticky note attached. The flyer advertised a crime podcast called *ShadowLands* with host Wendell Hawthorne. On the sticky note, it said, "I'm serious about my offer to have you on. Please give a listen and let me know." Hawthorne had repeated his contact info with an email and cell phone number.

"Who the hell is Wendell Hawthorne?" Nick said as he came around the peninsula to read the contents of the envelope.

"Quinn's professor. He wants me on his podcast."

"A podcast? When you said no to CNN?"

"Relax. I said no to him too." She eyed the flyer. "Which makes it strange he's still asking. How did he even find me here? Your address isn't listed."

"You think he's following you?"

"I haven't noticed him. Maybe he got the information out of Quinn somehow. Let's finish up here so we can get some rest, okay?"

In bed, he spooned up behind her in the dark and she felt his large hand cover her abdomen, a silent question. She placed her hand over his. His body was relaxed, his arms pleasantly heavy around her. Her heartbeat still thrummed in her throat and her head was full of gunfire. She waited, tense, to see if he would question her about another test, but he merely snuffled into her neck and went to sleep.

Annalisa lay awake, blinking in the dark. Cops had a name for this feeling: *wired*. She felt shorted out, exhausted but still sparking, unable to rest. She stretched her arm out carefully so as not to wake Nick and picked up her phone from the nightstand. The sudden burst of light in her face made her squint, and she angled it away from him. She typed Hawthorne's podcast, *ShadowLands*, into the search box. It returned a website that showed more than thirty episodes going back several years. The latest one was called "Cornflower Girl." She clicked the description:

The first note Dixie Chandler received from her eventual murderer seemed harmless, even sweet: *Your eyes are blue as cornflowers*, he wrote. He would leave her other notes, many of them disturbing, as he stalked Dixie around her college campus. University cops told her she should be flattered and to enjoy her secret admirer. Dixie changed her phone number, her hair color, and her address, but he followed wherever she went. When he killed her, she didn't see him coming because she'd been looking in the wrong places. The stalker wasn't a stranger. He'd been right in front of her all along.

Annalisa immediately did a second search for Dixie Chandler. The case came up with various headlines dating back five years ago. Dixie Chandler, age twenty, had been attending college in Lincoln, Nebraska, when she was found strangled to death in her own apartment. The killer was eventually revealed to be her English professor.

Literally right in front of her, Annalisa thought as she pictured the professor lecturing at the front of the room. She shivered as she replaced the phone on her nightstand. It was a long time before she slept.

EIGHTEEN

....

NICK WAS IN THE SHOWER WHEN SHE AWOKE AT DAYBREAK. Annalisa forced herself from bed with a groan. She stumbled over Nick's shoes on the ground, which were under his pants and shirt from yesterday, as though some supernatural force had evaporated him and left a pile of clothes where he'd been standing. "And he wonders why I won't move in," she muttered as she stooped to pick up the clothes. As she lifted his pants, his wallet fell out of the back pocket and flopped open on the ground. She rolled her eyes and bent again to retrieve it. As she did, she noticed the credit card receipt stuck in the billfold. She stopped, wallet in hand, listening to the sounds of the water running in the bathroom. This was her proof the last time, receipts for single-night hotel stays in town when he'd sworn he'd been working.

Trust your gut, Pops had advised her when she'd joined the force. *But trust the evidence more.*

She edged the receipt out from the wallet. TREADWELL JEWELER'S, it read. The total was more than six grand with tax. The water stopped. She shoved the receipt back in the wallet and the wallet in Nick's pants. When he emerged from the bathroom with a towel around his waist, she threw the clothes on the bed like they'd caught fire. He caught the gesture and grimaced. "I left them lying on the floor again, right?"

"No problem," she said quickly, ducking his gaze. She tucked her hair behind both ears, a nervous gesture that dated back to her childhood. "I made coffee but we're going to have to swing past my place so I can get dressed."

He looked to the dresser and the drawer he'd cleared out that still sat empty. "No problem," he echoed with a short nod. "Just let me get changed."

She escaped to the kitchen and poured a large cup of coffee. As desperate as she'd been to drink it a few minutes earlier, now she stood there staring into the brown liquid like it was a Magic 8 Ball. Nick had proposed to her the first time when they were both tipsy from cheap beer. She'd been in her first year of law school. He was a beat cop. Money was beyond tight. He'd slid a pop-top ring over her finger and asked her to marry him. Laughing, she'd said yes because she hadn't thought he was serious. The next morning she'd lain draped across him, still sleepy, and he'd traced an invisible line over her ring finger. "I'll get you a real one soon." She'd kept her mouth shut about her flippant answer. The longer she remained quiet, the more she warmed to the idea. Sure, she was young, but Ma had been pregnant with Vinny by Annalisa's age. *This is what you've always wanted*, she told herself. A home with someone. A family of her own.

"You want to be my wife?" Nick materialized behind her in the kitchen. She whirled around. "What?"

"I said, do you want to drive?" He gave her a funny look as he adjusted his tie. "On second thought, maybe I should. You look kind of pale."

"Uh, yeah, that's good. You drive."

A half hour and one change of clothes later, they hit the road in Nick's red sports car. He had money to spend now, she realized as she looked at the leather interior. All these years with no real debts, no dependents, and now he earned a senior detective's salary. *Wait*, she remembered. *Now maybe there is a kid.* She looked sideways at him as he drove. He didn't look like a father, or at least not like her father did in her memories, with a constant worried crease deep in his forehead. Of course, Nick wasn't trying to bring up four kids on a cop's salary.

"Have you talked to Cassidy recently?" she asked, trying to sound casual.

"We texted. She wants to meet up for coffee this weekend, but I told her I'd have to wait and see how things shake out here with the case."

Annalisa thinned her lips and looked out the window at the passing scenery. This, she did remember. Unpredictable hours. Ma kept home base functioning, kids in order, and food in the fridge for whenever Pops made it through the door. Both Annalisa and Nick worked those same grueling hours, the same erratic life of takeout and 2 a.m. calls. This morning alone, they'd both dashed out the door with only a granola bar for breakfast. If they had a kid, who would make it breakfast? Who would do car pools and soccer tournaments?

"Speaking of the case," Nick said, interrupting her thoughts, "you want to hit up Wade Armstrong first today?"

"You got a bead on him?" she asked with surprise.

"Ran him through the system. He has two DUIs, both of them more than ten years ago. Also, an ex-girlfriend took out an order of protection against him in 2006. It wasn't renewed past the original sixty days. Nothing recent on file, though. He runs a plumbing business with his brother, Matthew Armstrong. The address is over on West Thomas Street, if you want to check it out."

"Let's go knock on the pipes," she replied, settling back in her seat for the ride.

The area of Thomas Street listed as the address for Armstrong Plumbing turned out to be a residential block of identical three-unit brick buildings, not unlike Sam Tran's place from the night before. She knew they'd found the right place when she saw a white van with a cartoon strongman's arm flexing and holding a wrench stenciled on the side. "Must work out of the apartment," Nick observed as he pulled into an open slot.

They rang the bell for the ground-floor apartment, which corresponded to the business address. A heavyset white man wearing a gray sweatshirt answered. He had a droopy left eye and calluses on his hands. "I don't want any," he said bluntly when he saw them and tried to close the door.

Nick blocked it. "Detective Carelli, and this is my partner, Detective Vega. We're looking for Wade Armstrong."

"Wade's out on a call. I'm his brother."

"Matthew," Nick said, pointing at him.

"That's right. What do you want with Wade?"

"He's a witness to a crime and we'd like to ask him a few questions," Annalisa said.

"Oh, yeah?" Matthew's bushy eyebrows shot up. "What kind of crime?"

"A double homicide."

"Whoa, two people got whacked? Where?" He stuck his head out the doorway to look up the street.

"The Springwood Inn," Annalisa answered.

He looked confused for a moment. "Oh, you mean that thing at the motel," he said, less interested again. "That was a million years ago now. You're telling me you ain't caught the guy yet?" He said the last line slyly, like he knew they hadn't.

"We're still on the case," Annalisa pointed out. "When do you expect Wade to return?"

He shrugged one large shoulder. "Depends on how long the job takes. Could be hours."

"Do you happen to know if Wade has talked to anyone else recently about the case?" Annalisa asked.

"You mean the Asian PI? Yeah, he was here a couple of weeks ago."

"Do you know what they talked about?" Nick pressed.

"Nope. Didn't ask and don't care. Like I said, it was a million years ago."

"Wade said he was working at the Springwood Inn the night of the murders. That's when he saw the car—a blue Ford Taurus."

"If that's what he said, then that must've been what happened." Matthew glanced back into the apartment. "You want to leave a message or something for Wade? I've got paperwork I've got to get back to."

Annalisa could see the flicker of a TV behind him, some TV judge show. "That PI," she said, "he found evidence that Wade wasn't working the night of the murders. He wasn't on shift that night."

"That so?" His second eyelid came down to match the droopy one, and he regarded her with suspicion. "You're saying Wade lied?"

"I'm saying there's a discrepancy in the records. We'd like to ask him about it."

Matthew leaned against the doorjamb and licked his lips. After a moment, he smiled a little, almost to himself. "I can tell you what it is," he said at length. "You're going to laugh your asses off, I guarantee it."

"Try us," Nick said, deadpan.

Matthew grinned and licked his lips. "This was back around twenty years ago, right?"

"That's right," Annalisa said.

"Wade was married then to this gal named—I shit you not—Misty Waters. Only her parents should've named her Stormy because that lady had a temper on her. She threw one of her high heels at Wade once. Caught him right here and opened up a gusher." He indicated his temple. "He needed a dozen stitches to close it. Still has a scar."

Annalisa glanced at Nick. This had nothing to do with their case that she could see. "Get to the funny part, Mr. Armstrong."

"Well, she threw the shoe at him because he was running around on her. Wade always did like the ladies, and they liked him back. Sometimes, he'd use the motel as a meetup place. It was perfect because he worked there and he could fix up a key and sneak into an empty room, no problem. He and his lady friend would . . . you know . . ." He thrust his hips repeatedly at Annalisa. "And Misty would think he was at work. Which, I guess, technically he was." He grinned from Annalisa to Nick. "Funny, right?"

"So you're saying Wade was at the Springwood Inn the night Kathy Morrison and Stephen Powell were murdered, but he wasn't working. He was . . . entertaining." Annalisa did her best to keep any judgment out of her voice.

"That's what I'm betting, yeah. But of course he's not gonna tell you cops that because what if you brought Misty into it? He would've got another shoe to the face."

"Can you excuse us a second?" Annalisa jerked her head to the side, indicating that Nick should join her on the far side of the porch. When he joined her, she kept her voice low. "Are you hearing what I'm hearing?"

"Yeah. There could be one witness in the Powell-Morrison homicides that the police never talked to—whoever Wade Armstrong was sleeping with at the time."

She nodded. "And Sam Tran may have dug her up."

NINETEEN

··········

QUINN HELD AN EMPTY CARDBOARD BOX IN ONE HAND, AND WITH THE OTHER, SHE PRESSED THE DOORBELL SO HARD HER FINGER TURNED WHITE. She stood on the dilapidated porch to the apartment that Jason and Zach shared. They had the upstairs unit. A trio of girls lived downstairs; they'd tried to pretty up the stoop with a wreath on the door and a flowerpot full of fake mums, but it did little to hide the warped wooden floorboards or the peeling blue paint. When no one answered the bell, Quinn tried banging on the door. Eventually, Zach appeared, shirtless, his hair half on end. "What time is it?" he asked her as he let her inside.

"Time to get my stuff," she replied tartly as she pushed past him and started up the stairs.

"Huh?"

She started in the kitchen, where she took her barely used colander, the cheery yellow dish towel, and a half dozen spices. She placed them in the box and moved to the living room.

Zach stood there wearing pajama pants and a frown. "What are you doing?"

"Taking my things back." She'd gifted them a throw pillow to make their ratty sofa look more homey, and she plucked it from the couch. "Is Jason here?"

"No, I don't think so. He usually goes running around now—but then you know that."

Her cheeks burned. She did know it. She ignored him and went to the bathroom, where she started rummaging through the drawers for her things. Mascara, lip gloss, a comb. She'd been so pleased to leave this stuff at Jason's place. He was an upperclassman with an apartment. She was in a real, adult relationship. Turned out he was still a big child. She threw a hairbrush into the box with an angry toss and moved to Jason's bedroom. Zach followed and watched from the door.

"I heard you were looking into what happened to that girl. Sienna."

She opened the closet door and did not look back at him. "Where'd you hear that?"

"Around."

She rolled her eyes to herself. Natalie, probably. That girl talked so much her brain couldn't keep up with her mouth. She took a plaid flannel of hers off the hanger, and after a moment's thought, she took Jason's Illinois University sweatshirt too. Call it an asshole tax.

"Did you find out anything yet?" Zach asked.

She paused, balancing the box on one hip. "Why?"

He shrugged. "Just curious. I heard something the other day and it made me think about what happened to Sienna."

"What did you hear?"

"That biology professor—Hawthorne?—he left his last school after some girl reported him for creeping on her."

"Yeah? What school was that?"

"I dunno. I think it was in Texas, maybe. That's what I heard. Sienna and I both had him last semester, so he definitely knows who she is."

Quinn had a hard time imagining Professor Hawthorne dressed up in a gorilla suit at a frat party. "Okay, thanks," she said, dismissing him as she turned to the nightstand. She found a spare charger she wasn't sure was hers and a half-empty pack of gum. She took them both. She had a red nightshirt here somewhere, but she hadn't seen it yet. She looked around the unmade bed and then under it. Smelly sneakers and a dust bunny the size of a tumbleweed looked back at her. "Gross," she muttered, and went to Jason's dresser. One by one, she opened the drawers and went through them. T-shirts, boxers, socks, and jeans. No nightshirt. She was about to give up when she came across something solid.

She pulled it out and saw it was a phone. Not Jason's usual Android but a cheap, temporary one. What did Annalisa call it? A burner. Quinn's heart started pounding in her ears as she took out her own phone from her back pocket. With shaking fingers, she retrieved the series of anonymous text messages, barely allowing herself to look at them. She hit "dial" to call the number that had sent them and held her breath.

A moment later, the burner phone began to ring.

TWENTY

....

T HEY HAULED WADE ARMSTRONG IN FOR QUESTIONING. He wasn't what Annalisa expected after meeting his bigger, grubbier brother, Matthew.
Wade was shorter, with an athletic build, brown hair thinning a little
on top but still perfectly respectable for a man pushing fifty. He had a
friendly, open face, and yes, a faded scar at his right temple. They told
him no when he asked if he could smoke, so he turned a pack of ciga-
rettes around in his hands. "I'd like to help you," he said. "I would. But
I don't remember anything more about the night that couple got killed."

"We're more interested in your love life," Nick said.

Wade blinked in surprise. "I've been dating a woman named Patricia
Scarlotti for two years now. Why, did she say something about me?"

"Should she have?" Annalisa asked drily.

He tugged at his collar and gave a nervous chuckle. "Nothing that
involves the police."

"Back then, when the murders happened at the Springwood Inn,"
Nick said. "Who were you dating then?"

He blinked. "I was married."

"I know. That's not what I asked."

He looked from Annalisa to Nick and back again, then tossed the cigarette pack on the table in disgust. He scrubbed his face with both hands. "I told the truth about what I saw," he said emphatically. "I went out for a smoke break, and there was a guy there idling in a blue Ford Taurus. I didn't get a good look at him, and I didn't see the plate. All I can say is it was probably from Illinois because I would've remembered otherwise."

"Yes, we have your statement." Annalisa made a show of opening the folder and looking at a typed page. "But we also have the records that show you weren't working that night."

"Yeah, so I was off duty. It doesn't change anything."

"The woman in the motel room with you that night," Nick said, "what's her name?"

"I can't say."

"You can't say or you won't say?"

He fidgeted in his seat. "I'll tell you like I told that PI—I don't remember. I saw a bunch of different ladies back then. Maybe her name was Lila. Or Stephanie. Or Maria. You get the picture?"

"You cared enough about her to keep her out of it," Annalisa pointed out.

"I cared about saving my own butt. I'm not proud of it, okay? But my wife would've killed me if she found out, and I probably would've been fired to boot. It's not like I paid for that room."

"Where was the room?" Annalisa pushed a pad of paper at him. "Draw it for us, and include the spot where you saw the Taurus."

"Jeez, I don't know. This was like another lifetime." He took up the pencil and hunched over the pad, one hand holding up his head. He looked like a high school student who hadn't studied for the exam. Finally, he started sketching. "I generally picked a room down by the end on the first floor. That's where the dumpster was and we always rented those rooms last. So, if we were in here, that puts the Taurus somewhere in this row of spaces opposite the rooms. Probably about here." He drew a box to indicate the spot and turned the pad to show her.

The murder victims had been found on the second floor, above the spot where he'd indicated the car had been parked. If Brad Morrison had been watching his wife that night, he would've had a great view. "Okay, thank you," Annalisa said as she accepted his sketch. "Now back to your companion . . ."

He pushed back from the table with a frustrated groan. "I don't re-member. Why don't you believe me?"

"Who might remember? Your brother? A friend? Anyone else you might have told about this woman you were with?"

"It was on the down-low," Wade replied. "I didn't exactly advertise."

"Can you remember anything about her?" Annalisa asked. "Where you met, maybe? Where she worked?"

He answered with a helpless shrug. "I was drinking a lot back then. Seeing a lot of girls. Some of them, I met in bars. Others, I met when they came through the motel for one reason or another. These weren't exactly long-term deals, you know what I'm saying?"

"Yes, I get it," Annalisa said with a sigh. She narrowed her eyes at Nick, who'd had a similar relationship pattern there for a while. So many times, they'd be out to eat and she'd see a waitress give him a little wave, and she'd wonder if he was at it again. "Wait," she blurted, sitting up as a thought occurred to her. There was one person who might know this woman's identity. The woman who'd had a vested interest in tracking Wade's infidelity. "Where is your ex-wife these days?"

"Misty?" He put his palms flat on the table and shook his head. "Uh-uh. No way. I don't want to talk to her."

"You don't have to talk to her. We will."

He still looked reluctant. "Look, I haven't talked to her or seen her in years. If you really want to look the she-devil in the eyes, you can proba-bly find her at the hair salon she owns over in Pilsen. The place is perfect for her—it's called Head Games."

Nick and Annalisa exchanged a look. Wade sighed deeply and with regret, like a buddy in a horror movie watching his friend go into the woods to get murdered.

"You want my advice?" he said. "When you go, wear a helmet."

....

THEY LET WADE GO AND LOOKED UP THE ADDRESS FOR HEAD GAMES. Before they could depart, Annalisa got a message from the desk sergeant. She looked it over with a groan. "Problem?" Nick asked as he shrugged into his coat.

"Nina Osteen. She's the third open case on Sam Tran's desk. I've been ducking her calls and now she's apparently waiting here to talk to me."

"Okay, so you talk to Nina and I'll go see the infamous Misty Waters."

She raised her eyebrows at him. "You sure it's safe? What if she mistakes you for Wade and throws a shoe at you?"

"Nah." He tapped his knuckles against his skull. "I've got a thick head."

She couldn't argue with this, so she let him go and reluctantly went to meet Nina Osteen in the waiting area. It wasn't hard to pick her out, as the only other person there was an elderly Black man with a cane and a plaid hat. "Ms. Osteen?"

The woman looked up from her phone with an eager expression. "That's me." When she moved the giant purse from her lap and stood, Annalisa could see she was heavily pregnant. Her own stomach dropped at the sight. She swallowed against the queasy feeling and forced a smile. "I'm Annalisa Vega. Please come this way?"

Annalisa set Nina Osteen up with water and a packet of vanilla cookies, which the woman didn't touch as she started removing items from her giant bag and setting them on the table. "Thank you for seeing me," she said as she put out what looked like a journal with a faded purple cover, followed by a worn photo album and a notebook with colored sticky notes peeking out on all sides. "I heard that Sam Tran is dead," she said, pausing in her unloading to look at Annalisa.

"Yes."

"Murdered? That's what I saw in the news." Nina had huge blue eyes that seemed to take up most of her face. They were the same as the eyes of the young girl in the photo Sam Tran had in the file, and the same eyes of the missing mother.

"His death is being investigated as a homicide," Annalisa replied.

"That's so terrible. I know he had a teenage son. Benji, right?"

Annalisa was touched at Nina's concern. This was the first of Sam's clients who had expressed real sympathy at his passing. "That's right."

"So awful," Nina said, shaking her head. She had dark chestnut hair she wore braided and coiled like a crown. "Who could do such a thing?"

"That's what we're trying to find out."

"And you're looking into his cases, right? That's what they told me on the phone. I hired him to look for my mom, Charlotte Osteen."

"Yes, that's true, but—"

"He hadn't gotten very far with my case, but he promised to find out what happened to my mom. This is her, right here." She flipped open the photo album. "This is the last picture we have of her, from Christmas right before she disappeared. I was four years old then, so it's been more than thirty years."

"On New Year's Eve, right?" Annalisa asked as she accepted the album.

Nina looked relieved and she put a hand to her chest. "Oh, so you are looking into her case. Thank you. I don't have money to pay another investigator right now."

Annalisa didn't reply as she flipped through the photo album. They showed a happy family in what appeared to be the late 1980s or early 1990s. Nina's mom had big hair and wore a pastel tracksuit. The man, presumably Nina's dad, appeared only occasionally in the snapshots. He was big but skinny, with a mustache and glasses. He did not smile in the pictures, but Nina looked content sitting on his lap, wearing footie pajamas and clutching a stuffed elephant.

"I still have Bobo," Nina said, touching her finger to the elephant through the plastic sleeve. "He was a Santa present that year, and I was so happy to find him under the tree that I picked him up and did a dance with him right there in the living room. Mom had tied a fancy red ribbon around his neck, but you can't see it in the picture from the way I'm holding him. I know it was there, though. Isn't it funny, what you remember?"

"I'm sorry about your mom," Annalisa said as she set down the album.

"Dad says she left us. That she was drunk and went off with another guy. He says I don't remember how she would do that to us—go out and not come home for days. He's right that I don't remember. I do know she drank. To this day, I smell Bud Light and I think of her. I remember there were days my dad made breakfast because she couldn't get out of bed, and he said I had to be quiet because she was sleeping."

"Do you remember anything about the day she disappeared?"

"They were fighting, Mom and Dad. She wanted to go out to the party and he didn't want to go. He'd canceled the sitter she'd arranged. She said she'd go without him then, which I guess she did. But she never would have run off like that for good without telling us. Look at these pictures. She—she took care of me. She loved me."

"I'm sure she did," Annalisa said kindly as she looked again at the photographs. She thought of her own family pictures hanging in Ma and Pops's house, the truth they showed and then everything they didn't.

Charlotte's smile in the photos Nina had looked slightly too big. In one shot, she was in profile, sitting on the couch, her gaze tender as she looked at something out of frame. Nina, maybe. But the photographer had not centered Charlotte in the photo. She was at the very edge, almost cut off, and in the middle of the shot sat the end table with a ceramic Christmas tree, a bowl of peppermint ribbon candy, and a can of beer. "Your father reported her missing when she didn't come back?" Annalisa asked.

"He did, yeah." She sniffed and Annalisa stretched to reach the box of tissues sitting at the other end of the table. "The cops found a witness, a guy who said he'd seen her on New Year's getting into a car with another man. He said they were kissing."

"Do you know the witness's name?"

"Joey Fuller. I got a copy of his statement years ago. I made another copy for Mr. Tran, but I can give you one too if you need it."

"I'm sure it's in the file." She could pull the original police report if necessary, but she couldn't imagine it getting that far. Charlotte's disappearance was tragic but it almost certainly had nothing to do with Sam Tran's death. Annalisa felt a prick of guilt that she was leading this woman on, asking her questions like she meant to investigate a cold-case disappearance from thirty years ago. No way Zimmer would authorize the time even if Annalisa wanted to pursue it.

"I brought her diary too. My dad saved it for me. He gave me a box of her stuff when I turned eighteen. Some of her jewelry, her photos like this little album she made . . . her black leather jacket and her white boots with fringe on them." She smiled sadly. "I used to put them on and clomp around the house in them. They're too small for me but I kept them anyway. Probably they were too small by the time I turned twelve. Mom was tiny."

Annalisa fingered the fabric edge of the diary but did not open it. "I take it there's nothing in here about a boyfriend or her intentions to leave."

"Not a word. She wrote about how she wanted to quit drinking by the time I started school. She didn't want all the other moms thinking she was a lush. Every other day, it seemed, she promised to stop."

"But she didn't." Annalisa could guess the outcome.

"No." Nina sniffled, her eyes watering. "But let's say it's true that she went off with another man," she said as she dabbed at her eyes with a tissue. "Wouldn't she call or come visit? Wouldn't she send a note? She wouldn't tuck me into bed and leave like that forever. I don't believe it."

"It does happen," Annalisa said gently. Most missing people were missing on purpose. Sometimes they were unsafe at home and so they left without a trace. Sometimes they were ashamed or unhappy with who they were and they wanted to make a clean break. They rationalized that people left behind were better off without them.

"Not my mom," Nina insisted brokenly, but she didn't sound sure. She rested one hand on her swollen belly, the crumpled tissue clutched between her fingers. "I've looked for her on and off over the years, you know? I went to the bar where she was that night. I talked to her friends to try to . . . I don't know. Understand her better. I was looking for one person who could tell me for sure that yes, she had a plan to take off and leave me. Sorry, kid. Your memories are a fantasy. She didn't love you as much as you thought. But no one could ever tell me that." She looked at Annalisa, defiant, like she was daring her to say otherwise.

Annalisa couldn't imagine a friend telling this woman her mother had intentionally abandoned her as a child. "Maybe she meant to get in touch and then something happened to her."

"That's what Mr. Tran said. He said most likely she's dead, and was I prepared for that?" Her shoulders hitched. "I said she'd been silent on me for so long that her death would be welcome. I'd have a reason for why she didn't come back." She rubbed her stomach absently. "Whatever the truth is, I have to know it. I have to know if she was the mother I remember or . . . or someone else."

Annalisa could have told her that the truth wouldn't be that simple or that satisfying. She had the Pops of her childhood and the Pops she had to contend with now—the one who had cheated on Ma and then covered up a murder. Annalisa knew them both equally but could not bring them together in her head. She took a deep breath and leaned closer to Nina. "Ms. Osteen, I have to be honest with you. From the perspective of the Chicago Police Department, your mother's case is closed."

"Why? Because that witness, Joey Fuller, said she ran off?"

"Because it's been more than thirty years. Because it's not a crime for an adult woman to leave her family—at least not a legal crime. I'm sorry."

"Sorry." Nina's enormous blue eyes filled with tears again. "That's all I've heard for thirty-four years now. *I'm sorry.* Well, I don't want any more sorry. I want someone to find her."

"Maybe eventually you can hire another PI . . ." She trailed off as Nina began sticking her mementos back in her bag.

"My husband got laid off two weeks ago. He already thinks I'm chasing a ghost, and now we've got the baby coming. He doesn't understand. His folks are still around, still married. They live in Iowa and they can't wait to meet their grandson. All I can think about is when he's old enough to ask me about his other grandmother, about my mom . . . what am I going to say?"

Annalisa didn't have words to offer her because there were no words to summon. This was the problem. Nina had a blank space where her mother was supposed to be. "If I uncover anything useful, anything else that Sam Tran might have discovered about your mother's case, I'll be sure to let you know."

"Sure," Nina said, gathering her things, not making eye contact. "Thanks."

Annalisa remained in the room alone after Nina Osteen left. The law was clear on her duty. It helpfully divided the world into people whose problems she had to solve and those she did not, but the people on the other side of the line still needed help sometimes. Annalisa could not pretend she didn't see them, and it hurt to leave them behind.

A sharp knock on the door startled her, and she turned to see Nick poke his head inside the room. "Oh, good," he said when he saw her. "You're free."

"What's up?" she asked, rising to her feet.

"I found Misty Waters, and you're not going to believe what else."

TWENTY-ONE

....

NICK TOOK ANNALISA TO A DIFFERENT INTERVIEW ROOM, AND THE SMELL OF PERFUME HIT HER LIKE A FIST THE INSTANT HE OPENED THE DOOR. Inside sat a white woman, mid-forties, with brassy blond hair and glossy wine-colored nails. "Miss Waters?" Nick said pleasantly. "This is my colleague, Detective Annalisa Vega." He indicated Annalisa with one hand as he set a bottle of water in front of Misty Waters with the other.

"Charmed, I'm sure," Misty said, barely looking up as she leafed through a binder in front of her. She had full lips that matched the color of her nails. Annalisa did a quick check of the woman's shoes and was relieved to see they were low-heeled boots. Misty wouldn't be giving anyone a head wound today. "What year did you say this was again?" Misty asked Nick.

"Summer of 2000," Nick replied as they each took seats across from her.

Up close, Annalisa could see the binder held photos, printouts, and various receipts. Also sequins and stickers. "What's this?" she asked Nick under her breath.

"My records on Wade's activities," Misty answered for him. She flipped to show Annalisa the cover, which had a sticker on it that read SHITHEAD in fancy printing.

"Miss Waters did employ various private investigators to follow Wade Armstrong," Nick explained. "Lucky for us, she documented it all, and, uh, saved the records."

"You never know when you might need it for the lawyers," Misty said as she turned back to the place she'd been perusing.

Annalisa leaned over. "Is that glitter?"

"I like scrapbooking," Misty told her. "You got a problem with that?"

"Not at all." She was no longer surprised by any form of human behavior, even bedazzling the PI reports on your husband's infidelities. "We're looking for the name of a woman Wade was seeing at the Springwood Inn."

Misty snorted as she turned another page. "Who wasn't he seeing there? That dog hit on my own mother once. Ah, here we go." She took out a pair of red-rimmed glasses and looked closer at the pictures. "I think this is who you were looking for. The report says her name was Paula Polanski."

"Can I see that?" Nick asked.

"Knock yourself out." She sat back in her seat and folded her arms across her chest.

He turned the album around and Annalisa scooted closer to look. The PI report on Paula Polanski was thorough, including her name, address, and phone number at the time. Misty had affixed it to the page with sticker letters that spelled out SKANK. "This is the Springwood Inn, all right," Nick murmured as he examined the photos.

"And that's Wade." The pictures showed a younger Wade Armstrong and a dark-haired woman getting out of a silver car and walking into a motel room together. At one point, Wade was caught kissing the woman's neck and grabbing her breasts through her shirt.

Nick turned the page. "Looks like he was telling the truth about his smoke break." The PI had caught him hanging around the dumpster, smoking. His companion was apparently still in the room. "And look at that."

Annalisa looked where he was pointing on the page. One of the shots caught the back end of a Ford Taurus, which looked black or gray in the shot but could easily have been blue in reality. The plate was blurry but readable. Maybe they wouldn't need to bother Paula at all. Annalisa jotted down the plate number. "Please excuse me a moment," she said, getting up to go run the registration.

"Sure, whatever," Misty said. She looked to Nick as Annalisa left the room. "Does this mean you're going to arrest Wade for something? I'd love to see him fry."

Annalisa went to her computer to run the plate. While she waited, her stomach grumbled, complaining it was past lunch, so she felt around in her coat pocket for a mint or piece of candy. She found a mini chocolate bar and a folded piece of paper. She ate the candy as she unfolded the paper. It was the note she'd taken from Sam Tran's desk, the one that read *Sally Johnson, 1999*. She set it aside as the computer beeped the result of its search: the blue Taurus had been registered to Brad Morrison.

She practically sprinted back to the interview room. "Miss Waters, the pictures in your scrapbook . . . is there any way to tell when they were taken?"

"Sure, the date's right here on the report," Misty said, pointing to the printed paper she'd pasted in next to the photos. Annalisa held her breath as she leaned over to check, and there it was in black-and-white: the night of the Queen of Hearts murders. Brad Morrison had been at the motel.

TWENTY-TWO

············

O KAY, SO I'VE BEEN ABLE TO CONFIRM THE GORILLA GUY IN MULTIPLE PHOTOS
NOW, BUT I STILL DON'T SEE A BLACK CAT." Quinn sat cross-legged on her
bed, scrolling through Instagram on her phone. She found a bunch of
photos from people she didn't know by following the #DGN and #Hal-
loween tags. Time stamps weren't that helpful because the partygoers
didn't necessarily upload the pictures at the moment they were taken,
but near as she could tell, the gorilla man had not been present at the
beginning of the night, when the crowd was smaller and people weren't
as sloppy drunk. She spotted him lurking by the food table a few times
once the party was underway. At no point did she see him interacting
with anyone else.

"Are you sure there was a black cat?" Sarah Beth asked. She lounged on
Natalie's bed, flipping through a catalog. "This is cute, don't you think?"
She held up a page that showed off a black sweater with cutouts at the
shoulder. "But who orders anything from a paper catalog anymore?"

"My mom does." Quinn had a sudden pang of homesickness. Nights
like this when it was cold and windy outside and Quinn had to study, her
mom would bring her cookies and cocoa. *Can't focus when your tummy's
rumbling*, she'd say, and she would stroke Quinn's hair like Quinn was
still five years old. Mom and Dad never changed.

"So they print these for the geriatrics, then?" Sarah Beth asked, waving the catalog. "Don't they know they're killing the planet by cutting down all the trees?"

Normally Quinn would ask her to leave, but Natalie was across campus in the practice rooms, playing her flute, and Quinn didn't want to be alone. She abandoned her search for the black cat and thought about what Zach had said about Professor Hawthorne, that he had left his previous school after complaints from a student about harassment. Quinn got out her laptop to Google his name and found Zach had gotten the school wrong—Hawthorne had been a junior professor in Nebraska, not Texas, prior to his current job—but the only other item she found was that he'd placed third in his age group in a half-marathon four years ago. "Have you heard anything about Professor Hawthorne harassing any students?" Quinn asked Sarah Beth.

"You mean like groping them and stuff? Because sign me up." Sarah Beth gave a mischievous grin and popped off the bed to grab a half-eaten bag of chips from the top of the mini fridge.

"I'm being serious."

"So am I," Sarah Beth answered, deadpan, and Quinn rolled her eyes.

"I heard a rumor he might've gotten in trouble at his previous school, but I can't find anything about it online."

Sarah Beth joined her on the bed, chips in hand. "Check the big rate-my-professor sites. Message boards don't always show up in Google searches."

"Ooh, good idea." Quinn found him easily for their school, but he had a solid four-star rating and the comments were mostly glowing. Hawthorne makes biology seem fun! His lectures have real energy and humor. I almost didn't hate getting up at 8am to go to class. The most negative comment she found was Didn't totally suck.

"Try his other school," Sarah Beth suggested.

Quinn went to the site for his Nebraska campus and entered Hawthorne's name. "Nothing," she said, disappointed. "He's no longer listed."

"Let me see." Sarah Beth wiped her hands on her jeans and took the computer from Quinn. "The internet is forever," she told Quinn. "We should be able to find it archived somewhere." She was able to call up a version of the site from two years ago, and Wendell Hawthorne's name appeared under *H*. "Ta da," she told Quinn with triumph.

Quinn leaned in. "Two years ago, he'd already come here."

"They must not have taken it down right away. Let me check." She clicked a couple more dates from the archive. "Yeah, it looks like they pulled him sometime earlier this year. I guess it takes some time for the system to update when a professor moves schools."

"What's the last available version?" Quinn asked.

"Here." Sarah Beth handed her the laptop. "Ten months ago."

His rating stood strong, Quinn saw. The average was over four stars. The comments were much the same as the ones he had on his current site. Tough but fair. A total fox. Made the Krebs cycle not a total nightmare. "Oh my God," Quinn said when she got to the final comment. "Look at this." Wendell Hawthorne is a pervert. It was dated January of this year, so after he had moved schools. The user was listed as Anony111, but the avatar was a photo of a black cat.

A loud knock on the door made them both jump. "Quinn? Quinnie, are you in there? I just want to talk to you." Jason's desperate voice came through from the other side.

Quinn fell back on the bed with a groan. "Great," she muttered. "Now the whole hallway will know my business."

"Want me to get rid of him?" Sarah Beth asked.

"No," Quinn said with a sigh, forcing herself to sit up. "It's my mess. I'll clean it up."

"Quinn?" Jason knocked again, his whine plaintive.

She squared her shoulders and opened the door. "What?" she asked.

He grinned with relief at her appearance. "Babe, thank you. Zach told me you came by the place today and cleared out your stuff."

"I texted you. It's over, Jason."

"Yeah, but you don't really mean it." He moved in closer and she could smell he'd been drinking. "We're good together, you and me. You're my girl." He tried to put an arm around her and she ducked away.

"I do mean it."

He frowned. "Zach said you found some phone in my stuff. Something about sending you creepy messages? It wasn't me, I swear."

"I called the phone number. It rang."

"I mean the phone isn't mine. I've never seen it before."

"Sure," she said, not believing him. "Well, now you can go call some other girl with the phone that isn't yours, okay? I'm out." She tried to close the door on him, but he blocked it.

"You have to believe me. It's not my phone."

"It was in your underwear drawer."

"Yeah, but I didn't put it there."

"So who did?"

His brow furrowed. "I don't know. Could be a lot of people. You know we have guys over all the time. We barely lock the door. Come on, Quinnie, you've got to believe me."

"I don't," she said flatly. "And I want you to leave."

"Aw, don't be like that. You like me. I know you do." He started to push his way into the room, and she shoved back, hard enough to send him into the cement-block wall. "Jesus, what the hell?"

"I said leave," Quinn told him. "Don't contact me again, you understand?"

"Fuck you," he spat out.

"Not anymore."

"That's it. You listen to me—" He started charging at her, but Sarah Beth appeared as backup. She had her jacket ready and put a hand on Jason's chest.

"Jase, why don't I walk you out, hmm? Get some air?"

"Your friend's a real piece of work," he said, glaring at Quinn. "It wasn't even me!" He hollered at her as Sarah Beth started to drag him away. "You broke up with me for nothing!"

Quinn closed the door and leaned her back against it. Her heart was pounding. *You did it*, she told herself. *You said it's over.* She'd never had to break up with anyone before. It was kind of scary but also powerful. Talking with Sienna, hearing how helpless she'd felt with the gorilla man, made Quinn doubly committed to not taking shit from anyone.

Her phone rang on the bed and she went to retrieve it, prepared to tell off Jason yet again. But it was Natalie calling. "Hey," Quinn said. "Where are you?"

"I'm still in the practice room. My lips are blue, and now I have to walk home in this crazy wind. I was thinking of stopping to get ice cream. You want to split a pint of fudge brownie?" Natalie could eat ice cream in any weather.

Quinn shivered at the thought. "Not tonight." She drifted to the window, where she could see the bare tree branches waving in the breeze. "Just come straight home, okay? I have to tell you what happened with Jason."

"I'm packing up now."

Quinn saw a shadow outside, far below and across the path. It looked like a person. She blinked and it was gone. "Maybe you should take the safety shuttle."

"That thing takes thirty minutes or more to show up. I can be back in half that time."

"Nat, I'm worried it's not safe."

"I'll be fine. I can see outside now and there's Officer Ken. I'll be home in twenty and we'll talk, okay?"

"Okay." Quinn hung up the phone. She decided to take a hot shower and make a bowl of popcorn for when Natalie got back. She showered, changed into warm fuzzy pajamas, and popped the bag in the microwave. She watched the seconds tick down and checked her phone for the time. Natalie was late.

Quinn shook out the bag into a bowl and went to her bed, waiting for the moment when Natalie would come through the door. She ate some popcorn. Then some more. She checked her phone as worry started rising. She texted once and got no answer, so she moved straight to calling. Natalie's voicemail recording came on the line. *Hey, this is Natalie. Why are you calling me? If you want a response, send me a text.*

"Nat? It's Quinn. Where are you? It's been almost an hour and you're not here. Please let me know you're okay."

Quinn went to the window with her phone clutched in her hand. She looked at it every few seconds, willing it to ring or buzz, but it remained silent. *You're being silly*, she thought. Any moment now, Natalie's familiar shape would come into view.

The minutes continued to pass until one hour became two. Quinn paced the length of the room, chewing the inside of her lip as dread settled in her stomach. It was almost midnight. Natalie never stayed out this late without a predetermined destination. She always told Quinn where she'd be and what she was doing. She updated practically the whole world via social media on an hourly basis. The last image on Natalie's story showed she'd been at Pearce Hall, posing with her flute and some random girl with a bass guitar, just as she'd said. Then Natalie would have been heading home, just as she'd said. Only somehow, she never made it back to the dorm.

Quinn stared at her phone and tried to figure out who to call next. Because she had to admit the truth now: Natalie was missing.

TWENTY-THREE

....

ANNALISA MADE A STRATEGIC DECISION NOT TO CALL VINNY. If Quinn looped him in, that was fine, but she wasn't going to rile her brother in the middle of the night over something that might be nothing. She had no choice but to alert Nick, though, since he'd been lying beside her in bed when Quinn called. "Did you tell her to dial 911?" he asked now from the passenger seat of her car. They hurtled forward on the highway, doing fifteen over the limit, but the late hour meant the roads were mostly clear.

"No."

"No?" he echoed.

"Natalie is a legal adult. She could be a million places, all of them perfectly fine. You know as well as I do that no one is going to even file a report on this until she's been gone at least twenty-four hours, and maybe not even then."

"So this has nothing to do with the fact that Quinn's your niece and you want to make sure you're in charge of the scene," he said, nodding to himself. "Got it."

"What scene? When we have something that might resemble a scene, I'll be happy to hand it off."

"Sure." His face cracked with his yawn. "Let's find this girl so we can get some sleep."

Quinn met them outside her dorm wearing an oversized sweatshirt. The exterior light was on to illuminate the door, but the building was mostly dark, with just a few coronas of light visible around the window shades. She threw herself against Annalisa in a desperate hug. "Thank you for coming. I didn't know who else to call."

Annalisa hesitated before touching her hand to the back of the girl's warm head. "We'll find her," she promised. "But first you have to tell me everything you know about where she might have gone."

"I've called or texted all of Nat's friends and her boyfriend, Logan. No one has seen her. She told me she was coming back here after practice but she never showed. That was about nine forty."

"Practice?" Annalisa couldn't figure out what sport played in the dark.

"Flute practice. She booked one of the rooms in the music department. They're soundproof so you don't annoy everyone in the dorm when you play. She goes a few times a week."

Nick looked around at the shadowed quad and the silent sister dorm across the way. "Maybe she's still there. Have you checked?"

"No," Quinn said slowly. "But when we spoke, she was on her way out. I told her to take the shuttle but she wanted to walk. She said she was going to stop at the campus store to pick up ice cream. I don't know if she did or not."

"Okay, so we start there," Annalisa said. "Which way?"

"It closed at midnight," Quinn replied with a desperate edge in her voice.

"Still, we retrace the route Natalie would have been on. Can you show us the music hall?"

"Sure, it's this way," Quinn said, her determination apparently renewed. She fell into step beside Annalisa. Nick hung back, his flashlight out. He shone it here and there as they walked, pausing to look into trash bins. Quinn cast a look over her shoulder. "What's he doing? Natalie's not in a trash can."

"When you have no leads, you look everywhere."

"This is a shortcut," Quinn said, pausing to point to a left fork.

Annalisa stopped to evaluate. "Would Natalie have taken it?"

"Yes, probably."

"Okay, then we do that too." Annalisa started forward, but Quinn stayed rooted. Annalisa turned around as Nick caught up to them. "What is it?" Annalisa asked.

Quinn shifted from one foot to the other. "I haven't told you everything," she confessed. "That Halloween party? The one where the girl got attacked after? I was there."

"I figured as much," Annalisa replied. "Natalie too?"

"And Sarah Beth. It was a huge party. Everyone was there. But I couldn't say that in front of my dad. You know how he is." She looked to Annalisa for understanding. "He's so rigid about everything, especially since . . . well, that thing with Alex."

"Yes, I know."

"He sees danger everywhere now. I guess I've been trying to do the opposite. Pretend like everything is fine."

"But it's not fine?" Annalisa pressed gently.

Quinn swallowed. "You were right. That girl—her name is Sienna— she did get attacked behind the frat house. There was some guy in a gorilla suit who was molesting her upstairs at the party, and we think maybe he followed her into the woods. You can see him in pictures, standing there watching everyone, but he's got the mask on to hide his face. I thought I could figure out who it was, but I haven't been able to and now Natalie's missing and it's all my fault." She broke off with a sob and covered her face with her hands.

"None of this is your fault," Annalisa said as she slipped an arm around her niece's shoulders. "We're going to find Natalie and then I'll worry about the gorilla man, okay?"

Quinn gave a watery sniff. "I will die if anything happens to her."

Annalisa rubbed Quinn's shoulder in what she hoped was a reassuring gesture. "Let's go check the music hall."

Pearce Hall was large and imposing and gave the impression the architect had tried to evoke the feeling of a grand Greek building. The facade had four imposing columns at the front and fancy scrollwork at the top, but up close, one could see this was basic cement work and that it was attached to a typical redbrick building at the back. Annalisa tugged on the doors and found them locked. There was an electronic keypad and a place to scan identification. "Can you get in?" she asked Quinn.

"I don't know." She fumbled in her pockets for her student ID and tried it on the scanner. It answered with a red light. "No."

"I'll try around back," Nick said. "Maybe there's another way in."

Annalisa peered through the narrow glass windows on either side of the doors. There was a faint light on in the entryway but no obvious sign of anyone in the building. She turned and looked at the nearby surroundings. "What's over there?" she asked Quinn, indicating the building across the road.

"That's one of the main auditoriums," Quinn replied. "They hold large classes in there as well as theater and concert performances. Beyond that are the athletic buildings and the soccer field."

"Hmm." What Annalisa saw was the parking lot. She and Nick had arrived on the other side of campus, nearer to Quinn's dorm, but this was a separate main entrance, presumably to accommodate people arriving for the athletic games and fine art performances. Easy way in from off campus. Easy way out too. "Are there dorms down this way?"

"Not here, no. But there are cheap apartments that go to mostly upperclass students. My boyfriend—" She stopped, gritted her teeth, and started again. "My ex-boyfriend Jason lives there with his roommate."

"Does Natalie know anyone who lives that way? Maybe she went to visit."

"I told you I checked with all her friends."

Annalisa took another look inside the building. "Maybe she has a friend you don't know about."

Nick reappeared at the base of the steps. "I tried all the doors—nothing."

"She was leaving here," Quinn insisted. "That means she's somewhere else."

Annalisa didn't have a chance to reply because a sudden flash of headlights caught her across the face. One of the parked cars across the road had turned on its high beams. She shielded her eyes and stepped to the side for a better look. A figure was getting out of the car, and she saw now it was a black-and-white cruiser with CAMPUS POLICE lettering on the side. Officer Kent strolled over to them, a flashlight in hand. Annalisa hadn't heard the engine drive up, which meant he'd been sitting in the car watching them this whole time. Regardless, she was almost relieved to see him. More eyes looking for Natalie wouldn't be a bad thing.

"You're on private property," he called to them. "And it's closed."

"Detective Vega," she reminded him. "This is my partner, Nick Carelli."

Officer Kent shone his flashlight from one to the other, making them squint in turn. "You two want to explain why you're trying to break into Pearce Hall in the middle of the night?"

"They're helping me," Quinn supplied. "I'm looking for my roommate, Natalie Kroger. She was leaving here to come home a few hours ago, but I haven't seen her since."

"That so?"

"She said . . . she said she saw you," Quinn said. "On her way out."

"When was this?" he asked in reply.

"Just before ten o'clock."

"She's a little bit of a thing, right? Reddish-brown hair?"

"She had on a red jacket," Quinn told him.

He scratched his chin with his free hand. "Don't recall seeing her, but I've been all over the place tonight. Tell you what, let's take a look-see inside." He mounted the steps and went to the keypad, where he punched in a code. The door buzzed open in response.

Quinn rushed in before Annalisa could stop her. "Natalie? Nat, are you here?"

Annalisa followed her niece from room to room, but there was no sign of Natalie. She heard the heavy footfalls of Officer Ken behind her. "Looks in order," he said, shining his light around. "She's probably in some friend's room. Or with a boy. That's usually where we find 'em. Elsewise, they go into the city for a walk on the wild side. That's more typical on the weekends, though."

Annalisa was looking at the ceiling for cameras. "You have security cameras anywhere?"

"Not here. They've got them in the research labs because of the drugs and fancy equipment. Ditto the computer science building. There are two each that cover the parking lots, and that's it. Nothing in the academic centers, the dorms, or the student union." He gave her a tight smile. "Mom and Dad don't want their little chickadees under surveillance, and truth be told, neither does the brass."

Annalisa got his meaning immediately. "If you put up cameras, you're admitting there might be crime."

"Bingo. Of course, the minute they can't reach their little darlings by phone or FaceTime or whatever, they call up campus security to report them missing." He paused meaningfully. "Not one time has any of them really been missing."

"Let's hope that's the case this time," Annalisa replied. She went to find Quinn, who looked increasingly distraught.

"I keep checking my phone, but she hasn't replied to my texts. If she could reply, she would."

"We'll keep looking. Where's the campus store?"

Officer Kent joined them as they left Pearce Hall and walked back toward the center of campus. Quinn indicated a shuttered convenience store on the ground level of the student union. "This is it," she said. "But like I said, it closes at midnight."

Nick did a slow patrol of the area, looking behind the low brick wall, poking into the trash and recycling receptacles. Officer Kent stood around looking bored. Annalisa cupped her hands around her face and looked through the glass window of the store. "I see a camera," she announced. It was hard to see in the dim light, but she could make out the black lens and the steady red dot mounted on the ceiling near the register.

"Oh, yeah," said Officer Ken. "That one's just CCTV for the store. Not on our system."

Annalisa indicated the door to him. "Can you open it?"

"No. You need keys for that one. Janitorial staff would have one, but they're gone for the night. No way I'm rousting the supervisor to go after a college kid who hasn't been gone even five hours. We don't even know she was here."

Annalisa held back a curse and considered her options. She felt Quinn's anxious gaze on her and Officer Kent's self-satisfaction at watching her spin her city-cop wheels. "I know someone who works here," Quinn said after a moment. "My ex, the one I was telling you about? His roommate, Zach, works nights. He may even have been here tonight. You want me to call him?"

"Yes, that would be great, thank you," Annalisa said. Maybe this kid would know how to work the camera footage.

"Hey, Vega," Nick called to her. He had wandered away from the campus center, down the main path. "Come here a second."

She jogged over to Nick, who shone his flashlight into a trash can.

"What did Quinn say Natalie was picking up at the store?" he asked. "Ice cream, right?" He used one finger of his other hand to push aside the handles of a plastic bag. Inside sat a pint of fudge brownie ice cream, apparently untouched.

Annalisa pulled out a pair of unused gloves from her pocket and put them on before lifting out the bag. "No receipt," she said, disappointed. "But the purchase was recent. The ice cream is still mostly hard."

"Yeah? Look at this." Nick's voice had a new edge to it. He stood over the bin, shining his light inside.

Annalisa peered into the trash can to see what had been revealed under the ice cream. It was a black carrying case with silver hinges—the kind you might use for a flute.

TWENTY-FOUR

············

WHAT ARE YOU THINKING?" Nick asked her in a low voice as they stood over the trash can.

"My brother, Vinny, he hired Sam Tran to look into whoever was harassing Quinn. But Quinn and Natalie share a room. The slurs written on the door might have been for her, not Quinn. Natalie's also the one who said she thought someone was following her a couple of weeks ago."

"But Quinn got those texts."

"She said it was her boyfriend who sent them. She found the phone in his bedroom." The boyfriend would know Natalie, too, Annalisa reasoned. Maybe the guy wanted to scare both girls.

"You have proof that he purchased the phone?" Nick asked.

"We know the phone that sent the texts came from Walmart where he works. This new wrinkle with a missing girl might give us enough for a warrant to pull the footage to confirm it's him."

"Yeah, but is he good for this?" Nick nodded down at the flute in the trash.

"I don't know," Annalisa replied, frustration edging into her voice. "But it's stalking behavior, so I think we have to look into it." She glanced over to where Quinn was chatting with Officer Kent and saw a lone figure loping toward them in the mist. Quinn rushed up to hug him, so Annalisa deduced this must be Zach, the roommate who worked at the campus quick mart. She walked over to introduce herself.

Zach shook her hand, his face etched with concern. "Quinn says Natalie's gone missing."

"We can't find her at the moment," Annalisa answered lightly.

"She was in the store tonight," he said. "Bought some ice cream. She seemed fine to me."

"Did she say anything to you?" Annalisa wanted to know.

"Just that she was tired and was looking forward to going home and crashing. Oh," he added, casting a guilty glance at Quinn, "also that she was sorry about Jase and Q breaking up."

"Jase—that's Jason Wilcox, your roommate?"

"That's right."

"Is he home now?"

Zach looked again to Quinn. "No," he said after a pause. "When I left for my shift, he said he was going to talk to Quinn. I haven't seen him since."

"No idea where he could be?" Annalisa looked from Zach to Quinn, who looked at the ground.

"He showed up at my room asking to get back together," she mumbled. "I told him no. We—we argued and then Sarah Beth walked him out. I don't know where he went after that."

"Okay, let's leave Jason aside for now," Annalisa said, turning to Zach. "Can you get into the store to see the security camera footage?"

"Sure, I brought my keys." He jangled them in his pockets. The group followed him to the glass doors, which he opened, and then he flicked on the overhead lights. He went behind the counter and pulled out a laptop. "Let me fire this baby up."

Annalisa did a slow walk of the small store. A freezer in back held ice cream and frozen entrees. Cold drinks sat in the fridge section next to it, along with eggs, milk, butter, and cheese. The shelves held mainly junk food, peanut butter, and canned soup. Nothing looked disturbed or out of place. She went back to the counter to wait for the CCTV footage and her gaze traveled to the items stocked on the shelves behind Zach. Cold medicine, razor blades, and pregnancy tests.

"What time do you want to look at?" Zach asked.

Annalisa kept staring at the pregnancy tests.

Nick cleared his throat as he stepped up to the counter. "Whenever Natalie was in here. Around ten? Maybe start a little before that."

"Sure, here you go." He turned around the laptop and Annalisa forced her attention back to the task at hand. Officer Kent and Quinn crowded in with her and Nick to watch the laptop screen. It showed the convenience store in black-and-white. Zach, presumably behind the counter on-screen, was visible only by his hands and occasionally the back of his head. A guy in a black beanie and squarish glasses was buying an energy drink and a large bag of chips. The camera captured both the customers and the store behind them. The place was small enough to encompass the entire store in one shot, including the doors in the background.

"There she is," Quinn yelped as Natalie pushed through the doors and appeared on-screen. The time in the corner of the shot read 10:03 p.m. Annalisa noted a black backpack on the girl's back and the flute-carrying case in her left hand. They all watched as Natalie went to the freezer and selected her ice cream.

At the counter, Natalie smiled and chatted with Zach as she dug out her student ID to complete her purchase. The exchange seemed normal. Annalisa noticed a flash of light outside the store's large windows. Headlights, driving by slowly. Natalie took her purchase and went for the door. She met someone coming in as she was leaving and they said what looked like a friendly hello. "Who's that?" Annalisa asked. The figure looked tall and male, but he wore a hat and a scarf around his neck. The camera was too far away to see his face.

Zach squinted at the screen. "That's Professor Hawthorne. He teaches biology."

As the man bid goodbye to Natalie and moved deeper into the store, Annalisa could see Zach was correct. "Do professors often shop here?" she asked as Hawthorne perused the shelves. He selected what looked like some beef jerky and a bottle of soda.

Zach shrugged. "Sure, sometimes. Hawthorne especially. He lives near here."

"Here? Near the student housing?"

"Yeah, I see him sometimes walking his dog. A boxer named Rosie. She's real cute." He hit a button to stop the video as Hawthorne got to the counter to pay for his items. "That's it. That's all I have on Natalie."

"Keep it going a minute," Annalisa instructed.

Zach resumed the video and Hawthorne completed his purchase. He did not head for the door when finished. Instead, he went the long way around and appeared to stop near the freezer case, as if contemplating another item. Then he moved toward the door but managed to knock over a rack of greeting cards in the process. "Oh yeah," Zach said. "I forgot about this."

On-screen, Zach moved to clean up the mess. Hawthorne helped him right the rack and pick up a few cards. Then he said something and left as Zach continued to put the cards and envelopes back in their correct places. "Run it back, please," Annalisa said.

"The whole thing?"

"No, just the part where he knocks over the cards."

Zach rewound and Annalisa watched the mishap again. She could not be sure because the incident took place at the rear of the store, far from the camera, but it looked to her like Hawthorne moved his arm to hit the rack on purpose. But why? To distract Zach? To grab something without paying for it? A professor shouldn't need to shoplift.

"Wait," Nick blurted. "Go back again."

Annalisa looked at him. Maybe he saw it too. "What is it?"

But Nick let the video play past the crash of the card rack and Hawthorne's exit. The store was empty save for Zach hurrying to clean up the mess. "Stop it there," Nick said, and this time, Annalisa saw what caught his attention. There was a face at the door—a white male in a dark hoodie. He stood there for a few seconds watching Zach through the glass doors but did not enter the store.

"Oh, hey," Zach said, pointing at the face as he noticed it for the first time. "That's Jason."

"That's great and all," said Quinn, "but where's Natalie? None of this says anything about what happened to her."

"Probably back at your room by now," Officer Kent said. "You should go check. I'm going to head back to my unit and continue patrol. I'll keep an eye out for the girl and put the word out to the others that we're looking for her." He clapped Quinn on the shoulder. "Your friend will turn up, honey. They always do."

Quinn shrugged him off and cast a dirty look after him as he left. "It's like he doesn't even care."

"It's not a bad idea," Annalisa said. "To go check your room."

"No, I want to help look for her."

"It's dark, you're freezing, and we don't know where to look. Nick will walk you back, okay? I will call you if there are any developments. I promise."

Quinn let Nick lead her away without further protest. Zach tucked the laptop under the counter. "What now?" he asked. "Do you need me for anything else, or . . . ?"

"Let's check your place," she said abruptly. "Maybe Jason has turned up."

"It's your party." He turned off the lights and locked up the store. "We're three blocks off campus in this direction. But listen—you don't really think Jason could've done something to Natalie, do you? He can be a dick some-times, but he'd never hurt anyone."

"Right now, I think he could be a witness," Annalisa said as they walked. It wasn't the whole truth but it wasn't a lie either.

A pair of headlights caught them in the face. Officer Kent again. The metal bar that walled off the heart of campus from street traffic rose to let his car pass and he lifted his hand in greeting as he rolled on through. As the gate came down behind him, Annalisa turned to watch the taillights disappear into the night. Whatever car had passed outside the store ear-lier, the one whose headlights were visible on the CCTV—it had to be able to bypass the iron barrier as Officer Kent had, meaning it was driven by university personnel.

Quinn's voice came back to her. *She said she saw you*, Quinn had told Officer Kent. How could Natalie have seen him and he'd not noticed her? It was his job to notice things.

"You want to get going?" Zach asked, jolting Annalisa from her thoughts. He'd continued on a few paces ahead of her and then stopped when she hung back.

"Uh, yeah." She started to follow him when her phone buzzed. Nick.

We have a problem, he texted. The next thing was a screenshot from Quinn's phone, from the same anonymous number.

Too bad about the ice cream.

TWENTY-FIVE

....

*H*OLY *SHIT*. The words kept going through his head, occasionally escaping through his ecstatic grin as he bounced around the room. It worked. It finally worked. He'd thought about this scenario so many times, daydreaming, fantasizing when he should have been busy with other work, his mind shading in each section slowly, like a child bent over a coloring book. He kept opening the closet door to peek in at her because he could scarcely believe she was real.

She stiffened each time he cracked the door, going rigid against the zip ties he'd used to bind her hands and legs. She would have screamed except he'd taped her mouth shut. He had a cloth sack covering her head as a precaution. "If you see me, I'll have to kill you. So no peeking. You got that?"

She'd nodded frantically. She'd agree to anything he asked of her right now. He wished he could show her his face and let her know how easily she'd been fooled. How stupid she'd feel. How impressed she'd be that he could pull this off. She'd never seen him coming. He had been frustrated when he had to abandon the girl in the woods. Sienna. He knew her name now. Had seen her walking on campus and gotten a brief thrill at the sight of her injured face. But he'd made the right decision. He'd lacked the syringe, which meant he couldn't do to her what he really wanted.

He got out the instant camera and took a picture of the girl lying on his closet floor. She made a whimpering sound at the noise from the flash. If only there were a way to share it. He could put her on blast to the world. *Look at this girl*, he'd say. *Look at her Instagram and her Snapchat and her silly TikTok videos. Her hair is always sleek and shining. Her makeup precise. She smiles and giggles and you think she must be perfect—way better than you, you lowly toad. Look at her now. She has knots in her hair and snot on her chin. She's terrified and weak and pathetic. Who would envy her now? Who would ever want to be this girl?*

He could mark her forever if he wanted. He knew where the dissecting tools were and how to use them. He would get away clean, but she'd have to live with the results for the rest of her life. Whatever he was going to do, it would have to be soon. He couldn't keep her here for much longer. Quinn had called in her aunt and now there were at least two cops sniffing around looking for the girl. By morning, the story would be all over campus and he'd be unable to move her. He had to do it now, while it was still dark. He'd find somewhere private. Somewhere they could be alone.

He checked the drawer for his syringe and found it good to go. *Patience*, he told himself as he picked it up and stared at it. He couldn't use it here, where they might be discovered. He shoved it into his pocket and then got out the gorilla head, which he put on even though it restricted his vision somewhat. He didn't plan on taking off the bag on her head, but he didn't want to risk her seeing him. He didn't want to have to kill her. Not yet, anyway.

"Time to go," he told her as he yanked open the closet door.

She gave a muted shriek as he grabbed her legs and dragged her out. His parents always said he wouldn't amount to anything, but look at him now. Look what he'd accomplished. "Why can't you find a nice girl?" His mother had pouted at the holidays. "Put a ring on her finger." Maybe he could cut off one of this girl's fingers and leave it under his mother's pillow just for fun. He'd even put a ring on it to make her happy.

The girl lay curled in the fetal position, quivering like he was going to kick her or something. He sighed and got out the large laundry sack. A little thing like her, she'd fit in easy. "Remember the rules," he warned her as he pushed her lower half inside the bag. "No noise. You do what I tell you."

He pulled the drawstring tight over her head and went to check the window. No one was around. He ditched the mask under the bed and hoisted the sack with the girl in it over his shoulder. He carried her outside into the cold air, his eyes and ears alert for any sign of trouble. Near as he could tell, no one saw him putting her in the trunk of his car. He patted the syringe in his pocket and started whistling as he got behind the wheel.

He drove carefully. Waited at the stop sign. He was about to pull through when a silver car went sailing past without slowing down. He gripped the wheel when he noticed the driver was Annalisa Vega. *But she's leaving*, he told himself as he clocked her direction. She'd driven right by him and hadn't given him a second look.

He exhaled and started whistling again as he drove on. He didn't know why he'd ever been afraid of her. Annalisa Vega hadn't the first fucking clue who he really was.

TWENTY-SIX

....

I T'S NOT OUR CASE." Zimmer's office was about a thousand degrees since the heat had kicked in. Annalisa's boss had removed her jacket and unbuttoned her shirt collar and cuffs. She was using a file folder to fan herself as she gave Annalisa the bad news. Natalie Kroger's disappearance was not hers to investigate. "Your authority stops at the city limits, Vega. It's the state's call. Or campus security."

"And neither one is doing a damn thing right now." Annalisa stood, leaning forward to put her hands on Zimmer's desk. "If Natalie has been abducted—"

"If," Zimmer interrupted. "That's the big problem here. The girl is a legal adult. She's allowed to go where she pleases."

"Yeah, well, by all accounts, she wanted to get ice cream and go back to her dorm. Someone stopped her from doing that."

"You can't prove that."

"We found her flute in the trash . . ."

"I agree it's troubling," Zimmer said, setting aside the folder. "You told me the campus police are looking for her."

Annalisa thought of Kent's indifference. "Yeah, they're looking real hard."

Zimmer sighed. "What about this guy . . . Jason? He's in the wind too?"

"No one has seen him since shortly before Natalie vanished. We have him on camera in the area by the campus store where Natalie was last seen. According to my niece, Quinn, Jason had a burner phone he'd been using to send her anonymous text messages. The last one came in after Natalie vanished, and it referenced the ice cream."

"But you haven't found the phone."

Annalisa began pacing in front of the desk. She was wasting precious time recounting these details when she should be back on campus, looking for Natalie. "I accompanied Jason's roommate back to their apartment and he showed me where Quinn had found the phone in Jason's room. The phone was not there."

"So he took it with him."

"Probably."

"Probably?"

Annalisa hesitated. "The apartment wasn't secure. The lock to the back door has been broken for months and the boys did nothing to fix it." Young men completely self-assured in their immortality. "In theory, anyone could have come in and taken the phone. But they would have had to know it was there for the taking."

"Maybe they ran off together," Zimmer suggested. "Jason and Natalie."

"Maybe?" Annalisa halted and folded her arms. "If your 'maybe' is true, then everything will be fine. If mine is, a girl is in major trouble and no one is doing a damn thing about it."

Zimmer stretched forward and hit a key on her computer to wake up the monitor. "Not nothing. I have a call in to a buddy of mine—a trooper who works down in that area. I'll make sure the case is on their radar. Meantime, I got you approval for your warrant of the CCTV footage from Walmart. Turns out Jason's legal address is still in Chicago, so we have a work-around."

"That's . . . great." Annalisa tried to sound enthusiastic. Footage of Jason procuring the phone would be helpful in building a case if he was the abductor, but it wouldn't help find Natalie.

"Where is your niece right now?" The concern in Zimmer's eyes let Annalisa know she was taking the complaints seriously.

"She's staying off campus with a friend of hers, Sarah Beth McCarthy."

"Okay, good. Let's hope Natalie turns up hungover and unharmed. It's still the most likely outcome." Zimmer smiled, trying to make Annalisa do the same. "When I was seventeen, I hitchhiked to New York City to try out for Broadway."

"You what?"

Zimmer shrugged. "I thought it worked like a high school musical—just audition and get the part. My dad had to come haul my broke ass home ten days later. Mom didn't speak to me for a month. The point is, Vega, kids do stupid stuff all the time."

"There's the other girl, Sienna, who was attacked at the party," Annalisa reminded her.

"The one who wouldn't even file a report?"

"I don't think the campus cop was very interested in what she had to say. If I could go back there and talk to her—"

Zimmer held up both hands. "You have a case. Sam Tran's murder, remember? And from what I understand he may have uncovered a serial killer in Brad Morrison. I don't need to remind you what can happen when one of these guys crawls out from under a rock."

"No," Annalisa said, regret thick on her tongue. The Lovelorn Killer had murdered three additional people when he resurfaced after twenty years. Nick and Annalisa had narrowly escaped becoming victims as well. "We can put Brad Morrison at the hotel the night his wife and Stephen Powell were murdered. It's a far cry from proving he did it—or the other double homicide either."

"So? Go get more proof," Zimmer replied, dismissing her.

Annalisa went back to her desk, where Nick silently handed her a mug of coffee. She accepted it as she slumped into her chair with defeat. "The warrant came through," he told her, sounding more chipper than she felt.

"I know. Zimmer told me."

"Walmart is going to send me the footage." He perched on her desk and sipped from his own mug. "What do you want to do in the meantime?"

"Zimmer wants us to sweat Brad Morrison, see if he's good for the motel homicides."

"We can show him the pictures that put his car at the scene, but beyond that, we don't have much to press him with right now."

"That's what I said." Annalisa halfheartedly picked up the folder and opened it. The gruesome images of Kathy Morrison and Stephen Powell, naked and bloodied, lay on top. Annalisa felt for these victims, but they had been dead for decades now. A few more hours wouldn't matter either way. But they could mean life or death for Natalie Kroger. "I wish we had a legal way onto that campus," she muttered as she closed the folder.

"Maybe if something comes up on the Walmart video," Nick replied, not sounding too hopeful. "For now, do you want to take another run at Brad Morrison?"

"We need more before we talk to him again. More background, more details."

"That takes time."

"Yeah, but I might know a shortcut." She pushed aside the folder and dug out her notes from her conversation with Andrew Powell. The Powells had thought Brad Morrison guilty from the get-go, and they'd spent years fighting to hold him responsible. If anyone had dirt on Brad Morrison, it was Andrew and Amos Powell.

....

F INALLY." Amos Powell boomed the word like the preacher he was. He held his gnarled hands to the heavens. "Praise be to Him. Brad Morrison will finally be held accountable for the death of my son. I knew if I had patience that He would avenge Stephen and that poor Morrison woman."

"No one is being avenged just yet," Annalisa said. "We only want to ask a few questions."

"But the right ones. At last!" He widened the door, shuffling backward to admit them to his home. Annalisa noted his swollen knuckles and the orthopedic shoes on his feet. Whoever had killed Sam Tran and strung him up in a tree, it wasn't Amos Powell. "That private detective got my hopes up last month, and when I heard he was murdered, I figured it was because he'd got something on Morrison—something that would stick this time."

"Did Sam Tran talk to you about Brad Morrison?"

"Oh, yes, he was here for several hours in the war room."

Nick glanced at Annalisa. "The war room?" he asked.

"I'll show you." He beckoned them down the hall to a pair of glass double doors, which led to an office. Inside sat a desk with papers and folders layered like tectonic plates. Behind the desk were two large whiteboards with writing and photos tacked to them. She recognized copies of some of the crime scene photos—a close-up of the headboard showing the blood spatter, Stephen's wallet emptied on the ground, the queen of hearts playing card. There was even a shot of Stephen and Kathy lying dead in the bed, although it was cropped so as not to reveal their entire nakedness.

"Uh, this is . . . wow," Annalisa said, taking a deep breath as she absorbed his work.

"It's everything I have. Everything we've compiled on the case over the years."

Annalisa walked first to one board and then another. Her gaze fell upon a shot of Brad Morrison in a poker tournament. His hair was thicker, his face unlined. "When was this taken?"

"Two months before Stephen was killed." Amos walked unsteadily across the room to join her. "Look at the cards."

She had to squint. "They have cherubs on the back."

"Just like the one at the murder scene," Amos said.

"Well, not quite. These have a white background. The one at the scene has a blue background."

"I thought that too. But wait . . . wait." He went to the desk and started pawing through the folders.

Nick perused the boards and then looked at Annalisa with his eyes bugged out. His expression said, *Who the hell keeps pictures of their kid's murder up on display?* Aloud, he said, "I presume you know the police have checked into Morrison before. He has no record of violence. They searched his car and found no signs of blood."

"I have a theory about that," Amos replied. "Look over there at the bathroom photos. See the one showing the tub? The bottom was wet. Someone had taken a shower there recently. Maybe Morrison brought a change of clothes with him and cleaned up before he left the scene."

Annalisa had to give the old man credit. The theory was reasonable. "Brad Morrison thinks you did it," she said, curious how he would react.

He halted his search of the desk. "I know what he says. It's lies. He lies so much I'm surprised his tongue isn't forked. Stephen was my son, my flesh and blood. I would never have harmed him."

"You threatened to kick him out of the church," Annalisa replied. "Your own son."

Amos stroked his beard. "I regret my words," he said at length. "The Lord says you can repent up until your dying breath, but I'm not sure I will live long enough to apologize for what I did to my boy."

"Stephen was having an affair with Kathy Morrison," Nick pointed out. "That's a sin, isn't it?"

Amos closed his eyes against the truth, pain etched across his features. "It is. I urged him to stop. I—I begged. I threatened him. But he was lost, my son. Thanks to Brad Morrison he never had the chance to come home. I like to imagine that Stephen saw that the hour was upon him and he had a chance to admit his wrongdoing, to cleanse his soul." He glanced sorrowfully at the pictures he'd tacked up on the boards. "But the evidence says otherwise. The police believe they were sleeping when Brad entered the room and unleashed his savage attack. There are no signs that Stephen or Kathy put up a fight."

"For argument's sake," Annalisa said, "how would Brad have gotten into the room?"

"Maybe he can walk through walls." Amos's nostrils flared. "I hear the devil can do anything he wants."

"The devil," Annalisa repeated. "That's a bit much, don't you think?"

Amos locked eyes with her. "Who else would do that and walk away like nothing ever happened?" He gestured without looking at the board behind him. "Who could evade justice all these years? Drag my name through the mud? My son's name? That man is pure evil."

"I don't know what happens in the next life," Nick said. "But in this one, we need proof. If you have anything more than opinion that Brad Morrison is guilty of these murders, we'd love to see it."

Amos lurched to the desk again and shifted a few more folders. "Here," he said at last, thrusting one at Annalisa. "My other boy, Andrew, he's the one who found this. It's from that same tournament Brad Morrison was playing before the murders, but it's players at a different table. Look at the cards."

Annalisa looked at the photos and showed them to Nick. "They're the same cards," she said. "The ones with a blue background." She examined the photo again and saw something else. "This is interesting, Mr. Powell," she said. "It doesn't put the cards in Brad Morrison's hands, though."

"He was there the same time they were," the preacher protested. "That PI—Sam Tran? He thought it was good evidence."

"We'd like to take this photo with us, if we could," Annalisa said.

"Keep it. I have copies." He sank heavily into the leather chair behind the desk.

"If Brad Morrison is the murderer," said Annalisa, "why would he hire Sam Tran to look into the case?"

"To force me and Andrew to fight his lies some more. To corrupt my congregation and continue the devil's work." He gave a long exhale and rubbed his temples with one hand. "We can't explain evil. Merely witness it. Resist it." He made a fist as he tried to summon new energy. "Remember—the devil's greatest sin is arrogance."

Annalisa remembered the backward *p* Brad Morrison had written on the note he gave her. "In your investigations into Brad Morrison, did you find any evidence of a learning disability?"

His bushy eyebrows rose with surprise. "Now how in the world did you know that?"

"So it's true?"

"He had trouble in school. Nearly failed out. But they gave him some kind of nonwritten test that supposedly showed he's a genius." Amos snorted. "Maybe it's even true. He's fooled the cops all these years."

Annalisa looked around at his murder board and wondered how to score this sin, wallowing in his son's death to the point of ruin. "What if . . ." she said, taking a step closer to the pictures he had tacked up. "What if I told you there had been a second pair of murders at a different motel?"

Amos's eyes went wide. "Brad killed again? I told you, he must be stopped."

Annalisa scanned the photos for any more signs of Brad Morrison. She stopped in front of the one that showed him at the poker tournament, holding the cherub cards that did not quite match the one at the scene. Her breath caught at the sight of a familiar face and she leaned in closer. "Could we get a copy of this?" she asked Powell.

He heaved to his feet. "Of course. Let me get you a copy from the files."

Nick wandered over to stand next to her. "What is it?" he asked under his breath.

"Look at that guy," she whispered back. "At the table behind Morrison."

Nick squinted. "I don't know . . ."

"Imagine him without the goatee. That's Norman Tolliver, the owner of the Springwood Inn."

"No shit," Nick said. "Interesting." His phone buzzed and he dug it out. "Walmart sent over the footage from the phone purchase."

Annalisa waited while it loaded, leaning over Nick's shoulder to get a view of his phone. They both watched as a heavyset man bought a wet vac and went on his way. Annalisa noted the time stamp of 8.09. "This is it," she said as a figure dressed in black appeared with a burner phone in hand. The person wore a baseball cap, but it was plain to tell this wasn't Jason on the screen. The person was smaller and skinnier—a woman. "Stop it there," she said as the figure turned to offer up cash for the phone.

"You know her?" Nick asked.

"That's Quinn's friend. Sarah Beth."

TWENTY-SEVEN

....

"Have you seen my phone?" Quinn pulled her head out of her backpack and glanced across the bedroom to Sarah Beth, who lay on her bed with her laptop open. Sarah Beth's room looked like a Nordstrom had exploded, clothes and makeup on every possible surface.

"Hmm?"

"My phone. I can't find it." Quinn put the bag down and lifted papers from the desk in front of her, in case they were concealing her phone.

Sarah Beth sat up. "When did you last have it?"

"The kitchen, I think? Or maybe it was in the bathroom before I took a shower." Quinn hadn't slept in two days and her head felt disconnected from her body like a balloon on a string. She checked the kitchen, which was in similar disarray to the bedroom. Sarah Beth's father, a single dad with money to burn, had sprung for a ritzy two-bedroom condo for his only daughter. The girls had quickly learned that anything they wanted, Sarah could ask her father to supply. A new coffee machine? Tickets to a show downtown? Just ask Daddy Warbucks. Sarah Beth had everything she ever wanted and then some.

Quinn looked around in frustration at the blender, the espresso machine, the dirty dishes, and junk mail. "How do you find anything in this place?" she asked Sarah Beth, irritation starting to edge into her voice. *Be nice*, she cautioned herself. *Sarah's letting you crash here and the only other option is to go home.*

"Sorry," Sarah Beth replied as she dropped a pair of mugs into the sink. "The house cleaner doesn't come till Monday."

Quinn grabbed up a sweater from the kitchen chair. No phone. Only when she held the sweater, she saw it was too big for Sarah Beth. It was a man's pullover, black with a thin gray stripe. "Is this . . . Jason's?" She wrinkled her nose and took a whiff. It definitely smelled like him.

"Hmm? It might be, I guess, if he left it here."

Quinn couldn't recall a time they'd all been here together, but she decided to let it go. She had more pressing problems than Jason's laundry. "Can you try calling me?" she asked Sarah Beth. The ringing would tell her where the phone went.

"Sure." Sarah Beth took out her own cell and dialed Quinn's number. The two of them walked through the condo listening for the answering trill of Quinn's phone, but it never came. "Did you leave it on mute?"

"I—I don't think so?" Quinn spun in a helpless circle. Maybe she'd left the phone back at her dorm when she'd packed a few items to take to Sarah Beth's place.

"You can use mine if you need to make a call." Sarah Beth extended her late-model iPhone, which was encased in a Kate Spade shell.

"No," Quinn said glumly. She pushed aside a pink fake-fur coat to collapse on the sofa. "I'm worried about Natalie."

"She'd call me if she didn't reach you," Sarah Beth said reasonably as she perched on the arm of a leather chair. "You want to try texting her again?"

Quinn shook her head. "What's the point? We've tried a hundred times." She sat up as a thought occurred to her. "You could try Jason."

Sarah Beth looked wary. "Jason, why?"

"He was on the video from the store last night. He was there around the time Natalie went missing. Annalisa said they can't find him either."

"You think he took Nat?"

Quinn halted. Did she? The Jason she knew could be immature at times, but he'd never physically hurt her. Still, he'd bought the burner phone to send her those texts. "It is weird, don't you think?" she asked Sarah Beth. "He disappears the same time that Natalie does?"

"Yeah, but—" She broke off, a wrinkle appearing over her perfectly sculpted brows.

"What?" Quinn asked.

Sarah Beth bit her lip. "I might know where he is."

"What? How?"

"It's only an idea. But I remember Natalie saying something about how Logan and Jason and some of the other guys have this place they go to in the woods. They found it hiking one time and now they go back to party there. It's an abandoned cabin or something and Logan joked it was a serial killer's hideout because they found a rusty chain saw. The guys go there to drink and there's a firepit. Logan said they do stupid challenges like who can jump out of the tallest tree or make the biggest fire. Natalie said they would probably kill themselves one day and she made Logan promise not to go there anymore." She picked up her phone and began texting, her fingers flying over the screen. "Logan can tell us where the place is."

"You think we should go there ourselves?" Quinn's skin prickled at the very thought.

Sarah Beth paused to look right at her. "You want to do something, right? Instead of sitting around here all day? Natalie's our friend. She'd do the same thing if it was one of us who was missing."

"But—"

"We go to the place and look around. If there's any sign of Jason or Natalie, we call the cops."

Quinn looked around at the mention of a phone call. She felt naked without her cell.

Sarah Beth yelped as she clutched her phone. "He replied. Logan replied! He's giving me directions. He says the place is only about a half hour away. We can make it before dark, easy."

The knowledge that at least they'd be poking around in the woods in the daylight soothed Quinn somewhat. If Jason was at the cabin moping about their breakup, he would talk to her when she told him about Natalie. Maybe he'd seen something near the convenience store when Nat disappeared. She couldn't believe Jason would hurt anyone, let alone Natalie. Odds were they'd find him drunk off his ass and he'd be no help at all, but Quinn couldn't take another minute of the consumer-crazed chaos in Sarah Beth's condo. "Okay, I'll go. But can we stop by my dorm? I want to check for my phone."

"Sure, we can do that. It's practically on the way."

"Great, let's go then." Quinn got up and handed Sarah Beth her pink fur coat, to which Sarah Beth crinkled her nose.

"I can't wear that. We're going stalking in the woods, babe. You gotta blend like a hunter." She went to a closet that was stocked full of coats and sweaters, and she pulled out a camel-colored peacoat. "It's cashmere," she said with regret, "but emergencies call for sacrifices."

Quinn felt her face go hot. "All I have is my usual coat." It was a blue North Face jacket her parents had given her last Christmas.

"Um, let me see . . . Oh, here. Will this fit?" She pulled out a boy's army jacket from the back of the closet. "Someone left it here at a party and I just kept it, figuring he'd come back eventually. Never did."

Quinn put on the voluminous coat, whose sleeves covered her hands completely. She didn't have her phone. She was wearing someone else's jacket. She felt like she was disappearing. Sarah Beth looked her over, gave an approving nod, and linked her arm through Quinn's. "Let's go find our girl."

TWENTY-EIGHT

··········

Annalisa pressed the buzzer for Sarah Beth's condo so hard her finger turned white. She'd sent Quinn off with Sarah Beth thinking her niece would be safer off campus with a friend, and it turned out Sarah Beth was, at minimum, helping someone stalk Quinn by purchasing the burner phone. Now Quinn wasn't anywhere to be found. "She still isn't answering," Annalisa said as she checked her cell again. "It goes straight to voicemail."

Nick had his own phone out. "Sarah Beth has a silver BMW registered in her name." He walked over to eye the small parking lot next to the building. "I don't see it parked anywhere near here."

"Maybe she's off with Quinn. Or with Jason Wilcox." Quinn's boyfriend was still in the wind.

"Wilcox drives a black Jeep," Nick reported as he consulted the records. "He's got a couple of speeding tickets—big ones. He must've been doing well over the limit when they pulled him over."

"That's it?"

"That's it for Jason, yeah. But he has an older brother, Michael Wilcox. When Michael was Jason's age, he beat a fellow teammate with a hockey stick so badly that the other kid ended up with brain damage. Instead of graduating, Mikey's doing five years for assault in Wisconsin."

"Just because the brother's guilty doesn't mean Jason is." It came out defensive when she didn't mean it to be. Her own brother was doing twenty years for murder.

"Jason might not be violent," Nick agreed. "But potentially he has access to a weapon. His father owns at least three registered handguns."

Annalisa muttered a curse and kicked at the dead grass. "Guns. Stalkers. Now a missing girl. No wonder Vinny wants to lock Quinn up and throw away the key." The thought of Vinny made her remember something. "Vinny," she said. "He tracks Quinn's phone. At least he did when she was in high school. We could ask him to trace it. Of course, that means telling him everything that's been going on." He'd pop his cork, as their father liked to say.

"She's his kid. Wouldn't you want to know if your kid was in trouble?"

"We don't know that she is," Annalisa hedged, dreading the thought of fracturing her relationship with Vinny even further. "She and Sarah Beth could very well be off getting coffee. If I drag Vinny into this and it turns out to be nothing, Quinn might not speak to me for the rest of her life. Meanwhile, Vinny would have another complaint to add to my list."

Nick rolled his shoulders and squinted in the direction of the sinking sun. "If it were my kid—"

"But she's not," Annalisa interrupted him. "Your kid is fifteen and barely knows your name."

She regretted the words as soon as she said them, but Nick didn't say anything in reply. Then he gave an exaggerated nod, his gaze on the concrete slab beneath their feet. "You're right," he said finally. He looked right at her. "And yet I'd still want to know. What does that tell you?"

She scrunched up her face, her eyes shut. She drew a shaky breath. "Okay. I'll call Vinny."

He answered on the first ring. "What is it?"

"Hello to you too."

"Yeah, hi. I'm waist-deep in invoices and don't have time to chat. What's going on? Did you get a break in the case?"

He means Sam Tran, Annalisa thought with a twinge of guilt. She was so far from where she'd started she couldn't see Sam anymore. "Uh, not yet. I had a couple of follow-up questions for Quinn, but she's not answering her phone. Do you know where she might be?"

"Let me check." She waited through the pause. "The app says she's at

156 Bayberry Drive. That's her friend Sarah Beth's place. You want me to call her?"

"No," Annalisa said swiftly. "She's probably studying. I'll try her again in a bit, thanks."

"Wait—did you find the stalker? Why do you need to talk to Quinn?"

"Gotta run. I'll call you back in a bit." She hung up with Vinny and nodded toward the house. "Her phone's inside."

"Maybe she's there and just not answering," Nick suggested.

"Or maybe Sarah Beth took away her means of communication and drove off with her somewhere."

"We could put a BOLO out for Sarah Beth's car."

"Sure, and then what? Hope she drives past a patrol unit?"

"Well, we can get a warrant for her phone and trace it, but that will take time."

"Too much time," Annalisa argued. They would first need her financial records to get the phone number and provider, and they probably didn't even have enough cause to justify that search.

Nick considered. "You know," he said, "there is one number we're already authorized to trace, and Sarah Beth is the one who purchased it."

"The burner." She paused, thinking. "We don't know she has it, but it's missing and we know she bought it. Let's try it and see."

Nick was already dialing to get the trace going. A few minutes later, he checked the app on his phone and gave her a flinty smile. "We're up," he said. "The phone is working."

TWENTY-NINE

....

IN THE CAR, QUINN SAT HUNCHED INSIDE THE LOANER JACKET, STARING OUT THE WINDOW AT THE INCREASINGLY RURAL SCENERY AS SARAH BETH KEPT UP A STEADY STREAM OF CHATTER. "Logan's complaining that Natalie's ghosting him," Sarah Beth said with a hint of amazement in her voice. "Does he really not understand she's missing?"

"Who would've told him?" It wasn't like the cops were looking for her. She and Sarah Beth had run into Officer Ken on their way out of the dorm—where Quinn had tossed her room until it looked like Sarah Beth's place and still not found her phone. He'd stopped his cruiser and beckoned them over.

Any sign of your friend yet?

No, nothing, Quinn had replied, clawing back her hair from the wind.

He'd licked his lips and nodded like he'd expected this answer. *Where are you girls headed now?*

We're going out to—Quinn started to say "the woods," but Sarah Beth cut her off. *We're going out for ice cream,* she had finished for Quinn. *Take our mind off things.*

Officer Ken had looked from one to the other like he could hear the lie in Sarah Beth's words. Part of Quinn wanted to ask him to come with them, but he'd moved on before she could blurt out the request. *You girls better stick together. Safety in numbers, now.*

Hurtling down the one-lane road with Sarah Beth at the wheel, Quinn did not feel especially safe. "Logan better hope that Natalie's not ghosting him for real," Sarah Beth said. "As in, like, she's a ghost. Because the boyfriend is always the number one suspect."

"How could you say that?"

"Calm down, I didn't mean it."

"Natalie's fine. She's going to be fine, okay? And Logan is sweet to her."

"Okay, I get it," Sarah Beth said petulantly. "He's a number one, A-plus boyfriend and I'm the worst for even suggesting anything bad about him."

"Not him. About Natalie. It's not funny to joke about her being dead."

"Sorry," Sarah Beth said with more feeling. She reached over and squeezed Quinn through the sleeve of the coat. "You're right. She's going to be fine." She craned her neck over the steering wheel. "Does that sign say Bramble Road? That's our turn."

They turned left onto an even narrower road that sloped uphill. Logan had said to turn left again when they reached a rotting old recliner sitting by the side of the road. "There it is." Quinn pointed as she spotted it. Sarah Beth made the turn and slowed down as the trees thickened around them. They had lost enough leaf cover that some light still filtered in, but there were no streetlights visible. If they didn't get out before dark, it would be pitch-black.

"There," Sarah Beth said as she stopped the car in the middle of the road. "Look."

Quinn followed her gaze and yelped with excitement. "That's Jason's Jeep!" He'd parked half-on, half-off the road, pulled almost into a ditch.

Sarah Beth pulled her car behind the Jeep and stopped. Quinn hopped out even before her friend cut the engine. She raced to the front windows and cupped her hands around her face to peer inside the Jeep. She saw a plastic bag from a liquor mart on the front passenger seat and a pair of black gloves in back. Nothing to suggest Natalie had been with him in the car. "The hood is cold," Sarah Beth remarked from the front of the Jeep. "He's been here awhile."

"Which way is the cabin?"

Sarah Beth consulted her phone and glanced at the tree line. "Logan said there's a notch on one of the pine trees over there to show the trail. The cabin's about a quarter mile in." She walked to the trees and examined them. "I think this is the one."

Quinn did not move, now wary as the sky grew darker and the trees loomed like a thicket of giant scarecrows. "Maybe we should call Annalisa."

"And tell her what? We don't know anything yet. Let's find the cabin and see if Jason's there . . . maybe even with Natalie. Then we can call."

Quinn cast a doubtful look at the woods. "Assuming you can get service."

"I've got two bars. We're good." Sarah Beth set off down what passed as a trail. Quinn took a deep breath before following her. The sweet stench of decaying leaves made her nose itch. Whenever Sarah Beth moved a branch aside, it came back to whack Quinn in the face. She would have told her to quit it, but she didn't want to make any noise. She heard only the faint crunch of their shoes on the trail and her own heightened breathing.

Sarah Beth halted so fast Quinn bumped into her. "I think that's it," she whispered.

A crow hollered down at them, decrying their trespass, and Quinn grabbed Sarah Beth's arm. A dilapidated cabin, its roof partially sagged in, sat in a small clearing twenty yards ahead of them. Quinn did not see Jason or any other movement. As they crept closer, she saw the makeshift firepit Logan had mentioned—a circle of stones with charred wood at the center. Someone had dragged a couple of logs nearby to serve as seats. Quinn noticed empty beer cans and fast-food wrappers, signs of parties past, but they looked to be weeks or months old at this point, dirty and mashed into the forest floor.

Then she smelled it. Something burning. Something unnatural, like rubber or hair. "What is that?" she murmured to Sarah Beth.

"Look." Sarah Beth pointed at the chimney, where a small plume of smoke emerged. "There's a fire. Someone is here."

The birds had gathered high in the trees around the cabin, chattering loudly. Maybe the smell spooked them. Quinn hadn't really wanted to come out here in the first place, but now, with the truth steps away, she had to know. She left Sarah Beth standing by the trees and drifted to the windows at the front of the cabin. They were half-broken and filthy. The acrid stench grew stronger as she approached and her heart started hammering in her chest. She held her breath as she reached the window and forced herself to look inside. For an agonizing minute, she stood frozen, only her eyeballs moving as her gaze darted around the dim interior of the cabin. She saw a smoldering fireplace. A battered wooden table and a couple of ratty-looking chairs. Nobody alive. Nobody dead.

She exhaled in a fiery rush, her hungry lungs sucking back in air with relief. She turned to beckon Sarah Beth. "It's empty," she called in a stage whisper. Sarah Beth sprinted across the clearing to join her by the cabin.

"Someone had to set that fire," she said with a shiver.

"Jason, probably." His car was here, so he had to be nearby. The door to the cabin was made of wood worn gray and smooth with age. When Quinn pushed on it, it opened with a groan that reverberated over the hush of the woods. Quinn entered, followed by Sarah Beth. Quinn went to the fireplace while Sarah Beth poked around the perimeter.

"There's a bedroom," she reported as Quinn knelt in front of the dying fire. "But trust me, you don't want to sleep on that mattress. Gross."

The fireplace didn't have any accompanying tools, but someone had brought in a stick to poke it with, so Quinn used it to shift the charred log aside to expose the ashes at its center. Amid the cinders, she saw what looked like black hair, but not human—more like from a stuffed animal. She poked again and a gray finger rolled out, making her squeak and fall backward.

"What is it?" Sarah Beth came running.

"I think it's the gorilla costume."

"What? No. Jason wasn't at the party that night."

"Maybe he was." Quinn got to her feet and dusted off her shaking hands. "I think we should get out of here. We can call Annalisa and have her check it out." The burned gorilla suit was enough to be suspicious.

"Wait, look at this." Sarah Beth stood by the table, using her phone as a flashlight to illuminate the surface. Quinn saw a bunch of white paper and went closer to take a look. "It has your name on it."

Quinn snatched up the pieces of paper one by one. Some had been crumpled and smoothed out again. They had Jason's handwriting on them, and they all appeared to be drafts of a letter to her.

Dear Quinn, I'm so sorry. I screwed up. I hope you can forgive me for what I've done . . .

Dear Quinn, I know someday I'll be just a memory to you, and my regret is that it won't even be a good one . . .

Dear Quinn, I know I lied to you, but I'm not lying about this. I love you. You have to forgive me. Please remember what we had, what we were together . . . I feel in my heart that one day we'll be together again.

One letter just said "I'm sorry" over and over down the page. There was a ballpoint pen on the table, too, she saw. The tooth marks in the cap resembled Jason's collection. She had no doubt he'd been here and written these letters. But where was he now? She felt a sudden chill and realized the door had blown open. More than that, Sarah Beth, who had been standing beside her, was nowhere to be seen. "Sarah?" she called tentatively. No reply.

She set the letters down and a strong gust from the open door immediately took them, flying them around the cabin like bats. Quinn went to the door and looked outside. The sky had turned dusky purple. They would have to leave soon or it would be dark. "Sarah?" she called again, this time with more urgency. "Sarah Beth!"

She heard a scuffling noise behind her—the papers blowing—and turned around. Sarah Beth stood there with a funny look on her face. "There you are," Quinn said with naked relief. "Let's go, huh? This place gives me the total creeps."

Sarah didn't reply. She held out her right hand toward Quinn. Though the light grew dimmer, Quinn had no trouble seeing what Sarah pointed in her direction. It was a gun.

THIRTY

···········

NIGHT FELL AS ANNALISA AND NICK REACHED THE WOODS, THE DAY-BLIND STARS BEGINNING TO WINK FROM OVERHEAD. Nick at the wheel cast a dubious look at the tall trees rising up around them. "You're sure this is the way?"

"According to the signal, the phone hasn't moved. Maybe it was dumped here someplace." She sat forward, straining against the seat belt as though she could propel him to drive faster. The phone showed a little red dot in the center of the woods, unmoving like a homing signal. Or a sniper's target. "There," Annalisa cried as Nick's headlights caught Sarah Beth's BMW pulled off by the side of the road.

Nick maneuvered their car to the flat bit of forest's edge that served as a shoulder on the narrow road. Annalisa flew from the passenger seat and rushed the BMW with a flashlight in one hand and Nick's phone in the other. She was careful not to touch anything as she shone her light in and around the car. "Nothing," she said, disappointed.

Nick gestured at the other vehicle. "That's Jason Wilcox's Jeep in front of her."

"Quinn is here, then." Annalisa turned to study the woods. "She has to be."

He swiveled his head around at the dark woods. "Yeah, but which way?"

A swarm of black birds descended on the branches overhead, an avian orchestra chattering down at them as the creatures tried to shoo away their nighttime guests. "Toward the dot," Annalisa declared resolutely, her beam slicing the darkness as she began trekking into the woods. Nick fell into step behind her.

Her breath misted in front of her face, her nose growing cold. Brambly branches reached out to claw at her and she swatted them back. Nick muttered a curse when one of them caught him across the cheek. She stopped short when she saw it—remnants of a wood cabin that now resembled a weary cardboard box. Nick's breathing sounded low and rough near her ear. "I don't see anyone," he murmured.

"Something's burned," she whispered back. She glanced at the phone and saw the dot was still at least fifty yards away, deep in *Blair Witch* territory. Where the hell were the kids? "Let's check it out." She advanced with soft steps toward the cabin, but before she could see inside, she heard a girl's scream.

Someone yelled, "What the hell are you doing?" and then there was a gunshot.

Annalisa dropped the phone and took out her own weapon. She heard more than saw Nick running with her. She used her foot to kick open the door and she saw Quinn standing there, Sarah Beth across the room. There was a Glock handgun on the floor between them. "What the hell is going on here?"

"Auntie Anna," Quinn said, reviving her childhood name for Annalisa. Her voice quavered with emotion as she rushed to Annalisa's side. "Sarah shot me."

"I didn't!" Sarah Beth screeched. "It went off by accident."

Annalisa checked Quinn for injuries and found nothing but tearstains on the girl's face. "You're okay," she assured her.

Nick knelt by the weapon and then stood up again. Sarah remained behind him, shaking and hugging herself. "You have to believe me. I've never touched a gun before. I didn't mean to fire it."

Nick used his flashlight to scan the walls. "Looks like it hit over here and went clean through," he said as he found the small hole in the wall that marked the bullet's path. It had gone sideways out the east wall about two feet shy of the ceiling, which was nowhere close to the spot Quinn had been standing. Unless Quinn had suddenly changed positions, Sarah Beth had not been aiming for her.

Annalisa went to examine the bullet hole for herself. The splinters around the hole were fresh and pale. Markings to the left of the hole caught her eye. She shifted her flashlight and saw they were initials and years that had been carved into the wooden wall of the cabin. *T. B.*, read the top one, *2001. N. F.* the same year. *B. N. 2002, A. Q. 2003, L. T. 2004, O. K. 2006*, et cetera, up to the most recent carving, which read *J. W.* with the date from last year. She ran her fingers over the dates as Sarah Beth renewed her pleading.

"It was an accident, I swear. I found the gun under the bed in the bedroom. I brought it out here to show Quinn and then it went off."

"Where's the phone?" Annalisa asked, turning around again.

"My phone? It's here." Sarah Beth struggled to get it clear of her jeans pocket and extended it to Annalisa with trembling hands.

"Not that phone. The one you bought at Walmart. The one that's been sending Quinn the messages." Annalisa trained her light on Sarah Beth's face so the girl was forced to shield her eyes. "Don't try to deny it. We have you on video making the purchase."

"What?" asked Quinn softly. She took a step toward her friend. "What are they talking about?"

"I—yes, I bought the phone." She hesitated and let out a small sob. "I sent the texts. But that's all I did. I swear. The thing with the gun was an accident."

"Why did you send the texts?" Annalisa asked.

Sarah looked like she didn't want to answer. Her shoulders slumped. She twisted her hands together in agony. "I wanted her to think Jason sent them. I wanted her to freak out and break up with him."

"What? Why?" Quinn looked disgusted.

"So then maybe he would notice me. I was at freshman orientation too, you know. He was talking to me before you ever walked in the room. Then he saw you and it was like I fell into a hole."

"There's a zillion other guys on campus."

"Yes, but I wanted him," Sarah Beth explained with the certitude of a young woman used to getting whatever she wanted.

"Well, you can have him," Quinn said, her voice cold.

"No, I can't. Look at the letters. He's still in love with you."

"What letters?" Annalisa asked even as Nick stooped to pick up a piece of paper. She didn't think Sarah Beth posed any danger now that Nick had possession of the gun, but she also didn't let the girl out of her sight as she moved to join him. He showed her the handwritten messages. "Jason wrote this?" Annalisa called to Quinn.

Her niece was shaking off Sarah Beth, who had tried to hug her. "Get away from me!"

"I'm sorry," Sarah Beth said, crying openly now. "I never meant to hurt you. Not for real. When I saw your aunt text you that I sent the messages, I hid your phone. I—I tried to think what I could do to make it up to you. That's when I had the idea to find Jason. I thought if I brought the two of you back together, you might forgive me."

"You thought he had Natalie," Quinn said, and Sarah shook her head vehemently.

"No, no, I never believed that."

"You wrote that text about the ice cream. Don't lie to me. Do you know what happened to Natalie? Where is she?"

"What ice cream? I don't know anything. I swear."

Annalisa produced the screenshotted text from the night of Natalie's disappearance. **Too bad about the ice cream.**

"I didn't write that." Sarah turned deathly pale. "I swear I didn't write it. I left the phone at Jason's. Maybe he wrote it."

Quinn shivered and looked around. "Where is he, anyway?"

Annalisa agreed that this was a crucial question, and there was one other pressing mystery she had not solved. "We still haven't located the burner," she said to Nick. "You stay with the girls. I'm going to see if I can find out where it is."

"It's dark," he argued. "You shouldn't go alone."

"I don't want to leave them here by themselves." There had been at least one weapon hidden on the property. Nick followed her outside, where she retrieved his phone from the ground. She handed it to him to unlock it, but he just looked at her hand and did not accept it.

"We can all go," he said.

"Nick . . ."

"All of us or none of us," he repeated. "I'm not letting you wander into the woods by yourself in the dark."

"Okay, all of us," she agreed grudgingly. She waved the phone. "Will you unlock it now?"

He did but did not hand it back to her. "Looks like it's about seventy-five yards that way," he said, pointing. He turned and called over his shoulder, "Suit up, girls. We're going for a hike."

"Not with her," Quinn spat out. "I'm not going anywhere with her."

"You're both coming," Annalisa said flatly. She grabbed her niece by the arm and tugged her out the door. "You're with me and Sarah Beth can walk with Nick."

They readied their flashlights, Sarah Beth using her phone for illumination, and set out deeper into the woods. Nick led the way since he had the tracer app. "I don't understand," Quinn said as they picked their way through the trees. "If Sarah Beth had the phone, what's it doing out here in the woods?"

"Shh," Nick said. "We're getting close." He took about ten more steps and stopped, tilting his head to listen.

Annalisa shone her light ahead, trying to see, but a rising mist cut her light dead within a few feet. "Where?" she asked Nick. She pushed past both girls to join him.

He consulted the phone. "According to this, we're right on top of it. Check the ground. Maybe it's under a pile of leaves somewhere."

They fanned out, kicking at the leaves and pine needles under their feet. Annalisa stubbed her boot against a tall root and gritted her teeth against the shooting pain in her otherwise frozen toes. She edged farther away from the others, around a tall pine. The scent reminded her of Christmas and she paused for a second to inhale with her eyes closed.

"We could try calling it," Quinn called out. "Sarah Beth obviously knows the number."

"That's not a bad idea." Nick's voice floated out from the darkness behind her. "Let me try it."

Annalisa pushed onward. A sharp branch with thorns on it caught her jacket. She jerked away and stumbled, dropping her light in the process. As she bent to retrieve it, she caught a different smell. Something off. Something dead. With a dreadful feeling, she moved toward the odor. Her light beam wavered in the mist.

Shoes. That's what she saw first. Men's sneakers, hanging down in front of her. "Oh, God," she breathed. "No."

"Annalisa?" Quinn's voice, high and frightened, pierced through the night.

"Stay back!" Annalisa shouted. She raised her light to find Jason's gray face and the rope around his neck. In his pocket, the phone began to ring.

THIRTY-ONE

···········

During winter in Chicago, the night came like a blanket over a bird-cage, sudden and complete. The sun had gone to bed at four thirty in the afternoon, twelve hours earlier, and it wasn't near to reappearing as Annalisa drove the empty freeway back toward campus. Eyeballs dried from unending hours of wakefulness, Annalisa felt like she might never see daylight again. The girls slept in her backseat. Nick was still at work with his phone, mining its electrons for every last bit of information he could wring from their meager clues. They had all been printed and questioned extensively by the state cops who came to take Jason Wilcox's body away. He'd been dead about twelve hours, meaning he'd seen the last of the sun before Quinn and Sarah Beth ever set foot in the cabin.

"The gun was registered to Jason's father," Nick reported from her passenger seat. "Stands to reason Jason's the one who brought it up there."

Annalisa cast a look in the rearview mirror, where she could just make out the curve of Quinn's face. She didn't like to contemplate what other actions Jason could have had in mind. "He had the burner phone too." Sarah Beth had admitted planting it in his room as part of her frame job, but that didn't explain why Jason had taken it with him to the cabin.

"Speaking of, the dump came back on that," Nick said. "Only one number on it that wasn't Quinn's, and it was a call to Byron Lambert. Might be worth checking out."

"Don't bother," said a sleepy voice from the back.

Nick turned around as Sarah Beth leaned forward. "What do you mean?"

"I made the call when I couldn't find my regular phone. Byron's my TA for Professor Hawthorne's class. I wanted to know if he would let me hand in my lab report a half hour late."

"Did he?" Nick asked, curious.

"No," she said, leaning back with a heavy sigh. "He's kind of a hard-ass."

"Scratch off the hard-ass, then," Nick said to Annalisa. He rested his head against the seat and closed his eyes, looking defeated. "There's nothing linking Jason to Natalie's disappearance."

"Nothing yet." She signaled left to go to Sarah Beth's condo. As she neared the building, her taillights caught a familiar license plate on the car parked on the street outside. "Oh, crap," she breathed. "Here we go."

Nick was instantly alert. "What is it?"

"Vinny."

She pulled in behind him. He exploded out of his car before she even had time to cut the engine, his bald head covered in a black knit beanie and his olive complexion pink from cold or rage. "What the hell are you doing?" he hollered as he barreled up to the passenger door. "Where's Quinn?"

"I'm right here," Quinn said, rousing from the backseat. She got out into the cold to show him she was unharmed. "See?"

"It's almost five in the morning. I've been sitting here since midnight, where your phone says you're supposed to be. Only you're not here. Where the hell have you been?" He was yelling at his daughter, but the last question he aimed at Annalisa, anger flashing in his dark eyes. "Somebody better answer me."

"I'll get your phone," Sarah Beth said, apparently eager to escape from the family drama.

"Your coat," Quinn said as she looked down at the ill-fitting army jacket she had on.

Vinny looked too. "Where the hell is your jacket? This is no good for the cold."

"Keep it," Sarah Beth said quickly, and disappeared into her condo.

Vinny was still examining the coat. "This is a boy's jacket," he concluded with suspicion.

"Dad," Quinn said, pulling away and cutting him off. "I'm fine. I'm just tired. I want to go home and get some sleep, okay? I'm sorry you got worried, but you didn't need to drive down here just because I didn't pick up my phone. I'm not a child."

"You damn well are. You're my child, and I want to know what the hell is going on." He turned to Annalisa. "You didn't drive down here for no reason. Tell me the truth: What do you want with Quinn?"

Annalisa took a deep breath. "Well," she said, trying for optimism, "I caught your stalker."

The news seemed to jolt Vinny out of his ire. "What? How? Who?"

Quinn looked at the ground. Annalisa gestured at the condo. "It was Sarah Beth sending the texts to Quinn." She couldn't prove it yet, but she suspected the girl was probably behind the notes on the door too. "She wanted Quinn to dump her boyfriend so she could have him to herself."

Vinny's eyes bugged out. "For real?"

Quinn shrugged one thin shoulder. "I guess."

His expression turned to befuddlement. "Wait, so she was the one following Natalie too? Why would she do that?"

Annalisa glanced at Nick. She recalled what he said about how he'd want to know the truth if Quinn was his kid. "We don't know yet. Probably not." She paused. "Natalie is missing."

"She's what?" Vinny's voice boomed so loud a neighbor's light flicked on. Annalisa motioned for him to keep it down. He was not mollified. "What the hell do you mean, 'she's missing'?"

"I mean that no one can locate her at this time."

"That's it," Vinny said, grabbing Quinn's arm. "You're coming with me."

"What? No, I can't! It's the middle of the term. I have papers . . . I have class."

"Not anymore. I'll take you to your room and you can get your stuff."

Quinn sent Annalisa a pleading glance and Vinny dragged her toward his car. "Why did you have to tell him?" she cried. "You knew he'd do this. Dad, don't!"

Sarah Beth darted out with the phone, which Vinny snatched from her with one hand as he used the other to try to push Quinn into his car. "Vin, go easy there, huh?" Annalisa said, taking a step closer. He halted his struggle with Quinn to point at Annalisa with the cell phone.

"You keep out of it. I don't want to hear a word from you. Quinn's roommate disappears and you don't even give me a heads-up? What the fuck is that about?"

Annalisa opened her mouth to protest that Quinn had been perfectly safe the entire time, but of course, this wasn't precisely true. They hadn't even mentioned Jason yet. She shut her mouth again and put up her palms. "You're right," she said. "I should have called you."

"Yeah? Too late. I'm taking my kid and I'm going home."

He succeeded in wrangling Quinn into his car and gunned the engine. He drove off with Quinn's anguished face looking back at Annalisa, betrayal in her eyes. Annalisa shoved her hands in her pockets. "Great," she muttered. "Now they both hate me."

Nick rubbed the back of her neck with tender fingers. "You did the right thing."

"Yeah." However much Quinn might despise the idea, Annalisa agreed with Vinny that removing her from campus right now seemed like the right thing.

"Home?" Nick asked.

"Not yet," she said, and his expression deflated. "Food first." There had to be an all-night greasy spoon around a campus this size.

"Okay, I guess I could eat."

"Then I want to check with the university cops to see if they have anything new on Natalie."

Nick barely suppressed a groan. "Couldn't we just call them?"

"Yeah, but then I wouldn't be able to see their faces to know if they're bullshitting us," Annalisa said as they climbed back into the car.

"Zimmer's told us more than once to tie this case to Sam Tran or let it go."

"I think we have," she said as she started the engine.

He looked surprised. "What do you mean?"

"I mean we found Jason Wilcox hanging from a tree like Sam Tran. Doesn't that seem like the same MO to you?"

"You're saying Jason was murdered. Not suicide?" The state cops seemed to be leaning the other way. The recent breakup with Quinn was the precipitating trauma, and the repeated "I'm sorry" messages in the love letters Jason wrote read like a suicide note to them.

"Jason brought a gun to the cabin. I think if he was going to commit suicide, he would have taken the quick and easy way out."

"So why did he have the gun with him?"

"I don't know," she replied, troubled. "Maybe he did know something about Natalie's disappearance. Maybe he was afraid." Driving through the dark, she felt a tingle of fear too. If the killer was the same person, he had to be big and strong, able to hoist two large men to their deaths—not to mention smart enough to get away with it.

Nick located an all-night diner, and they wolfed down plates of cheesy eggs, hash browns, and bacon. Annalisa nodded at the waitress when she approached with the pot of coffee for a second refill. Nick frowned a little. "Isn't that a lot of caffeine?"

"As much as I can guzzle," she agreed as she went for a greedy sip of the strong brew. She eyed his mug, which was just as full. "I don't see you holding back."

"Yeah, but I'm not . . . you know." He gestured at her vaguely with his fork.

She hid her face in the mug. "I'm not either," she said. "At least not for sure." She knew she had to be kidding herself at this point. Her cycle was never this late. But what she didn't know couldn't hurt her.

"You could be," he countered. "Sure," he added when she looked up at him. He jerked his head. "There's an open drugstore right there. We've got the time."

She regarded him with horror. "I'm not peeing on a stick in a gas station bathroom."

"So we take it home with us," he said with exasperation. "At least then we'd know. Right?" He looked at her, uncertain. "I mean, don't you want to know?"

That her world could change forever? No, she'd had enough of that lately, enough for a lifetime. "It's a big deal, Nick."

"I know it is."

"I mean huge."

"I think I grasp that."

"Do you?" she said, annoyed. "You have a kid show up saying she's yours, and it barely puts a dent in your day. It doesn't bother you at all."

She'd be rattled—she was rattled—and he seemed maddeningly calm about the whole thing.

"Of course it bothers me. But it's not like I can change it. She's here. She's been here for fifteen years already, and I missed every one of them. You think that makes me happy?" He looked away, out the window at the dawn-streaked sky. "I always told myself I'd be a good dad—you know, better than the one I got."

Nick's father had shot and killed his mother when Nick was eight. Nick hadn't known his daughter until a few days ago and he was already better than that. She stretched her hand across the table to reach for him. "Of course you would be. You are."

He looked her over searchingly. "I mean, if you have doubts about me, about my potential here, I'd understand."

"No, that's not it." She worried about herself, not him. "I just—" He leaned forward, hanging on her every word, and she realized she had run out of excuses. She sighed. "I'll buy the test, okay? But I'm not taking it here."

"I'll buy it." Either he didn't trust her to follow through or he remembered what happened the last time she'd tried. They were far outside the city limits, but the Chicken Bandit was still on the loose somewhere. "You can get . . ." He broke off as he apparently realized he wasn't sure what to call the meal they'd had. They had been awake so long it was probably still dinner. ". . . the food," he finished as he stood up.

Annalisa paid for their meal and got another coffee to go—decaf this time. When she met Nick at the car, he didn't comment on her paper cup. He handed her a sack, and she immediately stuffed it into the console between them and closed the lid. He didn't comment on this either. She drove them back to campus, where she parked outside of police headquarters. Though it was early, the lights were on in the cement bunker and there were a couple of cruisers stationed outside. When they entered, she saw a young officer, barely older than the kids he patrolled, doing computer work at one desk. He looked up eagerly. "Can I help you?"

From the other end of the room, Officer Kent replied, "I got this one, Chapman." He rose from behind his desk, a mug of coffee in his hand. "Detectives, I hear you had some excitement up in Goodridge Woods."

Annalisa eyed him. "If you call the death of one of your students excitement."

"A tragedy," he said with regret as he indicated they should take a seat by his desk. "What brings you here? I'm sure the troopers have things well in hand."

"Oh?" Annalisa said as they sat. "What did you hear, exactly?"

"They're talking suicide. It's a shame, but not that surprising. With thousands of kids here, we lose a couple every year." He sipped his coffee and leaned back in his seat.

"First Natalie Kroger and then Jason Wilcox. You're losing them awful fast these days," Annalisa observed.

"I'm still expecting Natalie to turn up any minute, hungover and contrite." He gave her a tight smile over the rim of his cup. "They usually do, especially the freshmen—they're like puppies off the leash for the first term."

"But you're not out looking for her."

He set down the mug and regarded her. "We've got an alert out for the girl. Where precisely do you suggest that we look?"

"What do you know about the cabin up in the woods where Jason Wilcox was found?"

He shrugged. "It's abandoned property. I'm sure someone owns it, but no one has touched the place in years. Kids go up there to party."

"You ever been there?" Annalisa's gaze went to his nameplate to verify her memory. Officer Ken had a real name, and it was Owen Kent. O. K. had been one of the sets of initials carved into the wall of the cabin.

"Not in years."

"But you know the place?"

He waited a beat, looking first to Nick as if to ask, *Where's she going with this?* Nick kept his face neutral, his hands folded in his lap. Kent licked his lips before replying. "I've been there when I was younger, yeah."

"Maybe you can tell us about the initials on the wall, then."

He grinned. "Oh, that? That's like, a challenge. If you spend the night there all by yourself, then you win and you get to put your initials on the board."

"And you've done it?"

"Sure, once." He gave her a meaningful glance. "And that was enough. The owls and coyotes make an awful racket—someone even saw a bobcat one time."

So he knows the terrain pretty well, Annalisa thought. Aloud, she said, "Why do you think Jason would go up there to commit suicide?"

"Maybe he didn't want anyone around to stop him."

"There was something burned in the fireplace," Nick said. "Looked like maybe fake fur, possibly a costume of some sort."

"Black fur," Annalisa added. "Like from a gorilla." Quinn had told her about Sienna's claim of being groped at the Halloween party by a man in a gorilla suit. Annalisa had later seen the loose hand, possibly from a gorilla costume, at the site where Sienna said she was attacked. "Seems I recall Sienna mentioned something about a man in a gorilla costume being inappropriate with her the night of the party."

Officer Ken raised his eyebrows. "She didn't say anything to me."

"Did you say gorilla suit?" Chapman interjected from across the room.

Annalisa turned. "Yes, why?"

"Well, there's kind of a legend about it on campus."

"Chapman, don't waste their time with stupid rumors." Officer Ken looked annoyed.

"Go ahead and waste it," Nick replied, making a show of settling in to listen. "I love rumors."

Chapman looked to his boss, his expression chastened. "It probably doesn't matter," he said. "But Professor Massey used to do this thing when he was teaching the unit on the brain. He'd re-create an old psychology experiment. He took the class to the basketball gym and had one group of people wear red jerseys and the others wear white. Everyone else was told to count the number of passes that happened inside of five minutes and that anyone who counted right would get an automatic A on the next test. While the game was going on, Massey would put on a gorilla suit and walk through the court. After, everyone had to fill out a form saying how many passes they counted. They were also asked if they saw anything else on the court. Only like ten percent of people even noticed Massey as the gorilla. It's supposed to make a point about how your attention is more focused than you think—and why eyewitnesses can miss so much during a crime."

"No one cares about your psych class," Officer Ken interrupted.

"It was for bio, actually," Chapman told Annalisa and Nick. "Massey died a couple of years ago of cancer. One of the students thought it would be hilarious to show up to his funeral dressed in the costume. I know it sounds nuts, but trust me, Massey would've laughed his ass off over it. But when the student went to get the costume from Massey's lab where he kept it hanging, it was gone. There was a rumor afterward that he was buried in it."

Officer Ken gave a beleaguered sigh. "Thank you for that pointless offering. I'm sure when Professor Massey died, his family came to claim his personal effects. But naturally the story about being buried in a gorilla suit is much more entertaining."

Annalisa was still thinking. "Biology, huh? Who took over the classroom after Professor Massey?" She feared she already knew the answer.

"Hawthorne," Chapman said. He made a face. "He's okay, I guess. But he never dresses up in a gorilla suit."

THIRTY-TWO

....

QUINN'S EYES BURNED WITH UNSHED TEARS AS SHE SHOVED CLOTHES IN HER DUFFEL BAG. She kept her head down so she couldn't see Natalie's empty bed. Her friend was still missing, and here she was, running off like some coward instead of looking for her. Quinn's dad had given her fifteen minutes to pack up her whole life.

She jerked at a knock on the door. Had her father come to stand over her while she packed? No, he wouldn't knock. He would push right in. She swiped at her eyes with her sleeves and went to answer the door. To her surprise, Sienna stood on the other side. She entered the minute Quinn opened the door. "Where have you been? I've been texting you all night."

"I've been—busy." Quinn didn't have the energy to relay the whole mess with Sarah Beth and Jason. "I didn't have my phone."

Sienna took out her laptop from her backpack and stopped when she saw Quinn's suitcase. "What are you doing? Are you going somewhere?"

"My father says I have to come home."

"Like for a visit?" Sienna looked confused. Thanksgiving break was still more than a week away.

"Like for the rest of my life," Quinn replied, flopping onto her bed. "What did you want to talk to me about? I've only got a few minutes."

"Remember that post about Professor Hawthorne that you told me about—the one with the black-cat avatar?"

"The one that said he was a creeper, yeah."

"I traced the IP. The person who posted it wasn't at his old school in Nebraska. They're here on campus." She looked triumphant as she showed Quinn a bunch of numbers on her laptop screen.

"So? We still don't know who it is."

"We might be able to find out." Sienna sat next to her on the bed and clicked another window on her computer. "The IP address doesn't just match our school. It's coming from the biostat lab—the one with the fancy computers with the statistics software on them."

"Yeah, but anyone could've used them. You only need an ID to unlock the door."

"You need to sign up for time, though. There's a book by the door."

Quinn was more intrigued now. "So you have the time the post was made. If we find out who reserved time on the computers for that period, we might know who did it."

"And who the black cat is. If we find her, she might be able to tell us who the gorilla man was from the party."

"Look, Sienna . . ." Quinn took a breath. She had to tell the girl what she and Sarah Beth had found at the cabin. She explained about the fireplace and the costume they'd seen burned in it. She told her about seeing Jason hanging in the woods. "I hate to say it," she said, "but Jason might have been the guy who attacked you."

Sienna blinked. "Jason Wilcox? No, that's impossible."

"That's what I thought too. But then he had the costume . . ."

"He wasn't at the party."

"We thought he wasn't," Quinn corrected. "But maybe he was standing there the whole time."

"No, he wasn't," Sienna insisted, turning to face her. "Remember we searched for pictures from Halloween night."

"Yes, I know. The gorilla man was there, but you can't tell who's inside. It could be anyone."

"Anyone but Jason," she said as she picked up her laptop again. "I didn't limit my search to the Delta Gamma Nu party. I thought maybe the black cat could've been at a different party that night and then showed up late at DGN. Look, here's the midnight streakers' run on the main quad."

The pictures showed a bunch of naked guys, their private parts strategically blurred. They all wore masks of some sort as they raced across the quad in front of a gleeful, pointing audience. Some held beer cans. One had a fake axe. One wore a university hockey mask with the number 12 emblazoned on the side. "That's Jason's mask, right?" Sienna asked Quinn. "I remember thinking he was a dumbass for wearing something so identifying. He could've been suspended if they caught him."

Quinn took the laptop for a closer look. "That's his helmet," she agreed. She squinted at the torso and noted the pattern of chest hair and the tiny mole near the collarbone. "And that's Jason wearing it." She felt a hot rush of relief. Whatever else he might have been, her ex-boyfriend hadn't been a rapist. "But wait," she said to Sienna, "then why did he have the costume?"

"Maybe he knows who was wearing it." Sienna paused. "Or maybe someone was trying to frame him." She stood up. "Come on, if we can find the black cat, she might be able to tell us who was in the suit. She's our best lead right now."

Quinn looked at her half-empty suitcase. "My dad's downstairs waiting . . ."

"You're the one who said we should investigate. You dragged me into this in the first place. Now you're leaving me here alone?"

"I don't know what you want me to do about it."

"Come with me to the biostat lab to look at the book. Find the black cat like we planned. Maybe if we catch this asshole, your father will let you stay."

Quinn gave a soft, humorless laugh. "You don't understand. If I'm not downstairs in the car in five minutes, he's going to come looking for me."

Sienna considered a moment and then she smiled. "Okay, so then we give him somewhere to look."

············

QUINN HESITATED, CLUTCHING HER PHONE, AS THEY STOOD NEAR THE OPEN BACK OF THE FOOD DELIVERY TRUCK. The driver was inside, dropping off the day's ration for Paine Hall. "It's for the greater good," Sienna urged her, and Quinn tucked her phone in between two empty crates. They dashed off just as the delivery man came to close up the back of the truck.

"I pity that man when my dad tracks him down," Quinn said. They'd escaped from the dorm through the rear emergency exit. Her father would be none the wiser for at least a few more minutes. "And then when he catches me, I'll be dead."

"Let's not worry about that right now. You can crash with me if you need."

"You're not hearing me—I'm going to need a casket, not an air mattress."

Sienna stopped walking and looked genuinely concerned. "You think he might really hurt you?"

"No," Quinn said. Her father had never laid a hand on her. But then again, Uncle Alex hadn't spanked his girls either. "I just . . . hope this works out and we find this girl quickly. I mean, we don't even know it's the same black cat."

"I know. I feel it in my bones."

When they reached the biostat room, they found it silent and in shadow. Technically, it did not open until eight. A red light glowed on the electric panel governing access to the computers. Quinn held her breath as she tried her ID. The light switched to green and the door clicked as the lock opened. Sienna flashed her a grin as she yanked on the handle. "We're in."

Sure enough, as Sienna had predicted, there was a proctor's desk at the front of the room and an appointment-type book used to sign up for time on the various machines, which were labeled with numbers one through eight. "Which one of these was used to post the stuff about Hawthorne?" Quinn asked as she surveyed the computers. They were all powered down, but somehow the room seemed to hum with electricity nonetheless. The place smelled like warmed plastic.

"There's no way for me to tell," Sienna replied. "Could've been any of them." She bent over the appointment book and paged back through it until she reached the previous semester. "Looks like I was wrong. You don't book the time here, but you have to sign in when you arrive."

"Okay, so who signed in?" Quinn shivered and glanced back to the dim hallway.

"Uh, a guy named Ben Martin, and two girls. Tasha Swanson and Kia Huber."

"I don't know any of them."

"Me either, but we can look up Tasha's and Kia's pictures online to see if they look familiar. Maybe one of them will have pics in a catsuit."

The doors clicked open and they both jumped as a guy appeared. "What are you doing here?" he demanded. Quinn exhaled when she recognized Byron from the frat house. He recognized the pair of them as well. "Oh. If it isn't the girl detectives. Still looking for that earring?"

"No, just seeing if the computers were free today." Sienna flipped the book closed.

"They're not," he told her.

"How would you know?" Quinn asked.

He nodded at the proctor's desk. "That's where I sit. I keep track of the list." As if to underscore his point, he stepped around Quinn and took the book from where it sat near Sienna's hand.

"The man with the power," Quinn said, arching one eyebrow at him.

"The power to kick you out, at least. This place isn't even open." He pointed at the door. "Out. Now."

He stood there watching them until they had cleared the exit and walked out of sight. Quinn reflexively patted her pockets for her phone before remembering its fate. Her father was probably chasing it through the city right now. *I'm so dead*, she thought again. Out loud, she said, "Do you want to look up Tasha and Kia? We'll need your phone."

Sienna looked back over her shoulder. "What do you know about that guy?"

"Byron? Nothing. Why?"

"I don't know him either. But the weird thing is . . . I can't shake the feeling that he seems kind of familiar."

THIRTY-THREE

....

ANNALISA AND NICK CRASHED AT HIS PLACE FOR FIVE HOURS OF SLEEP. She cracked her eyelids open to the sound of him in the shower, and she could tell they hadn't gotten enough rest because he wasn't singing. She heard only the rushing water, and she pictured him standing, zombielike, beneath the spray. Not quite human herself, she rolled out of bed and tried to assemble an outfit from the meager clothes she kept at his condo. No socks. She would have to borrow a pair of Nick's, and when she opened the sock drawer to grope around for a dark-colored pair that might fit her, her hand bumped a small velvet box. She knew she should leave it where it was, but she was a cop: she wanted to see the evidence. She opened the box and made herself look.

The ring was beautiful. A platinum band encircled with tiny diamonds. Less flashy but no doubt more expensive than the one he'd given her the first time around. She had a memory of chucking the original ring at his head as hard as she could throw it and wondered what he had done with it after the divorce. Sold it? Buried it deep like nuclear waste? The shower shutting off made her shove the ring in the drawer and grab the first two socks she laid hands on. Only when she went to put them on did she realize they were slightly different shades of black. Already dressed in yesterday's suit, she cast a grim look at her mismatched feet before moving to the unoccupied bathroom to attempt to groom her wavy dark hair into something presentable. She used her hand to wipe off a circle in the middle of the steamed mirror. The woman looking back at her had a sallow complexion and layers of bruise-colored circles around her bloodshot eyes. She looked like the dead she was trying to avenge.

At the precinct, Zimmer did nothing to improve Annalisa's dour mood. "It's not a murder," she said when Annalisa made her case for Jason Wilcox's death being linked to Sam Tran's. "The ME is leaning suicide. No defensive wounds, no evidence that there was anyone else with him in the woods."

"Unless you count the two girls," Nick pointed out.

Zimmer didn't look amused. "You're saying they killed Jason Wilcox?"

"No," Nick answered. "But the place has evidence of a dozen recent visitors, Commander. There's empty bottles and condoms and all sorts of junk up there. Plus, the leaves on the ground would obscure any footprints."

"There's more," Zimmer said, her jaw tight. "They found a bloodstain on Jason's jeans."

"Natalie's?" Annalisa asked as she leaned forward with renewed energy.

"No way to know yet. The blood is female. Regardless, the state troopers have the case at the moment. If they decide there's enough evidence to say Jason Wilcox abducted Natalie Kroger, then the feds will probably get involved. Either way, it's not our case."

"You don't think it's odd that we start out investigating a hanging, and now we've got two of them?" Annalisa asked.

"People do unfortunately hang themselves, Detective Vega. Thousands every year."

"This boy had a loaded gun."

"And another thing," Nick added, "if we're supposing Jason took Natalie, what did he do with her? There was no sign of her at the cabin."

"I've asked the state investigators to keep us in the loop," Zimmer said, putting on her glasses to signal the end of the conversation. "When they figure it out, I'm sure they'll be in touch."

Annalisa and Nick waited for anything more but she said nothing further, just turned her attention to the paperwork on her desk. With a frustrated sigh, Annalisa pushed to her feet and returned to the bullpen. Nick followed and they sat at their desks across from each other, not speaking. Annalisa sorted through the files in front of her until she found the one on Sam Tran. She took out his picture and showed it to Nick. "Sam Tran might've been three nuns in a trench coat, he was so clean. We've been through his financials and his personal life. He had modest savings, no debts, no romantic interests that we can see. He didn't do drugs and there wasn't any alcohol in his place. By all accounts, he didn't drink."

"Except for what was found in his stomach."

"Right." She tapped the edge of the photo on her desk as she thought about this wrinkle. At that moment, one of the rookie patrol officers happened to be passing by on her return from the vending machine. Annalisa grabbed the woman before she could stick a Hershey bar in her mouth. "Chavez," she said as she literally reached out to take the woman's arm. "How'd you like to do me a favor?"

Melissa Chavez looked suspicious as she glanced at the mess of files across Annalisa's desk. "We're not allowed to do your paperwork."

"It's not paperwork. It's following up on an important lead in a case."

"If it's so important, why aren't you following it yourself?" Chavez would make a good detective one day. Annalisa's tension headache increased the pressure behind her eyes. Right now, she was counting on the fact that Chavez patrolled in Sam Tran's neighborhood. She forced herself to smile.

"I would, but there's too many for me and Carelli to track at once." She showed off Tran's picture. "It's not hard and it won't take you off your route. Just show this picture in the bars on your patrol and ask if this guy was in last Saturday night."

"What did he do?" Chavez asked as she examined the picture.

"He got murdered."

"Oh." She looked at the photo again. "That's too bad. He has kind eyes, you know?"

"I know," Annalisa said more gently. "And he was on the job at one point too. So, what do you say?"

Chavez still looked torn, like she didn't want to be climbing out of her car in the thirty-five-degree weather every two seconds. "Tell me why," she said.

"The vic was found with alcohol in his stomach," Nick supplied. "Only he kept no booze in his place."

"If he was drinking with someone Saturday night," Annalisa continued, "it could be the killer."

Chavez's brown eyes warmed with excitement as she realized Annalisa hadn't been shining her on; it was a real lead. "Okay, I'll do it. But you owe me."

"I'll buy you a drink," Annalisa promised. "You pick the place."

Nick watched Chavez walk away with Tran's picture. "That may be the best avenue we have right now. She could break the whole case."

"I hope she does," Annalisa said through a yawn. "Then maybe we can get some sleep. Besides, we still have more pressing concerns—like what happened to Natalie Kroger."

"You heard Zimmer. We have no legal justification to be back on that campus. Hell, your niece doesn't even live there anymore."

"I don't need a legal reason. I have a standing invitation." At his puzzled look, she dug out Hawthorne's flyer and the note asking her to be on his podcast. "I figure I'll tell him yes, and while I'm there, I can poke around some more, starting with the good professor himself."

"You have reason to suspect him of something?"

"Yeah, he gives me the creeps." She quirked an eyebrow at him. "Plus, Quinn said there's a rumor he groped some girl back at his old school in Nebraska. I'm going to check it out."

"No way Zimmer is letting you go to Nebraska."

"I mean on the phone, wise guy." She called up the university website to see where to start. Administration? The biology department?

"Speaking of phones," Nick said, pulling out a sheet of paper from his own desk. "I was looking back over Sam Tran's calls in the week before his death."

"We ran those down already. Nothing surprising."

"Yeah, but that was before we knew about Norman Tolliver being in the poker tournament with the deck of cards—the one with the angels on them? Tran called Tolliver twice before he died. We thought he was gathering the usual background on employees present the night of the murders, but what if Tran made the same connection we did?"

"Then that might be the reason for a second call," she agreed. "We should check it out . . . right after I call Nebraska."

Annalisa tried one number and the woman who answered transferred her to another department, where she was put on hold. Eventually, someone in records said she should try human resources and simply hung up on her. Annalisa dialed HR and promptly got put on hold there too.

Annalisa fiddled with the cord on her desk phone, waiting, and a slender young woman in a puffy pink coat caught her eye. "Uh, I think you have a visitor."

Cassidy waved as Nick turned around. She had a paper cup in her hand and a backpack over her shoulder. "I was in the neighborhood," she explained as she handed him the cup. "You like it with cream, no sugar, right? I hope I didn't put in too much." She watched him with anxious eyes as Nick took a sip from the cup.

"It's great, thank you." He gestured awkwardly at Kolcheck's empty chair at the desks next to theirs. "Would you like to have a seat?"

"Oh, I can't stay. My mom is expecting me. I just wanted to bring you the coffee and . . ." Her face turned bright red. ". . . to ask if you maybe wanted to join us for Thanksgiving dinner. I'm making the whole thing this year and I've gotten pretty good in the kitchen. Not gonna lie, though—the bird is kinda intimidating." She put up her palms with a nervous chuckle.

"Oh, uh . . ." Nick gave Annalisa a pained look. They hadn't discussed the holidays at all.

"Human resources, this is Malcolm Peterson," came a voice on the other end of Annalisa's phone. She would have to stop eavesdropping.

"Yes, hello," she replied, and introduced herself. "One of your former employees, Wendell Hawthorne, is a person of interest in a case we're investigating. I was hoping someone there could answer some questions about his time at your university."

"Wendell Hawthorne worked here from August 2016 until April 2020," the man replied.

"Were there any complaints against him during that time?"

"I can only confirm that he worked here for the duration of time I gave you."

"Listen, there's a girl missing at the university where he works now," Annalisa said, her impatience showing. "There's a rumor that Hawthorne may have had harassment claims made against him in the past. All I'm asking is whether you can confirm that or not."

"And I'm telling you that legally, all I'm authorized to tell you is that Dr. Hawthorne worked for us."

"If you have records, I can subpoena them."

He gave a dry laugh. "I'd like to see you try."

Everyone who watched *Law & Order* thought they were an expert these days.

She rolled her eyes at Nick, who was listening openly. So was Cassidy. "Fine," she said, "can you please give me the number for the biology department?"

"Look in the directory," he told her. "Under *B*. Have a lovely day." He disconnected and Annalisa glared at the receiver like it was Malcolm's head.

"No luck?" Nick asked diplomatically.

"I'll try the head of the biology department, but I'm not optimistic. It's like they've all been programmed with the same rote answer."

"Did that professor do something?" Cassidy asked.

"Nothing you need to worry about," Annalisa replied, giving Nick the eyes so he would know to get rid of the kid. This was no place for a fifteen-year-old girl to hang out.

"I'll let you know about Thanksgiving," Nick said, touching Cassidy's arm. "I may have to work. But you are sweet to think of me." He softened the quasi rejection with a smile, but Cassidy didn't seem to be paying attention to him. She stepped around him to get closer to Annalisa.

"We had a soccer coach at my school who turned out to be a perv," she said. "He got arrested for sending sexts to one of his players—her dad's a lawyer and he wasn't having it. But once she came forward, a bunch of other girls did too. Not just from the current team. He'd been doing it for years. Turns out half the school knew he'd been creeping on girls, and no one did anything about it. Can you imagine? Everyone knew the whole time."

Huh, Annalisa mused. *Everyone knew.* Quinn had guessed it was a former student who'd posted the message on the internet board about Hawthorne in the first place. If one student knew, maybe others did too.

THIRTY-FOUR

....

H E RESISTED THE URGE TO GO BACK AND CHECK ON THE GIRL. He'd moved her under the cover of darkness to someplace they would be alone, and it had been exactly like his imaginings. The drug worked like he planned, like he'd read about—she kept her eyes open but couldn't move as he touched her. A living doll. He'd tried various poses with her and taken pictures to remember his favorites. The best one was on the metal gurney, like from a real morgue.

Now came the hard part. He had to walk away. She'd been his, under his total control for more than forty-eight hours, and now he had to return her to the rest of the world. Whether she would come back dead or alive wasn't up to him. He'd left her locked up in the old building but he was hardly the only one who knew about the place. People were looking for her. If they got to the right place in time, then she would live. Part of him hoped she would so she could tell the whole story. All her little friends would be terrified. He'd been careful to wear a mask with her, a different one this time, just in case she did survive. She wouldn't be able to identify him, so she'd have to be afraid of everyone now.

He tried to breathe normally as he walked through campus. He nodded when he saw a guy he knew. The images of the girl, the feel of her, vibrated in his head. He felt like when the colors came on in *The Wizard of Oz*, like he could dance on the yellow brick road, and he worried others could see it on his face. ***Don't look suspicious***, he coached himself. ***Not too much eye contact, but don't look away. You're in charge of the situation. They don't know who you are.***

His palms sweated inside his pockets. He wanted to go back to the lab to see her. Already the high was fading, becoming a memory, and he knew if he touched her again it would come rushing back. But he couldn't risk going there in the daylight. He couldn't be seen near the place if he wanted someone to find her soon. He had to be as surprised as everyone when she was discovered.

He would have to find another source to make up new vials of the drug, which he planned to do soon. It wouldn't be long before they found Natalie, and she'd either tell their tale or take his secrets to her grave. Either way, Natalie Kroger was used up. Finished.

He was going to need another one.

THIRTY-FIVE

....

NICK AND ANNALISA HAD THEIR COATS ON, PREPARED TO GO TALK TO NORMAN TOLLIVER ABOUT HIS LAST CALLS WITH SAM TRAN, WHEN ZIMMER CALLED THEM BACK. From her somber expression, Annalisa knew it couldn't be good news. "What is it? Did they find Natalie?"

"I just got off the phone with a Detective Ray Davis from the fourth district."

"South side," Nick said, looking sideways at Annalisa.

"They had a robbery there early this morning about two a.m. at a 7-Eleven. A man in a rooster mask entered the place, held the clerk at gunpoint, and demanded he empty the till."

"Chicken Bandit," Nick said. "He hit again."

"Yes, well, this time he shot the clerk." Zimmer regarded Annalisa with serious eyes. "The bullets are a match to your gun."

Annalisa sank into the nearest chair as her legs went weak. "He shot someone with my gun?"

"There's more," Zimmer said, watching for her reaction.

Annalisa braced her arms on the chair. "What?"

"The bullets also match the shooting the other night at Sam Tran's place."

"So it was him who took a shot at me." She'd figured as much.

"The clerk's in the ICU. He may pull through. But needless to say, the case just went up a notch in importance again. Detective Davis wants to compare notes, and I told him I'd send one of you."

"I'll go," Annalisa and Nick said at the same time. She looked up at him. "I should go. It's my gun."

"That's why you shouldn't," he said gently. "You're not just working this case, Vega—you're a victim . . . and a target. Let me handle the conversation with Davis. If there's anything you need to know, I'll loop you in ASAP. You can go talk to Norman Tolliver like we planned."

"I like it," Zimmer said, sounding pleased at this development. "I'll tell Davis to expect your call, Carelli. Vega, watch your back. This idiot in the chicken mask is still out there."

"I'll be careful."

As they left, Nick looked at her with worried eyes. "Maybe I should go with you."

"And disappoint Ray Davis? I hear he's waiting for your call."

"I can call him from the car."

She shook her head and placed a hand briefly on his chest. "You're the one who should be careful, heading into Chicken Bandit territory. Norman Tolliver is what, sixty-five years old? He looks like an actual chicken."

She started for the door and Nick followed her. "Tran didn't have real defensive wounds," he protested. "Whoever got to him, he didn't see them coming—and he was trained to look for that sort of thing. For all we know, someone slipped him a Mickey at the bar."

"Okay, so I won't go out for drinks with anyone," she assured him, trying to get him to smile. It didn't work.

"Call me," he ordered her. "When you're done talking to Tolliver."

"I will." She rapped her knuckles lightly on the hood of his car. "Drive safe. And tell Davis to catch this SOB already. I want my friggin' gun back." Nick stood by the driver's-side door in the cold and watched her as she unlocked her own car. He didn't wave as she drove away.

Norman Tolliver did look like a chicken. The white tufts of hair on his head stood up almost like feathers, waving slightly as he tottered back behind his desk. He had a hooked nose that resembled a beak and his brown trousers did nothing to hide the frailty in his legs. The office looked like it had not been updated since the seventies. The wallpaper was yellowed and peeling, and the whole place smelled like old cigar smoke. Tolliver fell backward into his chair with an *oomph* and regarded Annalisa over the clutter across his desk. He had a large but outdated computer monitor with what looked like a coffee stain down the side of it, stacks of folders, receipts spilling out from the sides, a handmade clay paperweight clearly painted by a child. Two snow globes, one with the Springwood Inn inside of it, and an assortment of pens, pencils, paper clips, and other office supplies. The shelves behind him were equally strewn with junk—old photos, a baseball cap, books on hotel management, *Sports Illustrated* magazines from decades past, and, she saw now, a small gold trophy for winning a poker championship. She pointed at it. "Is that yours?"

Tolliver grunted. "Got my name on it. Must be mine."

"You play a lot of poker?" she asked.

"Used to. Not so much anymore." He gave her a suspicious look. "I thought you wanted to ask me more about that PI who came around here. Tran?"

"He talked to you more than once," she said. "We saw as much on his phone records."

"Sure, yeah. He called a couple of times."

"What did he want to ask you about?"

"Same as you. Asking about the murders. I told him the same thing—I don't know anything about who killed those people."

"But you do know something about the cards." She dug out the picture from the poker tournament in which cherub cards had been used. "Right?" she asked as she handed it over to him. "That is you."

He somehow turned a whiter shade of pale. "Yeah, it's me." He flicked the picture back across the desk at her. "So?"

"So Brad Morrison wasn't the only one who had a deck of those cards." She watched him carefully for any reaction. "When the queen of hearts showed up at the murder scene here, the cops must have asked you about it. No way you didn't recognize it."

"Sure, I recognized it. But it wasn't mine."

"Is that what you told Sam Tran when he asked?"

"Damn right I did."

Ah, she thought, so Tran did make the connection. "What else did you tell him?"

Tolliver shrugged. "He asked where my cards went. I said I hadn't the slightest idea. It was more than twenty years ago. I got a hundred decks or more." He opened a drawer and tossed an unopened package at her for proof. "I'm kind of a collector."

Annalisa glanced around the office and wondered where the line was between collector and pack rat. "You collect them, but you don't have the deck with the cherubs on it? That's kind of convenient, don't you think?"

"More like inconvenient," he scoffed. "If I still had 'em, I could show you to prove it wasn't me."

"Where do you think they went?"

"The hell if I know. I played a lot back then. We had a couple of games every week that we ran in the rec room here."

"Games with whom?"

"Jeez, I don't know. My buddies Stan, Lou, and Paulie were the regulars, but we'd take in whoever wanted to play that week. It didn't matter so long as their money was good."

She tried not to look disappointed. "Who else? Guests? Employees?"

"Yeah, sure, both of those. Like I said—if you had the dough, we'd give you a seat at the table."

"Come on, you must remember some more names." She had her notebook out, ready to take them down.

He snorted. "I can barely remember my kid's name half the time."

"Brad Morrison? Did he ever play here? He was at that tournament with you."

He looked guarded at the mention of the dead woman's husband. "I knew Brad, sure. But he didn't play here with us at the motel. I saw him on the circuit."

She decided to try playing to his pride. "Listen, whoever killed Katherine and Stephen went on to murder a second couple at a different motel across town a few years later. This wasn't some affair thing—this guy had a taste for it, you know what I'm saying? He's bent in the head. You spent hours with these guys, trying to read them, trying to see inside their skulls and predict their next moves. You're telling me no one stands out to you as maybe a little freaky?"

He gave a dry chuckle that made his chest rattle. "Hon, we were all a little freaky back in the day."

"I'm talking about the kind of guy who could bash two people's heads in and walk away whistling."

Tolliver sobered. Ran a tongue over his thin lips. "I told Tran—those murders nearly killed me too. You think people want to come vacation at a place where a couple of lovebirds got whacked? Business tanked for months. I almost lost my shirt. Only a loan from my brother-in-law got us through that year. I sat with the cops for hours, trying to help them. I told them everything I could because no one wanted this asshole more than me. They said it was a personal thing with the victims, that someone from their families followed them here and took 'em out on account of they were having an affair. That's what made people willing to come back. They heard it wasn't a random, crazy killer on the loose. Now you're telling me maybe it was?" He waved both hands at her.

"Not random. If the guy had your cards, you knew him." She stood up and leaned over the desk closer to him. "You looked him in the face and never knew."

A shadow of what might have been genuine fear passed over his face. "Maybe that's so. We had ex-cons working here from time to time. No one violent as far as I knew, but we didn't do extensive background checks. I always thought I was a pretty good judge of character. Like you say, look a man in the eyes and take a measure of him."

"You never had any trouble with anyone?"

"Thirty-seven years and I've only fired three people. A maid named Sindee with an *S* for drinking on the job, my own son-in-law for doctoring his time sheets, and a handyman named Wade Armstrong."

Annalisa's skin prickled at the familiar name. "Wade Armstrong?"

"That putz was using our rooms to bed his harem for free. Didn't clean up after himself either. So yeah, when I figured out who was doing it, I fired his ass."

Annalisa looked again at the trophy. "Did Wade Armstrong ever play in your poker games?" she asked.

He looked surprised. "You know, now that you mention it, I think he did."

Annalisa sat in her car in the parking lot as the sky deepened toward night. She looked to the end of the row of rooms where Wade had been with his girlfriend that night. Her car was parked approximately where Brad Morrison had sat in his blue Taurus, watching his wife cheat on him with another man. She wondered idly if Sam Tran had also come here and occupied this exact spot during his investigation and concluded he probably had. He struck her as a hands-on kind of cop. Somewhere, he had met his killer. Maybe here, where another killer had walked. She could imagine that night, darker than this one, a shadowy figure creeping toward the unsuspecting lovers in room 226. He would have been wearing gloves. He would have the murder weapon already in hand. *An aluminum bat*, the ME had guessed. *Maybe a pipe.* They had not recovered the weapon at the scene.

Annalisa jumped in her seat as someone knocked on the window next to her. She felt a chill when she realized it was Brad Morrison. How the hell did he find her here? Had she been followed? He motioned for her to roll down the window. Cautiously, she complied. "What is it?"

"Norm called me. Said you were poking around the place. Said you were thinking maybe Katherine was murdered by a serial killer." Passing headlights made his eyes go black for a moment. *Norm*, she thought. *Tolliver must still be in touch with his buddies from the circuit.*

"I can't discuss it with you," she told Morrison.

"Sure you can," he argued. "If it was a serial murderer, then you know it wasn't me."

She eyed him. That was one possibility. The other one could be that he was the serial killer. He had his own set of cherub cards and his Taurus was at the scene the night of the murders. But if he had motive to kill his wife and Stephen Powell, he had no obvious reason to want the second couple dead. Bonnie and Todd Adkins had never crossed paths with Brad Morrison that she could tell. She abruptly pushed open her car door, forcing Morrison to back up. "Over there," she instructed him. "Put your hands on the car."

"What?" He complied even as he seemed confused. "What the hell are you doing?"

"Making sure you're unarmed."

"I don't own a gun. I never have."

"Guns aren't the only thing that can kill a man." She patted him down until she was satisfied he posed no threat. Then she pointed at her passenger seat. "Get in."

"Are we going somewhere?"

It was freezing outside and she didn't want to have this conversation in the cold. Once they were both inside her car, she nodded at the row of rooms in front of them. "How do you like the view?"

His lip curled in a sardonic smile. "My wife was murdered here, Detective. How do you think I like it?"

"You lied to us," she told him flatly. He shifted to look at her in mild
surprise. "You lied to us and you lied to the cops back then. You were
here the night of the murders. We have pictures that can prove it."

"Pictures?"

"You weren't the only jealous spouse out for blood that night," she told
him. "Another woman hired a PI to tail her husband, and the pictures
he got show your car parked right where we're sitting now. It's a great
view of room 226. Did they leave the lights on? Could you see them in
the act?"

He put his hands to his head. "Stop."

"You must have been furious."

"I didn't kill her."

"Maybe you didn't plan it. Maybe you got here, saw what she was
doing, and grabbed something from your trunk. A bat, maybe? You were
only going to scare them, right? Bash in a few lights and show them how
angry you were. Only you couldn't help yourself when you got up there
and saw them naked together. You lost your shit and went wild on them."

"No," he insisted, swallowing hard, "I never went in. I never saw—"
He broke off with a choked noise and balled his hands into fists. "I never
saw them in the room. They had the curtains drawn. I knew what they
were doing. But I didn't go in there and I didn't kill them."

"You lied," she said again.

"Because I knew how it would look! You're proving it now, by accusing me. Yes, I did follow Kathy that night, but I didn't confront her.
I—I didn't want to see her with him. I saw him open the door and she
went into the room. Of course I knew what they were probably doing
in there, but I couldn't make myself go see for sure. I knew if I went up
there, it would be over. There'd be no going back. Outside, out here . . . I
could still have hope." He turned baleful eyes to her. "I know that sounds
pathetic."

Annalisa turned away. She knew this particular shame. She'd felt it
many times.

"Why do you think I hired Sam Tran to begin with?" he asked, his voice
hoarse. "Because I was here the night Kathy died. I sat here in the car and I
felt sorry for myself. I didn't have the guts to go up there and confront her,

so I just drove home and killed a bottle of Jim Beam. Maybe if I had stayed, if I had gone up there to talk to her, then she'd still be alive."

"What did you see?" Annalisa asked him. If he wasn't the killer, he was at least a witness.

His head lolled back against the seat. "I saw her get out of the car. She was wearing a red dress I'd never seen before. I didn't even try to hide the fact that I was following her. I think I wanted her to catch me, so she would have to confront me rather than the other way around. But she didn't even notice me. She went up those stairs and to the room like she was thinking only of him. The light was on inside, so he was already there."

"What about anyone else? Did you see anyone else near the room that night?"

"No." He paused, thinking. "The parking lot was about half-full. I saw a family with two little kids come back from someplace, maybe dinner or a fair, and they went to their room. The kids had balloons and they were laughing. I remember because I was thinking how I'd wanted kids with Kathy one day and now that wasn't going to happen."

"What about this guy?" Annalisa called up a picture of Wade Armstrong on her phone and showed it to him.

Brad looked at it a long time before he shook his head. "I don't remember him."

"He was staying in a room at the end down there by the dumpster."

Brad followed her gaze and squinted. "Was he . . . was he maybe smoking? I think I remember someone standing down there smoking but I didn't get a good look at him."

"He says he was, yeah."

Brad looked again at her phone, which he still held in his hands. "Is this the guy?"

"I don't know."

"I always thought it was Amos Powell who killed them. I—I bet my life on it."

It was true, she saw, taking in the lines on his face. Morrison and the Powells had spent the past two decades fighting each other over the murders. All the lawsuits and private investigators. So much time and money invested and nothing to show for it.

"What's his name?" Brad asked, still looking at Wade's photo, tilting it this way and that like he couldn't quite bring it into focus.

"Wade Armstrong. He worked here at the motel."

Brad nodded absently. "Yeah, I guess that makes sense. There was a blue van here and I think it said Armstrong on it. It had a cartoon strong arm on the side, like Popeye?" He flexed his bicep to demonstrate. "I remember thinking I'd like to have muscles like that to smash Stephen Powell's face open. Guess I probably shouldn't admit that now." He handed her the phone back.

She barely heard him. She was thinking about the van and the missing murder weapon. *Armstrong Plumbing.* The van would probably have contained pipe. Wade had access to the cards. He'd been present at the scene. "You need to excuse me." She hurried Brad Morrison out of her car and back to his vehicle. Then she phoned Nick. His voicemail picked up. "Call me when you get this," she said, unable to contain the excitement in her voice. "I think I solved the Queen of Hearts case."

THIRTY-SIX

....

ANNALISA DROVE PAST THE BUILDING WADE ARMSTRONG SHARED WITH HIS BROTHER, MATTHEW. Both units were completely dark, and she did not see the van parked outside. She idled across the street for a few minutes, trying to decide on a plan, when her stomach grumbled. Heeding the message for once, she circled around to the main road and parked by the nearest deli. A quick sandwich and soda, she thought. She could eat while she waited outside the Armstrong place for Wade's return. As she reached the door, she bumped into a tall, fit young man on his way out with a sandwich in hand. "Sorry," she said automatically, glancing at him. He had an unremarkable face, unshaven for several days, and dark eyes.

His lids flew open wide as their gaze met. This moment of recognition on his part, when she couldn't yet place him, made her palms tingle. *He knew her.* She instinctively shifted to block his exit as she studied his face.

"Wait," she murmured as his familiar build slowly penetrated her consciousness. Her gaze drifted down to the striped sneakers on his feet. *Shit.*

He shoved her hard, dropping his sandwich in the process, and took off running. Annalisa righted her balance and ran after him. He was fast, dodging pedestrians, moving them bodily out of the way so he barely slowed down. Annalisa knew she should call in the pursuit but even the seconds it would take to pull out her phone meant she would lose him in the dark. He turned a corner, disappearing from sight, and her feet pounded on the pavement as she struggled to catch up. When she rounded the same corner, he'd vanished. She halted, looking wildly around at the rows of houses crowded close together. She listened for his footsteps but heard only her own ragged breathing.

She slowed to a walk, peering into the side yards as she went. He could be anywhere. Just then, a dog started barking a few houses down, and she broke into a run again. She caught up in time to see him disappearing into the alley, a German shepherd trying to leap the fence after him. "Stop, police!" she hollered. She went one house down to avoid the dog and cut through the yard to the alley. Her suspect was just exiting out the other end, heading back toward the more commercial block where the shops and restaurants were. "Stop!" she yelled again.

Shockingly, he complied. She was so surprised that she stopped running too. She saw him freeze about thirty yards down the alley. Just as she withdrew her weapon and prepared to approach, he yanked something from his pocket and disappeared around the corner up ahead. She couldn't be sure what he'd pulled. Might have been a phone but could also be a gun. Her gun. It would be stupid to advance farther at this point—like walking into a trap. She hung back and crouched against the wall. She called dispatch to report what she'd seen. It didn't take Nick long to get the message because her phone rang in her hands almost immediately afterward.

"You found the Chicken Bandit?" he asked by way of greeting.

"I think so. He was actually patronizing the deli rather than holding it up, so, you know, I can't be sure. But he ran like he was guilty."

"If he was picking up food, he might live in the area."

"At least staying nearby, yeah." She eyed the windows around her. "I don't know where he went once he disappeared around that last corner, though."

"I'm en route with backup."

"Yeah, well, step on it, will you?" The shadows seemed to shimmer around her as she walked back toward the deli. "I'm like the Christmas goose out here."

"You take cover. This asshole's shot at you once already."

"I distinctly recall that, yes." She welcomed the bright lights of the deli and the return to civilization. Surely the Chicken Bandit wouldn't be stupid enough to hunt her here.

"Sit tight. I'm twenty minutes out."

"Let me know when you get here," she told Nick. "I'll be at the Armstrong place two blocks away."

"The Armstrongs'? Why?"

"I'll explain when you get here. Just hurry."

She drove the short distance back to the Armstrongs' building and found there was now a light on in the first-floor unit and a silver Chevy Malibu parked in the driveway. She ran a quick check on the plates and found it was registered to Wade Armstrong. As the info came back, she saw a man's shadow moving inside the apartment, faceless and silent given the distance and walls between them. This was how the killer had operated, she thought, in plain sight but somehow still invisible. The victims had been waiting twenty years for someone to recognize what they had seen in their final moments. The murderer didn't come in from outside the motel.

He was already there.

THIRTY-SEVEN

∙∙∙∙∙∙∙∙∙∙

ANNALISA PAUSED OUTSIDE HER CAR, HER BREATH FORMING WHITE PUFFS IN THE FRIGID AIR AS SHE READIED HERSELF FOR THE CONVERSATION WITH ARMSTRONG. A dark sedan drove past at low speed, like a shark circling, and she locked eyes with the middle-aged white guy behind the wheel. She wondered if this was one of the units Nick sent in to try to nail the Chicken Bandit. She kept one eye on the dark street around her as she crossed to the Armstrongs' building.

At the door, Matthew answered her knock, not Wade. He leaned his large shoulder on the doorjamb and looked down at her. "Wade's out on a call—a broken toilet for a family that's got just one bathroom. For us, that's like a lights-and-sirens kind of emergency."

This explained the missing van. "I get it," she said. "We had one bathroom for four kids growing up."

He jerked a thumb behind him. "You can come in and wait if you want. I picked up a bucket of chicken, and I'm expecting Wade any minute. You hungry?"

She followed him inside and the glorious scent of fried chicken hit her right in the gut. Her stomach resumed its noisy protests. "Ah, no thanks," she said, hoping he couldn't hear. "But you go ahead."

"I'll wait for Wade. Don't mind if I have a beer, though." He indicated that she could take a seat on the sofa as he went back to the kitchen area. "Are you a drinker, Detective?"

"Not on duty."

He peeked back in at her. "Still at work? At this hour?"

Had he really thought this was a social call? "It's like your job," she called back to him. "Emergencies at all hours."

"I'll drink to that." He grinned as he returned with a can of Bud, and he handed her a cold seltzer. "Here's to overtime."

She accepted the can but didn't open it. "You must carry a lot of stuff in that van," she said, trying to sound casual. "So you're prepared for different types of situations." She was trying to determine the types of pipe that the van might have inside it.

"Sure, we got all kinds of junk in there." He made a confused face at her. "Is that why you're here? To ask Wade about the van?"

"Sort of."

"You're still on that old case? The one about the couple that got whacked?" He sounded like he couldn't believe she was wasting her time.

"Your brother is a key witness."

He chortled in disbelief. "The only thing he was witnessing was some girl's ass."

"Well, we're wondering if someone might have broken into the van that night."

He halted with his beer halfway to his lips. "A break-in? Wade never said nothing about that."

"The murder weapon may have been a pipe. We were thinking it could have been stolen from his van. That's why I'm here. I was hoping to get a look at the kinds of pipe you routinely carry to see if any of them might be a match."

"We wouldn't have that old pipe around here today. Hell, we don't have that van either. Sold it more than ten years ago now."

"No, we're not expecting to see the same van or the same pipe. More like an example." She glanced at the door, hoping Wade would walk through it.

"Oh," he said, sounding chipper again. "If you want to see an example, I've got that back in the garage right now." He jerked a thumb in the direction of the rear of the house. "You want me to show you?"

She looked again at the door. It couldn't hurt, she supposed, although she was really more interested in the types of materials they kept inside the van. Plus, she wanted to see Wade's reaction when she asked him about them. "Sure," she said, relenting. "Let's take a look."

He didn't bother with a coat, proceeding instead with his low-slung jeans and a T-shirt. Annalisa cast a longing glance at the bucket of chicken as they passed it on their way out the back door. Matthew opened the garage and turned on the overhead light. They kept the place as a storage unit and workshop, she saw, with a bench at the back and various tools tacked to the walls. There were two toilets in the corner, a large metal toolbox, and plenty of pipes lying across almost every surface. She was careful to keep him in her sight, the open door of the garage behind her. "Is this what you're looking for?" he asked her, gesturing at the nearest pipe.

She picked up a copper pipe the approximate width of a bat. "Could be. What's this used for?"

"Oh, this beauty is used for about anything you could want." He picked up a length similar to hers and palmed it in a lover-like caress. "Showers, tubs, sinks—you name it. They're corrosion resistant and can last you more than fifty years."

"So you would carry this kind of thing with you in the van?"

"Sure, all the time. Wade can show you when he gets back. Man, I can't believe what you're saying that the killer might've used one of our pipes . . . Wade's going to freak when he finds out."

"Oh, yeah? Why is that?" She tested the weight of the pipe in her hands, imagining the killer raising it over his victims.

"Well, it's just . . . you're out on a job, minding your business, and someone grabs your stuff to use in a murder like that." He shook his head. "It's wild."

"Wild," she agreed. She put the pipe down and turned around to the open mouth of the garage. "When did you say he'd be back?"

"Any second now. We'll hear the van pulling up."

She tried to control her impatience. Of course the brother she wanted to talk to would be the one out on a job with the van. *Wait.* She stiffened and blinked several times. Wade was working, so he had the van. The night of the murders, Wade had been off the job. He'd been having sex with his girlfriend and then smoking by the dumpster. He wasn't working. If he wasn't working, he wouldn't have been driving the van . . .

which meant Matthew Armstrong had it. She blinked as the shock went through her. Matthew gave her an odd look.

"You okay there, Sarge? You look a little pale."

"I—" She heard a loud crack, maybe a gunshot, somewhere in the neighborhood. The Chicken Bandit? Her attention was torn, just for a second, but it was all Matthew Armstrong needed. The pipe was already in his hands, and he raised it high in the air. She had only time to gasp as the full force of it came down on her head.

THIRTY-EIGHT

··········

S HE WOKE UP FACEDOWN ON THE GARAGE FLOOR WITH BLOOD IN HER MOUTH.
Her head felt like it had been split like a melon and she was surprised not to see her brains splattered around her. The intense pain made
her want to close her eyes, surrender back to unconsciousness, but she
forced herself to stay awake. She wasn't dead yet, so Matthew Armstrong
had a different plan for her. He'd pinned her hands behind her back. She
flexed experimentally and determined it was probably plastic zip ties.

"Good, you're awake." He reached down and hauled her to her feet.

The sudden movement made her stomach lurch as the world spun
crazily around her. She heaved and would have vomited if she'd had
anything to bring up. Matthew Armstrong shoved her forward. "Where
are we going?" she asked hoarsely as she struggled to stay on her feet.

"Somewhere private."

She stopped moving, stalling for time. She'd told Nick where she
would be. He was due any moment. "You killed Kathy Morrison and
Stephen Powell. You probably did the Adkins couple too." His work no
doubt took him to various motels.

"Shut up and move." He jabbed her with something from behind. Her
gun, she realized. She'd lost another one.

"Does Wade know?" He'd be back soon too. Or maybe not. She only had Matthew's word on where his brother was.

"No, and he's not gonna. Enough chitchat. Let's go."

When she still didn't walk forward, he put his giant arm around her neck, squeezing the breath out of her. His voice, laced with the scent of beer, was low and angry at her ear. "Now."

He half walked, half dragged her from the backyard to the front. She wheezed and tried not to pass out. The streetlights overhead made her dizzy. *Think, think.* He was taking her to his car, she realized as it came into view. If she let him move her to another location, Nick would have no way to figure out where she'd gone. She'd probably be dead before he even realized she was missing.

"Fucking bitch cop," he said as she dragged her feet on the cement. "Should've left it alone."

Her deadweight meant he was forced to readjust his grip. As he loosened his hold on her neck, she had one chance. She opened her mouth as wide as she could and she bit him on the wrist—hard. He let out a whoosh of pain and his arm fell away. He didn't drop the gun, so she did the only thing she could. She ran.

Her vision blurred, trees and houses doubling. She sucked in air and kept going. It was awkward to run with her hands tied at her back. She could hear his footsteps, the *slap slap* of his shoes on the wet pavement, gaining behind her. There was no time to approach one of the houses and knock. He'd be on her before anyone could come to the door. She hoped he'd take a shot at her. In motion, she'd be hard to hit, and the noise of the gunfire would summon police attention to this location. There had to be units in the area. She pulled frantically at the ties holding her hands, the plastic biting into her wrists. The bonds held. Tears stung her eyes and she ducked right into a random yard.

She tugged on the door of a shed, looking for a place to hide. It was locked. She had to move on before he caught up with her. She slipped out the back to the alley, looking up and down, hoping to see a patrol car at either end. The place was deserted. She yanked harder at her bonds as she stumbled toward the closest exit. She was so disoriented at this point she didn't know which direction might lead her to the shops. "Ah," she gasped as her left hand tore free, taking a chunk of her flesh with it.

"There you are." Matthew Armstrong came crashing out of the bushes to her right. He tried to grab her but she was able to dodge him by slipping through the fence into the alley. This close, she could see the gun. If she could see it, he could hit her. She scrambled away from him, moving as fast as she could.

"Help," she called. "Help!"

She saw cars going by ahead. She could flag one down if she could just reach the street. She kept yelling as she staggered forward toward salvation. Armstrong caught up with her before she made it to the mouth of the alley. "Shut up," he growled as he grabbed her around the neck once more. She clawed at him with both hands but the anger and adrenaline from the chase had made him stronger. He started dragging her deeper back into the alley. "I should kill you right here." He choked her and her world started to go black.

Crack. Another gunshot shook the night, its sound magnified in the narrow alley. For a split second, she thought he'd shot her with her own gun. But no, he was falling. She could breathe again. He slumped to the ground as another bullet whizzed past her. She dropped next to Armstrong and squinted into the shadows in the direction of the shots. The Chicken Bandit, his mask in place again, was walking toward her with a gun in his hands. Probably the one he'd stolen from her. He'd tried for her but got Armstrong instead.

Her vision split again and there were two of him, wavy and blurry and heading her way. She panted and fought off the rising nausea. With a determined cry, she shoved her hand under Armstrong's body and yanked her new gun free from his weight. There was no time to determine which one of the Chicken Bandits was real. She aimed her gun at the left one and fired two rapid shots. She heard them hit something—she didn't know what—and then she promptly passed out again.

···········

W HEN SHE AWOKE THIS TIME, NICK WAS CROUCHED NEXT TO HER. "You're okay," he said, holding her hand. "You're going to be okay."

She tried to sit up. Armstrong. The Chicken Bandit. Searing pain wrapped itself around her head with the grip of an octopus. She moaned softly as she lay back down. "Armstrong—the other one—he's the killer. Queen of Hearts."

"I know. You took him out." He turned to indicate the man lying next to her.

"Not me. Chicken man."

"Yeah? Looks like you got him too."

She raised up just enough to see the other man lying twenty feet away in the alley, rubber mask still on. "He's dead?" That would be bad. They needed him to give up his accomplice.

"He's still breathing," Nick said as the spinning red lights announced the arrival of the ambulance. "Amazingly, so are you." He gave her a squeeze as the EMTs appeared with a stretcher. She got first dibs as they loaded her up and took her away. Chicken guy would have to catch the next one.

On the way, they asked her about her injuries. "I was hit on the head," she said. "Not shot."

"That's not what it looks like," the male medic said as he examined her arm. "You're bleeding."

The second shot, she realized. It must have hit her left arm. She hadn't even felt it until he mentioned she was bleeding, and now it felt like her shoulder was on fire. The motion of the ambulance made her sick. She closed her eyes as the female medic cut off her sleeve to attend to her wound. "The baby," she said softly. "This won't hurt my baby?"

She felt them freeze. "You're pregnant?" the female medic asked.

Annalisa still hadn't taken the test, but she was more than a week late by now. There was no other answer. She managed a tiny nod. She heard them relay this information ahead to the hospital. At the emergency room, the doctors seemed most concerned about her head. The bullet had merely grazed her arm and the wound was easy to close with a few quick stitches. Her head had a giant lump from the pipe and they were muttering something about a subdural hematoma. She got treated to a CT scan and a full neurological workup. She was waiting for the results alone in a dim room when Nick appeared.

"Hey," he said, standing near the bed. "How are you feeling?"

"Like I got hit with a lead pipe."

"Yeah? I heard it was copper."

"Mm, yes," she said, not opening her eyes. "It's anticorrosive. Good for another fifty years."

"Thank goodness so are you." He reached over and brushed a lock of hair out of her face. "Closing two cases in one night . . . that's pretty hot. You've got it going on, Vega."

She still didn't open her eyes, but she did reward him with a faint smile. "This turns you on, does it?" She was lying there covered in a mix of her own blood and that of Matthew Armstrong, along with road grit from the alley. She had a fat lip from where she hit the garage floor when Armstrong knocked her out and her shirt was half cut off.

They were interrupted by a quick knock and then the neurologist reappeared. She had a miniature laptop with her and a clipboard tucked under her arm. "Good news," she told Annalisa. "Your insides check out. You've got a definite concussion but no sign of a more severe hematoma. We'll be able to discharge you shortly, but you should rest at home for the next several days. Brain rest, not just physical rest."

Annalisa hadn't heard much beyond *home*. She clutched Nick's hand tighter and forced her eyes open. "What about . . . what about the baby? Is it okay?"

The doctor cleared her throat. "The baby. Yes. The nurses mentioned you said you might be pregnant, so we ran a blood test to be sure before administering the contrast agent." She paused. "The test was negative."

Annalisa wasn't sure she understood correctly. "Negative for brain damage?"

"Negative for pregnancy," the doctor said gently. "So you have nothing to worry about. Just rest your brain for a while and take the antibiotics for the injury to your arm. You'll be back to normal in no time."

She left, and Annalisa lay stunned and unmoving. Nick let go of her hand. "I thought for sure . . ." She trailed off, and he gave her a clumsy pat on the leg.

"I'll get the pills from the pharmacy," he said. "Then we can go."

She felt empty, like a ghost. She shuffled with Nick to his car, and he drove to her condo. She insisted on showering and he remained stationed on the other side of the bathroom door in case she collapsed. She discovered her period had arrived as she stood under the stinging spray. *More blood.* Normally she might take an ibuprofen for the cramps but the horse-sized pain pill she'd swallowed at the hospital meant she didn't feel much of anything at all. Nick tried to feed her canned soup and buttered toast, like she had a cold instead of a traumatic brain injury, but all she managed was a few bites. In bed, he slid up behind her. "Tell me if it hurts," he said as he enveloped her in a gentle embrace.

She shook her head and held his arm, stroking the soft springy hairs there. Tears burned in her eyes but she did not cry.

THIRTY-NINE

....

I'm not pregnant. Annalisa typed the words to Sassy from under the warm protection of her favorite comforter. Nick had deposited her there a half hour ago, after she gave her full statement at the precinct, and he'd given clear orders that she remain in the bed until his return. Sassy saw the text immediately, and Annalisa held the phone, waiting for her friend's response to appear. Instead, the phone rang in her hands. It was Sassy.

"You're not supposed to be reading."

Annalisa closed her eyes and turned her head on the pillow so it didn't bump the sore spot. "Jeez, did Nick tell the whole world?"

"He texted me this morning. I would have called earlier, but he said you needed sleep and I promised not to bother you. Are you okay?"

"I'm fine. I'll be fine." She picked at the edge of the comforter. "You saw my message."

"I saw." Sassy paused. "This is good, right? It's what you wanted."

"I know," Annalisa replied glumly. "I just . . . I thought I was. I was making the mental adjustment, you know? I don't understand why I was so late otherwise."

"Well." Sassy drew a long breath. "I've heard that stress can knock off your cycle. I skipped three months when Alex went to prison."

"You were thin. You didn't eat."

"Yeah, and two different guys tried to kill you last night."

"Nick told you that too?" Whenever she texted him, he replied with responses like k and u2.

"Nah, I saw the news. You know how they love the Chicken Bandit."

"Well, they can love him in jail now." She would bet the press would find him less fascinating now that the mystery was gone. Without his mask, Calvin Jones looked more like a pig—pale pink and snub-nosed with a round face and pointy ears. He'd had traces of her gum on his sneakers, like she'd planned. He lived near the alley where she'd shot him. Probably he'd heard her yelling and come running, hoping to finish her off. Instead, he'd saved her life.

"You want to come over?" Sassy asked. "I've got Oreos and wine."

"What about the girls?"

"Gigi's napping and Carla's at school."

"It doesn't matter. I can't drive." She sighed. "Nick took my car keys."

"Ha!" Sassy laughed. "It took that man twenty years, but he finally outwitted you. Let me see if I can get a sitter. I'll come to you."

Annalisa's phone dinged an email alert, and she read the message, half expecting it to be a test from Nick as to whether she was following instructions. Instead, it was Wendell Hawthorne. *Still on for recording tonight? I will meet you at my office at seven. I've got a studio in the basement.* Crap, she thought as she struggled to sit up against the pillows. The podcast. "Hey, Sass?"

"Hmm?"

"What if you got that sitter, but we went somewhere else instead?"

Sassy hesitated with her answer. "I don't know. Is it somewhere I could get arrested?"

"What? I wouldn't involve you in anything illegal. You know that."

"No, I'm suggesting Nick will slap the cuffs on me when he finds out I sprung you."

"Look, I'm not driving, texting, or reading. I'm following doctor's orders." Annalisa eased out of bed, wincing as her heart pumped extra blood to her head to make up for the fact that she was now upright. She was breathing. She was alive. This was more than they could say for Natalie Kroger, who was still among the missing.

"Somehow, I don't think Nick's going to see it that way," Sassy said, her voice heavy with irony.

Annalisa gritted her teeth as she pulled on a sweater. "Like you said, it's been nearly twenty years. He won't be surprised."

"Okay, let me work the phones. I'll call you back when I figure something out."

....

AN HOUR LATER, SASSY ROLLED UP IN HER KIA. She tossed sippy cups and board books from the front seat into the back as Annalisa opened the passenger side door. "Sorry, it's a little sticky," Sassy said, brushing her hand over the seat to remove some crumbs. "No one sits there anymore so it's basically become storage."

"It's fine." Annalisa fastened her seat belt and ignored the pain in her upper arm as she did so. "Who'd you get for a sitter?"

"The only one who's always on call—Grandma."

"You roped my mom into this?"

"This? What *this*? I thought I was just taking you to do some interview."

"Uh, yeah. You are." She didn't mention the interview was with a possible suspect in the disappearance of a college student.

When they arrived at campus, Annalisa still had a half hour before she met Hawthorne, so she asked Sassy to bring her past the university convenience store first for a snack. They parked as close as possible and hiked the rest of the way. Annalisa really wanted to get a look at the scene of Natalie's disappearance in the daylight, but she wouldn't mind a bag of chips. She selected salt and vinegar while Sassy picked out a chocolate bar. Annalisa added in some gummy candy at the last second. Her blood sugar had to be low. She was mildly surprised to find Zach behind the counter. His roommate, Jason, had just been found dead a couple of days ago. He seemed subdued, his dark eyes dull as he rang them up.

"Are you here because there's news on Natalie?" he asked.

"No, I wish I was," Annalisa replied. "Have you heard anything?"

He gave a disheartened shrug. "People are saying Jason did something to her. I don't believe it."

"I'm sorry about your friend," Annalisa said. She gave him the money and opened the gummy candy right there, devouring a small handful.

He put the rest of their items in a paper bag. "Everyone keeps telling me, 'Hey, at least when your roommate commits suicide, you get

automatic As for the semester.' Like that's a cool trade-off or something. Besides, it isn't even true."

"I'm sorry," Annalisa repeated with feeling. She extended the open bag of candy to him. "I know it's hard."

He waved her off. "Just went to the dentist," he said, gesturing at his mouth. "As if my life didn't suck enough already." He turned his face toward the windows. "There's a vigil scheduled for Natalie tonight, you know. With candles and stuff? Like that's going to help bring her home." He looked at Annalisa again. "I heard Quinn's family made her quit school because of what happened."

"She's still technically enrolled, but yeah, they took her home." If Annalisa could bring Natalie back, maybe it would mean freedom for Quinn too. Another reason to keep pressing. She cleared her throat. "I'm supposed to meet Professor Hawthorne to do his podcast," she said. "Have you ever listened to it?"

He made a face that might have been sympathetic embarrassment for her. "Kids listen to make fun of him. He thinks he's Mr. *CSI* or something, but he's just this dweeb professor spinning theories in the basement."

"Is that all the kids say about him?"

He froze and his tone became cautious. "What do you mean?"

"Quinn said maybe there was a rumor going around about him. That he might have been involved in a harassment incident at his previous school in Nebraska?"

He scratched the back of his head. "I might've heard something about it. Don't know any details, though."

"Is there anyone who might know more?"

"Why, is he like, in trouble for something?"

"Not that I know of. Just trying to get a read on him." She held his gaze until he started to squirm.

"Look, if you want to know about Professor Hawthorne, you should talk to his assistant, Byron. That dude is permanently glued to Hawthorne's ass. Beyond that, I know a guy whose sister went to the University of Nebraska. I think it was the same time Hawthorne was there. If you want, I can have him try to put you in touch with her. Maybe she knows more."

"That would be helpful." She shifted the groceries so she could give him her card. "Thanks."

The door dinged as they left and Annalisa pulled out Sassy's candy bar. Sassy narrowed her eyes in return. "An interview," she said with suspicion in her tone. "That's what you told me."

Annalisa thrust the chocolate into her friend's hand. "There's a girl missing," she said. "A friend of Quinn's. This is the last place she was known to be." She explained how Natalie had purchased the ice cream and they had found it in the trash can along with her flute. "No one has seen or heard from her since."

"How awful."

Annalisa indicated the route they had walked in from the east entrance. "We think the abductor may have chosen this point because it's an easy exit off campus from here."

Sassy scrunched up her nose. "But you found her stuff in the trash can up there," she said, pointing at the receptacle located up the hill. "And you say she was coming from the music building way down there, right by where we parked. Why not grab her then?"

"Huh." Annalisa thought this was an interesting point. She walked to the trash can where they had found Natalie's belongings. The sun had disappeared behind the hill, heading for the horizon, but it wasn't as dark as it had been the night Natalie vanished. "The trees over there offer good cover," Annalisa said, turning to speculate. "Maybe that's why he picked this spot."

Sassy crossed over the lawn to the cluster of trees Annalisa had indicated. "With as much money as it costs to go here, you'd think they could hire a groundskeeper," Sassy said, kicking at the leaves. She stumbled and cursed. "Crap," she said as she caught herself on the trunk.

"What is it?"

"Must be a root." Sassy nudged the leaves aside with her uninjured foot. "No, wait . . ."

"Don't touch it," Annalisa ordered as she saw the edge of a shoe come into view. She crouched down to examine it with her flashlight and determined it was a woman's gray slip-on shoe, size seven. She took out her phone to snap a photo. Quinn could probably answer whether it was Natalie's shoe or not. "Help me move the leaves," she said to Sassy. "Be careful and go slowly."

Together, they cleared the leaves from around the shoe, revealing two deep gouges in the soft ground. Annalisa knew immediately what they

were. Drag marks. Sassy wasn't a detective, but she understood the significance because her brown eyes grew dark and wide with fear. "You were right," she whispered. "He was here. This is where he took her."

Annalisa followed the direction of the marks with her flashlight beam into the distance. Uphill, toward campus. Not away from it. "Give me your purse."

Sassy looked confused, but she handed over her mom-sized bag. Annalisa put the remaining items they'd purchased from the convenience store into Sassy's bag, and then she used the empty paper sack to bag the stray shoe. She had Sassy hold the flashlight on the drag marks so she could take some photos of them too. "What do we do now?" Sassy asked her.

"We go to the interview. Up there." Annalisa fixed her gaze to the looming building at the top of the hill, the place where the drag marks seemed to be pointing. "The biology lab."

FORTY

....

In the basement supply room, Byron double-checked to make sure all the bottles had their labels facing outward, the way Hawthorne insisted they be stored. He adjusted a bottle of sodium hydroxide and paused again to study the array of chemicals. They were harmless on their own, but he could combine them in a way to melt off someone's skin or turn their blood to sludge. He touched the syringe in his pocket to reassure himself it was there. He felt itchy all over, his chest tight and his palms wet. He couldn't put off his plan any longer. The situation with Natalie Kroger proved as much.

"I know it was you."

He jumped a mile at the sound of her voice. When he turned, he found her standing there. The girl with the orange hair again. "You're not supposed to be down here."

"I couldn't figure out how I knew you at first, but I finally got it. Quinn and I, we checked with the girls in the biostat lab and none of them knew anything about that post about Hawthorne. Then it hit me—there was one other person in the lab that day. You."

"I don't know what you're talking about." He tried to bypass her but she blocked his path.

"You were there. Not just in the lab. You were there the ni—"

His hand shot out to grab her before he knew what he was doing. He clapped it hard over her mouth, fingers biting into her flesh, and her eyes flew open wide. "Shut up," he ordered her as she started to struggle. He had the syringe on him, and the moment her hand brushed his pocket, she started to whimper. He was so close and she was about to ruin everything. She gave him no choice. He dragged her back into the supply room with him and he shut the door. After a while, she stopped struggling.

··········

HE WAS ALONE AGAIN WHEN HAWTHORNE SHOWED UP IN THE LAB. It was spooky after dark—the huge windows totally black and the building silent as the grave. Hawthorne seemed to love it because he hardly ever went home. Byron paused where he was sweeping the floor. "Did you finish grading those exams?" Hawthorne asked as he scrolled through something on his phone.

"All set." Byron nodded to the table at the front of the room where the papers lay. "You want me to take them to your office?" His heart played pinball off his ribs, but he leaned against the wall, trying to look casual.

"No, I've got it." Still distracted, Hawthorne ambled across the room to retrieve the test papers.

Shit. Byron had to find another way into that room. He made a lame effort at sweeping, so deep in thought that he did not notice Hawthorne had sneaked up on him. The professor grabbed the back of his neck—not hard, but firm enough to make Byron jump. "You have to get under the desks," Hawthorne said, giving Byron a squeeze.

"Yeah, I will." Byron shrugged out of his grasp and slipped away. He kept his eyes down. He hated the powerless feeling he got whenever Hawthorne was around. Just the jangle of his boss's keys made Byron break into a cold sweat. But he had the upper hand now, he reminded himself. He knew where Hawthorne stored the data stick. A simple switch and Byron would be home free. He touched the hard edge of the syringe through his pants.

"When you're done here, make sure the studio is set up downstairs," Hawthorne said as he headed for the exit.

Byron's head jerked up. "You're doing a recording tonight?" It wasn't Tuesday, when Hawthorne usually recorded.

Hawthorne turned and favored him with a dazzling grin. "A real 'get.' Annalisa Vega is coming in for an interview." His smile faded as he looked Byron over from head to toe, his eyes lingering on the dirty smudge Byron got on his khakis during his struggle with Sienna. "Make sure you're gone by then."

Vega was coming here? Byron stood frozen with the broom after Hawthorne disappeared up to his office. He had less time than he'd imagined, and he had no desire to encounter her. But maybe he could find a way to use her to his advantage. Point her in the direction he wanted. He left the broom leaning against the wall. Hawthorne would carp about it, but after tonight, there was nothing he could do to Byron anymore.

Byron went to the basement of the building to the unused, windowless room that Hawthorne had co-opted for his podcast studio. It was probably intended to be a small meeting room or a library for old journals, but these days, everything was online. Hawthorne had put up foam padding on the walls to dampen sound. He'd spared no expense on the microphones, headsets, and audio mixer, but the professional-grade equipment didn't get him an audience. Last Byron had checked, Hawthorne had only two hundred subscribers. Byron paused in his straightening to consider this point. Either Vega didn't know enough to realize what a piddly little broadcast she was signing on for, or she had another reason for wanting to come here. The woman had busted a serial killer who'd eluded capture for twenty years. She wasn't stupid. Byron's hands started to shake as he neatened the chairs. He had to act and he had to do it now.

He opened the laptop and went to the audio settings, where he changed the input for one of the microphones. Then he closed out of everything and tried a sound check. Perfect. Hawthorne would eventually find the bug, but the delay would give Byron enough time to get into the office. He went upstairs to deliver Hawthorne the bad news. "One of the mics is on the fritz," he said from the doorway.

"So fix it," Hawthorne replied, irritated. He was looking at something on his computer monitor.

"I tried. No sound is coming out."

Hawthorne peered at him over the rims of his reading glasses. "Good help is hard to find," he said at length. "I'll check it myself."

Byron shrank back until he was pressed against the outside wall so Hawthorne didn't touch him as he stormed out the door. As he'd hoped, his boss was so preoccupied with the broken mic that he left the office unlocked. Once Hawthorne disappeared into the stairwell, Byron rushed into the office and to the desk. Hawthorne stored the data stick in the top left-hand drawer. Whenever Byron threatened to quit, Hawthorne would pat the drawer and smile.

Byron yanked on the drawer but it didn't open. He tried again and again until the whole desk shook with the force of his pull. Locked. He ran a hand through his hair, trying to think. Maybe he could force the lock. He opened the shallow drawer at the center of the desk, looking for tools. Paper clip, letter opener? He cursed himself for not realizing this barrier sooner. Of course Hawthorne wouldn't leave the data stick out where Byron could easily grab it. Byron sifted through the items one by one, eyeing the fine point of a pen, a stapler, a thumbtack. He tried the thumbtack, but it did nothing to loosen the lock.

Panic rose in him so fast he felt like he was drowning inside his own body. *Think, think.* He cast his gaze across the cluttered desk. There, half-hidden by a printed news article on Annalisa Vega, he saw a metallic glint. Keys. Hawthorne had forgotten to take his keys. Byron fumbled as he tried to find the one to open the desk drawer, sending them clattering onto the hardwood with a noise that seemed to echo through the whole building. He snatched them up and found a smallish one that appeared to fit the lock. Holding his breath, he slid it into the hole. The key turned and the drawer opened.

His momentary elation turned to despair as he saw the contents. Printed photos, some of them kinky. Papers he didn't have time to sort through before Hawthorne reappeared. And dozens of data sticks. Easily at least thirty. He started pawing through them, trying to remember any sig-nifying details on the one he needed, but there were too many duplicates of the same brands. His only chance was to try to take all of the black ones, and he started shoving them into his pants pockets as fast as he could. Blood roared in his ears. He didn't hear the elevator or the footsteps until it was too late.

"Hello." He looked up to see Annalisa Vega standing there with a woman he did not recognize. Vega regarded him with a quizzical expres-sion. "We're here to meet Professor Hawthorne."

Sweat beaded down the back of his neck. He nudged the desk drawer closed with his leg. "Uh, yeah. He'll be right here. I'm his assistant."

"Byron." She pointed at him as she said his name, and he felt it like a laser through his chest. She knew. She already knew.

"That's right." Byron felt the syringe again in his pocket. He had one play left and maybe just enough time to use it. Because if this was it, if he was going down, he planned to take every last one of them with him.

FORTY-ONE

....

ANNALISA REGARDED THE SKINNY, FLOPPY-HAIRED KID ACROSS THE ROOM. He looked like they had busted him in the middle of a murder. She could actually smell the sweat coming off of him. He wiped his palms on his pants and came around the desk. "Professor Hawthorne is checking the equipment downstairs. He'll be right up."

He tried to leave but Annalisa shifted to block his path. "Have you worked for him long?"

"This is my third semester."

"You must know him pretty well then."

Byron answered with a single short shrug, but he wasn't making eye contact. "Not really. Look, it's nice to meet you and all, but I've got to get going."

"Sure," Annalisa said easily, making no effort to unblock his path. "It's just, I've heard some rumors about Hawthorne going around the campus. I figured if anyone might know the truth, it'd be you."

The mention of the rumors got his attention. He looked right at her. "What rumors?"

"You tell me."

His gaze slid away from her to something on the wall. Annalisa turned to look and saw it was a teaching award from last year. Highest-rated class. From what Quinn had said, Hawthorne taught the large entry-level biology lectures. *Weed-out classes*, they used to call them. Hard, impersonal, and delivered in an auditorium full of students, they were designed to separate the ones who could hack it from the ones who failed out. The goal was to survive with a passing grade. Professors leading these classes didn't tend to be beloved, so it said something that Hawthorne had managed not only to hold the students' attention but somehow to win their favor. Byron saw her looking at the plaque. "He gets standing ovations, you know. At the end of the year? Kids actually get up and applaud him."

"Are you saying they shouldn't?"

"Oh, great, you've arrived." A booming, cheerful voice behind them interrupted the conversation, forcing Annalisa to turn from Byron to greet Professor Hawthorne. He'd come dressed for the part in a brown-checkered button-down shirt, a skinny brown tie, and a tweed jacket. "And you brought company. How lovely." He put one arm around Annalisa and the other around Sassy. Sassy made a face like she was contemplating a knee to his balls.

"My sister-in-law, Sassy, was kind enough to drive me," Annalisa said as she sidestepped his arm.

Hawthorne's eyes widened. "Sassy," he repeated. "You're Cecilia Vega—Alex's wife."

"Ex-wife." Sassy had divorced Annalisa's brother when Alex went to prison.

"Charmed, truly," Hawthorne said, taking her hand and bowing to kiss it. "I don't suppose you'd consider—"

"No." Sassy yanked her hand back. She didn't wait to hear what his offer was. She'd done zero interviews on the case that put Alex behind bars, and Annalisa figured she'd go to her grave with the epitaph NO COMMENT. "I'm only the taxi service."

"Very well," Hawthorne said with a regretful sigh. "But I'm afraid you'll have to wait outside the studio during the recording. Guests only."

Sassy put up her palms. "Fine by me."

Hawthorne appeared to notice Byron for the first time. "I've fixed the microphone," he told his assistant. "You are free to go."

Byron appeared relieved, almost desperate. He mumbled his thanks and attempted to flee the premises. "Wait." Annalisa grabbed his arm to stop him.

He jerked to a halt and stared into her eyes. "I can't help you," he said, wild-eyed. "I've never been to Nebraska."

Annalisa was so surprised at the non sequitur that she dropped her hold on his arm and he ran out the door. "You'll have to excuse that one," Hawthorne said drily. "He can be a bit squirrelly, but he's a proficient grader. Shall we head down to the studio and get to it?"

"First, is there a ladies' room I could use?" Annalisa tried to sound ingratiating. "The traffic took forever."

"Of course. Down the hall on your left."

Annalisa tugged Sassy along with her, like they were still in middle school and needed to schedule joint trips to the restroom. When they were out of sight, Annalisa whispered, "You look around while I'm doing the interview."

"What am I looking for?"

"I don't know. Anything that seems odd. Contact information for Byron if you see it. That kid knows something."

"What?"

"He said he'd never been to Nebraska, but I didn't mention Nebraska to him at all. He must know the story."

"Byron. Nebraska. Weird shit." Sassy nodded. "Got it."

Annalisa went back to Hawthorne's office on her own. She found him standing behind his desk, frowning at it, but he looked up with a new light in his eyes as she entered the room. "Okay, I'm all yours," she said, spreading her arms.

A strange little smile played on his lips. "Yes," he said. "You are."

They took the steps down to his studio, and Annalisa hobbled a bit on the way, as her hip was still sore from her adventures the day before. Before long, her meds would wear off and she'd be useless. Hawthorne took her to a small windowless room and locked the door behind them after they entered. "Don't want to be disturbed during the recording," he told her.

She took the seat he indicated and put on the headphones as he did. Her phone buzzed in her pants and she looked at it. A text from Nick. **Where r u??**

"Ah, ah," Hawthorne tutted at her. "You have to turn off all devices."

Annalisa hesitated a moment and then powered off the phone, showing him the black screen. He smiled at her. "Excellent."

They began the interview. He walked her through the Lovelorn case, but he seemed less interested in the serial killer's capture than Mr. Lovelorn's psychology. "Had he been abused as a child? Raised in a violent home?"

"Not that I know of. It's not really my area, though."

"He wrote the women elaborate love letters after he killed them. So did he love them or did he hate them?"

"He wrote the letters before he killed them," Annalisa clarified. "There was never any love."

"Still, he must have felt something. There was a reason he chose the women he did."

"I can't say what it might have been."

Hawthorne looked perplexed, or perhaps annoyed with her. "Surely you must have had to think like him, to get into his head, to understand how to catch him."

"He enjoyed torturing and murdering women. That's all I really needed to know." She shifted, uncomfortable. To probe the Lovelorn Killer's psyche meant she'd have to examine her brother's crime as well. She gave Hawthorne her single piece of hard-won wisdom. "Murderers can come from anywhere."

"Yes, yes," he said, leaning forward as he warmed to the idea. "You've been looking for one right here on my campus. Isn't that correct?"

"I can't comment on open cases."

"You can speak to the parts that are already in the papers," he argued. "That private investigator who was murdered, Sam Tran—you're looking into his death and it led you here."

"He was working a case here at the time of his death," Annalisa agreed.

"About a stalker." There was that gleam in his eye again. She decided to play along.

"Yes, some young women on campus were being harassed by an anonymous party. Sam Tran was hired to find the person responsible." Only, as she was finding, there was more than one person involved. Sarah Beth did the texting. Jason burned the gorilla suit up at the cabin—or someone wanted to make it look like he had. And where was Natalie?

"And did he?" Hawthorne uncurled toward her like a snake. "Find the stalker?"

"No." Annalisa held his gaze. "Do you have any ideas?"

"Me? How would I know?"

"You spend your life on or near the campus. You're at the heart of it. Obviously, you have an interest in crime and its underpinnings, Professor. Surely you have an opinion." She widened her eyes slightly, hoping she looked inquisitive, like a student hungry for the knowledge only he could provide.

Hawthorne grew coy, drawing back from her. "Well," he said at length, "the students play pranks on one another all the time, even cruel ones. The Greek hazing system is periodically investigated as a crime, as I'm sure you know. Moreover, the students are young, their hormones in full bloom, and often they're away from home for the first time in their lives. Sometimes their courting rituals go astray. Misunderstandings occur."

"So the stalker is just misunderstood."

"I didn't say that. In fact, I'm inclined to think he's a real problem. Even dangerous."

"Why is that?"

"Natalie Kroger." He waited for her reaction, and when she did not give one, he added, "She's missing."

"Ah, right," she said as if she had just caught on. "You know her. She was your student."

His face became pinched at the mention of this connection. "She was no more my student than anyone else's. I had her in a class of more than three hundred others. We never even interacted. My assistant, Byron, deals with the students more directly."

"But you know she's missing."

"It's all over campus. People talk."

"Hmm," she agreed, tilting her head to study him. "They do."

He held her gaze, squinting a little as if to try to figure out her angle. "Anyway," he said eventually. "I think the rumors that she's run off somewhere are wrong. I think she's been abducted."

Annalisa felt the air change. It was already stuffy and dry inside the little room. Now it felt devoid of oxygen. She parted her lips, trying to breathe evenly as she eyed the equipment on the table in front of them. The audio machine appeared on; it flashed when either of them spoke. If she could record a confession . . . "Interesting theory," she said, trying to inject a note of skepticism into her voice. *Make him prove it*, she thought. *Get him to brag.* "Why do you think Natalie was abducted?"

"She was a conscientious student. She had close friends, and they all say they haven't heard from her. Plus, her flute was in the trash."

"I'm sorry." Her pulse quickened. They hadn't released that information. "What did you say?"

"Her flute," he said, overly patient. "She'd been practicing with it in the music building right before she vanished. It was recovered from a trash bin on campus. But then . . . didn't you know that already?"

"Yes, but how did you find out?"

He gave a slow blink and that weird little smile again. "A journalist never reveals his sources."

Officer Kent, she thought. He was the only other person there. He might have leaked. Or Hawthorne knew the location of the flute because he'd put it there. "That's right," she said to him. "You were there when she disappeared."

"Me? No."

"Yes, I saw you on the convenience store video at the time she was buying her ice cream."

"I may have been in the store at some point, yes. I stop in sometimes on my nightly walks with my dog. But I don't remember seeing Natalie. Maybe . . . maybe she had a jealous boyfriend."

Had there been a dog that night? She didn't remember one from the video. "Natalie's boyfriend has been cleared. He was nowhere near the store that night."

"Someone who wanted to be her boyfriend, then. A young man she rejected. Or maybe that troubled student who committed suicide in the woods—Jason, I think his name was?"

"There was no sign of Natalie at the cabin. Where would he have taken her?"

"The woods are vast. Maybe she just hasn't been found yet."

"She clearly hasn't been," Annalisa agreed. "Not yet."

His smile turned thin. "Yet," he repeated. "That's what I like about these crime cases, the evolution of them, the sense of inevitability even when they might appear to be in suspended animation. They're like science in a way. You have evidence, you form a theory, and you test it. Is he the guilty party? Is she? You keep going until you have enough evidence to either prove or disprove your theory, and finally, you have a solution. What do you think of my analogy?"

"Mm, I see some parallels in what you're saying. But biology doesn't hide or keep secrets. It doesn't obscure the truth from the investigator the way a killer does."

"And that's what you think happened to Sam Tran? He got too close to someone's secret?"

"Someone here, maybe. Right on this campus."

He appeared to consider this. "Well, then, the killer was very foolish indeed."

"Why do you say that?"

"Because removing Sam didn't solve the problem. It merely amplified it. Sam is gone but here you are, still asking questions."

"That's right." She leaned over, close enough to smell him. "Here I am."

He did not get a chance to reply because someone started banging on the door from outside. "The sign clearly says 'Do not disturb,'" he grumbled as he removed his headset and went to answer it. When he opened the door, Annalisa saw Sassy standing there, her face white and her eyes dark with fear.

"Anna, you need to see this."

Annalisa moved as fast as she could to get out of the chair. "What is it?" Sassy only shook her head.

"Look here, we're in the middle of something," Hawthorne began, but Annalisa ignored him.

"It's upstairs," Sassy whispered to her as Annalisa took her arm. Hawthorne trailed them up the stairs and down the hall to the lab. Sassy closed her eyes and pointed into the room. "On the table at the front," she said. "Look."

Annalisa took a few cautious steps closer. Sassy had turned on the fluorescent lights, giving the room an overly bright, eerie glow. Annalisa saw there appeared to be a figure lying prone on the table, and as she neared it, she determined it was a skeleton. Life-sized, but a model. Someone had put a red wig on it and dressed it in a lab coat, which was buttoned at the navel. It was freaky looking, and Annalisa could see why Sassy might have been startled. "It's a prank," she said, turning around.

"Look at the ribs," Sassy told her from the hall.

"I don't know who could have done this." Hawthorne frowned as he joined Annalisa by the skeleton.

Annalisa saw it now, what had spooked Sassy so badly. Poking out of the rib cage where the heart should have been was a syringe.

FORTY-TWO

....

QUINN SAT ON HER BED, THE ONE SHE'D HAD SINCE SHE WAS SIX. Her parents were downstairs in the kitchen arguing in hushed tones about what to do with her. Her father was fine keeping her prisoner in her room indefinitely like some cursed Disney princess, but her mother thought Quinn should be allowed to return to school after the holidays, when "everything would have blown over." Quinn wondered if maybe she really was cursed. Her boyfriend turned up dead just after she'd dumped him and her roommate was missing. Quinn couldn't help but feel responsible, although she didn't see how. If she was the connection, if these bad things were happening in some way because of her, then she should be the one to fix it. But she hadn't even managed that much. She'd abandoned Sienna. They hadn't ever found the cat woman who'd posted about Professor Hawthorne. The burned costume at the cabin suggested Jason had been the one who attacked Sienna, but they had found that photo of him doing the naked quad run the night of the party. How could he be in two places at once? And none of this explained what had happened to Natalie.

Her essay on Greek civilization forgotten, Quinn let the laptop slide off her legs as she crawled across the bed to her window. It was dark outside and freezing cold. The windowpane chilled her face when she pressed her cheek against it. She hoped Natalie wasn't out in the elements. Her laptop chimed a notification from the chat program and she pounced on it eagerly. Her father had taken the phone, but he didn't realize she could use the computer to keep in touch with her friends. The message was from Zach. **Look outside.**

Puzzled, Quinn returned to the window. She had been looking and she hadn't noticed anything unusual. This time, when she put her face to the glass, she saw a light flash from inside a car parked halfway down her street. She blinked, wondering if she'd imagined it, but then it flashed again, like Morse code. She went back to the laptop. **Is that you??**

Yeah. I figured I shouldn't knock.

Smart move.

Can you get out?

Idk . . . why?

I'm looking for Natalie. Thought you might want to come.

Quinn bit her lip. She wanted to be doing something, anything, but she had no idea where to start searching. **Looking where?**

Campus.

They've already checked everywhere. No luck.

It took a few moments for his message to come through. **Not everywhere.**

Quinn looked at the closed door to her bedroom. She'd trained her parents not to come in over the past few days. Still, she formed a lump under the covers with some stray pillows and turned out the lights. Then she put on a large sweatshirt, a pair of knit gloves, and a beanie hat. She held her breath as she closed the door behind her with a soft click. She slunk down the stairs, avoiding the one that creaked, and edged along the wall, just out of her parents' view, until she reached the den with its sliding door. She escaped out into the cold night, exhaling finally into the misty air.

Zach flashed the light again and she ran toward it. Her father taking her cell phone meant he would have no way to track her, no way to know where she had gone. She felt giddy as she yanked open the door to Zach's beat-up old Ford Focus and plunked down in the passenger seat. "Let's go," she said.

Zach already had the engine running. "We're out of here." Stale heat poured out of the vents. The interior smelled like drying wool.

Quinn glanced at the side mirror to see her house disappearing into the distance. "How did you know where I lived?"

"You can find anything online." She must have looked alarmed because he turned his head and gave her a reassuring smile. "Your family got kind of famous there for a while, remember?"

"Oh, yeah." She relaxed into the seat. Reporters had camped outside their house for weeks after Uncle Alex got arrested. Of course her place had shown up on the news. "Where are we going to look first?"

"There's that small gymnasium down behind the smaller athletic field. It hasn't been used in years."

"It's locked up, though. Right?"

"Look in the back."

She twisted, and in the light of the passing streetlamps she could barely make out a pair of black gloves and a bolt cutter lying on the rear seat. She gave an uneasy laugh as she turned around again. "All we need is a ski mask and we could be committing a robbery."

"I have masks if we need them."

Her blood turned cold then and she put her hands to the heater, trying to hide her trembling. "What would we need those for?" If they found Natalie, they'd be heroes, not criminals.

"Hey, I don't know about you, but I don't need a vandalism charge on my permanent record."

"Right. Of course." She sat ramrod straight in her seat.

"I have another flashlight for you too," he said.

"That's okay. I brought one." She felt for it inside the enormous pockets of her sweatshirt. It was one her father had given her when she started school, one he'd ordered after seeing an advertisement on TV. He ordered many things that way. A knife that claimed to cut through other knives.

An indoor smokeless grill and a self-tanning spray that the TV swore was used by celebrities out in Hollywood. The products that showed up in the mail never lived up to the hype from the ads and invariably ended up gathering dust in the Vegas' basement. *This flashlight*, Dad had told her, *features an atomic-strength beam. Navy S.E.A.L.s carry it.* Quinn had rolled her eyes when she'd accepted it. How could he still be falling for the TV tricks? But now as she fingered the hard edge of the flashlight inside her sweatshirt, she thought maybe her father's gambles represented a kind of optimism, a form of hope. *This time, you can believe it.*

···········

THEY DIDN'T NEED THE BOLT CUTTERS TO GET INTO THE OLD GYM. Zach found a broken window and wriggled inside with no issue. Then he opened the door for her. They looked like *X-Files* characters, wandering around an abandoned building with flashlights, waving them this way and that, with no clear goal in mind. Quinn crashed into a hanging punching bag, which moved as she touched it, making her scream and drop her flashlight. Zach came running and he laughed when he saw her predicament. "Come on," he said as he helped her up. "There's nothing here."

"Where to next?"

"Grayson Hall."

The old 1970s-era dorm was being torn down to make room for a new one. They'd already put up fencing around it and brought in some equipment. Quinn kicked a deflated basketball on the way out. Their effort seemed more futile now. In reality, the gym had been empty only a few semesters, but it felt like no one had been inside for years.

They scaled the chain-link fence to check the condemned dorm. Here, there was a padlock on the door and Zach had to force it. He wore a ski mask to complete the job but Quinn just pulled up her hood. It was so big it nearly swallowed her head. Inside, they found only worn-out furniture and sad, cell-like rooms with tape still stuck to the walls. Quinn rubbed one edge with her finger. "She's not here." At that moment, Natalie felt so far away, it was almost like Quinn had made her up, like she was a character from a childhood book.

"There's still the old biology building."

Quinn wished he'd take the serial killer mask off. It frightened her to look at him. "That's all the way uphill. Natalie disappeared down here."

"Still gotta cross it off the list."

His determination won her over and they hiked up the hill—thankfully he took the mask off for this part—to the old brick building. Like the others, it was completely dark inside. Zach shook the front doors, but they were locked. "Let's try the back," he said as he pulled down the mask once more.

Quinn raised her hoodie with a shiver. "This place gives me the creeps." The old bio building was where they had once housed the monkeys for the science experiments, decades ago, before current standards for humane treatment came into being. Kids said if you walked by at night you could still hear the animals screaming.

The rear of the building was at least off the path, hidden by trees, so no one was likely to walk by and spot them. Zach went down the cement steps to try the basement door while she hovered at the top. "Locked," he muttered as he tugged it. There was no chain to cut, so his shears wouldn't work. He came up the stairs and craned his head back to see the full height of the building. "I bet I could get into one of those windows."

"Yeah, but how're you going to get up there?" She gestured at the brick wall.

"I don't know yet." He tried taking a running start and hurling himself at the building, but he caromed off like a bird bouncing off a window. He tried this several times and was still unable to get a grip or toehold on sheer brick. "If I can get to the ledge at the top of the door, I bet I can make it," he said, breathing hard.

"If you fall, you hit the steps and break your neck."

"I won't fall."

Quinn hugged herself as he balanced on the stone edges that lined the stairs to the basement. He was able to find an empty spot left by a crumbled brick to stick one toe in, which he used for leverage to hoist himself up until he could reach the cement facade over the doorway. He found two handholds on the elaborate, curled design. He hauled himself up and braced against the wall, his toes balanced on the thin ledge above the door.

Quinn felt sick just looking at him. "Be careful," she called.

"I—I got this." He stretched one leg across and reached the window ledge. Quinn screwed her eyes shut, unable to watch as he made the jump from one spot to the next. When she dared look again, he had both feet outside the window.

"Oh!" She gave a delighted cry and clapped her gloved hands together. "You made it."

"Yeah, I'm almost in. Just . . . one . . . sec."

Her heart was beating so fast, her attention riveted on Zach, that she didn't hear the footfalls behind her. "Hold it right there." A bright light trapped Zach in its glare. The power of this one truly did feel atomic. "What the hell do you think you're doing?"

Quinn recognized the voice even before he spun her around. They were beyond busted. It was Officer Ken.

FORTY-THREE

············

Professor Hawthorne reached over the skeleton to grab the syringe, but Annalisa shouted at him before he made contact. "Don't touch it! It's evidence."

He recoiled and gave her a puzzled look. "Of what?" he said, spreading his arms. "Some fraternity gag?"

She didn't know what the skeleton meant yet, but someone had taken care to dress it in a red wig. Natalie had red hair. "I need gloves and a paper bag."

"As you wish," Hawthorne replied, faintly amused as he started digging through drawers at the front of the room. He handed her a paper sack, lunch-sized, and a box of rubber gloves. She bagged the syringe. As she did so, she took time to study the skeleton. It did not look otherwise doctored, but it was posed in a faintly sexualized way, with one leg raised and the knees apart. The head had been turned to face the doorway so it was looking at people as they entered the room. Annalisa looked to the ceiling, where she saw nozzles for extinguishing any fires but no obvious cameras.

"The only eyes in this room are mine," Hawthorne said as he saw her looking. "My office is right down the hall."

"But you didn't see who did this?"

"No."

Sassy sidled up next to her. "What do you think it means?" she asked in a whisper.

"I don't know yet." She dug out her phone and found she had two voicemails from Nick. Wincing, she dialed him back. "Hey," she said. "Sorry I didn't get back to you. I was in the studio with Professor Hawthorne and my phone was off."

"Studio? You mean you actually went to that interview?"

"Sassy drove me."

"Figures," he muttered. "Are you on your way back now? I've got dinner."

She bit her lip and looked at the skeleton. "Uh . . ." There was a beep as a second call came through on her line. "Hold that thought." She transferred over to the other caller. "Vega here."

"Auntie Anna?" Quinn's voice sounded high and frightened.

"Quinn? Where are you? What happened?"

"I'm okay," her niece replied. "But, uh, I think maybe I'm being arrested."

Annalisa's headache surged back with a blinding ferocity and she gritted her teeth. "Tell me exactly where you are. I will be right there."

Sassy read her reaction and looked concerned. "What is it? What happened?"

"I need you to drive me across campus," Annalisa replied. "Right after I get some water to take another round of pills."

She moved gingerly toward the door, feeling around in her pockets for the pain medication. Behind her, Hawthorne complained as he gestured at the skeleton. "What am I supposed to do with this?"

"Leave it," she called back over her shoulder. She found a water fountain and took two pills, after which she and Sassy returned to Sassy's car and Annalisa relayed what Quinn had told her on the phone about her location.

"I thought she was home with Vinny," Sassy said.

"So did I," Annalisa replied darkly.

When they arrived at the obsolete biology building, Annalisa spied Quinn and Zach up against a campus police car, being watched by Officer Kent. He frowned at her arrival. "Don't think this situation calls for big-city law enforcement," he drawled, shining his flashlight in her face.

She put up a hand to stop the glare. "I'm here as Quinn's aunt. What's going on?"

"We were looking for Natalie," Quinn said.

"No one else is." Zach looked like a hangdog, kicking his toe at the pavement.

"That's flat-out not true." Officer Kent turned the flashlight on Zach. "Everyone's looking for that girl."

"Then how come no one's found her?" Zach shot back.

"And you think . . . what? She's in there?" Officer Kent whirled to face the old biology building. "What the hell makes you think that?"

Annalisa was curious too. She folded her arms and looked at Quinn. Quinn gave a half shrug. "We were checking all the buildings that are closed down and no one goes into anymore. We had to do something."

"People think Jason did something to her because of what happened with him up at the cabin," Zach added. "But I know him. He'd never hurt Natalie."

"Okay, okay." Annalisa made a calming motion with her hands. "Did you see inside the building?"

"No, we didn't get a chance," Quinn said. "He showed up to arrest us."

"No one's under arrest," Officer Kent snapped. "But you may face charges."

"Charges of what?" Annalisa asked, putting a hand to her hip.

"Breaking and entering."

She looked at the kids. "Did you break anything?"

They shook their heads. "We were just looking at the window, trying to find a way in," Zach said.

"There you go," she said, turning back to Officer Kent. "They didn't break and they didn't enter. What else?"

He scowled. "Trespassing, then."

"They're students here. It's their home. How is it trespassing to be on the outside of the building?"

"I found this one with a ski mask and bolt cutters," he said, giving Zach a little shove. "What do you think about that?"

"I think it sounds very stupid," Annalisa said, looking from Zach to Quinn. "But I don't think it's illegal or even against university policies." She looked to the dark and shuttered building. "Now, why don't we take a look inside?"

Officer Kent raised his eyebrows at her. "You want to do what now?"

"The kids have a point. No one has searched these properties, right? We're here now. May as well take a look."

"But they—I—we don't have keys." He sputtered and shook his head. "The place is locked up tight. No one's been in there."

"Yeah? I want to see." She hiked up to the front doors and found them locked, as Kent had said. Then she rounded the corner to the back where Quinn and Zach had been caught. Kent, the kids, and Sassy all trailed after her. She took out her own flashlight to examine the back door. "There are gouges on this lock," she reported. "It looks like someone tried to force it."

"It wasn't us," Zach said quickly.

"Like hell it wasn't," Kent returned.

"We didn't touch it," Quinn told Annalisa. "I swear."

Annalisa continued on with her search. The basement-level windows had bars on them. She tugged each one in turn until she reached the fourth, which came loose in her hands. It had been removed at some point and then rested in place again. Annalisa crouched further and pushed on the window itself. It flipped open easily. When she inspected the sash with her flashlight she saw smudges in the accumulated dirt. "Someone or something has been in through here."

"Raccoons, maybe. We get them a lot around here. Kids leave food in the garbage and they come raid the cans at night."

"Yeah? Did a raccoon also burn through these bars?" She touched the smooth end of one. "I'm going in."

"Anna, no," Sassy protested.

"Now you are trespassing," Kent told her.

"Then I suggest you accompany me," she replied to him as she prepared to wriggle feetfirst through the open window.

"If she's going, then so am I," Zach proclaimed.

"Me too," Quinn added.

One by one, the whole group went through the window and into the basement lab. A stack of old metal cages stood in the corner. Somehow the place still smelled faintly like chemicals and dead animals. Annalisa swallowed and pressed onward. "What all is in here?" she asked Kent.

"Labs, classrooms. The usual stuff."

The classrooms were empty, devoid of desks. A chalkboard at the front of the room spelled out GOODBYE in undated, handwritten letters. Annalisa's flashlight beam caught the dust and dirt gathering in the corners and a water stain across the ceiling. Officer Kent focused in on a dead rat lying near their feet. "No one's been here in years."

"What's that?" Annalisa heard a noise—like a scratching, maybe— coming from another room.

"Probably some critter," Kent replied.

They all waited, silent and listening. For several long seconds there was no noise at all, then the scratching came again, followed by what sounded like a moan. "That's no animal," Annalisa said, breaking into a run. She followed the moaning down the hall to the largest lab, and when she entered the room, she couldn't hold back a startled gasp. A young woman, presumably Natalie, lay spread out across a metal table. Her arms and legs had been strapped down but she had freed one foot and was scratching the heel of her shoe across the metal, making the noise they had heard. Annalisa rushed to the girl and started to free her.

"Natalie!" Quinn screamed from the doorway.

"Stay back," Annalisa called over her shoulder. "Call 911."

Quinn tried to get around her but Annalisa pushed her back. "Is she okay? Tell me. Please, is she okay?"

Dimly, Annalisa heard Officer Kent get on his radio to call for help. She worked quickly to free Natalie's limbs but the girl did not open her eyes. "Natalie? It's okay," Annalisa assured her. "You're going to be okay." Natalie was fully dressed, including her coat, making it difficult to assess what injuries she might have. Annalisa did not see any open wounds. Red marks circled the girl's wrists, indicating that she'd been bound there sometime before. Her skin was cold, almost blue, and Annalisa rubbed Natalie's hands to try to warm them up. "Help is coming," she said. She slid her fingers over to Natalie's wrist to check for a pulse. It was slow but steady.

Annalisa heard a sniffle and she turned to see that Quinn had crept closer again. "Oh, God," she hiccuped when she saw Natalie. "What happened to her?"

At the sound of Quinn's voice, Natalie moaned again and her eyelids fluttered. "She heard you," Annalisa said, beckoning her niece closer. "Keep talking."

Quinn took a stutter step forward. "Wh-what should I say?"

"Just let her know you're here." Annalisa cast an anxious glance to the windows. No lights or sirens outside so far. Officer Kent had disappeared, presumably to go open the front doors. They obviously weren't leaving through a basement window.

Quinn took her friend's cold hand. "Hey, Nat, it's me. I'm so glad we found you."

Natalie's eyes cracked open. She licked her lips. "Quinn," she croaked.

"Yes." Quinn was crying openly.

"He—he's real. Gorilla man."

"I know. I know."

Annalisa leaned in again. "Natalie, it's Annalisa Vega. I'm Quinn's aunt. We're getting you help right now, okay?"

Natalie closed her eyes again. She may have nodded slightly.

Annalisa hated to press her, but they had to know. "Can you tell me who did this to you?"

Natalie hummed a non-reply, seeming sleepy again. Quinn squeezed her hand.

"Nat . . . Nat . . . did you hear the question? Who did this?" When Natalie didn't reply, Quinn turned anxious eyes to Annalisa. "Maybe she doesn't know."

Natalie opened her eyes and looked right at them. "It was Jason."

FORTY-FOUR

....

ANNALISA SAW NATALIE JUST ONE MORE TIME, DURING THE FEW IN-BETWEEN
MINUTES AFTER THE DOCTORS HAD FINISHED WITH HER AND BEFORE HER PAR-
ENTS, WHO HAD FLOWN IN FROM TEXAS, ARRIVED TO TAKE HER HOME. Annalisa
did not press Natalie about the abduction; it was, as Zimmer had told
her multiple times, not her case. The troopers would get the pleasure of
interrogating this nineteen-year-old girl about her torture. Maybe the FBI
would get involved. Annalisa wanted to be sure, for Quinn's sake, Natalie
had fingered the right man.

Natalie had her own questions. "Why did he pick me?" Her voice
remained thin and scratchy, but her eyes were determined, boring into
Annalisa's.

Annalisa made a helpless gesture with her hands. "We don't know."

"There must have been a reason."

"I'm sure he had one. But it probably only made sense in his head." If
Natalie was correct and Jason was the kidnapper, then any hope of clar-
ity had died with him in the woods.

"Was it something I did?"

"No, of course not." Annalisa rushed to assure her. Natalie thinned
her lips and looked away. Wrong answer.

"If you don't know why, then you can't be sure."

Here was the crux, Annalisa knew. Natalie couldn't be sure either. She might never be sure of anything ever again. "The important thing is that you're okay," she said, trying to find the light. "You'll recover. You'll go back to your life and he can't hurt you anymore."

Natalie's hair rustled the pillow as she shook her head. "He could have killed me, but he didn't. My life, it's like a gift he gave back to me. Return to sender. Only he did things to me. Things I feel in my body but don't remember." The girl had come back with several different drugs in her bloodstream. No wonder she was foggy.

"You're sure it was Jason?" *Say yes.* Annalisa wanted to believe it was over.

"He wore masks the whole time so I never saw his face. But he kept me in his closet." Natalie's eyes watered and she sniffed. "I saw his hockey equipment with the name on the bag. It was Jason's."

Annalisa knew that the forensics team was at Jason's apartment now. If Natalie had been in the closet, it would be easy to verify. Annalisa heard voices outside the door. Someone was coming and she had precious little time left. "Remember, you're the same person you were before," she told the girl with a tinge of desperation, trying to impart some comfort or wisdom. "You're still you." They'd recovered Natalie's flute, her bag with all her books and papers. Her room was untouched and she could go back to it at any time. Natalie was saved.

Natalie looked at Annalisa with regret, like she was sorry to disappoint her. "No," she whispered. "I don't think I am."

....

ANNALISA FINALLY FOLLOWED ORDERS. She stayed away from the cases—those that were hers and those that weren't—and she convalesced in bed until the headaches disappeared. Nick brought her tea and chocolate cookies, grilled cheese and soup. They watched *The Price Is Right* and argued over the correct price of laundry detergent. He slept curled around her like a question mark and never mentioned the ring in his sock drawer. When, on the fourth day, he had to go to work again, she went looking for it. She pawed through an endless array of brown and black socks, eventually pulling them out, chucking them into the air one by one like an inept juggler. When the drawer lay smooth and bare, she couldn't deny it: the ring was gone. And why not? There was no baby. No family to build. She swallowed the lump in her throat and ran a hand over the empty space. Sassy's voice came back to her: *Isn't this what you wanted?*

She was lying on the couch in her sweats when her phone buzzed to life on its charger by the window. It had been silent for days, so she was intrigued enough to shake off her sloth and retrieve the message. Melissa Chavez had sent her an email with the subject line: *You owe me 27 drinks.* The text explained that Chavez had visited twenty-six bars before finding the one that Sam Tran had been at the night he'd died. *They have video*, she wrote. *Not sure it's what you'd hoped for, but it's attached.* Eagerly, Annalisa swapped the phone for her laptop so she could get a better look at the video. When she booted it up and retrieved the email once more, she sank onto the bed and prepared to see Sam's killer. A chill went over her when Sam appeared on-screen. He looked relaxed and calm, exchanging some dialogue with the female bartender that made her laugh. Annalisa wished there was a way to warn him of the coming horror, but all she could do was watch the video play. He sat at the end of the bar and ordered what appeared to be bourbon. He didn't check his phone or his watch. He didn't turn to the door when it opened like he was expecting someone. He drank slowly, occasionally lifting up the glass to look at it, swirling around the liquid. The Bulls were on TV. He followed along with one eye but otherwise paid no attention to anything around him. When he finished his drink, he ordered a second. When he was done with that, he put a fifty on the bar, thanked the woman, and left. At no point did he speak to anyone. At no point did anyone speak to him. Annalisa went back to the beginning to watch the whole thing again, this time focusing on the other patrons to see if anyone might be watching Sam or following him. Nothing.

Defeated, she closed the laptop and sank back into the pillows. Tran had been close to solving the Queen of Hearts case and probably would have busted Armstrong if he had lived. He had spoken to Jason in his investigation into Quinn's harassment, but nothing in his notes suggested that he thought he was a dangerous stalker. Could Jason have been worried enough to attack Tran anyway?

The windows went black by 5 p.m. as night greedily swallowed up more and more of the day. Nick came through the front door with a gust of frosty air and two paper bags of takeout Thai. Red curry for her and green curry for him. Annalisa picked at hers, still preoccupied by the failure of the video to reveal anything about Sam Tran's death. "Food no good?" Nick asked as he cracked open a beer for himself.

"It's fine."

He sighed. "Maybe you'll like this better. I called up the guy handling Natalie's kidnapping today to make some inquiries."

This did get her attention and she put down her fork. "You did? Why?"

"I was channeling you. Zimmer needs someone to holler at for meddling, right?"

She made a face at him. "What's the latest?"

"The lead is a guy named Ned Ledbetter."

"I don't know him."

"Me either," he said. "But I looked him up and his rep is good. Ex-navy. On the job fifteen years. Anyway, I called up his office and said I might have a lead for him, and he called back twenty minutes later."

She picked up her fork again and stabbed a pepper. "And do you? Have a lead?"

"I told him we'd heard that one of Natalie's professors, Wendell Hawthorne, had been suspected of harassing a girl at his previous school. He wanted to know if we'd IDed the student and I had to say no. He seemed interested, though."

"The press makes it seem like they're heavily focused on Jason."

"Yeah, well, they found Natalie's blood in his closet—right where she said she'd been held."

"Sure, but Sarah Beth admitted she waltzed right into Jason's room and planted the cell phone. That apartment isn't exactly Fort Knox."

"Vega. There's a difference between zipping in to plant a phone and storing a girl in the closet."

She stirred her food. "True," she said grudgingly. Her work phone buzzed from the other room, where she'd left it. "Twice in one day," she said, raising her eyebrows at Nick. "I'm popular."

"I wrote your number on the men's restroom wall. Said you were lonely."

She threw her napkin at him and went to take the call. It was Ned Ledbetter, and he wanted to see her in person. "Is it about what I found?" She had turned over the shoe and the syringe, and she figured she might have to make a formal statement to solidify the chain of evidence.

"It's about what I found," he said. "Shall we say my office, nine a.m.? I'll bring donuts and coffee."

As luck would have it, tomorrow was the first day she was cleared to drive herself again. "Make mine maple bacon," she told him. "See you there."

FORTY-FIVE

....

Nick insisted on coming with her. "I don't need a babysitter," she told him. "I dressed myself this morning and everything." After ten days of looking like an unmade bed, she had showered, put on a suit, and tied her dark hair back into a sleek knot. She was glad for this meeting with Ledbetter. She didn't want to face Zimmer and admit the Tran case had gone cold. Zimmer had put her on the trail of her friend's killer, and Annalisa had not found any answers. Now Zimmer, Tran's ex-wife, Lara, and his son, Benji, would have to live with her failure.

"I show up whether you ask for it or not—like a U2 album." Nick kissed her lightly on the cheek as she assessed herself in the mirror.

She rolled her eyes but reached back to touch his face with affection. "Okay, Bono. But I'm driving."

In the car, she put a nineties mix on loud and even rolled down the windows to celebrate her return to real life. Traffic was lighter than it might have been, as some people took the whole week of Thanksgiving off, and she let the accelerator free. Nick humored her, squinting in the frigid breeze, but she raised the windows when she noticed his cheeks turning pink. "About Thursday," he said, his voice raised over Sheryl Crow crooning about all she wanted to do.

Thursday, she thought. *Thanksgiving.* Her mother had already texted to ask if they should set a plate. Meanwhile, Annalisa was pretty sure that if she showed up, Vinny would boycott. "What about it?"

"I think I'm going to Cassidy's." He gave her a quick glance to see how she was taking it. "To her and her mom's place, I mean."

"Oh. Okay."

"You are welcome to come too."

She shot him a look. "They don't even know me."

"This would be a chance to fix that."

Fix that. God, she'd tried. She had memories of Thanksgivings from years past, Ma and Pops's place stuffed to bursting with people and food. Football on TV. Ma's kitchen steaming. Aunts arriving with trays of cookies. Kids running everywhere, and half of them named Tony. The memory glowed warm, inside and out, but now it seemed like a mirage, a flicker in the dark. She'd spent her whole life trying to get back to that place only to learn it maybe never existed. She had no idea how to fix anything.

"This is it," she said, spotting the address Ledbetter had given her. Inside, a young man at the front desk pointed them in the direction of a fit Black man in his mid-forties who nonetheless had the look of a man going through five divorces at once. His red tie was askew. His desk had three empty paper cups of coffee stacked one atop the other, file folders stacked at the front like sandbags at a levee, while Ledbetter cradled his phone between his shoulder and his jaw, talking to someone at the same time he was typing into a computer.

"Hi," Annalisa said, giving him a little wave but keeping her distance lest the file folders avalanche onto her feet.

"Gotta go," he said into the phone. He sucked in a deep breath and summoned a smile as he stood to greet her. "Detective Annalisa Vega," he said, showing off a perfect set of white teeth. "Live and in the flesh."

"Mostly alive," she corrected. "I'm still on leave."

"Yeah, I heard you notched another serial killer case." He shook his head as though he couldn't believe her good luck. "Those motel murders? People didn't even know they were connected."

"Someone did," she said, thinking of Sam Tran. "I was just following his lead."

"You're too modest. I took the FBI class at Quantico last summer," he told her. "Your name came up."

"Let me introduce my partner," she said, eager to change the subject from her to anything else. "Nick Carelli. He also worked the Lovelorn Killer case, you know."

"Of course," Ledbetter said, shaking Nick's hand. "We spoke on the phone."

"Speaking of," Annalisa said, "I gather whatever you've turned up couldn't be handled by phone."

He tilted his head like he was stalling for time. "I got those donuts you wanted," he said. "They're in the conference room." He led them to a small, windowless room with a long table that took up most of the space. There was an empty whiteboard at one end and several folders sitting on the table, along with a box of donuts and a carafe of coffee. "Please help yourself."

Nick poured while Annalisa assessed the donuts. Ledbetter had ordered two maple bacons and apparently guarded them with his life because the full dozen sat there, untouched, inside a busy cop station. "Sneaked them in at dawn," he said as though reading her mind. His chair squeaked as he leaned back in it as far as it would go. "Look," he said, "I'll be straight with you. My boss doesn't know you're here."

Annalisa paused with a donut halfway to her mouth. "And I'm assuming you want to keep it that way?"

He shifted uncomfortably and tugged at his tie. "We have a difference of opinion on whether to involve you. Also, uh, he used to be drinking buddies with your commander."

"Zimmer?"

"Right."

Annalisa snorted. "I feel sorry for him, then." Zimmer could outdrink men twice her size.

"Yeah, well, she really has opinions on whether to involve you." He pulled a file folder in front of him. "My feeling is that you're already involved."

"Okay, so shoot." She put down the donut, her appetite evaporated. "What is it?"

"Let me back up a second. We got the tox report back on Natalie Kroger and she had the whole periodic table in her bloodstream. Whoever took her, they doped her up pretty good. That's no doubt why her memory is hazy."

"She's given you nothing more on the abductor?" Nick wanted to know.

Ledbetter shook his head. "She's cooperative, but her statements haven't been of much use in elucidating her attacker. Most of my unit, including my boss, is fixed on Jason Wilcox."

"But you're not?" Annalisa asked.

"It'd be nice if it were that easy. Hell, maybe it is. But here's the thing. The tox screen turned up some funky stuff in Natalie's blood sample. They couldn't identify it right away. But a separate analysis on the syringe you found revealed traces of a paralytic drug. Once we had the chemical signature, I had the lab cross-check it against Natalie's sample, and they found she had the same stuff in her system. Her exam at the hospital showed multiple injection marks. The lab boys think the paralytic drug is homemade, like the kidnapper cooked it up in his kitchen. Jason Wilcox was going for a degree in sports management. He took a couple of physiology classes, but no chemistry. So I'm wondering, where'd he get the know-how to make the drug? And why didn't we find any evidence of it when we searched his place?"

"And how did he put the syringe in the skeleton if he was already dead at the time?" Annalisa mused.

Ledbetter pointed at her. "You see my problem."

"What does your boss say?" Nick asked.

Ledbetter sighed. "He says we'll find proof Jason made the drug if we keep looking. Maybe he bought it off the internet or stole it from a buddy."

"Was Natalie's blood on the syringe?" Annalisa wanted to know.

"No, no blood from her or anyone else. It doesn't seem like that particular syringe was used to inject anyone. We are checking it for DNA but that will take a few more days to get results. The only fingerprints on it belong to a student named Byron Lambert. He's an assistant teacher in the biology department, and he also stocks the shelves. The syringe is the same model purchased by the school for experimental labs, so it makes sense Byron's prints would be on the vial. We brought him in for questioning anyway."

"What did he say?" asked Nick.

"Nothing of value. But he was nervous, twitchy. Kept saying he didn't know anything. Like, he said it twenty times."

"When once or twice would be enough," Annalisa concluded. "Interesting. But he can't be the only one with access to the syringes."

"No, there's a whole list of people. We're going through them now. But one particular subject stands out." He pulled out a printed copy of Wendell Hawthorne's informational page from the university website. "I understand you were already looking into him."

"Yeah, we heard a rumor he'd harassed at least one student at his previous institution in Nebraska," Annalisa replied. "But when I called, they gave me the runaround."

"I got the same routine," Ledbetter said. "Lots of 'Legally, all we are permitted to say is that Mr. Hawthorne was an employee here.' But I get the impression they'd like to say more."

"So the lawyers were involved," said Nick, leaning forward on the table. "That suggests it's bad."

"Bad . . . but not too bad," Ledbetter answered. "If there was proof or even a police report, they'd happily pawn my questions off to someone who could say more. This tight-lipped legal mumbo jumbo tells me that it could have been very bad, but everyone involved feels like they dodged a bullet. They're keeping mum and hoping it continues to go flying on by. The discovery of the drug in the syringe and its link to Natalie was enough to get us a warrant for the entire biology department, though. We turned up some disturbing stuff in Hawthorne's office."

He pulled out another folder and pushed it toward her. Nick leaned over so he could look too as she opened it. Annalisa's gut clenched as she saw the photos. BDSM stuff. Men and women in kinky situations with masks and ropes. Some of the images reminded her of the Lovelorn Killer's work. The people in the photos were young, maybe late teens to early twenties, but nothing in the images looked outright coercive. In fact, they had the lighting and sheen of professional porn. "Odd to keep this at your workplace," she said, closing the folder. "But not illegal."

"No, but this could be." He took out another few pictures and spread them out so she could see them. They showed a slim young woman with a pink shoulder-length wig on. She had carefully done makeup with iridescent eye shadow and pink glossy lips. The pink fringe from the wig came down almost to her eyes, which were lined with big false eyelashes. In another picture, the girl cupped her breasts through the black bustier as she made a kissy face for the camera. She kneeled on a bed, but the wall behind her was blank.

"Who is she?" Annalisa asked.

"We don't know yet. But look here. We had this part of the picture blown up." He showed her another photo that had enlarged the foot of the bed by the girl's knees. There was a sticker or label of some sort on the bed. The letters were blurry but Annalisa could make them out. PROPERTY OF IU. "This is a student," she breathed with horror.

"Yes, but we don't know who or even if she's currently at the university. Professor Hawthorne says the images aren't his, that he confiscated the flash drive containing the photos from a student when they were using the stick inappropriately in class. The student never came back to collect it. He says he can't remember the student's name."

"Of course," Nick said flatly.

"I wish I could help you." Annalisa stared into the young woman's face. She did feel somewhat familiar, but Annalisa couldn't put a name to the face. "I don't know who she is."

"Well, there's more." He drew a deep breath. "We used this information to get a warrant to access Hawthorne's work computer. It's clean as far as any pornographic images, but his search history raises some troubling concerns." He took a piece of paper and handed it to Annalisa. Down the page, Ledbetter had highlighted in yellow the related searches.

*Annalisa Vega address, Annalisa Vega boyfriend, Annalisa Vega
shooting
Quinn Vega
Vincent Vega address
Lovelorn Killer photos
Death by strangulation how long
Alex and Cecilia Vega*

"He has ascertained your address, your partner's address, those of your family members, and your place of work," Ledbetter continued as she stared in horror at the search results. "He's entered some of them into maps to get the directions. He's also accessed pictures of you, your brother, and your nieces."

"Why? Why would he do this?"

"He says it was for a podcast interview he did with you. He was doing a background search."

"And for that he needed my address?"

"He says he wanted to drive around in your neighborhood, see where you grew up."

"He went to my parents' house?" She practically yelled the words.

"This is why I thought you should know," Ledbetter said. "We don't have grounds to hold him on anything at this point. He's searched public information and done nothing overtly illegal. He's a free man—one with an intense interest in you, it seems. But maybe he was trying to keep tabs on you to see what you found out about the case."

"What's this guy's deal anyway?" Nick asked as he retrieved a picture of Hawthorne from the file. "He's okay looking, makes a good living, has a bunch of teaching awards. Why's he messing around and harassing his students?"

"I had an English teacher in high school who used to write illegible comments on the girls' essay papers," Annalisa said. "Sassy finally asked him why he did that and he admitted it was because he wanted the girls to come see him after class. You know . . . alone."

"Please tell me they fired the guy," Ledbetter said.

"Got promoted to principal. That's how it goes with these guys. I was sixteen back then and couldn't do anything about it. But Wendell Hawthorne, I can do something about."

"Keep your distance for now," Ledbetter cautioned. "Let us handle Hawthorne."

She made no promises. Instead, she picked out the clearest photo of the pink-haired young woman. "Can I take a copy of this?" she asked. "My niece goes to school there. She might be able to ID this girl."

"Sure, I'll make you a copy. But keep it quiet, okay? I don't want to spook this girl, whoever she is, or alert Hawthorne we're digging around. Not before we figure out what the hell is going on here."

Annalisa glanced at the picture and back at Ledbetter. "You don't think Jason Wilcox was the campus stalker. You think he's still out there."

Ledbetter took his time with a reply. "I think," he said carefully, "Jason Wilcox can't be the end of the story. Not with so many questions left unanswered."

Annalisa and Nick took a donut for the road. Nick ate his from behind the wheel, which Annalisa conceded so that she could stare at the girl's photo some more. "I've seen her before," she said. "I just don't know where."

"We've passed a thousand kids over the last few weeks. She could be anyone. You should text her picture to Quinn and see if she knows."

"Good idea." Annalisa got out her phone, but it rang in her hands before she could snap a picture. The area code was out of state and the number was not one she recognized. "This is Vega," she said.

After a pause, a tentative female voice came on the line. "Detective Annalisa Vega?"

"That's right. Who's this?"

"My name is Emily Carpenter. My cousin Stephanie gave me this number from Zach Spencer. He said you wanted to know about Professor Hawthorne."

"Yes," Annalisa said, sitting up straighter in her seat. "What about him?"

"Well, I heard you were asking about him when he was teaching here in Nebraska. I took his class back then—five years ago, I guess it was? Anyway, he was funny. Everyone liked him."

"Yes, and?" Annalisa willed her to get to the point.

"He was always nice to me, so I, uh, I feel a little bad spreading more rumors about him. It's not like I know anything personally."

Annalisa closed her eyes, feeling the lead slipping away. "I see."

"Zach said you thought Hawthorne might be harassing a girl on campus. But that can't be right."

"Why is that?"

"The student here, the one he was creeping on . . . it wasn't a girl. It was a guy."

Annalisa thanked the young woman and disconnected the call. She stared at the photo in her lap as this new bit of information percolated in her mind. The face blurred and then came into focus again.

"Are you going to text Quinn?" Nick asked from behind the wheel.

"I don't need to contact Quinn," Annalisa said as she picked up the pink-haired image and held it in front of her face. "I know who it is."

FORTY-SIX

···········

Byron had chewed his thumbnail down to the quick. He paced his room at Delta Gamma Nu, floorboards creaking beneath his feet, and his laptop sat on his desk with seven browser tabs open, all to local news. He checked the window periodically to see if the patrol cars were rolling up to bust him. That state cop, Ledbetter, had gotten right up in Byron's face and accused him of taking Natalie. *It's your prints on the syringe, son. If we find even a hint of her DNA on that vial, you're going down.* Byron had thought he might vomit then and there in the interrogation room. But he'd somehow stuck to the story. He knew the truth. No way Natalie's DNA was on the syringe.

A flash of orange outside got his attention. Sienna. She was walking on the path toward the main campus. He felt a fresh wave of nausea at the sight of her. If her DNA turned up on the syringe, he'd be toast. *No,* he told himself. *They don't know about her. They won't be looking for her DNA.*

Sienna stopped and turned suddenly, like she felt him staring at her. He ducked to the side so she wouldn't see him. When he looked again, she was gone. He tried to breathe. She hadn't told anyone his secret. She had promised she wouldn't. But if Ledbetter somehow put her in that hot little room and got his face right up in hers, God knows what she would say. Byron had almost blurted out the truth himself. What he'd done. Who he was.

He wiped sweaty palms on his jeans. Thanksgiving was coming soon and everyone would leave. Everyone but Byron. He'd made excuses to his parents about why he couldn't come, but the truth was he wanted the silence and emptiness. When the campus was deserted and he could walk across it without seeing a single soul, that was when he felt most at home. He just had to hang on for a few more days.

Another flash of movement from outside. An unfamiliar car had turned onto fraternity row. It wasn't a cop car, but he couldn't see the driver. He left his room to go to the front of the house, where he viewed the street below from his lofty perch at the window seat at the top of the third-floor staircase. His stomach clenched when he saw the car had stopped in front of the house and two people got out. One was Annalisa Vega. He should have known she wouldn't leave it alone. Had Sienna told Quinn and then Quinn told her aunt?

He heard the front door open. Footsteps on the stairs. He had the irrational urge to hide under his bed like a child. He ran to his room and slammed the door, backing up until he felt his bed hit his knees from behind. He sank down and watched the door, listening as they grew closer. His eyes screwed shut, his hands in fists, he waited for their arrival like it was a physical blow. When the knock came, he gasped.

"Byron? It's Annalisa Vega and my partner, Nick Carelli. Could we talk with you a minute?"

He looked around desperately, but there was no way to escape. The window led three stories straight down. He forced himself to get up and move stiffly to the door, which he opened to admit them. He knew from the way Annalisa's gaze probed around his room, searching for evidence, that the game was over. The male cop went to Byron's open laptop on the desk.

"How long have you worked for Professor Hawthorne?" Annalisa asked.

It took Byron a moment to parse the question. He was watching the male cop squint at the laptop, taking in the search terms Byron put in for news headlines: *stalker, Natalie Kroger,* and his own name. "Uh, three semesters."

"What's he like as a boss?"

He jerked his attention from the male detective to Annalisa. "Everyone loves him. He's like a god around here."

"I'm asking your personal opinion of him."

"He's okay, I guess." Byron rolled his neck around to loosen it.

"You were working quite late the other day when I visited."

"I have classes during the day like everyone else. At night, I come clean the lab and do his grading."

Annalisa drifted toward his closet but did not open it. Byron's heart started pounding again. *Just get it over with*, he told her mentally. *Say what you know.* She peeked out his second window, the one that faced the rear woods.

"Is it usual to work multiple semesters for one professor?"

He shrugged one shoulder. "I don't know what other people do."

"But you keep with Hawthorne."

"I need the extra money." When the male cop backed off, Byron leaned over and shut the laptop with a slap of his hand.

"Yeah, I checked that on the way over here," she said, taking a step closer to Byron. "He doesn't pay you."

Sweat broke out over his upper lip. She was close enough to see.

"He did pay you the first semester, but not since. He's not paying any assistant this year—at least not on the books."

Byron said nothing. He looked at the empty stand in the corner where his guitar had sat. He'd sold it last month to avoid asking his parents for cash. "What is it you want?" he asked Annalisa.

She took out a folded piece of paper from her pocket. As she unfolded it, he caught a glimpse of pink and knew immediately what it was. He braced himself. "Do you recognize this person?" she asked as she held out the printed photo toward him.

"Wh-where did you get that?" he said in an anguished whisper. He'd never been able to find it.

"Police confiscated it from Wendell Hawthorne's office," she said mildly. "They're trying to identify the student so they can potentially bring charges against Hawthorne."

"Charges." Byron's head started to spin. He sank down onto his bed. It was everything he'd wanted and his worst nightmare rolled into one. No way Hawthorne would talk, so maybe if he kept his mouth shut, he could still make this go away.

"It's you," Annalisa said. "Isn't it?"

He covered his face with his hands. He nodded once. She came to sit next to him on the bed, still holding the picture. He'd ditched the outfit and wig the minute Hawthorne had shown he'd taken the pictures off of Byron's phone. Byron often wore a face mask for part of the cleaning duties, meaning he had to punch in a code when he wanted to check his phone. It was only six digits, easy for Hawthorne to see and memorize.

"Did Hawthorne take this?"

"No." His voice was barely audible. "I used a tripod."

"Then how did he come to possess the images?"

"He took them from me." He risked a look at her. "He does that."

"Why?"

"Ask him," he scoffed. "To have something on us. To make people do what he wants."

"Like for sex?"

He recoiled at the idea. "Not with me. I don't think it's a sex thing. I think he likes knowing secrets. You know, to lord it over you and shit. Like how he made me work for him for free or he'd send the copies to my parents and my brothers here at the house."

"He did it for power," she said, nodding. "I see."

"No," he replied miserably. "You don't. My life is ruined if you let this come out."

"You set up the skeleton in the lab with the syringe," she said. "Didn't you?"

What the hell, he thought. *It doesn't matter now*. He nodded again.

"There was a drug found in the syringe," the male cop said, frowning at him. "The same kind found in Natalie Kroger."

Byron jerked his head up. "I didn't do anything to Natalie."

"Your prints are on that syringe," Annalisa told him. "They were the only ones found."

"I touched it, yeah. I knew she was missing. I thought maybe Hawthorne did something to her. I'd seen him watching her a few times. He held her back after class the week before she went missing. I thought—I thought if I set up the skeleton with the syringe, you'd look into him more. Even if he didn't do anything to Natalie, he's still a creep."

"You had access to the chemicals used to make the drug," the male cop said. "You had contact with Natalie too. She was in the study section you led on Wednesdays."

"Plus, you were here," Annalisa said. "The night of the Halloween party. Another girl was attacked that night, and it started on the other side of that wall." She gestured behind his bed to the next room where Sienna had lain.

The male cop swaggered forward. "Got dressed up like an ape man for Halloween, right? You hung around downstairs for a while, looking for a victim, but you couldn't decide. Then you came back up here and found a girl passed out right next door to you. How convenient. So you decided to have a little fun with your needle."

"No," Byron said, his breathing unsteady. "That's not what happened."

"Tell us," Annalisa urged. "No more secrets, Byron. Tell us the truth."

"I wasn't the gorilla," he said. "I was the cat."

FORTY-SEVEN

....

THE STACK OF PAPER COFFEE CUPS ON LEDBETTER'S DESK HAD INCREASED TO SIX HIGH. He had a seventh in his hand as Annalisa sat across from him and prepared to pitch her idea. From the way he pinched the bridge of his nose with his free hand, she knew she could wear him down. He wanted answers; she had a way to get some. She needed Nick to show up with the materials he'd promised to secure so she could make the demonstration. "Let me get this straight," Ledbetter said. "Byron Lambert, dressed as a female black cat, was in his room alone at Delta Gamma Nu the night of the Halloween party."

"That's why he wasn't in any pictures. He didn't actually attend the party downstairs. He stayed in his room the whole time."

"Until he heard the gorilla guy next door."

"Right. He had heard Sienna go into the room earlier. He'd checked on her and found her passed out from too much alcohol. He rolled her onto her side, put a cup of water by the bed, and went back to his room. When he heard a second person go into the room and shut the door, he got worried. He went back to see that Sienna was okay and found someone in a gorilla costume sitting on the bed with her, preparing to inject her with a syringe. Byron hollered at the guy to stop and the two of them had a physical altercation, during which the gorilla man dropped the syringe. Byron picked it up and kept it."

"He didn't go to the cops." Ledbetter set his cup aside. "Instead he set up that freaky display with the skeleton."

"He couldn't identify the person in the gorilla costume, and the guy got away. Byron hit on the idea to plant the syringe on Professor Hawthorne to make trouble for him, maybe get him fired."

"So he would stop blackmailing Byron with the photos."

"Exactly," Annalisa agreed.

Ledbetter shook his head and blew out a long breath. "I don't know what you want me to do here. Legally, I don't know that there is much I can do. If there's proof that Hawthorne was using blackmail to force Byron to work for him for free, that might be enough to get him fired from the university. But if he says Byron wanted to do the work for extra credit or something, I don't know that Byron could counter that unless he has texts, emails, or other evidence of the blackmail. Plus, now we have him admitting that he had possession of the paralytic drug. I take this to my boss and they're not going to be interested in some phantom gorilla man—they're going to tell me to arrest Byron for illegal possession and possibly even the kidnapping of Natalie Kroger."

"Sienna confirms the presence of the person in the gorilla suit who tried to assault her—who maybe did assault her when she left the party."

"And that may have been Jason Wilcox," Ledbetter countered.

"Maybe," Annalisa conceded. "But Byron doesn't think so."

"Oh?"

"He says the gorilla man seemed familiar to him. His posture, his voice. He convinced himself it could be Hawthorne under there."

"But he can't say for sure."

"No, he can't make a positive ID. The gorilla head stayed on through the whole fight." She looked again over her shoulder to the door for Nick. To her relief, she saw him walking toward them with a bag in his hands.

"My point stands," Ledbetter was saying. "Byron's statements implicate only himself. We have no way of determining who was in the gorilla costume and what role this person may have played in what happened to Natalie."

"Did you get the stuff?" Annalisa asked Nick as he arrived at the desk.

"I had to try three different stores, but yeah." He pulled out a pair of gloves shaped like gorilla hands.

"What are those for?" Ledbetter asked, frowning.

"We know Byron can't ID the person in the gorilla suit. But he doesn't know that."

"You just said he kept his mask on the whole time."

"His mask, yes. But probably not the gloves." She held out the pieces of the costume to Ledbetter. "Here, put these on."

A balding guy at a nearby desk snickered as Ledbetter complied and put on the ape hands. Ledbetter made his gorilla hands into fists and shook them in the other man's general direction. "Laugh once more, Bigby, and I'll come over there and go King Kong on your ass."

"Now here's a syringe," Nick said, reaching into his bag and extracting a plastic-wrapped vial and needle similar to the ones stocked at the university. He took it out and put it on Ledbetter's desk in front of the other man. "Try to pick it up and uncap it."

After a couple of tries, Ledbetter was able to pick the slippery plastic up off the desk. The cap on the needle was tight, by design, and he had trouble getting his gorilla fingers around it with enough force to pull it off. Finally, he stuck the end in his mouth and yanked off the cap. He looked at Annalisa with a triumphant gleam in his eyes. "There. I didn't take the gloves off."

"Right, but you did put your DNA all over the cap."

He blinked in surprise. "Huh. If the cap is still in the room where Sienna was attacked . . ."

"We looked," Nick told him. "It isn't."

Ledbetter scowled again as he tore off the ape hands and threw them down on the desk. "Then what's the point of all this?"

"The guy had to either take off the gloves or put the cap in his mouth to get it off. Either way, he could have left traces of himself in that room," Annalisa said. "And now we have a witness—"

"Who saw nothing," Ledbetter interjected.

"Who can prove he was there," Annalisa corrected. "The person in the gorilla costume doesn't know what Byron may have seen or what evidence might have been left behind. His saving grace right now is that no one is looking. Like you said—your boss thinks it was all Jason Wilcox."

"And none of this proves it wasn't," Ledbetter told her. "So what's your plan?"

"We go public in a big way. Say there is a witness—someone dressed as a black cat the night of the party—and based on the cat's statement, we have a new forensic team prepared to analyze every inch of Delta Gamma Nu."

He had already started shaking his head before she finished. "No way my boss signs off on that. Sending a team costs money—money we don't have. Not to mention, if we're caught out on camera saying the campus stalker isn't Jason Wilcox, we're muddying the waters if it was him."

"You don't have to send the team," she explained patiently. "We just have to make the person in the gorilla costume think we're going to send them. Then we stake out the top floor of Delta Gamma Nu to see who shows up looking for evidence." Thanks to the media uproar over the Lovelorn Killer, Annalisa had numerous press connections. People who owed her. "Jason Wilcox is dead. There won't be a trial for him. This is maybe our one chance to get to the truth."

Ledbetter sank back down in his creaky seat, looking contemplative. "If we go on TV and say there was a witness at the party dressed in a kitty costume, people are going to figure out who it is. Not just the gorilla guy. We want him to figure it out, right? But all the other guys in Delta Gamma Nu are going to know who was in the room next door where Sienna got attacked. Byron's secret will be out—like way out."

"He knows," Annalisa said after a beat. She did not relish this part of the plan.

"And he's okay with it?"

"It's as you said—Byron looks like the guilty party here because he had the syringe. If anyone's facing charges in this thing right now, it's him. He's willing to do this to clear his name and get the guy in the go-rilla costume."

"That's great, but what about his personal safety? What if, instead of hunting around for lost evidence, the gorilla guy comes for Byron and tries to shut him up? Because there is definitely no room in the budget to protect a witness who didn't actually see anything."

"I've got it covered," Annalisa replied.

Nick looked sideways at her. "You do?"

"I do," she said firmly. She had it all worked out. Just as long as Vinny would agree.

FORTY-EIGHT

············

"More meatballs?" Carrie, Vinny's wife, asked Byron as he shoveled in the last bite. He'd put away a meal fit for a starving man. Next to him, Quinn picked at her food and sent Annalisa looks of silent suffering.

"No, thank you, Mrs. Vega," Byron said with enthusiasm. "I'm stuffed."

"I don't understand," Quinn said to Annalisa. "If you think there's evidence in the frat house, what are you waiting for? Why aren't you sending a team now instead of tomorrow?"

They had all watched the news and Ledbetter's press conference announcing that they were pursuing a new lead in the Natalie Kroger case, that there was a second unnamed victim. Sienna had already left for the holiday. She would be safe. Annalisa had made sure the cameras got a shot of her walking Byron back to her car. The gorilla costume was a better disguise than the cat woman getup. It was possible that Sienna's attacker already knew the identity of the person he'd grappled with on Halloween night, so Byron's presence at the police barracks would underscore the urgency.

"Tomorrow is the earliest the team is free," Annalisa lied as she reached for her water.

"I hope they find something," Carrie offered brightly. "Something that can put this whole mess behind us."

Quinn slumped lower in her chair, folding her arms. "We could go. All of us, right now."

Byron looked alarmed at the thought of returning to campus. Vinny shook his finger. "You're not leaving this house, you understand?" He'd consented to the whole thing when Annalisa promised that she, too, would stay in the house. *I'm putting family first*, she'd told him. *Like you wanted.* Quinn and Byron were both protected. She wished she could be staking out Delta Gamma Nu with Nick and Ledbetter, but she knew this was the only way to get Vinny to agree to shelter Byron.

"I made brownies," Carrie said. "I hope you saved room for dessert."

"I love brownies," Byron said at the same time as Quinn stood up and announced, "We're going to my room."

"We are?" Byron asked, confused.

She rolled her eyes and tugged him with her. "We are."

"Leave the door open," Vinny hollered as the kids went upstairs. A moment later, Annalisa heard a door slam. She hid a smile while Vinny made the sign of the cross and muttered something under his breath. He caught her amusement and kicked her lightly under the table. "Glad you find this funny. It's a good thing you never pulled this stuff when you were a kid. Pops would've taken you to jail and left you there."

"I did pull this stuff. Worse, even. You just weren't around to see it." Vinny had been out of the house by the time Annalisa hit her teenage years. "I carried a whole Walgreens cosmetics aisle in my bag to school. What Ma didn't see, she couldn't yell at me about. Sassy and I used to put on a whole new wardrobe before the opening bell."

Carrie rose to start clearing the table. "I once told my parents I was sleeping over at a cousin's house, and she said she was sleeping over at mine. Instead we went to a Pearl Jam concert. We were sixteen." She laid an affectionate hand on her husband's bald head. "Quinn wants to help her friend Natalie. I think that's admirable."

"It is," Annalisa said pointedly to Vinny.

He ignored her. "What if this scheme of yours doesn't work? What if the guy in the ape suit doesn't show?"

"Then we find some way to get a real forensics team in there. One way or another, we're going to nail his ass."

Vinny grunted. "For once, I'm happy to hear you talk like that."

Annalisa helped Carrie clear the dishes and load the dishwasher. Afterward, she found Vinny at the base of the staircase, looking up toward Quinn's bedroom with a worried expression. "Carrie says I can't keep her here locked up like Rapunzel," he said as Annalisa came to stand next to him. "That she'll only get angry with me and then leave anyway. But at least when she's under my roof I have some idea of what's going on. I can protect her. Isn't that what a father is supposed to do?"

Annalisa rubbed his arm. "Come on, let's go sit down in the den. Try to relax."

He let her drag him into the cozy room with an overstuffed couch and a television. Pictures of Quinn at younger ages hung on the wall and Vinny's gaze lingered over them. "So what's your endgame, then?" Annalisa asked him after a few minutes. "Keep her here until you're old and gray, and then take her to the nursing home with you so you can chase her around with your walker?"

He scowled. "Of course not. I just—I don't want to screw up again."

"Screw up how?"

He pinned her with a look. "You know." When she didn't reply, he chuffed and shook his head. "You know better than anyone."

"You mean about Alex?"

Vinny groaned like he didn't want to talk about it. He pushed off the sofa and began pacing the length of the small room. "About Alex. About Pops. About what was going on with Katie Duffy. I didn't know any of it, and I should have."

"Why? I was living in the house at the time and I didn't have a clue."

"You were a kid," he snapped. "A teenager, like Quinn. I was twenty-four, a grown man. If anyone should've confronted Pops, it should've been me. Alex shouldn't have gone over there. He shouldn't have had to deal with it. It—it should've been me." His anger evaporated and his shoulders sagged.

Annalisa got up and embraced him. "It's not your fault. It isn't."

It took him a minute to return the hug. When he did, his arms were first tentative, then strong around her. "It's not yours either," he said fiercely.

The words made tears burn in her eyes. She shook her head and he took her by the shoulders.

"You keep throwing yourself out there into these dangerous situations. Like you think you're disposable or invincible or that you just don't care."

"That's not true," she protested, her voice raw. "I care."

"Yeah? Then maybe you care too much. Me, I'm trying to protect one girl—you're out to save the world. It's not possible, Anna. You'll get yourself killed trying."

Annalisa's phone buzzed. All quiet here, Nick wrote.

Here too, she answered. But it's early yet. She imagined the gorilla man would wait until after night classes were through, until even most of the wild students had gone to bed. It would be a long night. Vinny must have sensed her thoughts. "I'll make coffee," he said.

Annalisa saw she had an email from Ledbetter dated more than an hour ago. *Here's the CCTV footage you asked for, he wrote. It's the same as you had told us earlier. Natalie buys the ice cream and leaves the campus store. There's no indication of who abducted her.*

Annalisa wrote back her thanks and went to find her laptop so she could screen the video from the night of Natalie's abduction once more. They knew from the ice cream in the trash that Natalie hadn't gotten far after her purchase. She intended to make a detailed timeline of events and who was where and when. First, though, a cup of coffee. She paused at the bottom of the stairs on her way to the kitchen, smiling a little at the noise coming from Quinn's bedroom. Quinn had put on music and Annalisa could make out muffled voices as well. Maybe Byron and Quinn would become friends out of all of this. *Everybody needs someone who's been through it*, she thought. *Someone who sees the parts of you that don't cast a shadow.*

FORTY-NINE

....

I DON'T GET IT," QUINN SAID FROM HER PLACE ON THE BED. Byron sat by her desk, spinning the rolling chair back and forth. "Who cares if you dressed up as Catwoman for Halloween? Mark Halloran went as Lady Gaga."

"It's not just Halloween. I dress up other times too."

"In girl clothes?"

He swallowed visibly and gave a single nod. "Yeah."

"Are you like, gay or bi or something?"

He looked at his hands and stopped swaying the chair. "I'm not anything as far as I know."

"What? You've never dated anyone?"

"Nope."

"But you must've had crushes?"

"Not really. I don't really notice that stuff."

She narrowed her eyes. "You're telling me there's no one on Earth who you think is sexy?"

He grinned back at her. "I think clothes are sexy."

"Mine aren't." She flopped back into her pillows with a groan. "My parents sent me to private school with uniforms my whole life, and now that I'm finally free, I can't even tell what works."

"Let me see your closet."

She peeked out from under a pillow. "You're serious?"

He was already on his feet. "Over here, right?" He opened the door and she got up off the bed to stand next to him. "Oof," he said, pulling out a conservative navy polka-dot dress she'd worn to Gigi's baptism. "Not this." He pulled out another plaid number from her school days. "This either. Jeez, you weren't kidding, were you?"

"I have other stuff. Like this." She picked out a pink dress with spaghetti straps and a hip-hugging skirt. Her high school boyfriend had certainly appreciated the length of it.

"It's okay for eighties night. Oh, but this." He selected a tight black sweater with a gold zipper at the back. "This has potential. Where are your skirts?"

She showed him. "You know, that guy Todd on campus—he wears skirts and makeup and stuff. No one bothers him about it."

Byron didn't look up from where he was going through her wardrobe. "Yeah, but have you heard what they call him?"

"I've seen him at the coffeehouse hanging around with people. He has friends."

"I have friends." The vehemence in his words took her aback.

"I—I know you do. I didn't mean to suggest otherwise."

His expression softened as he looked at her. "Look, my parents can't find out, okay? It would kill them."

"They might freak out, but I bet they'd get over it."

"Well, you'd bet wrong." He pulled out a leopard-print skirt and held it up to her body. "Your parents had just you and they were happy. My parents had me as a replacement."

"What are you talking about?"

He held out the black top and a red skirt made of imitation leather. "Try these on."

"First tell me what you meant by replacement."

He sighed and the clothes sagged in his hands. "My parents met in school—the same one we go to now. They were each other's first everything, at least that's how they tell it. They looked at each other and there was never any question they'd be together forever. They got married right out of school and had my brother, Patrick, and then a couple of years later, my sister, Mina. She's an environmental lawyer in California now."

"And Patrick?"

"He died."

"Oh," she said as she finally understood what he'd meant by replacement.

"The summer he was fifteen, he and some friends of his went swimming at the lake. One of the other guys started to drown and Patrick jumped in to save him. But he wasn't that great a swimmer himself, and anyway, there was a rip current and they both drowned."

"I'm so sorry."

He shrugged. "I never knew him. I was born a year later. My parents still have all his stuff, though—his baseball trophies, his soccer trophies. My dad always talks about how Patrick could beat him at golf by the time he was thirteen."

"A real athlete, huh?"

"I swim. My parents enrolled me in classes early, like before I could walk. Turns out I was pretty good at it, good enough to get a scholarship here, at least."

"But . . . do you like it?"

He looked at her blankly. "I don't know. It's okay, I guess. My parents like coming to the meets and cheering in the stands. I don't know what they'd do if I ever quit competing."

"Yeah, but you're not going to compete forever, right? You graduate next year. You're a chem major, not a professional swimmer."

"Try these on," he said, pushing the clothes at her.

He busied himself with her makeup bag while she changed, checking her supplies. When she put on the top and skirt, she smoothed her hands over her hips and faced him self-consciously. "Well?"

He turned and clapped with delight. "*Yas, queen!* See? You have some good pieces in there. You just need to find your style."

"What about shoes?" she asked him. From her desk, the laptop beeped with a new message alert. "Hold on a sec." She went to check it and found it was a message from Zach.

Did u see the news? Cops r talking to Hawthorne's asst Byron.

I know, she wrote back.

They said he's just a witness, but I think they r playing him.

She looked over her shoulder to where Byron was inspecting one of her lipsticks. What do u mean?

He's a sick freak.

"Who are you talking to?" Byron asked her.

"No one." She angled her body so he couldn't see the screen. **He's not a freak. He's nice. He saved Sienna at the party.**

Are u sure? Because I found something.

Her heart beat faster. **What?**

Something of his. Ur not going to like it.

Quinn's mind raced to imagine what it could be. The cops had searched Byron's place and Hawthorne's office—the whole biology building, even. Annalisa wouldn't have brought Byron here if they had found anything worrying. **There's nothing to find,** she wrote to Zach. **Cops searched it all.**

Not his swim locker.

"This color is perfect for you," Byron called over to her. "Or maybe me." He checked his face in the mirror. Quinn bit her lip.

Just tell me what u found. Or tell the cops. She almost wrote that Uncle Nick was on campus but then remembered this was supposed to be secret.

Can u come here & see what I found? It's about u.

She hesitated. Annalisa had been quite clear: neither she nor Byron was supposed to leave the premises. **U come here and show me,** she wrote to him. If it was important, she could take it to Annalisa straightaway. If it was just embarrassing, she could get rid of it. **Come around back to the basement door. DO NOT RING THE BELL.**

She held her breath waiting for his response. Eventually the text appeared on-screen: **On my way.**

FIFTY

....

NICK SAT ALONE IN A HARD CHAIR BY THE WINDOW. The lights were off and the only illumination came from the high moon outside. The frat kid's room he'd borrowed for the night smelled like old sneakers and cheap aftershave. On the wall, Nick could make out a poster showing the evolution of video game controllers, divided into boxes like some kind of Andy Warhol art. Nick had not owned any video games growing up. He'd been raised by his grandma, who hadn't understood such things, let alone been able to afford them. She also could not afford any fancy university. Nick had done classes at a community college during the day and worked nights at a bar. The good-sized room he sat in now, with its wood trim and built-in bookshelves, was the stuff of dreams.

He sat forward to stretch his back and texted Ledbetter, who had parked in the shadows down the block with a view of the front door. He was supposed to alert Nick to anyone creeping into the house, but he'd been silent so far. **Anything?** Nick wrote.

Negative, came the reply.

It was almost midnight. The house was quiet. Half the guys had gone home already. The old house played tricks, though, with a staircase that creaked with the wind. Twice he'd moved for his gun, his gaze trained on the door, only to relax again when no actual footsteps materialized. He yawned and looked outside at the cluster of trees where Sienna had been attacked. From this vantage point, he could see the edge of the makeshift path the students had carved. A flash of movement caught his attention. He moved so close his face could feel the cold through the window. There was a light moving around in the woods. He watched to see if it was a student tramping through the shortcut, but the light did not move in an orderly fashion. It remained in the woods at about the same position, appearing and disappearing almost like it was sending a coded message.

They're looking for something, Nick realized as a chill went through him. He and Annalisa had bet they could lure the attacker to the frat house in search of evidence, but they had neglected to consider he might search the woods as well. That was the scene of the second attack on Sienna. Nick made a snap decision to go investigate. Ledbetter was still watching the front of the house. If there was movement, he would signal.

Nick went down the stairs as quietly as he could. A lone light by the front door cast a diffuse glow, and he saw no one nearby. He crept through the house to the kitchen and out the back door. The flashlight was still bobbing around in the woods but he could not see who was holding it. He didn't dare turn on his own light. He entered the path taking care to tread softly, advancing steadily on his prey.

He heard leaves shifting; a stick snapped. Someone muttered a phrase Nick couldn't make out. A male voice. He saw a dark figure come into view and he reached at last for his own flashlight. "Stop right there," he commanded as he shone the light on the man. "Police."

The figure startled and shone his light right back at Nick. "Who the fuck are you?"

Nick stepped off the path out of the beam so he could see the man's face. It was that campus cop. What did Annalisa call him? Officer Ken.

FIFTY-ONE

··········

VINNY HAD FOUND A CLASSIC BEARS GAME ON TV. He was watching with the volume down while Annalisa sat on the other end of the couch, her laptop balanced on her knees and her notebook in hand. The footage from the campus convenience store that Ledbetter sent her contained the whole night, not just the short part Zach had shown her earlier. She watched students come and go, Zach's hands behind the counter ringing up their purchases. When the video got to 10:03 p.m., Natalie appeared and selected her ice cream. A minute later, as she chatted with Zach while he rang up her purchases, the headlights went past outside. The car was moving slowly and Annalisa ran it back several times to try to get a look at it through the glass door of the convenience store. It was a sedan, and the black-and-white markings suggested it was indeed a university police unit. Officer "Ken" on patrol. Why did he slow down when passing the store? She watched several times but could not see anything that might have attracted his attention—unless, of course, he was trying to see inside the store as he drove past.

Like in *Groundhog Day*, the video always progressed the same way. Natalie met Professor Hawthorne on the way out. The two exchanged words. Annalisa studied the interaction, which appeared cordial, but she noted Natalie gave the professor a wide berth as she moved around him to exit the store. Hawthorne turned briefly to watch her leave and then made his own selections. Then he knocked over the rack of greeting cards, forcing Zach to come out from behind the counter to clean them up. Hawthorne escaped into the night and a few moments later, Jason's face appeared in the glass door. He watched his roommate picking up the cards and then disappeared without entering. The next time anyone saw him, it was at the cabin where he'd been hanged from a tree.

Annalisa checked the time on the video. The whole thing took less than four minutes to play out. Officer Kent, Professor Hawthorne, and Jason Wilcox were all in the vicinity of the store around the time Natalie went missing. Natalie had said it was Jason who abducted her. Maybe she was right all along. Annalisa watched Zach return to his place behind the counter and stopped the video.

Vinny gestured at the TV. "Look at that! It was a late hit on number fifty-eight. Totally dirty."

Annalisa glanced at the screen to see the replay. Vinny was right. The play was over and the refs were mid-whistle by the time the defender launched himself at one of the receivers. But fifty-eight didn't have the ball, so the refs didn't notice. Only the cameras caught the hit.

Annalisa clicked her laptop to let the video continue. No sooner had she settled back to watch when a large guy in a dark baseball cap came in. He picked out a two-liter bottle of Coke and a stick of beef jerky. Annalisa frowned when the guy moved to pay; he was blocking her view of the door and she was trying to see through it to the outside.

"Are you blind?" Vinny shouted at the TV. "Defensive interference!"

"Isn't this game like twenty years old?" Annalisa asked him.

"That doesn't mean I'm wrong."

The guy on the screen had his ID out to pay. Annalisa wished he'd hurry up and get it over with so she could go back to watching the door. Her phone buzzed and she paused the video. It was Nick calling.

"What happened? Did he show?" she blurted as she answered. Vinny muted the TV and stood up to eavesdrop.

"I'm out in the woods behind Delta Gamma Nu," he said, his voice strange. "You're not going to believe what I found."

FIFTY-TWO

············

QUINN LOOKED OUT HER BEDROOM WINDOW AGAIN FOR ANY SIGN OF ZACH'S HEADLIGHTS. She mentally cursed her father once more for taking her phone. Zach couldn't text her when he arrived. She had to go to the basement and wait for him. God help her if he knocked or rang the bell. "I think, uh, I think I'm going to go get one of those brownies," she said.

Byron still had his phone, the lucky bastard. He was scrolling through it anxiously, looking at the headlines related to his visit to the police station earlier that day. "Hmm?" His head jerked up and he saw her lingering by the door. "Oh, yeah. That sounds good." He shoved his phone in his pocket and rose to join her.

"No, wait," she said, and he froze with a funny look on his face. She forced a smile. "I can bring you one."

"I don't mind. I could use something to drink too."

She couldn't think of a way to stop him, so they both went down to the kitchen. The clock on the stove said it had been more than an hour since she'd talked to Zach. He would be at her door soon. Byron admired her mother's collection of ceramic roosters while Quinn sliced up a pair of brownies. She nibbled the edge of hers while Byron wolfed his down.

"You have any milk?" he asked.

"Check the door of the fridge." She could bolt for the basement and leave him there. But if he went running to Annalisa, she'd be busted in a heartbeat. "I think I might watch TV downstairs for a while," she said, trying to sound casual. "In the basement. You don't have to come if you have studying to do."

"No, that sounds good. Can we take the brownies down? Or is your mom strict about that stuff?"

"It's fine." She repressed a sigh and watched as he gathered the tin of brownies and a tall glass of milk. "We'll be in the basement," she called to her father and Annalisa. "Watching TV."

She flicked the lights on and descended the stairs, Byron's footfalls heavy behind her. "Wow, nice setup," he said when he saw the large-screen television and sectional. "Our basement's just full of crap like boxes and old furniture."

She wondered if some of it was his brother Patrick's stuff. "What do you want to watch?" she asked as she picked up the remote.

"Whatever you want," he replied agreeably.

Quinn bit her lip as she looked over at him. Byron didn't seem remotely dangerous, but who knew what Zach had found in his swim locker? She found a *Project Runway* marathon and stopped there. "This okay?"

"Yeah, fine." For someone so into women's clothes, he didn't seem enthused. Maybe he was just tired. She hadn't slept a full night in weeks. She curled into the other end of the sofa and tried not to focus on the back door, which was now behind them. Byron ate a second brownie. The clock on the TV ticked off another few minutes and Quinn's anxiety rose like tidewater inside her. Zach would be arriving any second with the evidence. She had to get Byron out of there. "I'm kind of chilly," she said. "Do you think you could get my quilt from my bed?"

"Uh, sure." He glanced at the stairs. "Gives me a chance to hit the head."

She was awash with relief. "You're a doll. Thank you."

The moment he loped up the stairs, she sprang from the sofa and ran to the back door. She opened it to the cold night and looked out into the dark yard. "Zach?" she whispered. "Zach, are you there?"

No answer. She shivered and took a step outside to look around. "Zach?"

"Boo!" He jumped out from behind her mother's rhododendron and scared the living crap out of her. She barely muffled her shriek and then shoved him hard.

"Not funny," she said as he cackled.

"It was a little funny."

"Quick, show me what you've got." She walked backward to the open door, toward the light. He looked over her shoulder and whistled.

"Nice pad," he remarked.

"Thanks, now what is it you wanted me to see?"

He reached into his jacket and took out a manila envelope. "Check it out. This guy's been following you for weeks."

She accepted the envelope with shaking hands and walked it over to a nearby table. She tilted it upside down so the contents spilled out and gasped with horror when she registered what she saw. Instant pictures of her dating back to the beginning of the school year. Her and Natalie outside their dorm. Her sitting with Jason, his arm around her. Her walking to class. "I don't understand . . ." Byron had been stalking her and she'd never noticed.

"I told you he was a sick freak." Zach looked around expectantly. "You got any beer down here?"

At that moment, the door to the basement opened from above and Byron came down the stairs with her quilt in hand. "I assume this is what you meant," he said and froze when he saw Zach standing there. "What's going on?"

"N-nothing. Zach came by to check on me." Quinn frantically picked up the pictures and stuffed them in the envelope. She had to get upstairs and show Annalisa the photos.

"Hey, man," Zach said easily. "What's going on?"

"Nothing much," Byron replied. He set the quilt on the sofa and walked over to them. "What have you got there?" He nodded at the envelope in Quinn's hand.

"Zach brought me some class notes," she said in a rush. "I should take them upstairs."

"Now?" Byron asked. "I thought we were watching the show."

"Speaking of shows," Zach said, jabbing a finger into Byron's chest. "Saw you on TV with the cops today, my man. You're famous."

Byron moved away from Zach's touch with a frown. "Not really. I just had a conversation with them."

"They said you're some kind of big-shot witness." He looked slyly at Quinn. She looked at the door. Maybe she could run for it. "Is that what this is? Are you in protective custody?"

"Something like that." He turned back to look at the TV. "You want a brownie?"

Zach grinned. He poked Quinn this time. "I told you he wasn't a witness."

Byron turned back around. "What are you talking about?"

"You didn't see a fucking thing." Zach's smile vanished. "Because I was there and you have no clue who I am. The whole thing is a setup, right? Yeah, I figured."

"Zach." Quinn looked at the envelope with confusion. "I don't get what you're saying."

"I do," Byron said, staring at Zach. "It was you with Sienna that night. You're the gorilla man."

"Yeah, and this ain't a banana in my pocket." Zach reached into his jacket and showed off a gun. "We're all going out the back, real quiet-like." With his free hand, he plucked the envelope from Quinn's hands.

"You took the pictures," she said, realization dawning. "They weren't in Byron's locker."

"No, but they will be." He shoved her toward the back door. "Now move."

FIFTY-THREE

....

A TOOTH?" Annalisa said to Nick on the phone. "Whose?"

"No idea. It's adult-sized, no cavity. That's all I can tell you right now."

"What were you doing out in the woods looking for a tooth?" He was supposed to be in the frat house, waiting for the gorilla to show up.

"I saw someone with a flashlight hanging around near where Sienna was attacked, so I came to investigate. It turned out to be Owen Kent."

"Officer Ken? What the hell is he doing out there?"

"He says he saw the news and took our point about possible evidence left at the crime scene. He came to investigate. He's the one who found the tooth buried under the leaves."

Annalisa touched her tongue to her own front teeth, pondering the significance. "Bag it, I guess. And tell Kent to go back to base, will you? We don't need him spooking our guy."

Nick gave a mirthless chuckle. "I mean, I'll try, but he's pretty clear on the fact that he doesn't take orders from us."

"Just get back to the room, will you? The guy could still show."

"Back to ass duty," he said with a sigh. "Got it."

Annalisa hung up with Nick and found Vinny hovering behind her. "Well?" he asked. "Did he get the guy?"

"No, just a tooth." The whole tooth, and nothing but the tooth, she added mentally. *We've got to bust this asshole so I can get some sleep*, she thought as Vinny shook his head. *I've gone 'round the bend.*

She sat down and resumed studying the video. The large man was still at the counter where she'd left him, blocking her view of the door as he waited to pay. She sipped her coffee, which had gone cold, and resisted the temptation to speed up the action. The point was to watch everything that happened, no matter how small. The guy on the screen shuffled his feet and looked around. He appeared to be speaking to someone off-screen. Zach, maybe? He still hadn't paid for his items. Finally, he took the scanner, ran his ID through it, grabbed his groceries, and left. Annalisa frowned at the screen and set her cup aside. The bearded guy had rung up his own stuff.

She reran the video from the time he approached the counter, this time looking for any sign of Zach behind the scenes. He did not appear at any point. This was why it took the bearded man so long, she realized. He was waiting to be checked out and Zach wasn't there. Maybe he was in back getting stock. She waited and watched. Two minutes later, another customer came in—a ponytailed girl in a sweatshirt. She picked out some snacks and repeated the same waiting game the bearded guy had done. Eventually, she plunked some cash down on the counter and left. Annalisa checked the running time. Eight minutes so far since Zach had appeared on-screen.

The store sat empty for another six minutes. A trio of students arrived together, and they took their time picking out purchases, laughing and showing off items to one another. By the time they were ready to pay, Zach had reappeared at the register. She saw his hands and the top of his head when he leaned into the shot. But wait. She froze the video. His forearms were bare. Earlier, he had been wearing a black sweatshirt. Where had it gone? The running timer on the video said it was now 10:27 p.m. Zach had been unaccounted for since 10:06.

The girl at the counter tossed a bag of gummy candy on the counter, the same kind Annalisa had bought when she was last in the store. She had a flash of offering some to Zach and his decline. *Thanks, I can't. Just been to the dentist.* Maybe for a lost tooth?

Annalisa leaped from the couch and pulled out her phone. Vinny followed her. "What? What is it?"

She ignored him and dialed Nick. "You need to find Zach Spencer. Do it now."

"Jason's roommate?"

"Yes, the guy from the campus store." She pounded down the stairs to the basement, looking for Byron and Quinn. "I think he could be our guy. He went missing from the store for a chunk of time right around when Natalie was abducted."

Nick didn't ask more questions. "On it."

Annalisa halted when she saw the empty sofa in the basement. The TV was still on, playing at full volume. "Quinn?" she called, stalking around the room. She pushed open the bathroom door. "Byron?" Neither of them was anywhere to be seen.

Vinny had trailed her to the basement. "Where are the kids?"

"I don't know. Check upstairs."

He went to do as she asked while she checked the back exit. The door was closed and locked. She opened it and stepped out into the cold, biting wind. It swept her hair into her eyes and she clawed it away. Using her phone as a flashlight, she cast a look around. She found a muddy boot print, still wet, on the edge of the cement pavers. Quinn had been in slippers the last she saw, and this footprint was too large to be hers anyway. Byron had worn sneakers.

From the door, Vinny called to her. "I can't find them," he said, his voice tight. "The cars are both here."

"Think," Annalisa said, charging back toward the house. She went upstairs to the living room, pacing back and forth. "Where would Quinn go?"

"Back to campus?" Vinny guessed. "The last time she took off, it was with that guy Zach."

Her blood went cold. "Zach Spencer knows where you live? He's been here?"

"Sure," Vinny said, looking confused. "He came and picked her up."

Annalisa's phone rang. Nick's number flashed on the screen. "Quinn's gone," she blurted as soon as she answered. "Byron too."

"Well, they're not here," he said. "I'm at Zach and Jason's place, and it's completely dark. No one is answering the door."

She went storming back up the stairs. "Okay, then we need to get a BOLO out for his car."

"A black Ford Focus," he said. "It's here. I'm looking at it."

Her heart sank. "What if he has Quinn and Byron? Where would he go?" On the TV, the Bears were taking it to the Saints, running right through their defense, the same play over and over again.

"He's got to have a vehicle of some kind if he picked up Quinn and Byron. I'll check the records, see if he has access to another car."

The Bears running back tore through a line of defenders for another eight yards. "You keep going until they stop you," the announcer guy said. "Run it till it doesn't work."

Run it till it doesn't work, she thought. If Zach had been behind everything, then Jason was innocent. He'd been set up. Zach had probably intended to run the same scheme with Byron and Quinn. "The cabin," she said to Nick. "He's taking them to the cabin."

FIFTY-FOUR

··········

Q UINN'S SILENT TEARS DRIED ON HER CHEEKS AS SHE DROVE THE UNFAMILIAR
CAR DOWN THE DARK HIGHWAY. Her fuzzy slipper felt strange on the accelerator. Beside her, Zach kept a gun aimed at her ribs as he watched out
the window with growing impatience. "Faster," he ordered, and Quinn
nudged the speed over seventy-five miles per hour. She thought about
crashing the car, but Zach had clearly considered this already. He wore
a seat belt. Quinn had not been permitted to fasten hers, and Byron, his
feet and hands bound, lay across the backseat.

"Why are you doing this?" she asked.

"Because Jason wasn't enough. The cops are still looking for me, which
you should know. Your fucking aunt is leading the charge. Turn here."

The car fishtailed as she turned where he indicated. The cabin, she
realized. They were headed back to the woods. The woods where Jason
had died. Quinn tightened her hands on the wheel and tried to think.
"You really believe Annalisa will stop if you kill me? If you kill Byron?
Maybe you missed the headlines where she solved the Lovelorn case. He
thought he was going to get away with it too."

"Shut up." He jabbed her ribs hard with the gun. "Just drive."

"She probably already knows I'm gone."

"Good for her," he snapped, but he turned to look behind them. Quinn checked the rearview mirror again. No one was following them. "Make this left."

When they reached the edge of the woods, he ordered her to pull over and get out of the car. He made her stand in his sight while he leaned in and released the bungee cords from around Byron's feet. "Out," he ordered, waving the gun. "Now."

His hands still bound, Byron scooted awkwardly out of the backseat. Zach looked him up and down. "You know, I appreciate your effort to pin Natalie Kroger on Hawthorne, buddy. Too bad it didn't stick." He turned to Quinn with a sardonic grin. "Let's all learn from your mistakes, huh? Move it." He shoved first Byron and then Quinn ahead of him into the woods.

Quinn stumbled in the dark and caught herself on a tree. Byron couldn't help her because his hands were tied behind his back, but he moved closer anyway. "We have to run," he whispered.

Behind them, Zach stepped in and dragged Quinn back to her feet. "Keep going."

"Run where?" she whispered back. "There's no one here."

"He's going to kill us. Our only shot is to run hard in opposite directions. He can't chase us both."

"I can't—"

She didn't get to finish her statement because Byron veered hard to the left and took off into the woods. With a gasp, she ran the opposite way off the trail. Her left slipper fell off, then the right one. She could barely see anything and branches kept snagging on her clothes. Sobbing, she ripped her upper sleeve free and kept running blindly in the dark. Zach had the keys to the car, but her best chance was to run back to the road and hope someone else came along. Zach had been behind them on the trail. If she tried to double back, she risked running right into him.

Her feet were frozen. She could barely feel her hands. She stubbed her toes on a raised root and had to bite her cheek to still her cry of pain. She ran until her lungs ached from sucking in cold air. When she found a thicket of small pine trees, she ducked inside them and crouched down, panting. Her own harsh breathing made it difficult to hear anything else, so she deprived her lungs for a few precious seconds to listen, straining for any noise that might indicate Zach was following her. She heard only the ghostly sound of the wind in the trees.

She'd lost her orientation. Which way was the road? She peeked out and tried to guess. The moon was high and far away, its silvery light filtered through the canopy of naked branches. Her nose ran and she sniffed. *You can't stay here*, she told herself. *Pick a direction.*

Hesitantly, she stepped out from her hiding spot. She listened again for any sound of Zach. Nothing. She took several steps in the direction she guessed was west, back to the road. The crunching of the leaves at her feet sounded too loud, like someone unwrapping candy in a movie theater. She blinked back more tears and slowed her pace. Even the silence felt scary. She had the creeping feeling he was watching her from somewhere in the shadows.

"Ah!" She flinched when a branch snagged her collar and scrambled away from the prickly thorns. She touched her neck and felt wetness there. Blood. She wiped her fingers on her pajama bottoms and kept going. Eventually she saw something moving up ahead—a light in the dark. Her heart beat faster as she imagined Annalisa coming to the rescue and she had to force herself not to cry out. *I'm here! I'm here!* When she got closer, she peered around a tree and saw the cabin had appeared in the clearing, and now the light was inside it, still moving around. Zach, probably. She did not see Byron. For several minutes, she flattened herself behind the tree and debated her options.

Run the other way. This was the most obvious. Her legs felt like jelly. What if Byron was in the cabin? What if Zach was preparing to inject him with something?

Quinn crept toward the side of the cabin, keeping low and silent. When she got to the window, she peeked with one eye over the edge. Zach was busy taking stuff from his backpack and laying it out on the table. She saw Byron tied to a chair, his chin on his chest. She couldn't tell if he was alive. Zach had laid the gun down on the table to unpack his other supplies. Papers. A syringe. More bungee cords.

Byron moaned and moved his head to the side. He was alive.

She ducked down by the side of the cabin, her heart pounding. If she went in there, Zach would probably shoot her and pin it on Byron. If she wanted a chance to rescue Byron, she had to lure Zach out of the cabin. But how? She felt around in her sweatshirt pockets. All she had was a honey-flavored lip balm and a compact mirror she and Byron had been using to mess around with her makeup. She flicked it open and was glad it was dark enough not to see her reflection. She could throw it at a tree and maybe it would shatter. The noise might draw Zach out.

She tilted the compact as she considered and it caught the edge of a moonbeam, sending a white beam back into the trees. She wiggled it around as an idea started to form. She pushed to her feet and went back to the tree line, where she tugged the string loose from the hood of her sweatshirt. Then she walked to the spot opposite the front door of the cabin and tied the compact about chest-high so the mirror faced the cabin. When it was secured, she hunted around on the ground for a rock about the size of a lemon. She gripped it so hard her fingers hurt. She would have one chance to make this work.

She walked back to the cabin, positioning herself to the left side this time since it was closer to the door. Then she heaved the rock into the woods with all her might, aiming for the mirror. The stone ricocheted off a tree trunk with a loud *thwack*. Her stomach lurched at the noise and the door to the cabin burst open. Zach rushed through it, his gun in one hand and his flashlight in the other. She held her breath in agony. He stalked forward in the direction the stone had landed, shining his light into the trees. As she'd hoped, when his beam hit the mirror, it reflected back at him. He paused for a moment and then moved toward it, like a cat drawn to a laser pointer.

Now was her chance. She darted behind him and into the cabin. Byron was awake but gagged now with duct tape over his mouth. His eyes went wide at the sight of her. She put her finger to her lips and grabbed the syringe. She had no time to untie Byron. Zach would be walking back through that door in about five seconds.

She uncapped the syringe and moved to the side of the open door. She saw the beam from his flashlight enter the room before he did. Heard his footsteps on the porch. She raised her right arm over her head, and the second he appeared on the threshold, she launched herself at him.

FIFTY-FIVE

....

Zach roared as the needle plunged into his neck. The pain he barely felt; he vibrated with rage at this new disruption. He tried to shake her off, but she hung on, clawing at his face. For a petite girl, she was surprisingly strong. He cursed at her and slammed her backward into the cabin wall so her head cracked. The force was enough to make her lose her grip. She slumped to the floor, moaning, and he yanked the needle from his neck. His throat felt like fire and he glanced at the syringe before tossing it aside. She'd used up half the supply.

"What the fuck do you think you're doing?" He grabbed her and yanked her to her feet. Her eyes had trouble focusing, but she was awake. He shoved the gun barrel right up against her cheek and pressed so hard it would leave a mark. "I should shoot you right now. I should blow your brains out right here!"

Behind him, Byron made distressing sounds and struggled against the cords that held him to the chair. All he managed to do was hop around aimlessly. Quinn froze as Zach rubbed the gun on her face but didn't whimper or cower, which further inflamed Zach's fury. She was ruining everything. His finger was slippery on the trigger and he felt an almost unbearable urge to pull.

No, you can't. You can't shoot her. The voice in his head reminded him of the plan. He had to make it look like Byron was the stalker, which meant Quinn had to end up like Natalie. "You stupid cow!" He shoved her away so he wouldn't be tempted to shoot her. He had one more length of bungee cord, and he used it to bind her hands and feet together, hogtied. "Now I want some cooperation," he told her.

She turned her head away. *Bitch.*

He rubbed the side of his neck and bent to retrieve the syringe. "You should've paid more attention in class," he told her as he held it up. "You need a vein for this to work. Maybe you'll understand later when I give you a demonstration." He didn't have the full dose, but there should be enough to incapacitate her for a short time—long enough to let him do what he wanted. He turned to Byron. "And maybe you can watch." He leaned over and patted the guy's cheek. "You'd like that, wouldn't you? Sicko."

He went to the desk where the lantern illuminated the papers he'd brought with him. A typed confession saved time but wouldn't be as convincing as if Byron had written it by hand. Zach took the paper and went behind Byron's chair, where his hands were bound. He knelt to press Byron's fingerprints in multiple spots across the page. Byron struggled, trying to curl his fingers away from Zach, but Zach forced them back into place so hard he heard one snap. Byron gave a muffled yelp of pain.

"Stop it!" Quinn shouted from where she lay on the floor. "You're hurting him."

When Zach rose to face him once more, he saw the other man's face was wet with tears. "Aw," he said with mock sympathy. "I'm sorry." He rubbed the paper on Byron's face. Tears would be a nice bonus.

Zach returned the confession to the table and picked up the syringe again. He halted when he heard a distant noise. A siren? He rushed to the windows and peered out into the dark. Yes, a siren was approaching. More than one from the sound of it. "Shit," he screamed out the window. He repeated it several times for good measure.

"It's Annalisa," Quinn said, her voice taunting. "I know it is."

"You shut up!" He grabbed the gun and aimed at her. "I'll kill you both before she gets here."

Her eyes went wide and she did look afraid now. *Good.* "That—that's stupid," she said, her voice high and frightened. "Let us go. They'll go easier on you if you do."

"I said *shut your hole*. I need to think." He took the duct tape and put a stretch of it over her mouth. The sirens had stopped. No doubt he had an army of cops tramping their way through the woods toward him right now. It was all going to hell. He paced the length of the cabin. "I didn't even get to see her die," he muttered.

He looked at Quinn accusingly. Quinn stared up at him with huge round eyes. "I know what you're thinking," he continued. "What about Jason? Didn't I see him die? But Jason didn't count. That was business. I didn't want to do it, but he gave me no choice. He came home while I still had Natalie."

He checked the window, staying to the side, and he saw a line of flashlights advancing through the trees. Whatever his next move, he had to make it soon. Sweat broke out across his neck as he watched the lights get closer. He fired out the window—a warning shot. "Stay back!" he shouted. "Stay back or I'll kill them both."

The flashlights halted their progress. He'd bought a bit of time. *Think*, he told himself. *Think*. The syringe, the confession—they were all pointless now. He'd lost. That's how the story ended. He'd be nothing but another notch in Annalisa Vega's belt.

"Zach Spencer." A man's voice, loud and authoritative, crackled through a megaphone. "This is the police. We have the cabin surrounded. Throw out your weapons and come out with your hands up."

Zach risked a peek through the window. A pair of floodlights lit up the front of the cabin like Christmas and he could see nothing beyond them. He cursed under his breath and moved away from the window, stalking back and forth in front of Quinn and Byron.

"Zach Spencer. Come out with your hands up." The male cop repeated his orders. "We don't want to harm you."

Zach let out a dark laugh. They would shoot him the first chance they got. He stared at Quinn as an idea started to crystallize in his brain. He couldn't win this game, but he could even the score a little. He went to the window. "Where is Annalisa Vega?" he shouted, taking care to stand to the side where they couldn't see him. "I want Vega."

He turned back to Quinn. "The Lovelorn Killer didn't take her down," he told her. "He killed a whole bunch of people but not Vega. I get her, and they'll remember me forever no matter what happens."

Quinn looked horrified. She struggled against her bonds but it was no use. Zach knew how to tie a knot.

After a minute, a female voice came over the megaphone. "This is Vega. What do you want?"

It was her. He returned with caution to the window. "I have Quinn," he shouted.

"I know," she replied. "And I have about thirty cops out here. So I repeat: What do you want?"

"I want you to come in here."

He waited, his heart hammering. She made him wait a full minute for her answer. "You want to meet? You come out here."

"No fucking way," he hollered back. "You want to play with me? I'll make you a different deal. You come in here or I'll shoot her."

"No one needs to get shot," Annalisa replied.

"Sure, sure. That's why you brought all the guns."

"Let us help you," she said, and he broke into a hysterical laugh.

"You don't want to help me." He sobered and wiped his mouth with his sleeve. "You have two minutes to decide: come in here or I put a bullet in your niece's skull." He yanked at the cord holding her legs and arms behind her back until it came free and then tugged her to her feet. "Say hi to your auntie," he growled, shoving her into the window so the spotlights could pick up her face.

After ninety seconds or so, the megaphone crackled to life again. "Send out Byron," Annalisa said.

Zach had almost forgotten Byron existed now that he was no use to him. He turned to the chair and considered.

"Send out Byron and I'll come in," Annalisa said again.

Zach didn't see a downside to this plan. Anything to get Annalisa to walk unarmed through the front door. He imagined her face when she realized she'd been trapped. *Aim for her head*, he told himself. *She's probably wearing a vest.* He knew he'd only get one shot. Then the rest of them would come storming in, bullets flying.

He released Byron from the chair and nudged him toward the door. "Slowly," he ordered, keeping the gun at Byron's back. "I don't give a fuck if I have to shoot you." He had Byron open the door wide enough to escape. Zach watched him stumble toward the bright lights, his hands raised in surrender. What a pussy. He slammed the door shut and returned to stand near the open window with Quinn, using her body to shield his own. "Okay, you've got him. Now you come in here."

"I want Quinn to come out first."

He laughed. "No fucking way. You come in, then she can leave."

He detected some movement in the shadows behind the floodlights as the cops considered the request. He waited with growing impatience. "Hey, I did what you said. I gave you Byron. Now I want Vega."

Quinn moaned softly in protest and shook her head, like she was trying to signal her aunt it was a bad idea. Zach jammed the gun in her ribs. "Don't make a sound. Don't even blink, you got me?"

After another minute, he heard Annalisa's voice again. "Okay," she said. "I'm coming in."

He strained around Quinn to see, but the spotlights caught his eyes. All he could make out were the tops of the trees and some moving shadows. "No gun," he yelled out the window. "I want to see your hands."

He waited, breathing hard, and eventually he saw a female form with dark hair emerge from behind the lights. She was in silhouette and he couldn't see her face. "Hands!" he yelled at her again.

She raised both hands so her palms were even with her shoulders. "I'm unarmed," she called, and he heard that it was Annalisa. The trap was working.

"Slow," he ordered her. "No sudden moves."

She advanced one step at a time. "Don't do anything stupid," she said. "Just stay calm."

"I am calm!" He licked his lips and dragged Quinn backward with him so they were positioned by the door. Vega was getting closer. He listened hard for her footsteps on the porch. "Where are you?" he cried. "Get in here!"

"I'm coming. I'm almost there."

There. It was happening. The porch creaked, and his whole body went taut. Sweat poured down his forehead and into his eyes. Quinn sobbed behind the duct tape as the doorknob turned and he threw her to the ground so he'd have a clean shot. The door widened, bright white light spilling in, illuminating Annalisa from behind. He heard himself scream as the gun went off.

When he hit the floor, he didn't feel immediate pain. Only shock. He heard voices, people streaming in. He struggled to look up and saw a woman he didn't know staring down at him. She wore a speaker around her neck. "Wh-what?" he gasped as he tried to understand.

"Get the medics," said Annalisa from behind him.

He jerked his head to see and there she was. She'd come in from the rear somehow and she was wearing a headset. He'd been tricked. "Y-you shot me," he rasped.

She removed the tape from Quinn's mouth and hugged the girl close to her. "You wanted me to come in," she told him. "You didn't say how."

He let his head fall back on the floor. He couldn't feel his legs.

"He was going to kill you," Quinn said in a trembling voice.

Blackness threatened to overtake him. He tasted blood in his mouth as an EMT knelt to assess the gunshot to his back. As his eyes went closed, Zach heard Vega's reply, sealing his defeat: "He won't be killing anyone anymore."

FIFTY-SIX

....

S HE'D SOLVED TWO OF SAM TRAN'S OPEN CASES BUT NOT SAM'S DEATH ITSELF. To try to change this, Annalisa visited Zach in the hospital, hoping he might confess to Sam's murder. Doctors had removed her bullet from Zach's spine, but the damage was permanent. He would never walk again. She went primarily to ask him about Sam Tran, but she also sought deeper answers. He was barely legal, just eighteen months older than Quinn, a girl Annalisa remembered as a chubby-cheeked baby not so long ago. How could Zach have gone this wrong, this quickly? He was human, like her, like Natalie Kroger and Jason Wilcox. They were made of the same flesh, had the same beating heart. Annalisa hoped to see a sign that there was a person inside him worth saving.

He appeared harmless enough on the outside. His shaggy hair touched his shoulders now. His blue eyes were hooded and dreamy as he looked at her. In another life, he could have been fronting for a nineties boy band. He gave her a crooked grin when she asked about Sam Tran.

"That PI dude. Yeah, I saw him poking around campus asking questions."

"He talked to you?"

Another grin. "Nah. He never even saw me."

Annalisa didn't know whether this was the truth, but she had nothing to prove it wasn't. "Mr. Tran was found hanging, the same as Jason Wilcox." If Zach had murdered one, then he could have easily killed the other.

"I heard that. Where do you think I got the idea? It worked, too . . . for a while." He grimaced and shifted in the bed. "I had you fooled."

"Yes," she acknowledged. "You fooled a lot of people. Where did you get the recipe for the drug?"

"Internet. But I made my own tweaks." He looked proud of himself. She played into that.

"Smart. But how did you even get the idea?"

"Dahmer."

"Dahmer?"

He shot her a pitying look that she didn't follow his logic. "Jeffrey Dahmer? He was trying to make living zombies—you know, people who were awake but couldn't leave him. He just went about it the wrong way."

"But you figured it out."

"I got closer. But I didn't get a chance to finish my experiments."

The casual way he said the words gave her chills. He was right that Sam Tran hadn't seen him. Sam had been looking for a prankster, a jealous boyfriend. Zach Spencer was another species. She searched his face and found it young and smooth. Blank. Inviting you to see what you wanted.

"I don't get it," she said. "You're obviously brilliant. You had friends, a future. You could be anything you wanted. Why choose this?"

He looked at her with mild surprise. "Look at you. You caught the Lovelorn Killer. You could have written your own ticket—a book, a movie deal. You could have made millions off him. Instead you're just another foot soldier, a nobody. You think the badge makes you special, but it's so easy to obtain. How many of you are there in Chicago alone?"

"I'm the one who got you."

His face transformed, revealing the rage his victims must have seen. He tamped it back down and forced a plastic smile for her. "For now," he said. "But I think one day you may find you'll wish you'd killed me when you had the chance."

Annalisa didn't want to imagine a world where she wished a twenty-year-old kid dead. She got up and left him there. She'd found Jason's killer and Natalie's abductor, but in him, she failed to find any answers.

Maybe you have to make your own answers. Certainly, that's what she gleaned from wrapping up the Queen of Hearts case. She had thought that Brad Morrison and the Powells would be relieved to have an answer as to who killed Stephen and Kathy that night at the Springwood Inn. Each side had spent the better part of a lifetime blaming the other. In truth, the lovers simply had the unfortunate luck to cross paths with Matthew Armstrong. After so much blood, sweat, tears, and money, so much vitriol, she'd thought the truth would set them free. Instead, Amos Powell refused to accept it. "Brad Morrison was there at the motel the night Stephen and Kathy were murdered," he'd said, his arthritic hands wrapped around his cane. "You've proven it. Maybe he hired this Armstrong fellow to do the killing."

Annalisa had explained about the second motel murders, the deaths of the Adkins couple, but Amos wasn't having any of it. He vowed to hire another investigator to uncover a link between Brad and Armstrong. Annalisa had no choice but to leave Amos there with his yellowed papers and his stubborn insistence that he knew who was really responsible for the death of his son. Maybe it was easier for Amos to believe there was a reason for Stephen's death, some meaning in it. Maybe letting go of his anger would mean finally letting go of his son.

Now Annalisa was the one who had to let go. The Tran case had hit a dead end. She had had to face Sam's family and admit her failure. When Annalisa entered the conference room, Lara clutched her purse on her lap, as if for protection, and Benji put down his phone and looked up expectantly at Annalisa. She pulled out a chair across from them and laid down her files. Sam's family wouldn't get to see the details; they were merely set dressing to show that Chicago PD had tried their best to find Sam's killer. Annalisa explained that she had exhausted all avenues: Sam's finances were unremarkable, with no apparent irregularities; his business was intact; he had no romantic entanglements, no addictions, no debts or serious enemies. The one guy with a beef against him, the neighbor who'd argued over the parking spot, had a solid alibi.

"So that's it?" Lara asked when Annalisa had finished her recitation. "Case closed?"

"No, we won't close it." Closed suggested a resolution, and Annalisa had none.

"But you won't be investigating further."

Annalisa's cheeks turned hot. She cleared her throat. "We will rigorously follow up any new leads that come in," she said carefully.

"My dad would've kept going." Benji's wounded brown eyes held a challenge in them. "When I asked him why he didn't keep being a cop, he said cops didn't get to pick which bad guys they went after. He said that's why he went into business for himself: he could help people when the cops gave up on them."

"Benji, that's rude," Lara cautioned.

Benji slumped lower in his chair. "I don't care. It's the truth."

"He's not wrong," said Annalisa. "I wish I could keep digging. Lynn Zimmer wishes the same. The hard truth is that we have nowhere else to look right now."

"You'll have to forgive Benji," Lara said as she brushed a lock of hair from his eyes. He pushed her hand away. "This has been especially hard on him. He and Sam adored each other."

"Of course," Annalisa replied with feeling. "I am sorry I don't have better news."

Lara sniffed and nodded. When she raised her head, her eyes were clear. "Sam faced death many years ago with his cancer. When he beat it, he became hypervigilant—always looking for the enemy to return—but he also lived each day with purpose. With love. With honor." She brushed her son's hair back again, and this time, he let her. "I must believe Sam died the same way. Maybe this is truth enough."

When the Trans departed, Annalisa made one last pitch to Zimmer. "There's still the Osteen case," she said as she stood in the commander's office.

Zimmer leaned back in her seat. "Who?"

"Sam Tran's third open case. Nina Osteen hired him to find her missing mother."

"Right, I remember now. The mother disappeared in 1989," Zimmer said pointedly, emphasizing the year.

"I know it was a long time ago, but I could still check it out."

"Didn't you say that Sam only met with this woman one time?"

"Yes, but I—"

"And he'd barely started work on the case?"

Annalisa gave a resigned sigh. "Yes."

"Seems highly unlikely it's related to his death."

"It's still an open missing person case," Annalisa ventured.

Zimmer narrowed her eyes. "Then let Missing Persons deal with it." They both knew no one would touch a decades-old case without some solid new lead.

Annalisa gave a frustrated hum and braced her hands on the back of the nearby chair. "It feels like giving up," she said eventually.

Zimmer peered at her over the rims of her glasses. "You think I want to back off? Sam was my friend. I'd like to assign every detective in the city to his case. Hell, get every uniform out there too. Go door by door until we find a witness—someone, anyone who saw Sam with his killer that night. But it's been almost a month since he died. In that time, I've had ten fresh homicides and three dozen armed robberies come across my desk. What am I supposed to tell these people and their families? Sorry, we're busy?"

Annalisa recalled what Benji had said about his father, about how cops don't get to choose their cases. "It just doesn't feel like enough."

"I know." Zimmer took off her glasses and rubbed her eyes. "That's the thing they don't teach you. You hear horror stories about who did what to whom—babies shooting other babies. My training officer, he once had to arrest an eleven-year-old for murder, and the cuffs didn't fit around the kid's itty-bitty little wrists. 'You'll come home with blood on your shoes,' they'll tell you. 'You'll find out what the inside of a person's skull looks like.' And it's all true. You do this job long enough, Vega, and you think you've seen everything. What they don't say is that sometimes you arrest no one. Sometimes you find nothing. And that's the hardest part of all."

FIFTY-SEVEN

....

ANNALISA BOXED UP EVERYTHING SHE HAD ON THE TRAN CASE. When she came to the last item, the piece of paper she'd taken from his condo that read *Sally Johnson, 1999*, she paused. This was the one bit from Tran's notes she had not tied to any of his open cases. On a whim, she sat down at her computer to run the name and date. Plenty of Sally Johnsons, but no obvious matches. Dejected, she fished out the Osteen file and gave it one last look. There was a statement from Charlotte's husband, Mitchell Osteen, taken three days after she went missing. *I thought she was off somewhere, hung out to dry*, he said. *She did that sometimes. I'd accuse her of going out to get wasted, she'd deny that was her plan, and then when she got loaded up as usual, she'd hide out for a few days rather than come home to admit I was right.*

The witness, Joey Fuller, provided a statement too. He'd been parked in the lot across the street from the bar, changing a flat tire, when he saw a woman matching Charlotte's description leave with a man. *They looked real friendly. I saw them kissing by the door as they left. Then he helped her into his car and they drove off together.* He did not get a license plate. The best he could say was that it was a white sedan. The guy maybe had a beard. Or maybe he didn't. No way to be sure.

"Some witness," Annalisa muttered as she pressed onward. There were statements from some of Charlotte's drinking pals and people at O'Malley's Bar. They backed up Mitchell's statements about Charlotte's behavior. She drank, often a lot, and she'd crash with one of them for the night if she didn't think she could get home okay. Witnesses from O'Malley's party on New Year's Eve remembered Charlotte attending. Two different guys swore they kissed her at midnight, but a waitress claimed Charlotte had already left before the big countdown. This witness gave her name as Sarah Johnson. Annalisa sat up straighter as she registered the name. Sometimes Sally was a nickname for Sarah, wasn't it?

She looked across the desk at Nick. "How would you feel about lunch?"

He made a show of checking his watch. "It's ten past eleven."

"I'm buying."

He grinned and grabbed the coat from the back of his chair. "Then I'm eating."

In the car, she made a turn to take them south, and Nick swiveled his neck to look backward. "Something wrong with the food in our neck of the woods?"

"I have a particular place in mind, that's all."

She drove down near the lake's edge. Nick, who had begun shooting her speculative looks as their journey wore on, groaned when he saw the sign for O'Malley's Bar. "I know what this is. It's where that woman disappeared, the one Tran was looking into. Didn't Zimmer tell you specifically to move on?"

"She said I could keep going if I found a new lead."

"Which you haven't."

"How am I supposed to find something without looking for it?" She used her overly patient voice, trying to sound reasonable. Nick squinted like he wasn't buying it. She sighed as she cut the engine. "Don't you resent it sometimes, how we're told which cases to care about and for how long?"

"No," he replied immediately.

She raised her eyebrows at him in surprise. "No?"

He thought for a moment and then scooted closer to her. "Of course there are unsolved cases that eat at me. You want to close them all, right? But no. I need someone else making the calls because God knows I can't do it. I'd drive myself right off a cliff."

"It makes me nuts sometimes, how we decide. Who counts and how much. We've got budgets and time sheets and someone on the radio who tells us where to go. Charlotte Osteen's file is about three sheets thick. This was a person, a mother with a small child at home, and nobody even looked for her. I'm suggesting we take the length of one lunch to see what we can find. Don't you think we owe her that much? Don't we owe Sam?"

Nick stared straight ahead for a long moment. "Off a cliff," he muttered as he opened his car door. "And I'm riding shotgun."

Annalisa smiled as she joined him. "Yelp swears they have great fish and chips."

O'Malley's was only about one-third full but sizable enough to hold a crowd of more than one hundred and fifty, which was the estimated total from New Year's Eve the night Charlotte Osteen disappeared. Annalisa liked the overhead beams and the many photos on the wall. O'Malley's clearly catered to a regular crowd. She and Nick sat at the bar, where they both ordered the fish and chips.

"You know, these are pretty good," Nick said around a mouthful.

"It's the horseradish sauce," replied the female bartender.

"I'd love the recipe," Annalisa said. "Is the owner around?"

The bartender looked skeptical, then wary. "Mac?"

"Not O'Malley?" Nick joked.

She wrinkled her nose. "You know, I don't think so. But I don't know his last name. Everyone calls him Mac."

Annalisa showed off her shield. "Could we talk to him? I'd love to thank him for the meal."

The bartender went into the back and did not return. Instead, a white-haired, bearded guy in a plaid shirt came out. "A bit early for Santa, isn't it?" Nick said under his breath as the man frowned at them from across the bar. Annalisa smothered a smile.

"Lisa says you're asking to speak to me," the man said as he took her place behind the bar. "Mac Taylor. I'm the owner."

Annalisa shook his hand. "Your fries are delicious."

"Thanks," he said flatly. "They're free, of course. Compliments of the house. We always back the blue here at O'Malley's."

"Oh, no." She didn't come to shake him down for a free lunch. "They're worth every penny," she said as she produced her wallet. "I hoped to ask you a couple of questions. How long have you been the owner here?"

"Since 1981."

"I was looking at some of your photos. It looks like you throw a great party."

"We've had some barn burners over the years." He folded his arms across his broad chest. "What's it to you? You looking for a place for the Policeman's Ball?"

"I'm curious about your New Year's Eve event."

"That's more than a month off."

"New Year's Eve, 1989," she corrected, and he narrowed his eyes at her.

"This is about that lady. The one who went missing."

"You remember her?" Annalisa leaned in with interest. Even Nick looked intrigued.

"Sure, Charlie came in here a lot back then. Sweet gal. Loved her vodka tonics."

"Maybe a little too much?" Annalisa ventured, and Mac looked down at the bar.

"I never overserved her."

"Sure, you didn't."

"I didn't," he said, indignant. "She'd get other people to buy for her. A guy here, a guy there. Everyone was happy to buy for Charlie if she smiled at 'em just right. Not much I could do about that. If I caught her doing it, I kicked her out."

"And let her drive home?" Nick asked.

"She could walk from here," Mac replied. "Had a husband and a young kid a few blocks away."

"What about New Year's Eve?" Annalisa asked.

He shook his head. "Don't know what happened to her. It was crazy that night. She was here for the countdown is all I know. What happened to her after that . . ." He broke off with a shrug. "You people were supposed to figure that out."

"What do you think happened to her?" Nick asked, curious.

Mac picked up a rag and started wiping down the bar. "Nothing good," he said gruffly. "I heard she got in a car with some guy, a guy she met here. All I can say is it wasn't one of our regulars. They'd have never hurt Charlie like that."

"One of your waitstaff, Sarah Johnson, gave a statement about the New Year's Eve party. She said Charlie may have left early, before the countdown. The witness from outside seems to corroborate that fact, but we're hoping to talk to Ms. Johnson about what she saw. Do you know where we can get in touch with her?"

He grunted. "Try a psychic. Sally's dead."

She was called Sally, Annalisa thought. *So much for that lead.* She wondered why Sam Tran had thought her name important enough to write down.

"Anyways, if Sally said that about Charlie, she was wrong. Charlie was here for the countdown."

"How can you be sure?" she asked.

"I can show you." He jerked his head to the photos on the wall. They followed him over where he showed off two framed photographs. "These were both taken that night." One was a close-up of about six people with their arms around each other. Another was a huge crowd shot. The cameraman had stood on the bar to take the picture from above. "That's Charlie," Mac said, pointing to a woman in the front row. "She was here for the countdown because we take the group picture right after that. Where she went after, I can't say."

Annalisa leaned in. Charlotte "Charlie" Osteen was smiling with a drink in her left hand. She wore a white jacket with fringe tassels, a denim skirt, and white cowboy boots. Her right arm was around a burly, balding guy wearing a black T-shirt with the sleeves cut off along with a clip-on bow tie. "Who's this?" Annalisa asked Mac, pointing out the guy.

"That's Bill Powers."

"He looks friendly with Charlie."

"Sure. Bill's friendly with everyone. Or he was. He lives with his daughter over in Fort Wayne now."

"We're trying to figure out if Charlie left with a guy the night of the party," Annalisa said.

"Well, if she did, it warn't Bill. He closed down the place. Helped me clean up."

Annalisa frowned at the picture. "Do you think I could take this and make a copy?" She wanted to see if she could ID the other men in the photo.

"Sure, knock yourself out."

Annalisa took the photo off the wall. It had hung there long enough that the paint behind it was a brighter shade of green than its surroundings. She touched the border with one finger. "I'll make sure to get it back to you," she said.

They paid for their food and went outside to the car. Annalisa unlocked it but didn't get in. She looked across the road to the parking lot. "That must be where the witness was changing his tire. Joey Fuller." She stuck the photo in the backseat and went across to the lot. Nick followed her.

"What are we expecting to find here after more than thirty years?" Nick stuck his hands in the pockets of his overcoat as the Chicago wind picked up, screaming off the lake. Annalisa shivered.

"I don't know." She tried to imagine how it had gone down. "He got the flat on the road and pulled in here to fix it." She pointed at the street and then at the lot where they stood. The bar was about fifty yards away, but it had outside lighting and the streetlamps were plentiful.

Nick cocked his head. "Were the curbs like this at the time?"

She looked to where he indicated the traffic-calming barriers in the parking lot. "Not sure. Why?"

He moved to the entrance of the lot. "The witness, Fuller, he pulls his car in here."

"Van," she corrected.

"Van, okay. That's even weirder."

"What do you mean?" she asked.

"Well, he'd have to pull over this way, avoiding the curb. The spaces facing the bar are compact-only."

"So he parked across them rather than in them." She eyed the spots. "Plenty of room. Or maybe he didn't take a space at all, just stopped here in the middle. It was midnight on New Year's. Not like there were a lot of people at the pet shop or the hair salon."

"Yeah, okay, so we agree. The van was probably pointing south, like this. And then he gets out to fix his tire like so." Nick went through the motions like the van was really there. "There's just one problem."

"What's that?"

"You can't see the entrance from here."

"Wait, what?" Annalisa whirled around and saw he was right. From this angle, she could see the side of the bar and the entrance to its parking lot. Fuller's statement clearly said he'd seen Charlotte with some guy, kissing just outside the door, and then getting into a dark sedan together.

"Maybe . . . maybe he wasn't in the lot. Maybe he was parked on the street?" She backed up far enough so she could again see the entrance to O'Malley's.

"Or maybe he lied."

If Joey Fuller had lied, then Charlotte didn't get into a white sedan with some stranger the night she disappeared. But why make up the story at all? "Still think we're over a cliff?" she asked Nick as they went back to her car.

Nick had his phone out, checking something. He did not answer her. "Nick?"

He stopped walking and squinted at her in the bright sunshine. "Joey Fuller is dead. Died at Menard in 2005."

Her stomach dropped. "Menard? What was he there for?" The Menard Correctional Center was medium to maximum security, reserved for the tough cases.

"I'm checking."

They got in her car and she started the engine. Nick grimaced at his phone and she waited to put the car in gear. "What is it?" she asked when he didn't say anything. Her two potential witnesses were dead. The news could hardly get worse.

"Joey Fuller stabbed a woman to death in 1999," he said finally. He met her gaze and held it. "The victim's name was Sarah Johnson."

FIFTY-EIGHT

············

WHEN ANNALISA KNOCKED ON THE DOOR TO NINA'S APARTMENT, NINA ANSWERED HOLDING A BABY. "Oh my goodness," Annalisa exclaimed as she admired the little pink cheeks and tiny curled fingers. "How precious."

"His name is Charlie," Nina said as she admitted Annalisa to the apartment. "After my mom. He's three weeks old today."

Annalisa kept her smile frozen in place as she admired the infant. Babies were a fraught subject for her right now. A checkup with her regular doctor following her latest round of injuries had unearthed another possible reason for her late period: early menopause. *I'm only thirty-eight*, she had protested.

I'm not saying you're out of time, her doctor said. *I'm saying: if you want this, don't wait.*

Annalisa had tried to figure out how to broach the subject with Nick without making it sound like she wanted him for a stud fee. She didn't even know if he still wanted her. After all, he'd returned the ring and not said another word about it. "He's darling," Annalisa affirmed, and Nina glowed.

"My father is here to watch him while we chat. Dad?"

An older man with thinning hair appeared from the back of the flat. He broke into a big smile at the sight of his grandson. "Time to visit Pop-Pop," he said as he took the infant from Nina's arms. "We're going to watch a show about penguins."

"So." Nina turned to Annalisa with a kind of forced cheer. "You said you had news. Shall we sit?"

Nina had prepared coffee and cookies, but the food sat largely untouched on the coffee table as Annalisa relayed what she had learned. Joey Fuller had landed in jail for the first time at sixteen for attacking a fellow student with a tire iron over a dispute about money. An ex-girlfriend had taken out a restraining order against him in 1983, suggesting he'd been abusive to her. Then there was the murder he'd committed. In between, he'd worked odd jobs. At the time of Charlotte Osteen's disappearance, he'd been working on a fishing boat. Annalisa had been able to find a photo from the New Year's Eve party that showed Fuller in the bar. Mac had delved into his private albums to unearth it.

"So he wasn't changing a flat tire?" Nina asked as Annalisa showed her a copy of the photo.

"No, he was in the bar with your mom."

"But no one saw them together. You don't know he left with her."

"No, we can't prove that," Annalisa admitted. "With Fuller dead, we probably won't get a definitive answer. But I can tell you what I believe, and that is your mother did not abandon you. She did not get drunk and wander into Lake Michigan. A bad man set his sights on her that night and she was in the wrong place at the wrong time."

"But . . . what did he do with her? Where is . . ." She stopped to take a steadying breath. "Where is her body?"

Annalisa bit her lip. She'd lay money that Fuller took his boat out on New Year's Day, just far enough to dump the body. "We don't know. Unfortunately, his death means we'll probably never get all the answers."

Nina was quiet as she looked over the files and photos Annalisa had shared. "I knew she would never leave me voluntarily," she said softly as she picked up a copy of the photo from O'Malley's Bar, the one that showed the group shot of the countdown. She smiled at it. "My mom sure had style. Jewelry, clothes. Look at her in this cowboy hat. I could never pull that off." She glanced up at Annalisa. "My dad put a bunch of her stuff in a trunk and left it for me," she said at length. "Would you like to see it?"

"Sure," Annalisa said. She was off duty and had the time.

She followed Nina to the main bedroom where Nina kept the trunk at the foot of her bed. "I keep thinking I should get rid of it. It's just taking up space. Maybe now . . ." She opened the lid and took out a fuzzy pink robe. "I remember her wearing this. I remember how it felt against my face when I sat on her lap."

"She loved you."

Nina held the robe to her face and inhaled. "She loved drinking more," she said when she dropped the robe. "Maybe it wasn't her choice. Maybe she couldn't help it. Dad didn't want her to go out that night but she went anyway. If she'd just stayed home . . ." She shook her head and pulled out a small zippered bag, which turned out to contain makeup. She opened a tube and squinted at it. "You can see her lip prints on this."

She held it out to Annalisa to see. "Yes," Annalisa agreed.

"I know I seem crazy, keeping all this." She put the makeup down and pulled out a hat. "It feels like proof that she was real. She was here. She wore these clothes and used this perfume. When she disappeared, there was nothing left but her stuff, you know? We didn't have a body. There's no grave to visit. She was just . . . gone."

"That's hard."

"She got sober when she was pregnant with me. My dad told me that more than once. She stayed clean for almost two years." Her voice grew wistful. "I think it made him mad in a way."

"What do you mean?"

"Well, like she could be sober if she wanted it bad enough." She hesitated and admitted the next part in a small voice. "That she'd do it for me, when I was inside her, but not for him."

Annalisa considered this as she looked at the remnants of Charlotte Osteen's life. "I imagine she did the best she could."

"I wonder what she'd be now. Like, would she eventually have gotten clean and stayed that way? Would she have drank herself to death?" She pulled out a pair of white cowboy boots to admire them. "She was fun, sometimes, and funny. Charlie won't ever get to know her." She showed Annalisa the boots. "These are two sizes too small for me. I should definitely trash them, right?"

Annalisa opened her mouth to reply but then she actually looked at the boots. Charlotte had been wearing them in the picture in O'Malley's bar, the night of the party. The night she disappeared. "Where did you get those?"

Her sharp tone made Nina draw back. "They were just in the trunk with everything else. Why?"

Annalisa's stomach dropped as she looked at the boots. Maybe they were a different pair. "Let me just go check something," she said, excusing herself to go look at her file. When she saw the copy of the photo from O'Malley's, there was no mistaking it. Unless Charlotte somehow owned two identical pairs of white boots with fringe on them, these were the same boots she'd had on at the New Year's Eve party. She had made it home that night after all.

"Is there a problem?" Nina asked. She still held the boots.

Annalisa snapped the folder closed. "Your father," she said, "he ran a restaurant at the time your mom disappeared?" She remembered this from the file.

"Uh-huh. Down near the lake. It closed when I was about ten."

"What did they serve there?"

"Seafood, mainly. Why?"

Annalisa closed her eyes briefly. Seafood. Joey Fuller was a fisherman. His boat had sold to local restaurants. It was possible Fuller and Mitchell Osteen had known each other. But there were only two ways Charlotte's husband could have ended up with her boots: either Fuller killed her and returned the boots, or Mitchell did the job himself. Since Annalisa couldn't imagine why Fuller would have invented the tall tale about seeing Charlotte the night of the party unless he was involved, she figured Mitchell must have paid him to make Charlotte disappear. Fuller returned the boots as proof of a job well done. "Hang on for one second, would you?" she said, her voice overly bright. "I'm just going to grab something from my car."

Nina looked puzzled but she nodded. "Yeah, sure."

Outside, Annalisa grabbed gloves and an evidence bag from the trunk of her car. She looked up at the first-floor apartment and saw the silhouette of Mitchell Osteen in the front window. He was still cradling the baby on his shoulder. She shut the trunk with a slam and was surprised to find her vision had blurred. Her heart was pounding like it had when she discovered the evidence on her own father. *You have to do it.* She straightened her spine. *You have to.*

She went back inside and found Nina putting her mother's things away in the trunk. She cleared her throat. "Nina . . . I'd like to take your mother's boots for forensic analysis."

Nina paused with the bathrobe in her hand. "Analysis of what?"

"Any trace evidence might help us determine what happened to her." If Charlotte was wearing the boots when she died, they might have blood or even Fuller's DNA on them.

"Sure, okay." Nina still looked faintly puzzled. "If it will help." She held out the boots and Annalisa bagged them in a paper sack, which she then sealed and dated.

The sound of a newborn's cries grew louder as Mitchell Osteen returned to the room with baby Charlie. "I tried," he said, "but I think he wants something now that I can't give him."

"I'll take him," Nina said.

He looked at the bag in Annalisa's hands. "What's that?"

"They're taking Mom's boots." Nina patted her baby's back to soothe him, bouncing slightly. "For forensic analysis."

"What boots? Why?" Mitchell's jowly face turned pink like his grandson's.

"The white cowboy boots," Annalisa informed him, watching for his reaction.

He gave an intense scowl. "You can't take those."

"Dad . . ."

"Do you have a warrant?"

"Dad, calm down. They're mine, remember? I gave Detective Vega the boots. If she thinks it will help us figure out what happened to Mom, she can take anything she wants. Right?"

Mitchell was agitated and shook off his daughter's hand from his arm. "I don't like it. We have rights. They can't just come in here and take things."

"You'll get them back," Annalisa said. "I promise."

Nina waved one hand airily. "Keep them as long as you want. I don't need them anymore. Now, if you'll excuse me, I need to go feed this little one." She paused to clasp Annalisa's hand. "Thank you. Thank you for everything you've told me."

Annalisa could only nod. This poor woman had no idea what was coming for her.

Depressed, she dragged herself to her car. She put the boots in the trunk and left them there. It wasn't procedure, but she couldn't bring herself to detonate Nina Osteen's fragile happiness. Not yet. At home, Nick poured her a big glass of wine and sat with her on the couch. He had dinner simmering on the stove in the large pot he'd somehow moved into her place. She noted other signs of him in the room—his coat hung by the door. His shoes and boots on the mat. She might not have moved in with Nick, but he'd moved in with her. She sidled closer and he put an arm around her. "Tough day?"

She told him what she'd learned about Mitchell Osteen, about the telltale boots in her trunk. "I don't know what to do now."

"Nina wanted the truth," he replied. "That's why she hired Sam Tran."

"She doesn't want it," Annalisa countered swiftly. "Not if it's this. She's already lost one parent."

"Because the other one had her murdered," Nick pointed out. "Isn't that what you're saying?"

She leaned her head back. "Do you think Sam Tran knew? He spoke to Mitchell Osteen. He knew about Sarah Johnson's murder, so he probably knew Joey Fuller killed her. Maybe he figured out the truth and decided to leave it alone."

"Maybe Mitchell Osteen killed Sam to keep him quiet. Is that what you think?"

She shook her head dully. "No. He's physically weak. He couldn't have done it. Besides, Nina showed me pictures—the night Sam got killed, Mitchell was at her baby shower."

"Well." Nick took a breath. "If you don't log the boots, nothing comes of it. Right? Fuller's dead. The odds that we could build a murder case against Mitchell Osteen at this late date are slim to none."

Annalisa squeezed her eyes shut. Her own family had kept a similarly dark secret for years. *Keep silent*, the pact said, *and we'll be okay. The dead are lost and gone forever.* Annalisa had not kept silent, and the whole family paid a price. Life was not better, nor more peaceful. Just more honest. "I don't know," she whispered.

Nick squeezed her. "Well, tomorrow is a holiday anyway. You can take a couple of days to decide."

They were going to Cassidy's place to spend Thanksgiving with the girl and her mother, Summer. Nick had made the decision to go and regarded Annalisa with worried eyes when he told her the news. *Are you in too?*

She took his hand as they sat on the sofa. She hoped he knew by now: she was in.

FIFTY-NINE

....

Annalisa wasn't sure what she expected Summer to be like. Nick's women were not always conventionally good-looking. She herself had too large a nose, caterpillar eyebrows, and riotous dark hair that defied any styling. She eyed him as they knocked on the door of his daughter's house. He looked disgustingly handsome in his green sweater and charcoal-gray wool coat. Just as the door opened, he took her gloved hand and squeezed it. His daughter, Cassidy, broke into a huge grin when she saw them standing there. "You're here!" She wore an oversized blue apron and an oven mitt on one hand, but neither stopped her from launching herself at Nick. He let go of Annalisa to embrace her.

"Hey, kiddo. The turkey smells great."

She wrinkled her nose. "It's still not done. I've been cooking since seven this morning." At the noise of a motorized wheelchair, Cassidy turned and indicated the woman sitting in it. "You know my mom, Summer." She was thin with light brown hair. "And that's her best friend, Melanie." A dark-haired woman looked watchful and wary as she hung back from the group, acknowledging Annalisa and Nick's arrival with a simple nod.

"Thanks for having us for dinner," Nick said as he handed his coat to

Cassidy. He removed the bouquet from Annalisa's hand so she could do the same. "This is my partner, Annalisa."

"Also his ex-wife," Annalisa said.

"I told you he was married," said Melanie from the archway. Somewhere she'd acquired a glass of wine, and Annalisa envied her for it.

"You'll have to excuse Melanie," Summer said as she rolled backward to allow them into the front room. "She has a different kind of terminal illness than mine—every thought in her head comes directly out of her mouth. I can only presume someone will kill her for it." She said the words without rancor, and Melanie's smile said this was a well-worn joke between them.

"Canapés, anyone?" Melanie asked, producing a tray from the kitchen.

"Shoot, is that the timer?" Cassidy asked as she ran past Melanie.

"Do you mind if I . . . ?" Nick indicated he would like to go after Cassidy.

Summer waved him on. "Please. Neither of us can help her."

Annalisa accepted a glass of wine from Melanie and the three women sat in the front room together. Annalisa nibbled a piece of cheese and looked at the art on the walls. There was one striking painting, a close-up of a woman's face against a yellow background done in Roy Lichtenstein's style, only the woman had purple hair that gave her a modern sensibility. Her eyes were downcast and pale blue tears leaked onto her face.

"You must think I'm horrible," Summer declared, taking Annalisa's attention from the painting.

"What? No." She'd tried not to think about Summer much at all.

"I did know he was married," Summer said bluntly. "Back then. To be fair, he didn't really try to hide it."

Annalisa took another slug of wine. "Yeah, he didn't do much to hide it on my end either."

"I should have told him about Cassidy. I just—by the time I figured out I was pregnant, I hadn't talked to him in months. I knew he wasn't looking for a commitment. Not with me."

"Yeah? With me either."

"I tried to find him once, when she was about five. I went to three different police stations until I found the one he'd worked in, and they told me he'd moved to Florida. I took that as a sign that I'd done the right thing. But maybe . . . maybe it was just the easy thing."

Melanie reached out and held her friend's hand. "It wasn't easy," she told Annalisa.

"No, I don't imagine it was."

Summer took a breath. "I don't want his money. I have life insurance to pay for Cassidy's schooling. And you don't have to worry about taking her in or anything like that. She's going to live with Melanie."

Annalisa looked toward the kitchen, wishing desperately that Nick would return. "Maybe . . . maybe you should wait for Nick to talk about all this."

"I've told him already."

Annalisa jerked her attention back to Summer. "You . . . have?"

Summer nodded. "Now I'm telling you."

Annalisa decided to just lay it out on the table. She set her wine aside and leaned forward toward Summer. "I see. Do you mind if I ask why?"

"You're his partner. I mean . . . not just at work. Right?"

"Yes, but—"

"We're making the same bet," Summer said steadily, cutting her off. She glanced to the kitchen, where Nick was laughing at something Cassidy had said. "The bet that he's changed. I'm risking my whole heart here." She teared up as it was Cassidy's turn to laugh. Melanie squeezed her hand. When Summer spoke again, her speech was labored. "You . . . you know him best. So I'm asking you to be straight with me . . . Is he worth it?"

Nick popped his head out of the kitchen. He'd somewhere found his own apron, rubber gloves, and science goggles. In his hands, he held a carving knife and fork. "The victim is a small-game fowl," he said, "weighing about fifteen pounds. I'm going to begin with a Y incision."

A watery laugh escaped Annalisa. "Yes," she said.

··········

AFTER DINNER, ANNALISA HELPED CASSIDY CLEAR THE DISHES. "Dinner was excellent," she told the girl, and Cassidy wrinkled her nose.

"The turkey was dry."

"My mother says that's why God invented gravy." As she returned for the stuffing, Annalisa caught Nick checking his watch under the table for the third time. "Do you have a hot date?"

They were in a good enough place that she could say this and he didn't blanch. He did make a funny grimace, though. "No, I . . . ah . . . I thought maybe we could do dessert at your folks' place."

Annalisa took her phone from her pocket to check the time. It was going on six o'clock, which meant her family would be putting up Ma and Pops's Christmas tree—a form of controlled chaos that usually resulted in someone nearly electrocuting themselves with a string of lights. She also found she had a half dozen texts from her brothers and Sassy, each featuring different foods from Ma's table. The close-up of the lemon bars made her waver. "I don't know . . ."

Cassidy's face fell. "Do you have to go so soon?"

Annalisa looked to Nick, who this time did blanch. She made a snap decision. "Tell you what," she said. "Why don't you come with us?"

"Really?"

"Sure. There will be two dozen people there, easy. I have a niece about your age who just went through the whole college application process last year. Maybe she can give you some pointers." They had talked during dinner about how Cassidy was beginning to look at schools.

Cassidy's brightened mood faded as she took in the disarray of the table. "No, that's all right. I should stay here and clean up."

"Nonsense," said Melanie as she reached over to take the platter from Cassidy's hands. "You cooked. I'll clean."

Cassidy turned anxious eyes to her mother. "Mom?"

Nick got up and stood behind Cassidy, putting a hand on her shoulder. "We'll take good care of her. I promise."

Summer's eyes misted over. She still looked hesitant but she nodded. "Okay," she said, the word barely a whisper. Cassidy flew from Nick's touch to embrace her mom.

"I won't be late," she said.

Summer struggled to put an arm around her daughter. "Have fun."

On the drive to her parents' house, Annalisa looked at the girl in the rearview mirror. Cassidy was quieter than she was used to with teenage girls. "Quinn, my niece, is thinking about majoring in history, and maybe doing prelaw. Do you know what you want to study?"

"I was thinking about science or medicine. I could be a doctor or a researcher." She stared out the window at the passing scenery. "I know it won't be soon enough to help my mom, but maybe I could find a cure or treatment or something that helps other people in the future."

"I see." Annalisa saw Nick's hand clench into a fist on his knee. He said nothing. "That's an admirable goal," she said to Cassidy. "What does your mom think about it?"

"She wants me to go to an art school."

The painting in the living room, Annalisa realized. "That's your work," she said. "The art your mom has on her walls."

"Some of it, yeah."

"You don't want to keep going with it?" Annalisa said lightly. "You're clearly very talented."

"What's the point? Painting is fun, but it doesn't help anyone."

"I don't know about that. Your mom obviously loves looking at your paintings. Why else would she hang them on the walls where she can see them every day?"

"Yeah, but it won't keep her alive." Cassidy had hunched down inside her coat.

Annalisa's heart went out to this girl. How hard it was to live with a broken family. How little you could do to fix it, no matter how desperately you wanted to. "You know what I think?" she said, emotion raw in her voice. Cassidy heard it and met her eyes in the mirror. "I think you're right. We absolutely need doctors and scientists and medicine to keep us alive. But art? That's part of why we want to live."

The Vega clan welcomed Cassidy with their usual boisterous greetings—hugs all around. "We thought you'd never get here," Tony said as he embraced Annalisa, which she found strange since she hadn't known she was coming until about a half hour ago.

"There better be a lemon bar left," she warned him.

"There's like three dozen. You know Ma."

Annalisa looked across the room to where Sassy's girls had her mother deep in conversation about My Little Pony. Six of the creatures were lined up on the table and her mother was taking a quiz on the ponies' names—and failing. Annalisa went to hug her mother around the shoulders.

Ma reached back to pat her cheek. "What's all this for?"

"For you," Annalisa said simply, bestowing a noisy kiss that made her nieces giggle.

Ma pulled free and put her hands on her hips as she studied the colorful ponies. "I know that one is Hanky Panky. Which one is Sunny Bottom again?" The girls collapsed in a gale of laughter.

Annalisa had connected Quinn and Cassidy, but when Cassidy excused herself to use the restroom, Annalisa took the opportunity to check in with Quinn. "How are you holding up?" she asked, tucking a lock of hair behind the girl's ear. Quinn ducked her head.

"I'm okay."

"Yeah?"

"Yeah," Quinn said with more certainty. "Dad is letting me go back to school next semester."

"Hey, that's great," Annalisa agreed.

"I think it helps that Professor Hawthorne won't be there." At Annalisa's curious look, Quinn took a deep breath and continued. "Byron told the whole story. Hawthorne's out. They fired him."

"Wow, good for Byron."

"Mm-hmm. It meant his parents found out, though . . . you know, about his thing with girls' clothes."

"How are they taking it?"

"Well . . ." Quinn gave a small mischievous smile as she dug out her phone. "He's home with his folks for Thanksgiving. I got this from him a couple hours ago."

Annalisa looked and saw a photo of Byron in a red sequined top, blond wig, and eyeliner. He was standing in front of a beautifully cooked turkey, ready to slice it with a knife. He'd captioned the photo, "If looks could kill . . ."

Quinn put the phone away. "He says his parents are so glad he's alive, they don't care what he's wearing. He doesn't know how long that will last, but he's taking advantage while he can."

"Smart kid."

From the other room, Vinny shouted her name. "We need help in here," he added. "Should we go with the angel on top this year or the star?"

This was an old battle. She'd always liked the angel since it looked like her—Pops had purchased the tree topper for just that reason—and for the same reason, her brothers abhorred it and rooted for the gold star each Christmas. "You know my feelings," she hollered back as she went to find them in the front room. "Angel or bust."

Vinny had one tree topper in each hand. "Okay, then you have to put it up there."

Annalisa eyed the decorated tree. The family had picked a big one this year, at least ten feet. "Is there a ladder?" she asked as she approached it with trepidation.

"Look, Auntie Anna," Quinn said. "There's something caught."

Annalisa looked where Quinn was pointing and saw a gold thread tangled in the branches. Some ornament had unraveled. She tried to free it and discovered the string was caught on something other than the tree. "What is this?" With her fingers, she followed the thread from the tree and around the corner and then stopped in surprise. It kept going down the hall.

The rest of the family trailed after her as she continued past the hall table with the ceramic Christmas trees on it and around the corner into the den. She gasped when she saw Nick kneeling there with the other end of the string. It was tied to a ring. The ring. "After everything," he said, "I figured I had to do this here, in front of them." He nodded behind her to her family. "If you shoot me down in front of all these people, it'll be what I deserve. But I'm hoping you won't. I'm hoping you realize I've changed. I'm hoping you realize I'll ride shotgun no matter how high the cliff."

Annalisa looked at his shining eyes. Then she turned to see her family crowded into the room behind her. They had cleared a spot for Pops to wheel himself to the forefront. She looked to him, at his grizzled face, and realized she still cared what he thought. He frowned but gave her a tight nod. Yes. Emotion welled up in her and she turned her gaze to Vinny, who had his arms around Quinn from behind. He'd hold her tight as long as he could. He, too, managed a nod. Even Cassidy had her hands clasped together, hanging on Annalisa's answer.

We'll take good care of her, Nick had promised.

Annalisa turned to him. She wiped her eyes and laughed a little as she knelt down close to him. He smelled amazing, like he always did. "Well?" he prompted her in a low voice. "What do you say?"

She said the first thing that popped into her head, the answer that had been forming in the back of her mind for weeks now but she hadn't realized it until this very moment.

"I know who killed Sam Tran."

SIXTY

....

S HE ALSO SAID YES. Eventually. Of course she did. Who else but Nick would be accompanying her to Lara Tran's house on what was ostensibly their day off? Traffic was light the day after Thanksgiving and the drive took less time than usual. For once, Annalisa regretted the swift commute. She was in no hurry to make this journey. From the dismayed expression on Lara's face when she opened the door, Annalisa saw Sam's ex-wife felt the same. "Thank you for seeing us," Annalisa said as she and Nick removed their shoes at the door.

"Of course. I've made tea."

"Where's Benji?" Annalisa asked, looking to the stairs.

"In his room. Do you want me to get him?"

"No, no. I think it should be just us for now."

Lara took them to a dining room painted in a soothing shade of pale blue. A bright spray of daffodils sat on the table, their cheery yellow welcome but out of season. "They're fake," Lara said when she saw Annalisa looking at them.

Annalisa touched her fingertip to one and felt it was fabric. "A convincing illusion."

Lara poured the tea. "So," she said, sliding a cup to Annalisa. "You said you had news about Sam."

"I do." Annalisa left the tea untouched and looked at Sam's ex-wife, the woman he'd loved so dearly until the end. "I think maybe you already know it, though."

Lara shook her head, denying the words, but tears appeared in her eyes. "I don't know anything."

Nick produced a tissue and handed it to Lara. She took it and closed it in her fist. "Sam's cancer had come back," he said gently. "Isn't that right?"

"No."

"Yes," Annalisa said. "We confirmed it with his doctor this morning. Sam got the news about five days before his death." The fist-sized hole in Sam's apartment. The bruising on Sam's hand. Annalisa bet these told the tale of Sam's reaction. "It was his worst fear," she continued. "The enemy was back."

"He did everything right," Lara said. "His diet and exercise were military precise. He followed everything the doctors told him to do and then some. It wasn't fair."

"No," Annalisa allowed. "It's not."

"Sam made a plan," Nick said. "Didn't he?"

Tears streaked down Lara's cheeks. She looked beyond them out the window. "He didn't tell me."

"But you suspected," Annalisa persisted. "You must have. We couldn't find anyone who wanted to kill Sam. He was alone drinking the night he died. There was no one else with him. The letters on his chest that spelled 'pig,' with the backward P, it wasn't backward because someone with a learning disability wrote it. Sam wrote it himself." She paused, leaning back in her seat. "He took his own life."

Lara swiped at her cheeks with the tissue. "Sam's insurance policy, the one for Benji, it has a suicide clause in it. When I saw it, I suspected what he'd done." She raised tearful eyes to Annalisa. "He was trying to provide for his son."

"I know," Annalisa said with sympathy.

"He gave his own life, whatever was left of it." She looked suddenly alarmed. "You won't tell them, will you? You won't tell the insurance company what he did?"

Nick and Annalisa exchanged a look. "I'm very sorry," Annalisa said at length. "We have to file a report on what happened. Sam's case remains open otherwise."

"You'll undo everything he wanted," Lara protested. "What he died for."

"Benji has you," Annalisa replied. "He'll be okay."

"How am I supposed to tell him?" Lara had started crying again. "How am I supposed to tell my son how his father died?"

Annalisa thought of the Queen of Hearts case, now closed because of the clues she'd followed from Sam Tran's file. She thought of all the other neat folders in Sam's office, all the people he'd helped and the answers he'd found. She thought of Zimmer, who carried her friend's discharge from the police force like a second shield. She thought of Benji and the weeping woman in front of her, who'd clearly loved Sam even if she couldn't live with him. No one so loved was truly lost. "You'll have to tell Benji the truth about how his father died," she acknowledged. "But it won't be what matters."

"You don't know that," Lara said hoarsely.

"I do." Annalisa reached over and squeezed her hand. "Because of how he lived."

Lara made one last plea. "Will you at least talk to Lynn Zimmer? She loved Sam. If—if she says the report has to stand, then we'll live with it."

Annalisa glanced at Nick. *I need someone else to make the calls*, he'd said. Maybe this time, Annalisa did too. "I'll talk to her."

SIXTY-ONE

....

S HE WAITED UNTIL THE END OF SHIFT, WHEN THE COMMANDER SAT ALONE IN HER OFFICE. Zimmer never hurried home. She didn't have anyone there waiting for her. Her life was here, at the precinct. Annalisa didn't know if Zimmer had deliberately chosen this path or if it was a series of smaller choices along the way. Annalisa was grateful for her boss's steadiness, but she did not want to end up in the same place. "We need to talk about Sam."

Zimmer cocked her head and leaned back in her seat. She looked curious but not surprised. Maybe she already knew. Annalisa took a seat and laid out the evidence she'd found that Sam Tran took his own life. "Lara Tran is asking us not to file a report so that Benji can get the insurance money like Sam wanted."

Zimmer blew out a long, slow breath. She had stayed behind the blue line when Sam was forced out. She played by the rules, always. "We don't have proof, exactly," she countered. "We have a theory."

"We know enough." Annalisa paused. "Don't we?"

"What we have is more an absence of evidence than evidence of anything in particular."

Annalisa folded her arms. "What would Sam do, if he were here?"

"File it," Zimmer said without hesitation.

"Doesn't that mean we should?"

"Sam and me, we didn't always agree on everything. We didn't agree where the lines were." Zimmer brooded in silence for a moment. "Type it up," she said finally, with grim determination. "Then give it to me."

Annalisa sat there a moment longer. This was what she'd wanted, right? To have someone else make the call. Zimmer sat ramrod straight, staring at the wall behind Annalisa. "Yes, ma'am," Annalisa murmured at length.

She rose stiffly and went to her desk. She typed up the final report on the death of Sam Tran. When she was done, she cast a look at Zimmer's office. Her boss stood still, contemplating the plaques on her wall. Annalisa printed the report but did not hit "submit." She reached into her bottom desk drawer to pull out a sealed evidence bag, the one she'd been keeping from Nina Osteen. She hadn't submitted this either.

She took the report and the bag into Zimmer's office. Zimmer turned and watched as Annalisa set the printout on Sam's death on her desk. "What will you do?" Annalisa asked. She already knew the answer, but she wondered if Zimmer would admit it.

"You've done your part, Detective. You've submitted the report to your superior officer. Now I will . . . evaluate it."

Annalisa nodded. She took off her badge and gun and put them alongside the report. Zimmer looked stricken.

"Vega, no . . ."

"It's time. It's past time."

"I'll file the report," Zimmer said grimly. "If that's what you need."

What I need, Annalisa thought with a touch of wonder. How long since she'd even considered it. "I joined up to follow Pops," she said, bowing her head. "We know how that worked out. When his path fell away, I kept going. Like I could prove I wasn't him."

"You're not."

Annalisa nodded. She could acknowledge this now. "You've been a great boss," she said with feeling. "Really. But what you were saying about the lines, about you and Sam. I guess I fall on his side. I want to make the calls." She took a breath. "Who knows? Maybe I'll go into business for myself."

"You mean private investigation work?"

Annalisa shrugged one shoulder. "I know an office that's available." She could do worse than following Sam Tran.

Zimmer said nothing for a long stretch. "Have you talked to Carelli about this?" she asked finally.

"No." Annalisa sighed and cast a look out at Nick's empty desk. "But he won't be surprised. We have to split up now anyway since we're getting married. I brought him a going-away present . . ." She set the boots in the evidence bag on the edge of Zimmer's desk. Nick wanted someone to make the calls. This was her last one. Whatever happened to Mitchell Osteen after this, Nick and Zimmer could decide.

Zimmer gave her a questioning look. "You're sure I can't talk you out of this? I hate to lose you, Vega. You're one of my best people."

"You haven't lost me." She extended her hand and Zimmer just looked at it for a time. Reluctantly, her boss moved to shake. "You're one of my best people too."

Zimmer's eyes got wet. "Get out of here."

"Yes, ma'am."

Her phone started ringing as she left. Nick. "Hey," she told him, her step lighter as she moved through the station. "I have some news."

"I have some news too. What do you think about Bali for the honeymoon? I found a screaming deal."

She paused one last time on the threshold to look at the crowded desks, the coffee station, and the plaques and posters on the wall. When she'd joined, she'd imagined her own name up there one day, but now she knew the real price. Her gaze lingered over the faces one last time. "I think . . ." she said to Nick. She turned on her heel and smiled into the phone. "I think you should book it."

ACKNOWLEDGMENTS

This is somehow my eighth book and I am unbelievably grateful to the wonderful folks at Minotaur Books for allowing me to continue to do what I love. Many thanks to my intrepid editor, Sallie Lotz, for wrangling this beast of a novel. The book is stronger for her input. If you're reading this book, that's probably due to the hard work of my terrific publicity and marketing team, including Kayla Janas, Mac Nicholas, and Danielle Prielipp. They are creative and amazing!

Thanks as always to my terrific agent, Jill Marsal, for wise counsel and advice.

I am especially grateful to readers, many of whom I've heard from and whose comments, questions, and concerns are always a joy. I love that a shared passion for the written word connects us all.

As ever, this writer gig is way more fun if you are a member of #Team-Bump, even when Bump doesn't happen to be in the book. Thank you for your feedback and encouragement. I am blessed to have a crackerjack squad of betas that includes Katie Bradley, Stacie Brooks, Ethan Cusick, Rayshell Reddick Daniels, Jason Grenier, Shannon Howl, Suzanne Magnuson, Robbie McGraw, Michelle Kiefer, Rebecca LeBlanc, Jill Svihovec, Dawn Volkart, Amanda Wilde, and Paula Woolman.

Thanks as always to my wonderful family, especially Brian and Stephanie Schaffhausen and Larry and Cherry Rooney, for love and support.

Finally, if inspiration starts at home, I am the luckiest writer on the planet because I live with two inspirational human beings: my marvelous husband, Garrett, and our phenomenal daughter, Eleanor. They are the source of all my joy.